PRAIS[illegible]
AFTER EVERYONE ELSE

"*After Everyone Else* brings us back into the life of Bailey Edgeworth, Leslie Hooton's memorable, sparkling character from her first novel, but Hooton is such a gifted writer and natural storyteller that this story brings us new twists, new drama, new terrain, all in that witty, emotional resonant writing style. And, always, at the heart of Hooton's writing, there is an exploration of the past, how we are made, and how family and love open up new possibilities that we never expected."

— KEVIN WILSON, *NEW YORK TIMES* BESTSELLING AUTHOR OF *NOTHING TO SEE HERE* AND *THE FAMILY FANG*

"Hooton weaves together the past with the present and the nuances of marriage and mother/daughter bonds with tremendous depth. Readers looking for a big-hearted book that strikes the right emotional chord will devour this one."

— ROCHELLE WEINSTEIN, *USA TODAY* BESTSELLING AUTHOR OF *THIS IS NOT HOW IT ENDS*

"Warm-hearted and witty, *After Everyone Else* grabs you from page one and takes you on a journey of mystery and celebration as it explores relationships between mothers and daughters, brothers and sisters, husbands and wives. Leslie Hooton does it again!

— JANE L. ROSEN, *NEW YORK TIMES* BESTSELLING AUTHOR OF *ELIZA STARTS A RUMOR* AND *A SHOE STORY*

"With *After Everyone Else,* Leslie Hooton has delivered another gem of Southern literature: funny but heartfelt, plot-driven yet profound. I can't wait to see what she gives us next."

— AMY GREENE, NATIONALLY BESTSELLING AUTHOR OF *BLOODROOT*

"Marriage, mother-daughter bonds .... and murder. Acclaimed author Leslie Hooton's new novel *After Everyone Else* packs a powerful punch. Alternating between the past and present, what begins as a mystery quickly deep dives into the intricacy of relationships. Hooton doesn't miss a beat as she deftly explores how far we go to protect those we love—a Must-Read."

— LISA BARR, *USA TODAY* BESTSELLING AUTHOR OF *WOMAN ON FIRE*

PRAISE FOR *THE SECRET OF RAINY DAYS*

"Leslie Hooton, her writing vibrant and alive, so wonderfully harkens back to the grand tradition of southern storytellers. She writes with that potent mixture of humor and grace, and *The Secret of Rainy Days* has all the makings of a book club darling, a story that you can't help but share with someone else. This is a book suffused with a lifetime supply of "lucky dust," that intangible quality that makes you want to be close to it."

— KEVIN WILSON, *NEW YORK TIMES* BESTSELLING AUTHOR OF *NOTHING TO SEE HERE* AND *THE FAMILY FANG*

"*The Secret of Rainy Days* is a coming-of-age novel that is both deeply moving and beautifully crafted. Witty and charming, *The Secret of Rainy Days* is a gem.

— PATTI CALLAHAN *NEW YORK TIMES* BESTSELLING AUTHOR OF *BECOMING OF MRS. LEWIS* AND *ONCE UPON A WARDROBE*

"Equal parts funny and profound, *The Secret of Rainy Days* will have you laughing and crying both at once. Leslie Hooton's extraordinary second novel firmly establishes her place as a major new voice in Southern literature.

— AMY GREENE, NATIONALLY BESTSELLING AUTHOR OF *BLOODROOT*

"Heartbreaking and heartwarming, *The Secret of Rainy Days* examines the intricacies of small town livin' ('OKOP'—Our Kind of People). It is a coming-of-age tale chock full of Southern charm, love, tragedy, and unbreakable family ties. Leslie Hooton's world brings us colorful, witty characters and intricate friendships–those we choose, and those who choose us. *The Secret of Rainy Days* is a reminder that you can escape your roots but never really leave. And yet...if you look hard enough–all the answers are right there under the 'Welcome' mat."

— LISA BARR, AWARD-WINNING AUTHOR OF *FUGITIVE* COLORS AND *THE UNBREAKABLES*

"In distinctly Southern prose, Leslie Hooton captures the complexity of family dynamics and the difficulty of sudden loss in her sweeping sophomore novel. *The Secret of Rainy Days* explores what it truly means to come home again, especially when we think we have left forever—and how, sometimes, it's the most difficult days and the lessons they bring that teach us who we truly are. Fans of coming-of-age stories will find themselves immersed in every page."

— KRISTY WOODSON HARVEY, *NEW YORK TIMES* BESTSELLING AUTHOR OF *UNDER THE SOUTHERN SKY*

"The world that Leslie Hooton creates in *The Secret of Rainy Days* is both big-hearted and wise; it is a celebration of lasting love and friendship and an exploration of family ties and the many losses and secrets along the way. Hooten's eye for memorable details and her sharp sense of humor is a delight."

— JILL MCCORKLE, *NEW YORK TIMES* BESTSELLING AUTHOR OF HIEROGLYPHICS AND *LIFE AFTER LIFE*

"Like the best Southern novels, *The Secret of Rainy Days* reminds us when searching for your place in the world, you may find it where you least expect it. And that sometimes to move forward, you have to go back to where you came from."

— COLLEEN OAKLEY, *USA TODAY* BESTSELLING AUTHOR

"Hooton utilizes vivid description, a strong sense of place, and unparalleled comparisons to paint an accurate portrait of life in the South, both complex and multilayered."

—***SHELF UNBOUND***

PRAISE FOR *BEFORE ANYONE ELSE*

"*Before Anyone Else* is a wonder of a debut novel, a coming-of-age love story set in the fast-paced and often cut-throat Southern restaurant world, with flesh-and-blood characters that live and breathe. Bailey Ann Edgeworth is an unforgettable heroine, and Leslie Hooten is an immensely gifted writer. I can't wait to read the next one."

— AMY GREENE, NATIONALLY BESTSELLING AUTHOR OF *BLOODROOT*

"Like a good tasting menu Leslie Hooten's *Before Anyone Else* is full of delicious contrasts and dazzling surprises. It is also wonderfully suspenseful as we watch the fragile and intrepid Bailey make her way in the complicated world of restaurant design. Hooten understands so well how love and work are often intertwined. A splendid debut."

— MARGOT LIVESEY, *NEW YORK TIMES* BESTSELLING AUTHOR OF *THE FLIGHT OF GEMMA HARDY*

"Romantic and deeply moving, *Before Anyone Else* by Leslie Hooton, is a curl-up-on-the-couch debut novel that keeps the fire burning and the pages turning."

— LISA BARR, AWARD-WINNING AUTHOR OF *FUGITIVE COLORS*

"With *Before Anyone Else*, Leslie Hooton announces herself as a natural-born storyteller, a writer who can evoke character and place with such finely-tuned details that you find yourself pulled completely into the world that she has created. It's a sharp examination of work, how it defines us, how it consumes us, and how much it takes to find meaning beyond it. It's a beautiful book.

—KEVIN WILSON, *NEW YORK TIMES* BESTSELLING AUTHOR OF *NOTHING TO SEE HERE* AND *THE FAMILY FANG*

"*Before Anyone Else* is the romantic debut we have been waiting for, a coming-of-age novel that is both deeply moving and creatively beautiful. With wit and dazzle, Leslie Hooton takes us through both a love story and the cutthroat restaurant business. With charm to spare, this novel is a powerful story with a dose of hostess gold woven in for good measure."

—PATTI CALLAHAN HENRY, *NEW YORK TIMES* BESTSELLING AUTHOR OF *BECOMING MRS. LEWIS* AND *THE FAVORITE DAUGHTER*

After Everyone Else

also by leslie hooton

The Secret of Rainy Days

Before Anyone Else

after everyone else

a novel

Leslie Hooton

Keylight Books
an imprint of Turner Publishing Company
Nashville, Tennessee
www.turnerpublishing.com

After Everyone Else

Cover design by Emily Mahon
Book design by William Ruoto

Library of Congress Cataloging-in-Publication Data
Names: Hooton, Leslie, author.
Title: After everyone else / by Leslie Hooton.
Description: Nashville, Tennessee : Keylight Books, [2022]
Identifiers: LCCN 2021038336 (print) | LCCN 2021038337 (ebook) | ISBN 9781684428397 (paperback) | ISBN 9781684428403 (hardcover) | ISBN 9781684428410 (ebook)
Subjects: LCGFT: Novels.
Classification: LCC PS3608.O5985 A69 2022 (print) | LCC PS3608.O5985 (ebook) | DDC 813/.6—dc23
LC record available at https://lccn.loc.gov/2021038336
LC ebook record available at https://lccn.loc.gov/2021038337

Printed in the United States of America

For Robert,

For pulling me back from the proverbial ledge time and time again with your "chill" attitude. Can you please do that from heaven?

"We've lost our way,
What shall we do?"
—Alexander Pushkin

"Patience, patience, patience, is what the sea teaches. Patience and faith. One should lie empty, open, choiceless as a beach—waiting for a gift from the sea."
—Anne Morrow Lindbergh

After Everyone Else

NOW

The doorbell rang once. Then twice. And then a third time, like an impatient diner demanding his first cup of coffee. I opened the door fearing the worst. It would be worse than I could even have imagined.

"Yes?" My mind instantly went to my daughter.

"Are you Bailey Edgeworth?" I nod. "Bailey Edgeworth, you are under arrest for the murder of Elliott Graemmar."

The two uniformed police officers looked at me to determine how much of a threat I was. A petite, middle-aged woman, and they had interrupted my sidecar—my signature cocktail—so yes, I was probably very menacing. The tall officer read me my rights and then the shorter officer who had kind eyes brought his handcuffs out.

"I need to call my husband. And my attorney," I said in an octave I did not recognize. "And what about my phone and purse?" Did I already ask that? At this point I couldn't keep basic facts straight.

"You need to let us cuff you first and then you can show us your phone."

"You don't really need handcuffs, do you?"

"Handcuffs are standard," the tall one said. "You need to cooperate. You can call your attorney after you're processed."

I pointed to my phone. He put on gloves and then put my phone in a plastic bag.

Cooperate? I was paralyzed with fear. I had no idea how to act.

The drive to the police station seemed to take forever. There was booking and fingerprints, and they put me in a cell until they put me in an interrogation room. They let me call Jake, our business attorney. Finally. They brought me up to some drab, windowless room. It looked like the room that time forgot. It could really use some fresh paint and some interesting lighting choices. I laughed to myself. I could hear my husband, Griffin, saying "You've just been arrested for your ex-husband's murder and you're designing the interrogation room already?" I would've immediately answered back "occupational hazard." I design restaurants for a living, I just couldn't turn off my vision thing. Not even when the stakes were so high. And they were.

I heard "Well, if it isn't Mr. Fancy Pants." I assumed that my attorney, Jake Fein, had arrived. He walked into the interrogation room with another man who I'm guessing was the detective.

I jumped up. "Jake!" I was about to rush over to hold on to him as the detective blocked me. "Ma'am, sit down or I'll have to restrain you."

"What sort of evidence do you have against my client?" Jake said.

I'm not sure the last time he'd been in a police station, but his demeanor was cool like a batch of Griffin's summer gazpacho.

"It looks like your client has been very busy committing a murder," said the detective, who was soft-spoken and handsome.

"I'm waiting on the evidence, detective," Jake said.

"I am so glad you asked that question, counselor. It seems your client's DNA was found all over the victim's apartment. Her DNA was found on shards of glass. It was found on a knife, and there was DNA found on the victim himself. Samples of her blood were found in his apartment as well. Very strange for a couple who have been divorced for twenty years, don't you think? Then there's the apartment footage."

We watched about twenty minutes of footage showing the comings and goings. I wanted to see the rest of the tape. I wanted to see who else I might see coming and going. I knew who I was looking for.

For the first time since his arrival Jake looked at me, and I felt the need to fill the silence.

"I didn't do it."

The detective almost smiled as Jake gripped my shoulder.

"Stop. Talking. Now." I did as I was told.

"What is the bail, detective?"

"Oh it's going to be pretty high. Ms. Edgeworth—yes, I know who you are—is famous. I'm guessing she's rich too. But you're in luck. Judge May is on the bench tonight. So you can go plead your case with her."

"Detective, would it be possible for my client to wait here?"

"No, she will be returned to a cell."

For the first time, but not the last, my confidence was shaken.

"Did you call Griffin?" I asked as they led me away.

"I already have," Jake said, and we exchanged meaningful glances as to why my husband wasn't here with me now.

"Who the hell are you people?" Jake asked, looking back and forth from me to Griffin. "Just what the hell has happened to you two?"

These were good questions. I was asking myself the same things, sitting safely in Jake's soundproof conference room, wiping the black ink from my fingertips. I had just made bail. Secrets stretched between Griffin and me like the width of the conference room table. Strangely, our love stretched that distance too. Our love, the enduring bond . . . for now. Griffin and I had survived so much and yet here we were.

"It's epic, Mom," Charlie used to say proudly when she called me Mom and not Bae like her dad. On a day when she actually liked me. My precious daughter. So difficult. So challenging. So fragile.

"Who wants to tell me what's going on?" Jake questioned, slowly moving his neck from side to side as if working out a sore muscle. It was the first time I had ever witnessed Jake doing anything slowly.

"I just don't buy this murder charge, Bailey. I know you. I know you both. Bailey, you called me, not Griffin, from jail. Griffin, you took your sweet time getting here. In my line of work, there is always an 'aggrieved party.' So back to my original question—what is going on between you two?"

On my side of the ledger, flashing in neon signs, Griffin had kidnapped my only child about five years ago. On Griffin's side of the ledger, there was my possible infidelity, nude pictures, and the aforementioned murder charge. My complaint was the only actual infraction. Griffin's hand pointed at me.

My eyes fixed on my husband.

"Really?" Jake asked. "Bailey—what have you done?"

It'd been a long night. It'd been a long week. It'd been a long ordeal. It could've been worse. So much worse. Like when I confessed to Griffin that Elliott had proposed we meet alone to discuss the exchange of pictures.

"Elliott was threatening to publish nude pictures."

"The dead man I helped you divorce?"

I nodded.

"When did he take pictures of you, twenty years ago?"

I shook my head in the negative. Jake just cocked his head, looking at me as if I had not understood the question.

"If Elliott had taken pictures of me twenty years ago and I still had those boobs, I would've published them myself," I said, trying to diffuse the situation with humor like I always did. I was afraid to look at Griffin.

"When?"

I had never seen Jake discombobulated before, but then again, I had never been arrested before.

"What the hell, Bailey? Did you kill Elliott?"

"Bae, we need to level with Jake," Griffin said finally.

"Yes. A little honesty would be nice between friends," Jake agreed.

"Charlotte," I said in a clipped response.

"Elliott took nude photos of your daughter?" Jake seemed confused.

"For God's sake, Jake! No," Griffin said. "Elliott's son and Charlotte took pictures. Bae acted unilaterally and went to talk to Elliott to try and persuade him to give the pictures to her."

I glanced over at Griffin. His most searing indictment was that I had acted unilaterally. It had become a tortured action in our marriage history. He knew that it would sting and throw me off-balance. My nerves were frayed. Sitting in a cell for a few hours and being charged with the murder of a man you hadn't seen in twenty years until the night of the murder would do that to a person.

I tore my gaze away from my attorney. And my husband. Instead, I looked down at the traces of ink residue still on my fingertips, wondering if by getting my fingers clean I could make this whole mess go away. Yes, I had motive. Yes, I had opportunity because I was in New York last week. When it happened.

"How far were you willing to go to get the pictures back?"

"We should have gone together. Why couldn't you just wait?" Griffin interrupted, looking at me. Finally.

That was the question I hoped Griffin wouldn't ask. I didn't want to tell him.

Jake raised his eyebrows in a quizzical fashion. I didn't mind Jake thinking the worst of me. I was sitting on an airtight alibi that I would tell no one, not even Jake or Griffin, unless I could be certain that the two people I loved most in the world had alibis too. And I knew for a fact that both of them had been in New York the night of Elliott's murder.

Griffin had absolutely no reason to be there. He didn't know that I knew he had been there. A simple charge at the Starbucks near Elliott's apartment was the tip-off. Just who goes by Starbucks to grab a grande Americano if they're contemplating murder? Then there was Charlotte, our twenty-two-year-old daughter. She could be so impulsive. Like me. She lived in New York. She couldn't even remember what happened the night of the murder. My worst infraction was lying to Griffin about Charlotte's "condition." What a shitstorm the last seventy-two hours of my life had become. If I had to take a murder charge to protect either one of them, I was ready. Bring it on.

THEN

TWENTY-THREE YEARS AGO

Griffin slid my cocktail—a sidecar—to me at the bar. Along with the blue velvet box.

I hadn't opened it, but I was very aware of its contents. I had seen it on two other occasions. Griffin had been waiting for me to say the simple word "yes." I just hadn't been able to say it. About that time Annabel walked in and took her place beside me. Griffin placed a cocktail napkin in front of her, pocketing the box.

"Better make it club soda. I'm knocked up."

The news, proclaimed in a way only Annabel could, was like a giant bomb exploding in my mind. I no longer thought about the question that sat between Griffin and me, but about the news Annabel had just, well, delivered.

"You're having a baby?" I asked. I hated the term "knocked up." I couldn't exactly tell how Annabel herself felt about the news.

"Yes, I am. Mr. Monroe has planted his flag."

I laughed. It was not only about her indelicate way of saying she was having a baby, but how upset Griffin would be that for nine months Annabel Whitney Monroe would not be drinking.

"Bailey, grab us a table. I'm starving. I need to return a couple of calls and then I'll join you. Can you be my plus-one at a gallery opening tonight?"

Griffin and I exchanged looks. "We're not done here," he told me.

"I know." I moved to a table to wait on Annabel. This would be the third time. I guess after the other two sweeping proposals, Griffin just figured *What the hell, it's Tuesday, let's see what happens.*

The first proposal happened only a month after my divorce was final.

We were in Martha's Vineyard. I was so excited, and then at sunset, with the orchestration reserved for a Vivaldi concert, he dropped to one knee and produced the navy box. Before he uttered a single word, I said, "Oh, shit."

"Is that a good 'oh, shit' or a bad 'oh, shit'?" Griffin asked. There was a long pause.

"We have got to stop coming to Martha's Vineyard," I replied. "I love you so much Griffin. It's just a little too soon. Too fresh. I'm not sure I am quite repaired."

"I get it. Timing was never our strong suit." He stood up and put the box back in his pocket. He took my face in his hands and kissed me. It was one of those kisses. His kisses. The kind that reached way back in my memories and made me smile, the kind that hinted of a future. That as long as we were together, it would be okay. The kind that just stood still in the present.

I smiled up at Griffin. For the majority of my life I had been kissing this man. In the beginning they were forbidden kisses; later they became stolen. Some were during the saddest times of our lives, others during great highs, still expressing a connection that our words had a hard time doing. But in all those years, none had been inconsequential. Not even today. And yet I could not say the word or even let him ask the bloody question.

Unlike the first time we were here at Martha's Vineyard, which ended in disaster, we ended up making love and talking.

"I thought it may be a little too soon. But I wanted to make Martha's Vineyard right for you," he said, as the moon hung over us through the big windows.

"You know, Griffin, you have made my entire life right for me."

The second time he proposed was a few days before the following Christmas. It was becoming his favorite time of year. I think in part because that is when I redid his condo and gave him his first Christmas tree.

This proposal had all the trappings of one of those Hallmark movies. Except for snow. We were in Atlanta, after all. But we had a fire, our favorite champagne, beautiful flowers, a delicious meal, and dessert. This time he did get the question out. But it was our first holiday together, and I was still a little gun-shy.

"You're not making this very easy," Griffin said later, as he and I washed my mother's Christmas china so it would be ready for Christmas Day.

"I never have, Griffin."

"Touché." That time, we did not make love.

❧

When I got home from the gallery opening Annabel had dragged me to, after the aborted third proposal attempt, Griffin was waiting up for me.

"We need to talk," he said. I sat next to him on the sofa and took his hand in mine. He pulled it away.

"I think you need to move out and find your own place," he stated, so matter-of-factly. It scared me.

"Is this because of what happened earlier tonight?" I asked. But I knew the answer. I knew his patience had grown thin.

"You can't even say the words, can you? It's the third time I have tried to ask you to marry me. Clearly, you don't want to get married." He was angry. I didn't blame him.

"It's not like that at all!" I protested.

"Well, what the hell am I supposed to think, Bae? I've asked you three times. And you've turned me down. Three times. Yet you rushed into marriage with Elliott. Maybe you just don't love me like that."

"I have been in love with you most of my life."

"You have a funny way of showing it."

It was all I could do not to cry. How did things get so messed up? I took a deep breath in and out. I knew that I had to tell him all my secrets. Come clean. I just didn't know how.

For a little while, we both just sat there, counseled by our own thoughts and our own bruised feelings.

"It has never been about marrying you. It's what comes next," I started. My voice faltered under the weight of what this discussion meant.

"What do you mean? We're going to live happily ever after." Griffin smiled, but only briefly. He was trying to make it okay for me even now while realizing his own heart could be in pieces by the end of the night. This was something I had not planned or rehearsed. In fact, I had become rather successful in never acknowledging the fact but instead playing it for humor. Raised by wolves, I frequently said. I often said I raised myself. Never would I dare utter the word that swirled around the edges of my brain. *Motherless.*

"Griffin, I'm talking about a family. Having a baby."

He turned to me and looked genuinely shocked. "You mean, you don't want children?"

"I do want children. But think about it, Griffin. Most girls grow up with a mother. They either choose to emulate their upbringing or do the exact opposite. Me? I am just one big, empty slate. I didn't even have friends growing up to see how their mothers interacted with them. In fact—"

Griffin interrupted. "You have excellent role models. Reggie and Elle are really good mothers. You can ask them questions. And there are books on the topic. And you have me."

"Do you realize there are a million decisions a mother makes every single day on her own? What if he's taking an extra-long nap? Should you wake him or let him sleep through dinner? Will that spoil his bedtime sleeping? This is rapid fire. You have to make decisions in the moment. And you may not like this, but I want to work."

"I'll be more hands-on than your dad."

"When the baby is behind the bar and an orange or pineapple hits him in the head, you're going to explain that to social services?" I laughed briefly at the mental image of our baby behind the bar with some plastic contraption protecting him. I noticed Griffin did not laugh.

"We will hire somebody."

"Like a nanny? Are we those kind of people?"

Griffin was becoming increasingly harder to read as we lapsed further into an unwanted silence.

"This has been worrying you for a while." Griffin said this as a statement.

"No shit, Sherlock. I can hear it now: 'She can design restaurants, but she can't even raise a child.'" It was late. I was tired. There was so much more I could say but I didn't think either of us could handle it tonight. At the end of the day, it turns out a mother is pretty indispensable.

"I think you turned out pretty well."

"I disagree. I never had friends growing up. Just you, Henry, and Daddy. Is that what you want for our child? I don't. It was never a picnic."

Suddenly, all the lonely hours I spent by myself came flooding back. *How am I supposed to be a woman? What will happen when I become a woman? How do I know when a boy likes me?* Why, when I was on the verge of marrying and motherhood, had the loss of my mother decided to rear its head? In many ways it was as if she had just died. Her body bleeding out between Griffin and me. Or was it just me? The long arm of the past coming back to ensnare me. To accept it. And how could I explain that to Griffin?

I got up and headed for the guest bedroom I once occupied, before I was divorced from Elliott, abiding by his stupid rule that in order to get my alimony I couldn't "sleep" with Griffin until the divorce was final. It was humiliating signing that affidavit but rewarding. I lingered on the threshold, looking at the person I loved before anyone else. It had always been one of my favorite things to do. Gazing at Griffin. Even tonight it brought me comfort.

"You've given me an idea. I think I need to talk to the girls. I'll still sleep here tonight." I found myself reluctantly closing the door, but I heard Griffin.

"All I know is our children will have two parents who love one another and that's a pretty damn good start." Griffin was confident.

I sat on the edge of the daybed. All my insecurities were manifested in having children. I secretly imagined my own parents murmuring the same things to each other when their love was young, as they themselves embarked on parenthood. My mother probably went into having children with the idealism reserved for the young. The milestones she would certainly witness. Even imagining the wistfulness of growing old with my dad. But she didn't.

That was before her cancer diagnosis. Before she was too sick to dream anymore.

Elle was getting home from the office. She was working on a big deal. On these nights, her nanny would stay and get the kids fed and tucked into bed. Reggie had gotten her three children down for the night. You've got to love friends who put in full days but are still there for you when you need a three-way conversation. I could hear in the background Elle's shoes hitting the floor, a cork popping open a bottle of wine, and the quiet sounds of a struggle as she wiggled out of a bra. I had a visual of her doing all three at once. She was talented that way.

I told them that Griffin wanted me to move out. I told them about the three aborted marriage proposals. They were surprised. I started crying, opening up by telling them about my insecurities regarding motherhood. Elle waded in first. Of course she did.

"Suck it up, Bailey. Listen, when you set up a 529 for your kid's college tuition, just set them up with another fund for therapy. If you're really worried, make them sign confidentiality agreements so they can't write a nasty book about you. I will even draw it up."

"If you weren't around, who would you want to raise your children?" Reggie asked.

"Griffin." It was startling how simple that question was to answer.

"Well, marry the damn boy!" Regina commanded. "Besides, Elizabeth and I are not getting any younger to wear bridesmaid dresses. I do know you will have a proper wedding this time. Complete with us. Because how can you not?"

"Yes. No running off to a ratty courthouse. Said the person who spends a lot of time in a ratty courthouse," Elle said.

"Guys, I am a failure at this marriage thing. And I don't feel confident about being a mother. It is not like I had a mother set an example. What if I screw it all up and lose Griffin?"

"You won't. He loves you. Who else has that kind of patience to ask you to marry him three times? Put a ring on it Bailey, while we still have our youthful glow."

We all laughed. A lot. That was one of Elle's greatest gifts. Reggie, who had lost her own mother during college, was more thoughtful. She offered measured reassurance and sympathy that I didn't know I needed. In addition to the word *motherhood*, the word *cancer* had somehow seeped into my brain. Reggie offered the kind of compassion that led her to be a nurse in the first place.

They assuaged my biggest fears. Elle and I both were drinking wine, and as the night turned into a new day, we got sillier and sillier. I loved them both for their unique gifts and perspectives. We laughed, we cried. And then we hatched a plan.

I tiptoed into our bedroom the next morning. I sat down on the floor watching Griffin sleep. I loved the fact that no matter how worried I could get, he could always sleep. His hair was in his face.

"I know you're here. You girls were certainly long-winded last night."

I smiled. His eyes were still closed. I wondered if my heart would ever stop expanding when it came to this man.

"Did you get the problems of the world solved? Or at least our problems?"

"You know us. We always think we have the answers. But sometimes we don't. I've got to fly to Charlotte today. But if you still want, I will move out when I get back."

"I just need to know that you love me."

"You think we are going to make excellent parents and yet you wonder if I love you? Seriously? You do know that you are firmly grafted into each and every memory I have in my possession. Yes, some are sad, but most are happy. I have my favorites. Some I wish I could do over. And yet . . . Griffin, I wouldn't trade any of them for the world."

His eyes fluttered open, and he looked at me. And smiled. He considered what I had said as he combed through his hair with his fingers.

"So, am I naked in any of these memories you have grafted together in your brain?" He was definitely fully awake. I rolled my eyes.

"Listen, I wasn't kidding about having a plane to catch. But I think it would be a good idea if we went to Martha's Vineyard next Thursday for a long weekend. Away from the distractions here. Away from work. We can talk all this out. Figure out where we go from here. Make some decisions."

"You aren't coming home this weekend?"

"I can't. They have this big antique and estate consortium on the first of the month way out in the middle of nowhere in North Carolina and I need to go check it out. But today is Wednesday. I'm just talking about a week." I wasn't lying, but I was certainly stretching the truth.

"I'm not even sure Elaine has availability."

"I texted her already. Our room is available." I smiled. Now he was moving around.

"You checked with Elaine before you checked with me?"

"I know how much you love Martha's Vineyard."

I watched him as he hoisted himself out of the bed. He pressed his whole body into mine. This was always my undoing.

"I really need to go."

"Just think of it as adding to all those memories in your little brain." I was a goner. But there were certainly worse ways to go. And I would add this "last time" of having sex as a single woman to my reservoir of precious memories.

I found Griffin in the bar at Elaine's. Concocting recipes. New drinks.

"Hey." I leaned over the bar and kissed him.

"You want to sample something I've been testing? I am starting to really like these infused vodkas more and more."

I dodged his question. "Sure," I said, but added, "Let me start with some water. The plane ride was bumpy."

In truth, I was nervous. The confidence I'd possessed this morning talking to the girls was evaporating. We had been so busy during the last week planning our wedding that I had little time to worry about the outcome. I now knew why bridegrooms got nervous when popping the question. I hadn't stopped to consider the ramifications from Griffin's point of view.

I got up and walked to the window. Workers were outside erecting an arbor for an outdoor wedding. The lawn looked freshly mowed. Griffin brought my water to the window and looked outside to see what had caught my attention.

"Looks like somebody's getting married this weekend," he said. I nodded.

"We are," I said quietly, and then louder, with shaky conviction. "We are."

He shot me a curious look, took the glass of water out of my hand, and gulped it down. He sat at the table and considered what he would say next. I joined him. I wasn't sure if I should let him talk or if I should just launch in with my plan. This was the only part that I had no control over. Griffin could have a major freak-out and leave. This was walking on the high wire without a net.

"What do you mean, exactly?"

"Will you marry me Griffin?" I debated, and then I got up and fell to one knee and took his hand. He pulled it away.

"We can't get married right now. Nothing's been planned!"

I took a deep breath. And then another. It was now or never. "Everything has been planned. I never went to Charlotte last week. I flew to New York. The girls and I shopped for wedding dresses, bridesmaid dresses . . ."

"You never went to Charlotte? You and the girls concocted this?"

I couldn't tell if he was impressed, horrified, or both. "Once that was taken care of, we flew here, and Elaine has been helping us with flowers and the food and everything else."

"You wrangled Elaine into your plan?" He was measuring each word now, which let me know that he was not exactly overjoyed. Each question was laced with just the slightest anger.

Our words retreated. I wanted to be measured with my words too. As much as I wanted to explain and offer details, I practiced restraint. It was hard. But necessary. I knew, like me, Griffin did not like surprises. And this was a doozy.

"You planned the entire wedding in a week?" I nodded. He pondered this for a moment.

"Well, even if you did all that, I can't. I don't have your ring. Or anything to wear."

"Yes, you do." I stifled a little smile. "I took your suit out of the closet while you were in the shower." I paused. "Henry's coming tomorrow, and he is bringing the little blue box."

"We're both going to be gone from the restaurants. You trusted Henry to bring your ring?"

I could tell entrusting my brother with the ring was the least reassuring element for Griffin.

"He said he knew where you kept it."

"You stole my suit?"

"No. I borrowed it. It fits you well and I used it to buy another one. Of course, you'll be able to wear the suit after the wedding." I laughed a little.

"What does that mean?"

"That's just a little bridesmaid humor. No matter how hideous or pastel the dress is, brides always reassure their bridesmaids they are selecting dresses that can be worn again after the wedding. It's never, ever the case. I'm sorry."

Conversation ceased again. The airways of my throat were constricting slightly. My best hope was that Griffin was just too dazed by the organization of everything to get too angry.

"So, you left nothing to chance?"

"The groom. We left the groom to chance."

He actually made a little smirk. "So this is what you and the girls were talking about in that marathon conversation before you left?" Griffin deduced.

"Actually, no." I pondered how to begin this next part. "Do you realize I am the same age as my mother when she had me? When they found the cancer?"

He looked at me. The preamble to the next part of the conversation. I was about to start again when Griffin got up and pulled his chair next to mine. He took my hand in his.

"Bae . . ." He was trying to find the words.

"Have you ever heard of the BRCA gene? I could have it and pass it to my children. This is important." I let the seriousness of all this sink in. "Regina still has friends in the oncology department at Sloan Kettering. She pulled some strings and had me tested."

Griffin considered all of this information. The anger receded while we were left with our silence. I did everything to try not to change expressions. I certainly did not want sympathy to creep into our conversation.

"Whoa. Why didn't you talk to me about this?" he said finally. "You know, like after the first or second proposal. You can tell me anything."

"I know. It was like my brain was covered with a counter full of ingredients. I just didn't know how to choose the ones that worked. When I talked to Reggie, with her medical background, my true fears became clearer."

"I just thought you were concocting this diabolical little wedding plan." He said it matter-of-factly without anger or humor.

"No. We mainly talked about motherhood. My mother would've been expecting her second child at this point before the cancer. If I am carrying this gene, there is a 50 percent chance I can pass it on to my children."

Griffin waited for more.

"They posed all these questions about motherhood. Even if I am not caring that gene, who would I want to father my children? Who would I want to raise children with? And if something were to happen to me, who would I want to be responsible for my children? The answer was always the same. You."

Our conversation suspended for a time. Like a rain delay during a baseball game. And like the rain, it left the atmosphere heavy in its wake. I tried to diffuse the situation with humor. His eyes had clouded over with tears.

"Then we hatched our diabolical little plan." I smiled.

"If it's worrying you, maybe we should skip the wedding and go get you tested."

"When I find out the results I would like us to be married."

He leaned over and kissed me. He was everything I had ever asked for and more.

"I have to decide by Saturday?" he asked.

"Actually, by tomorrow morning. We have an appointment tomorrow morning at nine thirty at the courthouse to get our marriage license. But just so you know, that still gives you the option of showing up. Or not."

"Talk about pressure. Without sounding like a total jerk, this is a lot."

"I know. Everyone knows that this wedding may or may not happen. And it's just our little group. Our family. I really won't hold it against you."

"Where is your suitcase?" Griffin asked.

"I thought it was bad form to sleep together before the wedding."

"Now that contribution was Reggie and Elle." Griffin's phone buzzed. "That was Reggie. She wants to meet up."

"Go easy on her. She helped me get to the place that I wasn't scared to marry you, become a mother, and take the test." I got up to leave. Griffin hadn't let go of my hand. He brought it to his lips. For a moment, time stood still. But at that moment, Gabrielle, the florist who did all of Elaine's arrangements for her restaurant, was bringing in a beautiful arrangement of peonies, tulips, and roses for our wedding. She turned around to make a quick getaway.

"It's okay Gabby. Griffin knows."

She brought the arrangement over for both of us to have a quick look before placing it on the bar.

"Am I the only one staying here?"

"Yep. Just you and all those thoughts in your head." I gave him a quick peck on the lips before I could change my mind about staying with him.

❧

I was waiting for Griffin sitting on the bench outside the registrar's office. It was quarter to ten. Griffin, who is always on time, was fifteen minutes late. I wished I'd had a cup of coffee. But there is not a Starbucks to be found on the entire island. Maybe that's why Griffin liked the place so much. The island dwellers knew how to put their foot down to most forms of progress. I watched the clock on the wall make an entire rotation. 9:46. I had to come to terms with the fact that neither one of us could make unilateral decisions about our wedding. I would let Griffin make the proposal, get down on one knee, and then use the plans I had made already. Then I saw the top of his head. He was even carrying a cup of coffee. He sat next to me.

"Thought you could use this." He handed me the coffee.

"Have I told you I love you?"

"You can't tell me enough, and if I go through with this little plan of yours, you will be personally required to say it every single day. And just because I'm here does not mean that we are getting married tomorrow. But you are right—we can get a marriage license and then get married later, and not in some herky-jerky fashion."

"As long as the marriage license doesn't have some statute of limitations on it," I deadpanned.

"Who's going to marry us? Who's going to be my best man? And where are you taking me on a honeymoon?"

"Elaine. She is now an officiant. Henry is going to be your best man. The girls insisted on being bridesmaids. I can walk myself down the aisle. As far as a honeymoon, it is customary that the groom takes care of that. But I am willing to waive all of that since you didn't know about the wedding to begin with. Seriously, we really can't take a honeymoon right now. I actually do have to be in Charlotte next week. I rescheduled everything so I could buy a wedding dress and plan the wedding."

"No honeymoon? I'm out of here," Griffin said with a smile. Somehow our ease and equilibrium had been restored. For the first time in a week, I exhaled.

"I know this is not exactly how you would've wanted it—"

"Not by a longshot," Griffin interjected.

"But it *is* what you want."

"What's going on the rest of the day? Since you have the itinerary and I don't."

"Henry's family, Lea, and Hank are getting in sometime this afternoon." I had not asked Lea to be a bridesmaid because she had just given birth to their daughter. "You can spend the afternoon coming up with a nuptial cocktail." I looked at him expectantly.

"Don't push your luck."

"Point taken. Just don't make one called 'Beginner's Luck.' Been there, done that." I smiled. Even if we didn't get married, I realized it would be okay. "Since it is just a small crowd, Elaine and I planned a little garden party—which, of course, we can still have if we don't get married."

"This whole weekend is starting to feel like a 'wedding optional' kind of thing." For the first time since I met him at Elaine's yesterday, he actually laughed.

"I can't believe you didn't invite Annabel or Mac."

"Just family. And considering my first wedding debacle, this is quite the crowd."

"So just the party tonight?"

"Yes. Gabrielle did a fabulous job on the flowers."

"And what do you propose I wear to this little garden party?"

"Your suit has been returned to your closet in your hotel room. Along with the suit for the wedding."

"Our 'optional wedding' you mean. How did you do ALL OF THIS?"

"I have spies on the inside." I laughed. They called our names then, and we got our marriage license. And then we walked out into the sunlight, looking like a couple on the threshold of getting married.

Martha's Vineyard at twilight was magical. The heat of the day had retreated, giving way to a cool breeze that required wearing a wrap. The cicadas had come to provide a symphony of sounds. And if that weren't enough, Elaine had engaged a trio of musicians to punctuate the evening with romantic music. I looked at all the people who had gathered. Elizabeth and Regina cornered Griffin, no doubt giving him a pep talk. As usual, it looked like Elle was holding court—a drink in one hand and gesturing madly with the other—while Reggie, sipping her wine, waited patiently for her turn. I was so grateful to their spouses, who had stayed home to look after their children. I would have to do something extra special for Dave and Robbie. Henry and Hank were making their way through the offerings of food. I could tell from my brother's face that he approved of Elaine and her culinary abilities. Lea had gone upstairs to nurse Maggie.

Elaine walked over and handed me a cocktail.

"What is this?"

"Just something Griffin came up with this afternoon. He said to tell you it is called 'Wedding Optional.'" She winked as she said it. Everyone seemed to be enjoying themselves, except Gabby. She was busying herself removing wilted flowers or brown petals. I trotted over to her.

"Stop it. Here. Drink this. You are now officially our guest!" I handed her the drink Elaine had handed me.

"I love doing your flowers. I think they turned out rather well. I love the fragrance of white orchids and white lilies."

"You are so talented!"

"You *do* think you'll get married tomorrow, don't you?"

"Who knows? You know men. I hope so."

❧

I woke up with anticipation. I woke up with butterflies. I woke up with an eagerness to see how the day would unfold. I woke up with a sense of wonder only a child on Christmas morning would possess. I let the happiness of the day envelop me like a hug. I realized I couldn't care less what happened. The thing I cared the most about was Griffin. And after seeing him linger and give a toast to our guests, I knew we would be okay. I had never seen Griffin speak in public before, as he always deferred to Henry or me. He shouldn't. He was eloquent, earnest, and short. It was perfect.

I looked at my freshly manicured fingernails and toenails. Both Elizabeth and Reggie had insisted.

"Just because this isn't a full-fledged wedding doesn't mean we don't take our responsibilities seriously," they had said in unison. Over Bellinis earlier in the day, we had our nails and toes done.

I had reminded them both that this was still wedding optional.

"Just as long as at some point you have a honeymoon. That should be a requirement," Elle had said.

The other thing that remained an open question was what to do about my suitcase. Should I leave it in case things go bad, or bring it to Elaine's? I decided that regardless of what happened, I was going to spend the night with Griffin.

Just as the sun ducked behind a billowy white cloud, our guests assembled. I craned my neck and saw two men at the altar. Things were looking up. Reggie walked down the aisle first, followed in close succession by Elle. I had selected bridesmaid dresses in a shade of blush. The pale pink color coordinated nicely with their bouquets. For my dress, I had selected a beautiful white crêpe de chine with lace appliqués from the waist down. When Griffin saw me, he cocked his head.

As I started my processional, Griffin walked—no, ran—to meet me. He grabbed my hand and we started walking down in a more deliberate fashion.

"I really saved your ass today," Griffin said with a grin.

"Who's to say I didn't save yours?" I responded.

In mid-stride Griffin threw his head back and laughed. "Let's go take the 'optional' out of our wedding."

As the sun set, it left behind a beautiful canvas of blue, pink, and golden shades that only nature's paintbrush has access to. And with that, on this May evening, we were pronounced husband and wife.

When Griffin slipped the wedding band on my hand, it was I who received the surprise. It was a vintage wedding band that I had seen while shopping with the girls for Griffin's wedding band the week before. It was exquisite. I turned to them, smiled, and then looked up at Griffin.

"Let's just say those spies of yours are double agents." He smiled. He explained later that Reggie had seen the look on my face when I tried it on and secretly bought it for Griffin to give to him when they met.

The trio of musicians were back playing a slightly zippy set of music tonight. Griffin had been right. This was a magical place. A magical setting. I didn't want to leave. I didn't know who to throw my bouquet to because everyone was married, so I handed it to Elaine.

She took the bouquet to her nose and breathed in the fragrance.

"I'll do the honors and officiate at yours," I joked, considering I never saw her with anyone. But as I turned to join my husband, just as quietly, Gabby came up to Elaine and they laced their fingers together.

"So where are your suitcases tonight?" Griffin asked, playfully.

"Upstairs."

"Good," Griffin said. "Happy?"

"I am happy. I know this is not exactly the wedding you wanted, but did it turn out okay for you?"

"Bae, it was just perfect." He bestowed on me a prolonged marital kiss.

NOW

I followed closely behind Griffin as he unlocked the door to our house. I had lost track of time. Going to the police station, being booked, getting released, and then going back to Jake's office, it had to be the middle of the night. But when I looked at my watch, it was only eleven thirty. I guess that *was* the middle of the night for me. Unlike the rest of my family, I had turned into an early bird.

Like homing pigeons, we headed for the kitchen.

"We need to call Charlotte," I said.

"It's late. We should probably call her in the morning." Griffin said.

"Hello, have you met our daughter?" Griffin handed me a bottle of water while I washed the ink off my hands.

"If she finds out that I have been arrested for Elliott's murder on social media and not from me, I will never hear the end of it. It will become the source of unending writing material for her." I plopped my purse on the table and retrieved my phone.

"I'll call her. If it is me at this time of the night, she may think something's happened to you and will call me back," I continued.

"That's terrible, Bae," Griffin said, getting a glass of water.

"But true," I said. Charlie's phone went to voice mail.

"Hey, it's me. I need you to call me back. It's urgent." I hung up. Within a few seconds she called me back.

"Did something happen to Dad?" I had her on speaker phone. I met Griffin's gaze in silent acknowledgment. Our daughter may have preferred her dad over me, but I was the one who knew her the best. I was the one who knew what she was fully capable of. That's what scared me.

"No sweetie, I'm fine." Even now, the little hairs on the back of my neck bristled in jealousy. How normal is it to be jealous of your daughter's relationship with your husband? Her father had an ease with Charlotte that had been lacking between us almost from the beginning. Of course, I had not always approved of the buddy-buddy relationship they had established. When it counted, it had been Griffin that had stepped up to be the mercenary—but even then, that brought them closer together.

"Charlotte, have you heard in the news that Elliott was murdered?"

"Duh, Bae. It's been all over the news up here. Have they gotten anybody yet? That person deserves a ticker-tape parade," my irreverent daughter said. Calling me Bae was always a giveaway.

"It might behoove you to keep your opinions to yourself." I paused a moment. There is not a moment or a chapter in any of those parenting books that prepares you to utter the words I had to speak out loud.

"I've been arrested for the murder of my ex-husband."

I could almost feel Charlie's expression on the other end of the line. Her eyes growing big, her mouth refusing to shut.

"Oh my God."

That was it. My news had rendered Charlotte silent. The three of us stayed connected for a little longer. Finally, she said, "What can I do, Mom?" It was one of the nicest things she had said to me in a while.

I went upstairs to shower. I slid to the floor. Collapsing under the weight of the water, under the weight of secrets. Collapsing under the weight of lies. Collapsing under the weight of weariness. And it was just beginning.

Neither my husband nor my daughter had asked me if I had done it. If I had killed Elliott. I was hoping that one of them would ask. In keeping with some of those crime shows, it was a clue that the person doing the asking was innocent. I was pretty much in the same place I started. Not knowing if my husband or our daughter had done it.

Griffin must have gotten worried about me because he walked into the bathroom and grabbed a towel for me.

"Are you okay, Bae?"

I shut off the water, not realizing how long I had been in the shower. I was losing track of time. Losing track of reality. I stepped out and Griffin wrapped a towel around me. It might have appeared to be a very intimate gesture, but it was one of survival and generosity. I didn't even brush my hair. I walked over to the bed, still wrapped in the towel, and folded myself up in the sheets. Griffin slid in next to me and whispered, "So, what did you do while you were in the jailhouse?"

"I thought about the first time we were together. Not the very first time. But the time we could be together after my divorce became final."

I reflected back on it again. How he had pulled me up off the sofa and we had walked together to his bedroom. I had never slept there before. I remember feeling shy, but only briefly. We shed our inhibitions—along with our clothing—between kisses. We lost control. We lost our good manners. We lost track of time. The thing we didn't lose track of was our desire. It had come back with such gusto. We couldn't touch each other enough. We couldn't exchange glances enough. It felt good. It felt right. It felt like home. We were each aware that it was a blessing. I loved Griffin with everything I had. As much as I hated it, I returned to the reality of now.

"I'm still angry at you for going to that idiot's apartment alone, but I believe it's going to be okay," he said. I wanted to believe him. I wondered if my relationship with Elliott would ever stop haunting me.

❧

I walked past a throng of reporters into Jake's office. When I opened the door to the conference room, I noticed Jake and I were not alone. At the head of the table across from me sat a very handsome black man. With flawless dreadlocks. It was obvious to me he was in a custom-made suit. Without saying a word, it was clear this man was in charge.

"Bailey, this is Floyd Potts. Floyd is perhaps the greatest criminal defense attorney in the country."

"Jake, do you really think I need the greatest criminal defense attorney in the country?" Before Jake could answer the question, it was Floyd Potts who provided the answer.

"I wouldn't be here if you didn't. Let's get to business."

I would later find out that Floyd's retainer made Jake's retainer look like the price of an ice cream cone.

"May I see your phone, please?" Floyd began. I handed my phone to Jake, who then passed it to Floyd. He examined it and then looked up at Jake and me.

"Why are there no text messages between you and your husband? The first text message is from the day you were arrested." He asked again as if I were having trouble understanding. Jake just stared at me.

"I periodically delete a whole string of text messages. We text each other several times throughout the day and I just wanted to free up some room," I answered.

For a moment no one said a word and no one moved. Floyd lifted himself from the chair with aplomb.

"She's lying. She's wasting my time," Floyd said.

Jake intervened, his eyes pleading with me to take the situation very seriously.

"Okay," I nodded. And just as gracefully Floyd sat back down.

"Bailey, let's just get a few things straight. I do not care if you murdered your ex-husband or not. That is between you and our sacred Savior. My job is to provide you the best defense. I don't lose. I hate to lose. In order not to lose, I need to know the truth. I will not tolerate lying. Shall we begin again? Why are there no text messages between you and your husband?"

"I deleted them. We had a big fight. During the course of those exchanges, Griffin said he would kill Elliott. I was afraid that they would arrest Griffin."

Jake looked worried but Floyd had barely moved a jaw muscle.

"It's nice of you to care so much about your husband. I find that highly unlikely. Given the fact that it is your DNA all over Elliott's apartment."

I remembered just twenty-four short hours ago I was sitting in this very office, smugly knowing I had an airtight alibi. Even now I wondered how airtight an alibi has to be to combat DNA evidence. I also saw both men waiting for me to proceed. I reminded myself I was on the clock. I needed to stick to the facts. I just wondered how to tell the facts that did not seem so damaging to anybody in my family.

"I was there to retrieve the pictures and collect Charlie's things." I waited.

"Did you get them?" Floyd asked.

"No. When Elliott gave me the manila envelope, it was empty. There were no pictures inside. Elliott seemed as shocked as I was. And mad."

"Was there any kind of disagreement during the course of the exchange?"

"Well . . ." I stopped. "Yes. We got into a terrible argument. I accused him of hiding the pictures."

"There was blood found at the murder scene that matched yours. Why was your blood in your ex-husband's apartment?" I knew the answer.

"When I opened the manila envelope, I got a paper cut. I thought I wiped all the blood away."

"Evidently not. Why is your DNA all over his apartment?" Floyd asked.

"We tore up his apartment looking for the pictures. That's when we got into an argument. That's why my DNA is everywhere. I haven't seen the pictures but Charlie verified they had been taken," I explained.

"Does your husband know about the pictures?"

"Yes."

"Did he find out before or after you went to New York?"

"Before."

How could I make them understand with these silly one-word answers? Everything I had done was to protect my family. I needed to protect my daughter. I needed to protect her future. I needed to get it right with Charlie for once.

I felt the need to fill the vacuum.

"I have an airtight alibi," I told them. I'd had visions of delivering this line with much more bravado twenty-four hours ago. Like the waning minutes of the final scene in the *Legally Blonde* franchise.

"Why didn't you tell us this last night, Bailey?" Jake intervened.

"Because she is still not telling us the whole truth," Floyd said simply. "But we will entertain this. What is this airtight alibi of yours, Bailey?"

I couldn't believe Floyd was so blasé about my alibi. I couldn't tell if he was just taking it all in or if he had some fresh injections of Botox.

"I was at my acupuncturist. Amy will vouch for me. After I left acupuncture, I went back to my apartment."

"Did you see anyone at your apartment?" Floyd asked.

"No." I said.

"It's helpful. But not exonerating. You could've hired someone." I really didn't understand what he meant. It finally dawned on me.

"You mean like a hitman? I can provide all my bank statements. There is nothing to support my hiring a hitman. I wanted the pictures. I didn't want Elliott dead," I stated.

"Most people do not write checks to 'Hitman R US,'" Floyd shot back. "But I am starting to believe in your innocence. You just don't have the true instincts of someone committing a crime. Something has come up that requires my attention in New York. Let's reconvene in a few days." He stood up to leave, just as gracefully as before.

"You can't just leave! I'll tell you what you want to know. Does this thing in New York have to do with me? Is there any way to get the pictures back?"

And like a gazelle, Floyd Potts moved quickly out the door, leaving both Jake and me in stunned silence.

I walked into the quiet house. Something about being in Jake's office made me feel dirty. Although I had taken a shower last night, I felt the need to get clean again. I went upstairs and started kicking off my shoes and removing my blouse. I opened my closet door, and sitting on the floor was Charlie.

"Shit, Charlie! You scared me. What are you doing down there?" But I had a pretty good idea.

Some people come out of the closet. But this closet had been the site of many meetings. This had been the setting of some heated arguments, some hot sex, and secrets we did not want prying ears to overhear.

It was also the setting for some moments between Charlotte and me. When she was young, when we would play make-believe, when it rained and the only safe place was here in "Mommy's Fort." We had shared some heart-to-hearts about love and sex. And shed a few tears.

It was my fortress of secrets. It was my fortress of sorrows. It was my fortress when I had fallen short. As a wife. Certainly, as a mother. It was the place where I could bear my disappointments in private. The disappointments I had experienced. The disappointments I had rendered. I became emotional once I had Charlie. I kept there a box of Kleenex and glasses for wine, which were the only indicators this served as more than just a closet.

I readjusted my top and sat down with my legs folded beside her. I saw the faint traces of blue color still present in the landscape of her blonde hair. When she had gotten it done, I had told her it looked like she was coloring her hair gray. I had laughed. Charlotte had not, stomping off in a huff. When she came to me about a week ago, I wanted to fix things for her. I wanted to get it right. Parenthood was always a work in progress, wasn't it?

"I flew home this morning. It's all over the news that you hired Floyd Potts as your criminal defense attorney. There is rampant speculation in the New York tabloids that your DNA is all over Elliott's apartment. You do know that this guy is a shark. He has never lost a case. Even for the guilty."

That was the thing about my daughter. She may have looked just like her dad, but she was all me. She had needed to get that off her chest. She probably had even practiced all the ways in which she would deliver it. She may have been twenty-two years old, but her eyes looked frightened and pleading the way they used to when she was little, and we would shut the closet door to protect us from the monsters in the outside world. If only we could do that now.

I remember when she came to her father and me and told us she wanted to be a writer. I had rolled my eyes. But I'd also read some of the pieces that she had written in high school and college. Unfortunately, most had been about her tortured relationship with her mother—fictional, of course. Only I knew that most of it was true. It always hurt me. I told her at the time that it was all fine and good, but she would have to get a real job.

"Why can't you be like other parents and say follow your bliss?" she had asked.

"Sprite, you need to follow your bliss but just make sure it comes with a paycheck," Griffin had joked. His wonderful way with her. "Sprite" was her nickname. It fit her. Like all good nicknames.

I was always seen as the killjoy. And yet Charlotte did just that. She had gotten an internship with the *New York Times*, which had turned into a part-time position her senior year. She was on her way to being able to write her own ticket. I was so proud of her. I wondered how these revelations and lurid photographs would affect her job as a serious journalist. Her life.

"You know the New York tabloids. Don't believe everything you hear."

"Well, it sounds like you need Floyd Potts."

"I'm fine. How are you doing? How is Bishop?"

"I'm okay. Going to meetings. Bishop knows everything. I know how lucky I am to have Bishop. He sure has put up with all my crap. Does Dad know?"

"He knows what I told the police. He knows about the pictures. He knows I went alone to collect them at Elliott's. He doesn't know you had been drinking."

Charlie made a bad face.

"Do I have to remind you what happens when we keep secrets?"

"Nope. Been there done that. I have a T-shirt to prove it. I know I've complicated things between you and Dad. I just wish we could've gotten the pictures back."

We were both silent. I removed a fugitive thread from her jeans. I slid the pocket door closed.

"We will just deal with the pictures if and when they come out. When you give your statement to the police, just tell them you were at your dorm. I want Elizabeth to go with you."

"Won't the police think it strange that I wasn't staying with you?"

"For once, our unique mother-daughter relationship plays in our favor. How many years have you been in the city? You've never stayed in my apartment. As you pointed out yourself, we are not that kind of mother-daughter who have slumber parties together." I half smiled.

"You're right. Hey, did they book you and get your fingerprints?"

"Just like on *Law & Order.*" I tried to smile. Tried to alleviate her worry.

"There were times you would've paid good money to have me in prison."

She stood up, stretching her long legs, and gave me her hand to help me.

"Mom, I know you did not commit that murder."

"That is one of the nicest things you have said to me." I paused, "wait a minute how do you know that? "

"Because. My neck was bothering me, and I went for acupuncture and they said you had been there the night before I finally got sober. And I guess that's when I noticed my neck was bothering me," she said, as if she had personally cracked the case wide open. I had been trying to get her to go see my acupuncturist because of all those untold hours she spent at the computer.

She walked to the door and came to an abrupt stop at the threshold of the bedroom. She turned around and looked me in the eye.

"Oh my God. You think Dad did this."

"Hold up there, Nancy Drew!" I grabbed at her shirttail and pulled her back into the bedroom and sat her on our bed.

"I don't need you snooping around. This is not one of your creative writing assignments," I said. "Besides, you need to look at the facts of the case. Your dad was here. He's the one with the really tight alibi. Think about it. They would just say he was trying to take the rap for his wife because my DNA was found in Elliott's apartment." I lied to my daughter about my husband. I knew it was only a matter of time before his alibi collapsed . . .

Charlotte pondered this. After a few moments, she nodded. "You're right. I hope I didn't make things too difficult with Dad."

"I think we've been through worse." I managed to smile.

"Speaking of which, I'm working on the memoir. The more I write the more I just love your book title."

When she had come to me not long after rehab, she had shown me all her journals. Pages and pages detailing her return to sobriety. I saw the word *smashed* at the top. I told her that was already the title of a memoir I had seen that dealt with teenage drinking. And that she should stay away from the word *lit* because that was taken by an author named Mary Karr. I proposed the book title *Trashed*. Instead of commenting, she asked me how I knew so much about teenage drinking and memoirs. I told her I wanted to see what alcohol was like from her point of view. But mainly I just needed to be close to her, and this was the only way I could do it. The memoirs broke my heart, but ultimately, they brought me understanding.

"So, if this trial doesn't kill me, I suppose your memoir will." I managed a small smile.

"You're being so dramatic. I'm twenty-two. I'm more mature," she said. This actually made me laugh. Most of my closet was full of things older than she was.

"I'm hungry. I think I'll call Lucy and see if she wants to grab dinner." She got up to leave, pulled her phone out of her pocket, and walked away.

I wondered if Charlie had stayed in her dorm room all night. I knew my daughter was a blackout drunk. I could ask her a million times if she did it and she wouldn't have a clue.

THEN
TWENTY-THREE YEARS AGO

When I returned to the hotel from my day scavenging and shopping in a giant field at the Emporium Consortium, I noticed my room service tray from breakfast was where I left it that morning. This was a pet peeve of Griffin's. It amused me because he turned into a persnickety connoisseur who liked upscale hotels when he traveled.

When I opened the door, I quickly realized that the tray had not belonged to me but to my husband. He was sprawled out on the bed with his computer. Glancing at me, he smiled and said, "Surprise! Of course, it doesn't equal a surprise wedding, but then what does?"

I hated surprises, but my heart leapt nonetheless. In fact, it felt like I was on a roller coaster and had gotten to the top, when you throw your hands in the air and shout with unrestrained joy. It had been over a month since our wedding, and I realized, at that exact moment, how much I had missed him.

He came over to meet me. I walked into his arms. I walked into his kisses. I walked into his love. His hands began roaming and I stepped away.

"Wait. I'm hot and sweaty."

"Not a problem," he said. And it wasn't.

Afterward, we stayed connected. "Okay, what's the matter?" Griffin asked.

"Nothing." I wanted to say everything. But we had a policy not to bring our problems to bed. This was one of those things people tell you, like, don't go to bed angry, that very seldom really works. Or at least it didn't for us.

"Bae. I know something's wrong. Just tell me," Griffin prodded.

"Are you sure?"

When he nodded, I started again. "Everything. Everything is wrong. This guy is impossible. Cliff Rushton is synonymous with so many restaurants in this town and yet I just can't please him. I have pitched him several ideas and he's hated every one and makes me try again. I'm starting to lose my confidence. In New York, everything is possible. I know Atlanta. I don't know Charlotte. Maybe I'm losing it. Maybe my vision has finally run out. His restaurants are all successful. He wants to do something different. Hey, maybe you can help me figure it out," I said, pleading with him.

"Don't look at me. I don't have your gift with the vision thing, Bae."

"I'm just running out of ideas. He wanted something sexy, so I pitched what I thought were good ideas. He hated them. And then he wanted me to incorporate his favorite color. His favorite color is white. How do you make that sexy?"

"That's your area of expertise. And I just gotta say, talking about another man when we've just made love is making me a little jealous."

"Don't be. If he is as hard to read on a date or in bed, I would run the other way. The problem is he is very successful. He found his sweet spot. Great food, good price point, and very accessible. But now he wants this new upscale place. He has disliked every idea I've presented to him. No wonder he is on wife number four. I am really glad you are here."

"Well, if my wife wasn't going to come home, I figured it was up to me to come to her."

"Thank you, Griffin." I meant it.

"The pleasure has been mine so far. Why don't you jump in the shower? I need to give Henry a quick call."

We ended up going to Cliff Rushton's Italian bistro. Griffin studied the menu.

"It is a rather expansive menu. And the price point is very reasonable. It's nice. Perfectly nice."

I laughed. Griffin would've made an excellent Southern woman in a prior life. He could always say one thing that sounded like a compliment, but I knew it was just a put-down wrapped in a very subtle way.

"I know. It's buzzing and loud, but he wants something different."

"Why break it if it doesn't need fixing?" Griffin asked, as our food and another round of wine arrived. In mid-bite, Griffin lifted his plate.

"Swap." This was becoming our practice. We would both order different entrées and then exchange midway through. It was the culinary version of "who ordered it best?"

We took a taxi back to my uptown hotel. Griffin wanted to go by the bar, which we did.

"Now this vibe I like," Griffin said as he sipped his cognac.

"I know, right? Cliff hates this."

"May we declare a moratorium on any further discussion of Cliff Rushton and just enjoy being together?"

I touched his hand. It startled me. I was unaccustomed to seeing a wedding band on his finger.

"I've got to get used to this. But it looks good on you."

"You think so? I got married in a fever. And then my wife never came home."

"I'm here now." I watched him down his cognac and grab my hand, and we proceeded to end the day as we had a few hours earlier.

When I woke up Sunday morning, I was in the lovely place of being half-asleep and half-awake, not sure which one I was ready to commit to just yet. The smell of us hovered around me. My perfume and Griffin's clean soap scent commingled, reminding me of home.

Our bodies had not always been monogamous to each other, but our hearts were another story. Entirely. My heart had found its home when I was young. It never strayed. At least not too far. Or for too long. For all those years I questioned where Griffin's heart belonged; it had not budged from wherever I was. I smiled and felt lucky.

I decided to make my commitment known. I gently nudged Griffin. Nudged him to wake up. Nudged him to be a participant in the joy I felt.

"It's Sunday morning, Bae," he mumbled, wanting to sleep just a little more.

"You can sleep in next week when I'm not home," I said.

"Well, when you put it like that . . ."

I saw a sleepy grin cross his face. He smothered me with kisses. Enveloped me with hugs and blanketed me with his love.

After we showered and dressed for the day, there was a place I wanted to take him. He looked underwhelmed when we arrived at our destination. Looming before us was a cinderblock building. Its maximum occupancy was about sixty-five people, including the bar. It was a restaurant. But not any restaurant. It might have looked like a dive, but to me it was heaven.

We opened the door and put our name on the waiting list, because at this place, there was always a waiting list. Griffin spoke first.

"Ah, the smell of cooking bacon and greasy hash browns. It takes me back."

I knew he was thinking of Daddy's restaurant. While we were waiting, he looked around. The inside was no more appealing than the outside. It was a little hole-in-the-wall that was probably built in the early 1950s, escaping all code mandates like electrical wiring and air-conditioning. It stood like an attractive nuisance in the middle of Myers Park and Eastover, two of the most prosperous areas in Charlotte. When we were seated, Griffin ordered scrambled eggs, hash browns, bacon, and buttered toast.

"I think that says I'm all in," Griffin said as he drank coffee. Our food arrived a short time later and we both began eating madly. We did not come up for air, nor did we exchange plates.

"I take it we're not here just because of some positive Yelp reviews," Griffin said as he devoured the last slice of his crispy bacon.

"I was thinking . . ." I began.

"Oh brother. I knew this morning was going to cost me. I just didn't know how much." Griffin smiled.

"This would be a perfect time for you and Henry to jump off the color wheel and open the diner idea I had. Edgeworth's."

"For the record, it's *your* idea."

"I thought you were on board. It's a perfect time. Henry and Lea have just had a baby, we haven't started a family, and it's been a long time since you and Henry opened the next big thing," I said, laying my argument on thick. "People would be hungry for this kind of food. During the week they serve a mean hamburger. Supposedly the best in town. And there is an extra benefit to you." I waited to see if I had piqued his interest. He stopped eating long enough to meet my gaze.

"If I'm designing for you and Henry, it keeps me in town." I finished my bacon with a triumphant smirk.

"That was the most compelling argument you've made thus far. But just because the timing is right for you doesn't mean it is right for Henry and me."

"Don't tell me you are resting on your laurels."

"No. It's just not a good time." Griffin paid the check and we left so he could get to the airport. But it made me wonder—why wasn't it a good time?

❧

My Monday morning meeting with Cliff had filled me with dread. I laid out my ideas on the round table in his office that we had come to use as our official meeting place. As I placed my plans on the tabletop, a manila folder caught my eye. Certainly, the two names at the top caught my attention. Bender and Bender—and right underneath, in his signature handwriting, Nick Gallagher. My nemesis.

I carefully slid the proposal out to take a closer look. Bender and Bender had been Julian's most formidable competition, and when we were both interns with Julian, Nick Gallagher had been my stiffest rival. I had won the coveted position to work with Julian in his prestigious restaurant design business, and Nick had taken a job with Bender and Bender. I had lost a few jobs to Nick lately. Male clients. One told me it was because I had gotten married and would probably have a kid soon and then where would he be? I couldn't believe that this opinion was still so pervasive. But it was. I had to prove myself even more. I couldn't resist seeing what Nick had proposed to Cliff.

Nick's proposal looked entirely different than mine. It made me wonder if we were pitching for the same restaurant. But underneath Nick's name was the name of Cliff's new establishment. It made me wonder what Cliff had told Nick. It was a solid proposal—I would expect nothing else. But it wasn't sexy. And it sure as hell wasn't white. I quickly slid the proposal back into the envelope and resumed setting up my own proposal. About that time Cliff walked in.

"What do you have for me today?" He was in a jovial mood. I fanned over the table with the ideas.

"What do you think? This is how I made your white sexy. I used dark wood to contrast." This had become our practice. I would lay out my ideas and let Cliff study them.

"I was thinking we could introduce another color. Like green. I know you like green."

He held up the green juice he was drinking, which he told me was courtesy of his fourth wife. From his smallish sips, I could tell he wasn't a fan. I tried to keep my emotions in check.

"Green and white. Not really sexy."

"You're supposed to make anything sexy," he said. *I'm not a miracle worker*, I thought.

"What about a deep azure blue? That may lend itself to a sexier vibe," I suggested.

"Okay. What if you play around with your little ideas and we can reconvene on Thursday? I need to take this phone call," he said, as he summarily dismissed me.

I left his restaurant feeling demoralized. I had thrown every idea I had on the table. He liked none of that and yet he wanted me to keep at it. I wondered if he would even pay his bill if we did work together. I needed to regroup and see what I could come up with in the azure family.

I was starting to feel like a failure. I wished I had another job that I could just throw my energies into. I had purposely put off a few meetings with prospective clients to deal with Cliff, who came highly recommended. In all my time working with Julian I had not experienced this. Most people revered Julian. I hadn't seen him at the beginning of his career when he was still proving himself. Part of me wanted to just go home, but the other part wanted to stay and prove myself to this man who really didn't know what he wanted.

Before I could spiral too far downward my phone buzzed. It was Griffin. He usually didn't call during the day, so it alarmed me.

"Is everything all right?" I ask.

"Yes. Everything is fine. I'm just touching base. How are you?" There was an artificial lift in his voice.

"I'm just fine," I said. I looked for the words to fill our silence. "Okay. I think we're doing it again. Not communicating. We have got to stop this."

"You're right Bae. How are you really?" He chuckled.

"Okay. I just had my latest meeting with Cliff and he rejected my most recent proposal. But he's not ready to walk away. I feel like shit."

"See? That was pretty good communication, Bae. But I'm sorry," he said, and I felt his love all the way from Atlanta.

"He wanted me to make white and green sexy. I proposed azure instead. We're meeting on Thursday. I don't know if I can pull it together. I might be here another weekend. But after this proposal, I am walking, no matter what."

"Good for you. Stick to your guns," Griffin said. "I probably should get going."

"Wait, how are—"

And I heard the phone line go dead before I could catch him to ask him what had been on his mind.

I didn't go back to work. I went to lunch at a restaurant not owned by Cliff. I observed the happy patrons. Some laughed. Some were drinking wine. Others were whispering secrets. I felt like I stood out like a sore thumb.

I didn't work that afternoon either. I called Griffin before the night-time crowd at his bar.

"Hey, you never did tell me what was going on with you. What's wrong?"

"Nothing really. Just some broken things that need to be fixed," he said. "I just hope you're coming home soon."

"I hope you don't mean us. And yes, regardless of what happens with Cliff," I said.

"Never," he said, and he laughed. I could tell he appreciated my calling. "I love you, Bae."

"Back at you," I said.

ঔ

On Wednesday I found some really cool azure lanterns that looked vintage. I inserted those into my proposal and removed all the white because it was throwing the whole scheme off in my opinion. If Nick Gallagher could go off the reservation, so could I, in order to make it look right. I had always tried to not only listen to what a client said but to interpret what they meant. Oftentimes it could be two different things.

I called home, leaving the part about Nick out, and told Griffin I would be home tomorrow after I finished the proposal.

"I love you Griffin," I said, as I got ready to go to bed early.

"That's what keeps me going. Call me from the airport."

I let it alone, but I could tell something was troubling my husband.

After I pitched my proposal, Cliff and I agreed to give him a few days to think about it. This time he did not ask me a single question or propose a single addition or subtraction to the plan. I didn't know if that was a good thing or not. I almost didn't care. When I got to the airport, I called Griffin and found out what had been on his mind.

"I've just really hated to bother you, Bae. I'm just going to say it. We're going to have an intervention for Henry in the morning. He is drinking again, and it's gotten out of hand." Griffin waited.

"What the hell? How long has this been going on? Does Lea know? Are you sure?" I pounded Griffin with questions. Henry had become so mature. He had had two children since the first intervention. How could he still be battling demons? I realized he was an alcoholic.

"I'm not really sure how long. I noticed he had a drink at our wedding. But I couldn't be sure if he was just carrying it or what. It was our wedding, Bae. I didn't want to upset you or get into a fight with Henry."

"That was over a month ago!" I said.

"I know. But it has escalated. About a month ago he came in smelling like a distillery. Lea came to me. She wanted an intervention," Griffin explained.

"Well, she's never been to an intervention," I said. Besides the estrangement from Griffin after I married Elliott, that had been the single worst day of my life. I still had scars.

"She just doesn't know whether Hank should be a part of it," Griffin told me.

"No. Hank is eleven years old. He doesn't need to be in the middle of his family's warfare. It's too raw. What happened? He was doing so good. It's been so long." I felt helpless.

"He's an addict. That's how it works sometimes. But we need to nip it in the bud, sweetie." I had never heard Griffin use a term of endearment and it seemed strange. It underscored how upset he was. How much he needed me. He bore the pain alone.

"I'll come to the restaurant as soon as I get home . . . honey," I said, trying out my own endearment. Griffin laughed.

"That just sounds silly." Griffin was still laughing.

"Well, it didn't sound silly when you said 'sweetie.' This marriage thing isn't as easy as it looks."

"I thought you would be an old pro, seeing as this is not your first rodeo. Besides, I'm much more sentimental than you are."

"I'm willing to let that marriage comment slide only because you are correct about being sentimental. But I do love you." I hung up the phone and prepared to fly home to who knows what.

❧

I made two stops before seeing my husband. First, I stopped in to check on Daddy. I always said "hi there." I never knew who he saw when he looked at me. Most often he probably saw my mom. Seldom did he see me, his daughter. And sometimes the recognition had such a hard time penetrating his boarded-up brain that he just saw someone who looked familiar. I never held it against him but loved him that much harder.

My next stop was to see my brother at NOIR. I took a seat at the bar. I remembered when they opened this place. It had been Henry's salvation. Could the thing that brings us salvation ultimately be our demise? I caught his attention and he came around the bar and kissed my cheek. He showed no outward sign of dissipation. Not like the last time.

"What brings my sister to my humble establishment? I thought you had practically moved to Charlotte." It was a fair comment.

"I can't get a decent sidecar in Charlotte."

"Well, if you're looking for that you came to the wrong place. Trouble in paradise so soon? I thought you had broken in your bartender," he said good-naturedly, as he put down a cocktail napkin.

"I'll have another one with him. No worries." After a little more conversation, I said, "I better get back to my bartender." But I purposely left my drink untouched. When I made it to the door I turned around. I watched my brother down my drink in one gulp. It made me sad. So sad. It wasn't even Scotch, his favorite.

I walked into VERT and sat at the bar. I leaned over and kissed Griffin. We were not big into PDA, but exceptions could be made.

"You may not be sentimental, but I never mind you kissing me," Griffin said as he handed me a drink.

"I can't. The flight was bumpy, and after seeing Henry . . . it just turned my stomach." I relayed my exchange with Henry.

"Addicts are clever. Lea thinks it goes back to when they hired this guy named Chester. He was trouble. He washed dishes at NOIR. He was caught stealing, among other things. We've gotten rid of him, but the damage . . ."

I pushed my drink away. Just looking at it made me sick. "If it hadn't been Chester, it would probably have been someone else," I said.

"You're probably right. Let me do a few things and we can go home together." I watched Griffin speak to a few of the workers. I then watched him speak to a few patrons. In many ways he was very much like my dad. He may be hurting but he was also taking care of business.

When we got home, I rolled my suitcase to the bedroom. Griffin followed me and sat on the edge of the bed, taking his shoes off. I turned around.

"Let me make you feel better." I started kissing Griffin and undoing his shirt. I wanted to take the pain away. I let my hands roam.

"Whoa, Bae. I just can't tonight. Can I have a rain check?"

I stopped and sat next to him on the bed. This had been only the second time he had refused me; the other time was at Martha's Vineyard so long ago, when our actions led to very bad decisions. He must've remembered it too.

"This thing with Henry. It's all on me this time."

I looked at him bewildered. No intervention sex was still the rule of the day.

"Last time, I was in this with your dad. I know Lea wanted this, but as you said yourself, she has no idea," he continued.

My phone buzzed. It was a text from Reggie. I stared at it for a few seconds. Griffin noticed.

"Do you need to get that?"

"It's nothing," I said as I watched Griffin roll his eyes.

"Is this something that can wait until after the intervention?" he asked.

"Most definitely." I tucked Griffin into bed like I would a small child. I was exhausted myself, so I turned in not far behind.

When I walked into the kitchen the next morning, Griffin was staring into space. He didn't even notice I was there. Seeing the toll it was taking on him was actually making me physically sick. I threw up in the sink. The sound jolted Griffin.

"Are you feeling okay?" Griffin jumped up.

"Yes. You're not the only one who's a little jittery," I said.

"We need to take two cars. I'll be the one to take Henry to rehab." And I realized that my dad had taken Henry to rehab the last time and Griffin had tended to me.

"Are you worried about me? I'll be okay."

"Maybe I'm worried about me. We're men now. The stakes are so high."

"You and I are going to be just fine," I said in my most authoritative voice. "We looked after Daddy. We'll look after Lea and the children if we have to. Now let's go and get this over with."

A little while later, Henry came bounding into Griffin's office, unaware of what was about to happen. He was surprised to see me. When Lea walked in, it dawned on him that this was more than a family meeting.

"Well, shit. Fuck you, Griffin! You need to get a life. No. You need to get out of *my* life. This is all on you, brother." It was Hank who locked the door, keeping his father inside. It would be Griffin who took the brunt of it this time. Griffin started.

"You're like a brother to me. You have been my brother since we came into the world. But I just can't take it anymore. You get yourself clean or we are finished. Done. I can buy you out in a heartbeat, and I will. I won't look back." I have never heard Griffin so serious. It scared me.

"Bravo, Griff," Henry said. "But you don't have the nerve to do it. Why don't you focus all your considerable energies on your wife, not me?"

"Just stop it Henry," I interjected. "You're in your thirties. A lot is at stake. Is this the way you want Hank and Maggie to remember you? Because if you don't straighten up, you're going to lose your wife and children." I sat down. My legs were about to betray me.

"I really thought when you got your guy you would be a happier, more fulfilled person, little sister. I guess not. I guess Griffin really doesn't do it for you since you work all the time."

I was about to get up. Henry could make me lose my temper faster than anyone. Siblings. But instead of Daddy, it was Lea this time who stood up and separated us.

"Bailey's right. If you don't stop drinking, I won't let you near the children. I don't trust you with them."

Then something unexpected happened. Henry began sobbing. I almost got up to go comfort him, but Griffin held me back.

"Your tears will not stop me from taking the children away!" Lea exclaimed. I had never heard or seen this side of Lea. Then again, I had never seen her as a mother until now.

"Yeah, Dad. It may have been you and me before you married Lea. But . . ." Hank couldn't finish. He started crying. Henry continued sobbing.

"Fine." It was barely a whisper. A silent resignation. Hank took a few strides to his father and hugged him. Griffin joined them. I watched the looks pass between Henry and Griffin and then I saw the looks pass between Henry and his son. I started crying. It broke my heart. This intervention was so different from the first. It was full of uncertainty. I guess each intervention has its own DNA. Last time we were young and full of dreams. Now we were older. Supposedly wiser. An eleven-year-old shouldn't have to see such things. He certainly shouldn't be a part of an intervention. Hank should be playing with Legos. Should be testing recipes in the kitchen with his dad. Watching Henry, Griffin, and the man-child Hank leave together made me sad. I wanted to be hopeful. But I was scared. Scared for my brother. Scared for Hank. Scared for Griffin and what these memories were doing to him.

I went home with Lea. I knew the drill and I hated knowing the drill simultaneously. We did a thorough search of the house for drugs and alcohol. Every time we found a bottle or a bag of pot, Lea stopped as if each discovery hit her like a slap. After I was sure she was going to be okay, I went home to wait for my husband to return.

I sat at the kitchen table in silence. I had never prayed or thought much about it. But I offered one. A rudimentary one. Asking for help for Henry. Asking for some peace to be restored to Lea and Henry's home and marriage. Asking that the stress and strain would not be too much to bear for Griffin. And yes, that I would be a better wife. The last few months had not been my finest. What was a prayer anyway? A wish? A desire? A want? Maybe it was as simple as a thought. Or a hope? Because I hoped with everything I had that we had seen the last of addiction. I prayed that I would never have to attend another intervention. What is that saying? Be careful what you pray for?

❧

I heard the familiar sound of the key turning. I met Griffin at the door. He walked into my embrace. No words were exchanged between us. There had been so many words thrown around, like weapons, during the intervention. We allowed the silence to soothe us. We were in no hurry to break apart. Griffin stepped back and kissed me. It was a tender kiss.

"What is that I smell? Have you been cooking bacon?" Griffin asked.

I nodded. I didn't tell him I had gone through a whole pound of bacon just to fix a few slices that were crispy the way he liked. I wanted it to be right for him tonight.

"Yes. I was waiting to scramble some eggs. Breakfast for dinner?" I asked, taking his hand and leading him into the kitchen. I had placed the bacon in the middle of the banquette.

"That sounds perfect," Griffin said, grabbing a slice. He was probably starving; he hadn't eaten all day. "This took more time than before. More red tape. Henry told me it had been redecorated since the last time."

As I was scrambling the eggs, I briefly wondered who would choose a career in decorating rehab facilities.

We ate in silence. Occasionally I threw out an easy question. Are the eggs okay? How did I do with the bacon? He nodded or mumbled a single syllable. The day had literally worn him out. I wanted to jump into the silence and fill it with questions, mainly to ask about the condition of Griffin's own welfare, but I showed restraint. My meager gift to Griffin was some eggs, bacon, and silence. He finally finished and stood up to take his plate to the dishwasher. I put my hand over his.

"Just leave it. Let me clean up the kitchen," I said, standing up. He nodded as if I granted him a benevolent request.

"Thanks Bae. I think I am going to take a shower and turn in." He squeezed my hand and disappeared. I heard the shower turn on and I was grateful for my menial task of loading the dishwasher. I sent up another prayer. It was a plea, really. More urgent than the last. It was for Griffin. That he would be safe.

I went back through the condo to turn the lights out, and I sent quick texts to Lea to check on her and the kids, and to Reggie and Elle, giving updates. By the time I got into bed Griffin was already asleep. His hair was still wet. I slid into bed and turned out the lights. Just at that moment, Griffin put his arm around me. His simple act almost undid me.

When I awoke to a brand-new day, I noticed Griffin's arm was still draped around me. Had neither one of us moved during the night? I decided to just stay put; a gesture I was not entirely certain was for me or for my husband. I heard him stirring.

"Bae, you awake?" he whispered, moving closer to me if that were possible.

"Yeah. Are you okay?" I asked, turning my whole body to face Griffin.

"Yes. Thanks for last night," he said, opening his eyes finally.

"It was nothing," I responded, realizing the bar for me had been set pretty low.

"Yes, it was. Is it too late to collect on that rain check?" It took a minute for it to register what he was referring to. I moved to be over him and moved the fugitive hair out of his eyes.

"Never," I said, and I proceeded to kiss him. Tenderly. Gently. Kindly. Touching him in the exact same fashion. My eyes never left him. It was romantic. And necessary. For both of us.

When we were done, neither one of us made any motion to move. For a moment I wondered if we were going to stay in bed all day. To linger. To tarry. To piddle. It would've been nice. I would not have declined. After what seemed to be a sufficient amount of time, Griffin propped himself up onto pillows.

"Bae?" Griffin looked at me. I thought he might suggest a repeat. A day to play hooky.

"What did Reggie text you about the other day? You looked serious when you looked at your phone."

I wondered if he had forgotten. I had hoped maybe he might. It was too soon for reality.

"You really want to know?" He nodded.

"When we were in New York planning the wedding, Reggie made me an appointment to get tested for the BRCA gene with one of the doctors she used to work with. The results came back, and he can see me." It was a mood killer.

"When?" he asked.

"Tuesday."

"Whoa. That's a lot of incoming, Bae," he said, running his fingers through his hair.

"I know. I'm sorry. I can go by myself. I know you're busy," I offered.

"Of course not. I want to go with you. Are you okay with that?" he asked, squeezing my arm before throwing back the covers to get up. I wondered if I should have kept it to myself. Made the trip alone. But I was trying to do better. Not keeping secrets and all that. I got up too and joined him in the bathroom. We were looking at each other in the mirror.

"I just want it to be okay for you," I said.

"I want it to be okay for *us*," Griffin corrected me.

I nodded and wondered if there would ever be a time that my heart stopped expanding when it came to this wonderful man.

"You know, Henry is not the only one with addictions," he said. When I arched an eyebrow, he continued, "No offense, but you have your own addictions, Bae." When I didn't object, he continued. "You're addicted to work. A workaholic. Do you know how many days you have spent at home since we got married?"

The answer was once. He knew it. I knew it. But that was the thing about Griffin. He could level a charge so damning but without any traces of bitterness or anger.

"I know. But you did come to see me." It was a lame defense.

"That was about a month ago, Bae. Part of it is you're addicted to success. I think that's why this thing with Cliff in Charlotte has thrown you for a loop. He didn't just fall at your feet. He's playing hard to get, so you're playing harder. Tell me something. From the time we got out of bed until this very moment, have you checked your emails to see if you have heard from Cliff?"

I frowned. Not only had I checked my emails, but I had also checked Nick's Instagram account to see if he had announced any new projects.

"Guilty. I guess Nick got the job."

Griffin's expression completely changed. "That explains a lot. Nick Gallagher, your old nemesis. You are not going to get every job. It doesn't mean you are not the best. We both know you are." And he smiled when he said it. Talk about being killed with kindness.

"It's hard working by yourself. It's hard being a woman. You know some of these guys have actually told me that they can't hire me because I just got married and I will probably have a baby and lose my edge?"

"There are Neanderthals everywhere," Griffin said. "I've got to go to the market. Shopping for NOIR is a whole new level. I'll try to get home early so we can have a proper dinner. I'll bring a bottle of Sausalito's finest." He pecked me on the cheek and disappeared into the closet to get dressed.

I needed to get dressed too. Check on Lea. Check on Daddy. I studied my reflection. Everything that Griffin had said was right. I had been a crummy wife. I thought about Henry's mantra in AA: One day at a time. I thought of Sausalito. While Martha's Vineyard was Griffin's favorite place, Sausalito had been mine. I loved our time there together. It reminded me of how neither one of us thought of work. Of designs. Of finances. Just each other. And how we were rambunctious and uninhibited in our love. I smiled. I wanted to recapture those moments again.

ॐ

When I got to Lea's she was still in her pajamas. So was Hank.

"Have you guys had breakfast?" I asked, stepping over toys. They both shook their heads, so I went to the refrigerator to look for eggs and bread. After I plated their food, I looked around. Something caught my eye. Dirty clothes.

"Do you mind if I start a load of laundry?" I noticed both Hank and Lea were sitting at the bar in the kitchen, eating—devouring—their eggs.

"You don't have to do that," Lea protested.

"No worries. I may not cook like Henry, but I can certainly do a load of laundry." I poked my head out and smiled at them.

"Where is Maggie?" I asked before I turned on the washer.

"She just went down for a nap before you got here," Lea said. Having a baby and a growing boy led to a lot of dirty clothes.

I hugged Lea in a tight embrace and topped off her coffee. I walked around the bar until I was facing my nephew.

"You know, I just forgot something," I said, and I embraced Hank in a bear hug that he immediately tried to wriggle out of.

"Come on, Bae. I'm almost twelve!" His protests were lackluster. He needed a lot of hugs after what he had endured yesterday.

"I just can't wait to hug you in public." I smiled, picking up one last baby rattle.

"Not gonna happen," Hank said. He finished his eggs, rinsed his plate, and put it in the dishwasher. I nodded, impressed with my nephew.

"Well done," I told him, giving him a last hug.

"That was Dad. He always taught me to clean up after myself." We all let the mention of Henry hang in the air for just a moment. These people missed him mightily. Maybe it was a good thing I didn't get the job in Charlotte.

"You should see his room. I always tell him he's got the cleanest room of any boy I have ever met," Lea informed me. We all smiled.

"That was definitely not the case when your dad was your age!" I laughed and tussled his long hair before leaving.

I arrived at the memory care facility a little before eleven thirty. The sound of music filled the air. Cole Porter, the Gershwins, and Irving Berlin. Most of the residents had smiles on their faces. This music was their music. It was familiar. True to form, Daddy looked like a conductor from his wheelchair.

"Hey there," I said, approaching Daddy.

"Well, honey. So glad you made it. I saved the last dance for you." He was clearly delighted to see me. Of course, he thought I was his wife. I kissed his cheek and then I twirled him around on the imaginary dance floor, laughing with him.

After a few numbers, I felt someone tapping my shoulder.

"May I cut in?" It was Griffin. Daddy released me, clearly delighted at all the happy activity. We swayed together, and after a little bit Griffin whispered, "You still can't dance." Griffin, too, was enjoying himself.

"Only horizontally," I said, as Griffin showed a sly grin. "I didn't know you were coming by to see Dad," I told him.

"I plan to take you up on that later. I come to see Hank every day about this time. After the market. He's like my dad." Griffin embraced me closer.

"No," I said, remembering something, "he's your father-in-law." A big smile stretched across Griffin's face. He hadn't thought of that before.

"I'm really family now. Legit." Before we could continue, the residents started clapping.

"Kiss her! Kiss her!"

Griffin dipped me and then he gave the people what they wanted. But it wasn't just a peck on the lips. It was a bona fide, deep kiss. When I came up for air, I realized I was a little dizzy. Griffin didn't release me until he knew I was steady.

"That's what your kisses do to me," I said. He smiled.

"Would you like to stay for lunch?" Jeri, the senior nurse, asked us.

"Maybe another time," Griffin suggested. We moved to the doors to leave.

"Now who are they?" I heard Daddy ask Jeri.

"That's your son-in-law, Griffin, and your daughter, Bailey."

"You've got to be kidding me," he said aloud. I turned around and saw him smile as he gave his customary response.

&

I spent the day reading and responding to emails. Still nothing from Cliff. I composed several emails in my mind over the course of the day but never sent any of them.

It was late when Griffin came home. I had taken a shower, put some under-eye concealer on, and spritzed some perfume in some naughty places.

"Sorry I'm late. Trying to remember how to juggle three restaurants. I know I promised to cook dinner but I brought something from the restaurant instead." He kissed me. "You smell good. I did remember to bring you a couple of bottles of Sausalito's finest."

"No worries," I said as I set the table and put the two wineglasses in front of him to fill.

"Cheers to my favorite dance partner," Griffin said as he clinked our glasses.

"Haven't you become quite the toastmaster?" I said, sitting down and drinking the wine but also reveling in the memories that it stirred. "This is still my favorite wine. And a memory of one of my favorite times," I said as I began devouring my poached salmon in dill sauce.

"Mine too," Griffin agreed easily. Any uneasiness resulting from the morning's conversation had dissipated. I complimented him on the fish and our easy banter returned.

"Any news from Cliff?" Griffin asked tentatively.

"Cliff who?" I joked as I brought our dishes to the dishwasher.

"Let's go recapture Sausalito." Griffin was never subtle. I turned the lights off and we proceeded to get a little rambunctious, testing out some new moves and revisiting the best of Sausalito. Into the wee hours of the morning.

When we were packing to get ready to go to New York on Tuesday I almost canceled. For the last couple of days, I was starting to feel like a real human again. I was worried about the test. Worried what we would do next. I worried about Griffin. He had so much on his shoulders lately. He didn't need a wife predisposed to cancer. I worried about him more than I worried about myself.

Griffin had already arranged for the girls to meet us after the test. He was going to take us all to dinner. Again, I found myself in a prayerful position. I wanted the test to be negative. Not so much for myself, but for the best man I knew. He occasionally squeezed my hand during the flight, and I could tell he was worried.

Dr. Napolitano had run the test when I had come for the wedding planning. He was a preeminent oncologist at Sloan Kettering, where Reggie once worked and probably would again when her children were older. He was meeting us in his office at four thirty to go over the results. He had requested I come early to do a follow-up blood panel and urine test and mammogram. Reggie said he was nothing but thorough.

A little after quarter to five, he came in with a folder. He sat behind his desk. I was glad he wasn't taking my blood pressure because it would have been through the roof.

"Bailey, I ran the panel regarding the BRCA gene. You do not have the BRCA gene. Which I guess is a double blessing considering . . ." he paused.

We both sat there catching our breath. Trying to take it all in. Griffin spoke first.

"Bae does not have the BRCA gene, but there might be something else?"

"What do you mean 'something else'?" I asked.

"You don't know? You're pregnant, Bailey. It didn't show up in the genetic testing, but it did show up in the exam today," Dr. Napolitano said, and finally a big smile broke across his face. It was all I could do to try and comprehend everything he had just said. It all seemed like such a doozy.

"Bailey's pregnant?" Griffin repeated.

"Yes, I thought you knew that," he said, as if we were stupid.

"No. How far along am I? Is the baby okay?" I asked.

"Bailey, I have no idea. You would have to go to your gynecologist. I'm afraid I'm not an expert at that," said the preeminent oncologist in New York. I thought a minute.

"I have to be five or six weeks along. Maybe the day of the wedding, or . . ." I thought about it. "It had to have happened when you were in Charlotte. I mean . . ." I paused to look directly at Griffin. "You surprised me, remember? We were sort of flying without a net if you get my drift." After Elliott, I had stopped taking the pill and was now using the ring but had forgotten to put in a new one after my last period. I guess the surprise was on us.

"You've been drinking," Griffin said, worried.

"I think some of that is okay in moderation. But you will want to check with your doctor," Dr. Napolitano advised.

Talk about incoming. This was big news. But there was other news that I had been dreading telling Griffin.

"I am so glad that I was able to deliver such good news!" The doctor stood up, ready to dismiss us.

"Thank you, Dr. Napolitano. Is there any place we can talk?" I asked him.

"You could use my office for a bit. I need to see another patient at the hospital. Give my best to Regina and tell her nobody has come close to taking her place. She can come back anytime," he said, leaving us alone.

When we were by ourselves, Griffin looked stricken.

"This is my baby, right?" he started.

"Really, Griffin?" But I knew I was just buying time.

"I know. But what is it?" His eyes were pleading with me.

"This isn't the first time I've been pregnant," I said. We sat in silence for what seemed to be a long time. I didn't want to frighten him, but I wanted to present it in the best possible way.

"I didn't know you and Elliott were even trying to have children," he said.

"Good Lord, no. I never even thought about having a child with Elliott," I scoffed. I watched Griffin and his brain go crazy.

"Was this something that happened back in college? Were you raped? Did you . . ." His voice trailed off.

"No, no—I didn't have an abortion. Why does your mind always go to someplace dark?" I asked.

"Bae—"

I interrupted him. "No. I had a miscarriage." When I was sure he'd put his eyes back in his head I continued. "I had a miscarriage with the only other man I have ever slept with." The answer was perfectly obvious.

"Me? When?" he asked.

"Do you remember when we closed up Daddy's house? That morning?" I said.

"I didn't hear you complaining," Griffin said, waiting for more.

"I didn't. But again—without a net. I didn't even think about it. Several weeks later, I got these terrible cramps. Or what I thought were cramps. I thought, 'I'm going to have to go to the emergency room.' But I went to urgent care instead—"

Griffin interrupted. "Who took you to urgent care?" he demanded.

"I took myself. They told me it wasn't period cramps after all. That I was suffering from a miscarriage. I just had to wait till it was over and then I went home," I explained.

"Where were Reggie and Elle?" he asked.

"They were off with their boyfriends. It was the weekend," I said.

"You didn't tell them?" Griffin seemed shell-shocked.

"What was there to tell? One minute I was pregnant and the next I wasn't. I hadn't had sex with Elliott yet. It would've taken them about one minute to figure it out. Let's face it, all roads lead back to you." I smiled.

"Why didn't you tell me?" he asked.

"What was there to say? 'I'm pregnant. Now I'm not'?" It happened so long ago, but I realized it was fresh news to Griffin.

"I know. But maybe it would've made us do some things differently." Griffin sat silently.

"And me not marry Elliott and go through all that?" I asked.

"I will feel a whole lot better when you get checked out by your doctor," he said, taking my hand.

"Both of the girls have had miscarriages. It shouldn't be a problem. But I didn't want us to get to the appointment and have to fill out the box where it asks 'Have you ever been pregnant?' and have that conversation then."

"A baby. Wow!" Griffin let the happy news bubble to the surface. "This appointment turned out so much better than I thought. Let's go meet the girls." He grinned from ear to ear.

When we sat down at the restaurant, he purposely ordered sparkling water for both of us. It took my girls about two seconds to figure it out.

"Oh my God, you're pregnant!" they yelled in unison.

"It must've been a honeymoon baby," Reggie said slyly.

"I'm about six weeks along, I think," I said.

"Poor Dr. Napolitano, he's the one who tells us you're having a baby along with the other news. He's the most buttoned-up guy I know," Reggie said, and laughed and ordered a bottle of real champagne. My favorite. I had a glass, citing doctor's advice. My phone buzzed. The three of them stared at me, daring me to interrupt our happy festivities. Only later in the night when I was by myself did I check the text that informed me that Cliff wanted to hire me. Shit.

As the night wore on and the laughter overflowed, I watched my husband visibly change. The stress, the strain, and all the unsettling events of the past few days were slowly erased from his face like he had used some newfangled pricey serum. Internal happiness, I have decided, is better than any topical preventative.

I thought about the times that I had thrown up and wondered if that was just a sign of morning sickness. I hoped that, unlike the last time, it was the sign of a healthy baby. Our hands touched each other during the evening. The girls were eager to give advice.

"I think you should hire a baby nurse. Will you turn the second bedroom of the condo into a nursery? Where will we stay?" Reggie asked.

"Maybe they can just put the baby in their room when we come to visit," Elle said to Reggie. "We definitely need to find out when the baby's coming so we can arrange our schedules.

"And Griffin, you better start looking now for a push present!" Elle added seriously. Griffin and I exchanged bewildered looks.

"Come on," Reggie chimed in. "I bet that friend of yours, what's her name . . . Isabel?"

"Annabel," I corrected her.

"I can guarantee you one damn thing—she got her push present with her baby!" Reggie finished. It occurred to me that Annabel and I would have children the same age. That sounded fun. I was starting to realize all the things I didn't know.

"I tend to agree with the girls. If a present is involved, Annabel would want one!" Griffin noted, trying to get a word in edgewise. And for the first time in a very long time, I understood what the phrase "drunk on happiness" meant.

NOW

I was left alone in the bedroom. I had to admit it was nice having Charlie home. Even for a day. Even out of pity. Especially when she believed my innocence. I texted Griffin.

C's home. I peeled off my clothes to take a shower. The answer was swift.

I know. I will bring dinner home was Griffin's reply.

Thanks. I added a *love you.* When no reply came back, I jumped in the shower. It was unlike Griffin not to respond. It was his custom to say *love you too* or *ditto* or *same here* or, if he was really busy, he would send a thumbs-up emoji. He knew how I felt about emojis, and he did it to make me smile. There was nothing today. I tried to not let the lack of response get to me. But it did.

When I walked down the stairs, I thought maybe Charlie had met up with Lucy because it was so quiet, but when I entered the kitchen, there they all were on their devices, reading things off the Internet. The Four Musketeers. When I walked in, it looked like I had caught them in the act. And I realized they were reading press reports to each other.

There sat Lucy, Charlotte's best friend; and Lucy's boyfriend, Thompson, my friend and sometimes collaborator in the restaurant business, Mac Whitney's son. Lucy was the friend I hand-picked for Charlie. Her mother, Sally, had become one of my dearest friends. Charlie had been through everything with Lucy. And Bishop, Charlie's boyfriend, was sitting with them too. He had really been through the good, the bad, and the god-awful with Charlie. My guess is even when they had broken up, he was never really out of the picture. Like Griffin and me.

Bishop was difficult to describe. He was tall and lanky and said very little. His sunny disposition could pull Charlotte out of any funk she was in. He reminded me so much of Griffin. It was hard for me not to have a special affinity toward him. And he was back. Even after all the shit Charlotte had put him through. I knew for a fact Charlotte's heart was never completely indifferent to Bishop. It was Bishop who Charlie called. Bishop who dropped everything and flew to New York. Bishop standing by her. Always. I watched as Bishop touched her hand when she read a troubling article about me on the Internet. When Charlie twisted a piece of her hair between her thumb and index finger, a nervous habit, he gently pulled her hand away.

I caught her watching him when she thought he wasn't looking and no one else was. Had I been that obvious to Griffin when I was young? I loved that man as much today as I ever did. I hoped I hadn't done anything to jeopardize his love for me.

"Hey guys," I said.

"Bailey!" Bishop stood with his impeccable manners. What mother doesn't love a boy with beautiful manners?

"Sit down, Bishop," I told him. I had never liked the kids to call me "Mrs." It was complicated because I kept my last name for my work and, if I am being honest, to put just a little distance between me and the gargantuan Color-Wheel Boys, the nickname my brother and Griffin were given as partners in their three successful restaurants, NOIR, VERT, and BLANC.

"Hi, Bailey—my mother's coming over," Lucy said. She was still wearing the work shirt from her father's office, Cunningham Dentistry. She had split the summer: the first part she had been a camp counselor at her childhood camp in Virginia.

"Wow. It's like a celebration. Or a wake," I joked, giving Lucy a hug. It was strange how I felt I had more leeway with expressing emotions to Lucy than my own daughter.

"I just thought you might like a little moral support," Charlie said. I tried not to show how much this meant to me. This had been the second nice thing she had said to me over the course of a few hours. "Besides, I didn't have enough time to get 'Free Bailey' T-shirts printed!" she laughed. Our eyes met and locked for the briefest of moments. I was too cautious of her glibness. Griffin and Sally walked in together through the back door.

"I'm so sorry!" Sally Cunningham said, pulling me into an embrace. "I wish there was something I could do to help you get out of this fix." She finally let me go. Sally was a crackerjack estate attorney. But she had given up working when her children came. It'd been one of those things Charlotte had thrown in my face when we would have one of our battles. "Why can't you be more like Lucy's mom?" she would ask, inflicting the most damage. Sally often said Lucy wished she had been my daughter. I used to joke and say we always want the kind of mother we don't have. We think everyone else has the cool mom, until one day she told me, "I *do* have the cool mom. I just wish I had the mom who was home." It had crushed me. If I had a dollar for every time she said it, I could've put her through college single-handedly.

I walked over to Griffin to give him a quick embrace. He stepped away.

"I need to unpack dinner before it gets cold," he said. I nodded. I helped him pull out silverware, plates, and serving spoons. We had a full table. And happy noise. Charlotte hated being an only child. She held me personally responsible. She didn't hate it nearly as much as I did. That had been her father's call. But tonight, we laughed and chatted about summer plans. Lucy rolled her eyes about working for her dad.

"I hope I get something more exciting next summer. Not working for Chad. We can't all be Charlotte Hardwick and work for the *New York Times*. One of these days I am going to be *the* friend to someone famous," Lucy said. The hours fell away. It felt good to laugh with these people, whom I loved dearly. My phone buzzed several times and I hadn't even looked at it.

"Don't you think you better look at that?" Griffin said.

Jake wanted me in his office "first thing in the morning ASAP." Charlotte had read it and said, "Doesn't Uncle Jake know he's being redundant?" I laughed. She was such a smart girl, but she could also be a smart ass. That was one of her most endearing qualities.

When everyone had left, Griffin and I were alone in the kitchen. He was cleaning up.

"Let me do that. I don't mind," I offered.

"Thanks Bailey. I think I will go take a shower," he said. That did it. He never called me Bailey. I hated this artificial politeness. It made me sick.

As we turned in for bed, I tried again. I reached to embrace Griffin and give him a kiss. He pulled away.

"I just can't, Bae." He looked helpless.

"You can't or won't?" I asked him.

"It's just going to take me a little time," he said finally.

"Is this because of Elliott?" I asked.

"Well, the thought of you going alone to meet your ex-husband isn't exactly a turn-on," he said, slipping under the covers. At least we were sharing the bed. There had been times when we hadn't.

"What did you think was going to happen with Elliott. I wouldn't jeopardize us. I wanted those pictures. I thought it would be better with just Elliott and me. You know how he feels about you. I did it for Charlotte!" My voice rose.

"I know," he said, after a time.

"If there were any other way, I would've done it."

"I know," he said again. Neither one of us made a motion to turn out the light. The conversation was still not done.

"This is really not the time for you to go off the rails. I need you, Griffin," I said. It sounded like a plea.

"Jake said the same thing. He asked me if I was in it for the duration. I just thought you had learned the lesson about making unilateral decisions," he said, without giving an answer. I hadn't realized he and Jake talked about the case.

"Are you? Are you in for the duration?" I asked him, sounding more like pleading.

"I will get there. It's just going to take some time. We should have gone together," he said, and he turned his nightstand lamp off.

I wanted to ask him how long. But I thought it best to end our conversation on a hopeful note. I cut my own lamp off. Darkness immediately enveloped us. But I couldn't go to sleep. Griffin had still not told me that he had been in New York the night of the murder. I wondered if he would really let me be convicted of a murder I did not commit.

❧

By the time I had gotten dressed, Griffin was already gone. I found Charlotte in the kitchen, finishing the breakfast she'd obviously shared with her dad.

"Dad made you some French press," she said, barely looking up.

"Stop reading that stuff," I chastised, grazing her shoulder.

"It's brutal. One of the headlines reads 'Will Bailey Edgeworth Design in Prison Stripes?' And that's just one." Charlie looked up. "They don't mention my pictures. Thanks Mom." She managed to smile.

"Thanks for coming home and arranging the little gathering last night!" I changed the subject.

"The flight was expensive. You better pay your Visa bill," she joked. I knew that I was my daughter's very own ATM.

"Does Bishop know the whole story?" I asked.

"Yeah. Lucy doesn't know about the drinking. I figured Bishop was Fort Knox, as you like to say," she said. I smiled. Talk about history repeating itself. Right about then, the back doorbell chimed. Charlotte got up to inspect.

"It's Mrs. Harper. She's carrying roses, so unless she has a snake or hidden camera, I think you're good." Charlotte excused herself to get dressed. I went to the door.

"Harriet. Come inside." I noticed she looked uncomfortable.

"Bailey, I just didn't know what to do. Sally told me you love flowers. I grow roses. I don't believe that trash. I just wanted you to know that we were thinking about you and praying for you," she said nervously.

Harriet Harper went to church with Sally. It was the church that Griffin and I had Charlotte baptized in. Occasionally I would go with Sally when I was troubled.

"I just wanted to show my support." I was touched.

"Harriet, that is so nice of you. I love roses. You can't get these from the florist. I really appreciate it," I told her. We both sat in the awkward silence. Charlotte came bounding back in.

"Hello Mrs. Harper. I'm Charlotte. I'm a friend of Hayden. Tell him hello," Charlotte said in her best manners. I could tell this pleased Harriet.

"I will, Charlotte. Mrs. Cunningham tells me you are working at the *New York Times* this summer. That is so impressive. Maybe you can straighten them out!" She may have been awkward with me, but I could tell there was some connection with my daughter. "Well, I better go—I just wanted to drop these off," she said suddenly, and she headed back out the door.

"How do you know Mrs. Harper and her son?" I had forgotten his name.

"Hayden. He's been in and out of rehabs. A bit of a druggie. We shared joints and Adderall a few times. But as you know, those aren't my drugs of choice. I tried to help him," she said matter-of-factly.

"Well, that's nice of you Charlie," I said.

"I probably shouldn't have said anything. They don't call it AA or NA for nothing. My Uber will be here soon," she said.

"I'll take you to the airport," I offered.

"I think we both know you have somewhere else to be. Besides, he's pulling up now." I followed her to the front door. Not before I noticed she was wearing one of my tops. "I'll text you when I get there!" And then she was gone. Without a hug. Without me being able to thank her. Without a warning. Charlotte's departure left my heart full and sad at the same time.

As I drove to Jake's office, I reflected on Harriet's visit, and her son Hayden. Most of us carry our own burdens without any idea of what is weighing others down.

⁂

Both men were waiting for me when I walked into the conference room. As I sat down, Floyd Potts turned on a video screen.

"This is the building footage of the comings and goings the night Elliott was murdered. We're going to look at the tape together. You are going to tell me if you recognize anyone," he instructed.

"I will, but it's been a long time since I lived in this building," I said.

"Understood. But you may see something that I miss," he said, and he started the footage. But then I saw it. I recognized Griffin's hoodie and his bracelets. Lady Jane, Elliott's first wife, stepped off the elevator. They exchanged greetings and left together. There were many hoodies coming and going. I tried not to register recognition.

"Wait. Rewind back just a little bit," Jake requested. He looked at me when he said it. We watched the rest of the video in silence. Floyd motioned for Jake to turn on the lights.

"Other than yourself at the beginning of the tape, did you recognize anyone?" he asked. "Like that man in the hoodie." I couldn't tell if it was a question or statement.

"Floyd, I just don't know. Hoodies are pretty de rigueur in New York," I pointed out, and Jake looked at me and then Floyd.

"Jake, did you recognize anyone?" Floyd pressed on. Jake looked at me again as if he was being disloyal.

"He looked familiar. I mean, he could pass as Griffin's double," Jake said.

"What is it with you people and my time?" Floyd was angry. "Of course, it was Griffin. Why didn't you tell me, Bailey? How many times do I have to tell you this is serious? I'm guessing you've known this whole time and that's why you were withholding your alibi. I'm also willing to bet that Griffin doesn't know you know. Who is the woman he met? How am I doing?"

"It was Griffin. Her name is Jane Turner. Lady Jane. She was Elliott's wife before we married. They recently remarried. I know he was in New York the night Elliott was killed. He doesn't know I know. I sure didn't know he was meeting Jane, and what does it matter, Floyd? What if he was there? It's my DNA that's all over the place," I admitted.

"Why don't you tell me what you know," Floyd requested.

"I knew he was there because there was a charge on my Starbucks app. Upper East Side. For a grande Americano the night of the murder. Griffin doesn't know I know. The other thing I know is that Griffin wouldn't let me take the blame for something he did," I explained.

"You may be the only person in history that gets wrongly convicted due to DNA evidence. But if it was your husband, he may have just committed the perfect murder. That better be all that there is. This is going to be a hard case unless some other evidence comes to light."

About that time Floyd's phone buzzed. Then Jake's. And then mine. I heard Floyd's exchange. "That was your friend Elizabeth. They have called your daughter in for questioning. She thought it a good idea for me to be with her. I can't represent Charlotte, so I recommended an associate."

"I really appreciate that. She has a tendency to talk too much." Floyd looked at me with a knowing nod. Jake stopped him.

"I have to head to the police station. There is an inconsistency with Griffin's statement. His initial statement said he was in Atlanta, but Lady Jane has contradicted him, so the police want to bring him back for questioning. The police might not have realized it was Griffin, but Lady Jane was happy to comply." Both men left together, leaving me alone.

My daughter was being questioned about the night of Elliott's murder when she was so drunk she doesn't remember, my husband had just been caught in a lie to the police, and I still didn't have the compromising pictures of Charlie. I closed my eyes. Would this nightmare ever end?

ꕥ

I was out in my office when the phone buzzed. It was Charlie.

"I just got back from the police station."

"What did you tell them?" I asked.

"Not much. The attorney Floyd sent was pretty slick. He didn't let me say too much. I just told the police that I was in my dorm waiting for Bishop to come. Let's be real, that's about all I can remember. I was so trashed. It made me so scared."

"I'm sorry, Charlie. I'm sorry that I ever brought Elliott into any of our lives."

"I'm sorry you are going through this. I'm glad Dad is in the clear."

"About that. Your dad had to change his statement. It seems he was in New York the night of Elliott's death meeting with Desi's mom."

"He lied to the police?" Charlie said, and then, "You're not surprised? You knew, didn't you?"

"Yes," I said.

"You are protecting Dad, aren't you?"

"I'm protecting you too, Charlie."

❧

"Bae. Have they found the real killer yet?"

"Sweetie, you work for the *New York Times*. You would know better than I would."

"The paper wants me to work more than part time my last semester. They said that if I did a good job it could turn into something permanent." She waited. These sorts of conversations didn't often happen between Charlie and me. We didn't talk every day. But when we did it was something about our professions. We had a mutual respect in the job we each did.

"Oh, Charlie, that is really exciting. How would that work with school?"

"Bailey, the buzzkill. I would juggle my schoolwork with my job at the paper," she said as if it were no big thing. I had to smile. I was bursting at the seams with pride, but I was also too scared to show too much.

"No, you have it all wrong. I am very proud of you. I just don't want too much stress on you."

"You mean so I won't fall off the wagon again," Charlie snapped.

"I didn't mean that at all. I just want you to enjoy your last semester of college. Like normal people."

"You of all people should know we are not normal people. If I'm anything like you, Miss 40 Under 40, I will have a Pulitzer by the time I'm forty. Unless I publish the memoir, with your title, and earn a book award in my late twenties."

"I certainly hope you plan to dedicate that memoir to me. Because if it weren't for me you wouldn't be screwed up and have enough material to write a memoir." I found myself laughing and I heard Charlie laugh too.

We shared the same dark humor, and sometimes that was the only thing that kept us connected.

"Good one, Mom," Charlie said. I knew she was smiling because she called me Mom.

"Don't worry, I'll include in my dedication that it was you who gave me my first box of pens." She remembered her birthday present as a happy memory. I remembered it as another one of the tortured memories between us.

"Well, I guess I had better go and get back to work. Let me know if you need anything, Bae." She was gone. But it was as if she still wanted to talk. That desire brought me comfort.

❧

I decided to take a shower before Griffin came home. The law office made me feel dirty, nasty, and guilty.

I threw off my clothes and jumped in the shower. I let the hot water beat down my back. Washing me clean. Washing me free from this nightmare. After getting dressed, I noticed that our dirty clothes were overflowing. I rarely did the wash myself anymore. Griffin handled it. I was gathering up my dirty clothes when I noticed. The gray hoodie. I looked at it for a moment. I wondered if I should pick it up with my brush. Would it contain Elliott's DNA? Should I wash it? Maybe Griffin knew I didn't kill Elliott and that was why he hadn't told me. He hadn't been privy to the conversations with Floyd Potts and knew the evidence against me was stacked up like this pile of dirty clothes.

Suddenly Griffin was standing over me. I jumped.

"You're doing laundry?" he asked as I quickly sandwiched the hoodie between other dirty clothes so it was hidden. Maybe he had forgotten to wash it with all the drama over my arrest and Charlie being home.

"Yes. I was going to start a load of laundry. Is there anything else you need to throw in?" I tried to sound casual. Maybe it was Griffin who thought I was acting guilty.

❧

"Would you take the load down for me?" We both looked at the pile as if it were a bomb about to explode and we would get hit by shrapnel. I started the load, including the hoodie, while Griffin put dinner on the table. I poured myself a glass of wine and started eating. I noticed we ate in silence. I put my fork down. The noise caused Griffin to look at me.

"Well, who's going to go first?" I asked. "How was your day?"

"Why didn't you tell me you had an airtight alibi?" Griffin asked.

"How do you know about my alibi?" And then it dawned on me. "Of course. Charlie told you."

"She couldn't wait to call me. She yelled at me for letting you take the blame."

"You mean Charlie cared? She'd rather you go down for murder than me?"

"She also told me you knew I had been in New York that night. Why didn't you say anything? How did you know?"

"Because you charged a coffee to my account. And reloaded my card. Thank you for that, by the way. Your pal Lady Jane gave you up."

"Why didn't you say anything?"

"Because I will do whatever it takes to protect you and Charlie."

"Well, aren't you and your daughter a pair of Nancy Drews." He smiled.

"We think we are. Is it time for a game of 'Who Is the Murderer'?" This drew a suppressed laugh from Griffin.

"Yes. I was in New York. I was going to meet with Lady Jane to see if she would give me the pictures. We met in the building and then went to Starbucks around the corner to chat. She didn't have them. If it were up to her, she would burn them. She dislikes Charlotte as much as we dislike Desi. I knew better than to ask Elliott, so I left. I took the next plane out."

"Floyd has already hired a private investigator. Maybe it's a good thing we never had any more children. No telling what the bill is going to be for Floyd's defense." I watched Griffin's expression change. "I didn't tell you anything because I was trying to protect you and Charlie. But I didn't kill Elliott either, even though I wanted to. I cut my finger on the manila envelope and that's why my blood is in his apartment. We looked around his apartment to see if we could find the pictures. We didn't, so I left."

"Just how far were you willing to go to get the pictures back?" It was still tugging at Griffin's heart.

"I loathe Elliott. I wanted to protect Charlie. To protect her career. This may be fine for Hollywood but not for someone working at the *New York Times*. I wouldn't do anything to jeopardize us. Or our family."

We sat in silence a little while longer.

"You probably thought when I married Elliott, my marriage to him was going to be the hardest thing for you to get over. You never knew I would be implicated in his murder. I've asked you to do a lot when it has come to me."

"I'm still pissed that you went alone," Griffin said, stretching his arm across the table and touching my own. It was these connections that had gotten us through some of our toughest domestic turbulence.

"Did Charlie tell you her news?" I asked, changing the subject. He shook his head.

"The *New York Times* has asked her to stay on. I am so proud of her."

"She takes after her mother."

"You're coming on pretty strong."

"Is it working?"

In truth, we hadn't been together since this ordeal happened.

When he got into bed, he kissed me. He hadn't really kissed me since the arrest. He looked at me and his eyes were tender. They reflected the years of moments like this between us. We had been in bad places with each other—when I was upset about something, when I was sleeping in a separate bedroom, when Charlie asked me if we were getting a divorce. We had always found our way back to each other. Tonight was no different. I brushed the hair back from his eyes after we were done. We made no effort to break apart.

THEN

TWENTY-THREE YEARS AGO

Griffin and I were in an examination room with Dr. Sutton, my gynecologist. I had made an appointment as soon as we returned home.

"Do you hear that?" she asked in her soothing tone. "That is the baby's heartbeat." I couldn't believe that sound was coming from inside me.

"Wow. You are amazing, Bae," Griffin said, squeezing my hand tighter.

"I'm pretty sure I couldn't have done it without you," I said, trying to suppress a huge grin and having no success whatsoever.

"Soon, we can see the sex of your baby, if you want?" Dr. Sutton asked.

"I just know we are going to have a little boy. I just feel it," I told them.

"I want to be surprised," Griffin said, and I let him have his way.

"Go ahead and get dressed and meet me back in my office."

When we got back to Dr. Sutton's office, she explained some more of what we could expect.

"You are about seven weeks along. I would put your due date around April 1," she said clinically.

"April Fools' Day? Our baby is screwed!" I exclaimed.

She laughed. "Give or take a few days. We're on the baby's schedule at that point."

"So between the Ides of March and April Fools' Day," I said, shaking my head. But it was Griffin who had all the serious questions.

"Do you think it's a good idea for Bailey to work? Can she drink? Can we—"

"Yes. I think it is a fine idea for Bailey to work. One cup of coffee each day is fine, but I would avoid alcohol. And as far as having sex, certainly. You are not going to hurt the baby. But Bailey, I would not fly after about the seventh month. Or early in the eighth month at the latest."

I did the calculations in my brain. Against my better judgment, I had accepted Cliff's job. We were almost in September. If I could do all the installation by the end of January or the beginning of February, it would be okay. That would give me plenty of time.

We went home and proceeded to begin allowing our love to include our baby. We were both amazed by how love could do this. Create. I would never get over what our bodies did for love. What they do for love.

Afterward, neither one of us was in a hurry to get up or dress.

"This is really quite something," Griffin mused. "We made a family."

I smiled at him. There was something almost reverential in the way he said it. Said the word *family*. I knew it was not inconsequential.

"What do you think about the name Jack Hardwick? I think that sounds all-American. Or what about Robert Hardwick? Rob?"

"Those are great names," Griffin said, clearly pleased. "I would really like to use the name Anderson after your dad. But what if it's a girl?" He laughed. I was touched that he wanted to use Daddy's name. But I had always known how he felt about Hank Anderson Edgeworth.

"It will never be a girl. Girls don't have souls until they are my age. We're most definitely having a boy," I informed him.

"I thought about what you said. About my addictions. About me being addicted to success. I hate to admit it, but you were right. I just have a more socially acceptable addiction than Henry does. But I promise you, I am going to maintain a healthy work-life balance. You always have the ability to call me out on my shit."

Griffin smiled and rewarded me with his kisses, which I would never grow weary of. Except when I was hungry. Which was now.

I had been good for my word. Every Friday afternoon, either at two o'clock or four o'clock, I would fly back to Atlanta. On Sunday, I turned around to go back to Charlotte. But during the hours that I was in Atlanta, I did not utter Cliff's name. It was Cliff and Cliff's project along with Griffin's observations that taught me the meaning of balance. But it was hard work.

On Saturdays when I was home, I would go visit Daddy and then go by NOIR to see Henry. Henry was doing so much better. I had grown to appreciate my brother's counsel and friendship. It was just before Christmas and Henry and Griffin had prepared a special holiday nine-course tasting menu for NOIR including Griffin's signature cocktail of a "Brandy Alexander eggnog" and a main course of lamb with organic mint and cucumber glaze and a chocolate trifle with raspberry and Grand Marnier sauce for dessert.

"Well, look at us, little sister," Henry said as he placed a cappuccino in front of me. "Here we both are facing the holidays and neither one of us is drinking. Talk about a Christmas miracle." I smiled. The fracture that occurred in his family was mending. He looked good. Healthy. I knew it was still a one-day-at-a-time proposition but none of us would take his sobriety for granted. Especially Henry. He worked hard at it.

"And if we're talking Christmas miracles, don't think I haven't noticed that you have been in town every weekend since you started on that wretched project with that jackass client."

"Let's just say you aren't the only one with big addictions. My husband had his own little intervention with me when we found out I was pregnant."

"Why wasn't I invited to that intervention? I would've loved to put in my two cents' worth about how screwed up you are." Henry laughed.

"Why do you need an intervention? You tell me that every day," I said. "I am glad you are back in good form."

"I'm going to enjoy my front-row seat watching you balance your commas and prepositional phrases: Bailey Edgeworth, visionary, versus Bailey Edgeworth, wife and mother. That should be fun. I think you're going to need someone like me to pull you back from the ledge."

"I think you have job security there. You are the best brother. I am proud of you, Henry." And I was.

Griffin and I made a trip to New York before the holidays to see the girls. They were delighted at my expanding girth. They were surprised that no one in Atlanta was giving me a baby shower. I had to remind them that Annabel was my only female friend and she had just had a baby herself. A girl, who she named Whitney. Her maiden name. I knew Reggie and Elle well enough to see that they were concocting a scheme.

"Now don't go planning a surprise baby shower. I'm still working, you know," I reminded them.

"I think a surprise baby shower is perfect. I mean, I would think the woman who planned her own surprise wedding would be on board with the idea," Griffin said happily.

I still had some surprise Christmas presents for Griffin. I had wrapped several baby onesies, a couple of rattles, and a copy of *The Giving Tree* and tucked them under the tree for Griffin, from Santa. I knew he would read the book immediately and cry. This was such a Griffin book. Christmas morning, as he unwrapped all the presents, he got choked up and looked at me squarely in the eye.

"How am I going to cook Christmas dinner if I am a blubbering mess? I love you, Bailey Edgeworth, sometimes Hardwick!"

I laughed and went over to him, taking his dear face. I kissed him long and lovingly. I kissed him with all the desires that our bodies had shared.

ঔ

It was mid-January. Cliff's installation for his new restaurant, Bravo, would be complete in the next few days. Which was a good thing because Dr. Sutton had moved up my due date. Cliff and I were having our weekly meeting as we walked around the restaurant. I was impressed. The combined elements of white and deep azure tones with the dark wood did give off a sexy vibe. I had to do a little legwork to find paintings that would underscore the rich tones and offset the white. That was the one good thing about Cliff, though. Once he hired me, I was able to choose as I wanted. I had found four paintings at an estate sale in the Eastover section of Charlotte. Apparently, the woman living in this big house was a patron of this artist. I found two more paintings at galleries in the South End section of Charlotte. I had them reframed and hung throughout the restaurant. The paintings supported the cozy feel I was trying to create. The light fixtures were white. I just couldn't use white more without throwing the vibe I was trying to create off-balance.

"When do you think you'll have the grand opening?" I asked as we were finishing up.

"If you think you'll be done in a couple of days, then maybe in two weeks. Have a soft open on a Thursday and the grand opening on the following Saturday. Before we go any further, I want you to take a look at the menu and sample a few of the dishes Ken came up with." He said it as a statement. I was about to protest, but it was one thirty in the afternoon and the baby needed lunch. We sat down in a booth and Cliff motioned for Ken to bring the dishes over. I noticed he offered a glass of water in the azure barware I had selected. I took a bite of the halibut. The chef had also featured two versions of gnocchi—a meat version and a vegetarian variety.

"A braised beef gnocchi. And the vegetarian has a red pepper and cream sauce. Let me know what you think," Ken explained, and then he left us to try everything. The braised beef had a tangy sauce very similar to a sweet-and-sour sauce, but it was lighter and fit perfectly with the beef.

The red pepper and cream sauce was just delicious. However, the gnocchi itself was doughy and chewy. It almost ruined the rest of the creation.

"The gnocchi is made in-house," Cliff offered.

"I sure as hell wouldn't tell anybody," I said, having let my guard down. I recovered. "What I mean is that the beef is so tender and juicy and the sauce complements it perfectly. The red pepper and cream sauce is one of the best I have ever eaten. You are going to get dinged on the gnocchi, though. The halibut is some of the best I've eaten." I suppose Cliff took what I said to heart. I guess being from a family of chefs gave me a viewpoint that he respected.

"But you like the flavor?" he asked, leaning in to take a bite off my plate.

"Yes. The flavors are wonderful."

"I see what you mean by the gnocchi. I'll get Ken to work on it. Would you be willing to sample again?" He put his own fork down and took the napkin to his lips.

"Cliff, you don't know me very well. I never turn down food."

At this, he laughed. "And to think I almost hired Nick Gallagher," he said freely. We had come a long way since those early encounters when we both left frustrated and out of sorts. "Providing I can get the gnocchi worked out, do you think we could have a soft opening in two weeks, followed by the grand opening the following Saturday?"

I looked at my calendar and saw that was the last week of January. Perfect.

"That sounds great, Cliff. I think it came together really nicely." He nodded and smiled.

"Hey, could I bring a plus-one to the grand opening?" I asked. Cliff paused and grinned from ear to ear.

"I thought you were pretty much carrying around your plus-one with you," he said, pointing at my belly. I had not told Cliff I was pregnant, nor had he asked, but I suppose at this point it was obvious. And then he laughed.

"Bailey, you forget. I've been married four times. You don't survive four marriages without learning a thing or two about women. You never mention weight. Never." He laughed and then got serious. "I really wasn't sure how you were going to incorporate those paintings. But I like what you have done. You have made the restaurant look smaller. Cozier. It's better than I hoped it would be."

We had had a bumpy start to be sure. I worried that he didn't trust me or would second-guess his decision not to hire Nick. And I kept my promise to Griffin. I hadn't worked a single weekend. I had achieved a successful work-life balance here in Charlotte.

The next morning before I started work, I paid a visit to an upscale women's fashion boutique called Thrift. It was anything but. It was perhaps the most celebrated store for women's clothes in Charlotte. It was owned by Mimi Thrift, who was said to have amazing taste.

I strolled into the store, allowing my eyes to roam over the merchandise. A harried young salesgirl came up to me. It surprised me because it was barely ten o'clock in the morning and she already seemed out of breath.

"Can I help you?" she asked, regaining her composure.

"Yes, I am looking for something to wear to a grand opening," I told her.

"You came here?" She sounded exasperated.

"Yes," I responded, although that was perfectly obvious. "I think now I'm about a size 8. Maybe a 10." I usually wore a size 2 or 4. That was pre-pregnancy.

"You came here? I don't think we have anything for you here," she said. I was beginning to think I was in that scene from *Pretty Woman*, when Julia Roberts strolls into a high-end store and they refuse to sell her any clothes.

About that time a sophisticated and well-dressed woman in high heels breezed in, wearing large sunglasses as if they were a statement in and of themselves. To my surprise she approached us. "What seems to be the matter?" she asked in a commanding voice. The young woman answered her.

"She is looking for something to wear. Here." I hated being referred to as "she." I assumed this was Mimi Thrift.

"Bailey Edgeworth. I am looking for something to wear to a grand opening." I handed her my business card.

"You came here?"

"Yes." I was not going to be intimidated.

"We don't carry maternity attire," Mimi said, handing her satchel, which looked like mine, off to the young woman. She extended her hand. "Mimi Thrift."

"Yes, I'm pregnant, but I don't like maternity clothes. They are just garish. I have made it through my entire pregnancy without succumbing. Can you help me?" For the first time Mimi laughed.

"Garish. That is exactly how I would define maternity wear." She pretended to think about her merchandise. I say "pretended" because women like that—like me—know exactly how they want to proceed. She strolled over to a neatly grouped column of dresses and pulled out a beautiful frock. I guessed it was a Missoni, based on its wild coloring. I owned a vintage Missoni that I had purchased a few years back at Stock Exchange, a consignment store located in Peachtree Battle. I loved it. I'd worn it to Mac's grand opening in New York.

"I'm not sure I want to draw that much attention to my belly," I pointed out. I also wasn't sure I wanted to take any attention away from Cliff.

"I understand," she said, as her eyes continued their visual travel around her boutique. Our gazes landed on the same dress at the same time. It was beautiful. She pulled it out for a closer look. "What do you think about this dress?" she asked. It was a cream Valentino.

"What's not to like?" I asked, straining to get a look at the price tag.

"Why don't you try it on and see what you think?" she offered.

"So that is how you reel them in!" I laughed, but I was already in a dressing room. Being pregnant had made me much more modest. Clearly she understood and closed the door.

"Let me know when you have it on. No one has tried it on yet," she called.

Getting a close-up look at the price tag, I knew why. It looked good on me. I opened the door. "This is what happens when a beached whale models Valentino. I don't know . . ." I said, but I knew I was going to buy the dress.

"You look lovely. And after the baby comes you could get a fun belt and cinch it in or take it in at those side seams," she suggested. I had already come to that conclusion myself if I was going to spend this kind of money. I put my clothes back on and they felt a good deal frumpier next to what I had just worn. Moving to the cash register, I spied a beautiful blouse hanging by itself.

"You've got good taste. That would fit you now and after. It is a YSL size 6." She smiled. I frowned. At the rate this was going, these purchases would be classified as Griffin's push present. She wrapped both garments up like she was wrapping her grandmother's fine china. "You said you had a grand opening. What for?" she asked.

"For business. I design restaurants." In many places, a high-profile job for a visibly pregnant woman might be looked down upon. But Mimi Thrift struck me as the kind of woman who would appreciate vision and work ethic. She just nodded.

"For Cliff's new restaurant." She said it as a statement rather than a question.

I nodded slightly. The world could be a very small place, and I did not like to mix business with pleasure. I had done that with Elliott. I would never repeat that mistake again.

"I'm the first," Mimi said offhandedly. It took me a minute to catch her drift. And then it dawned on me she was the first Mrs. Cliff Rushton. I wondered if I would run into any of the rest while I was here. Mimi carefully took my garments out of the shopping bag bearing her logo and transferred them into a nondescript bag. "Much better." She thought for a moment and added, "What sort of jewelry will you be wearing?" I was relieved that she had changed the subject.

"I have a pair of peridot and diamond earrings that my husband gave me." I smiled to myself. I may be the only woman in history who received the same pair of earrings from two different husbands. I didn't count Elliott, although he was the initial giver. Griffin had bought them from Lady Jane because he knew that I loved them so much.

"Perfect. Here is my card. If you want the cool belt or anything else, I can text you pictures." I bet she could.

"I think I've done enough damage for a long time," I said, hoping the dress dazzled Griffin as much as it did me.

ঔ

"Wow" was Griffin's response two weeks later when I opened the door to greet him to go to Cliff's grand opening. I hadn't shown him the dress while I was home. I was not the kind of girl who needed constant compliments on my appearance. I was not the kind of girl who needed affirmation of Griffin's deep devotion. I was not even the kind of girl who got homesick, really, and yet . . . seeing my husband before my eyes, I decided at almost eight months pregnant maybe I was that kind of girl. It certainly felt good to be wanted and desired.

"You like it?" But it was clear he did.

"I wish we didn't have to go to this opening," Griffin said, embracing me. We kissed as if we were not going to a grand opening.

"Let me take a quick shower and change and I'll be ready," Griffin said, disappearing into the bathroom.

ঔ

I tried to lower expectations for Griffin as we entered Bravo.

"It isn't really white. It isn't green. But you worked your magic, Bae." Griffin nodded as he looked around.

There was a happy buzz, which was one of my favorite sounds in all the world. I had fallen in love with the sound of Saturday nights in Daddy's restaurant, I had loved it at each of the openings of Henry and Griffin's restaurants, and I even loved it at Elliott's. The sound to me was more intoxicating than champagne.

"You must be Bailey," a blonde bobbed woman said, extending her hand. "I'm Cliff's wife, Cheryl."

I shook her hand and made a mental note that she looked remarkably like the first Mrs. Cliff Rushton, Mimi Thrift. "I just love it. And I love what you're wearing."

"I've had this for a while," I said, committing to a lie that two weeks could constitute "a while." I introduced Griffin to Cliff and then Cliff took the floor to make a toast. He was a very polished toaster. After an acceptable amount of time, Griffin and I made our excuses and went back to our hotel.

Griffin devoured my kisses and everything I had stored up for him. He showed more enthusiasm than he did for any offerings in Cliff's restaurant. It took some maneuvering, but somehow, we made it work. Afterward, we lay spent, with smiles on our faces.

"One hundred percent," I remarked, and remembered how after each and every opening we always ended up like this doing the "horizontal tango."

"Not quite. There was VERT," Griffin said, remembering the second opening during my disastrous divorce and Elliott's crazy demand that I could live with Griffin but in order to receive my money, we couldn't have sex. I don't know how I agreed to such a thing, but I had felt so poor and like such a failure. It was money that I had rightly earned, so I had agreed to it. It seemed easy until it wasn't. I had to sign an affidavit regarding my abstinence. Then and only then did I receive my check.

"Well that was a court-ordered kibosh. And for the record I hated it as much as you did," I said, turning to face Griffin.

"Not possible. If you recall, I took out my checkbook on many occasions," Griffin laughed.

"Why do you think Elliott made that demand in the first place? He practically hated me at the end. And he had been unfaithful while he was doing all those drugs," I said.

"Are you kidding? He was so controlling of you. He was obsessed with you. I don't want to talk about Elliott anymore. I will say I was afraid for your safety for a while."

"Not too bad, especially with a baby on board," I said, wrapping Griffin's arms around me.

"This baby better get used to his parents loving each other," Griffin said.

"You said 'his.' Are you coming around to the fact that we are having a little boy?" I asked. But we were both drifting off to sleep after a lovely evening.

❧

As we approached the condo, it felt different. Like the feeling you have when you have gotten robbed. I realized my sinister thoughts were all unfounded when the door flew open and there stood Regina, Elle, and Annabel. Smiles covered their faces just like robbers' masks.

"Surprise! Welcome to your baby shower!" they said in unison as Griffin and I walked in. I noticed my husband was wearing the same smile they had on their faces.

"You really weren't kidding about a surprise shower!" I said, watching the three of them, being grateful for them.

"Actually, we told you we were having a surprise shower early on—you just didn't listen," Griffin said and embraced me and then all three women. He seemed surprised to see Annabel. I noticed there were no presents.

"I don't know much about women's showers, but shouldn't there be gifts?" I rolled my luggage into the bedroom.

"Oh, honey. Your friends told me the situation was dire when they got here," Annabel said as she was pouring everyone a mimosa except for me. Her daughter, Whitney, had been born three months prior and Annabel had chosen not to nurse her baby. I always joked with her that it was a matter of alcohol versus breast milk.

"Except for that baby crib with some green and white gingham, there are no signs of a baby. You are in deep shit." Annabel took a sip from her glass.

"I just figured I would buy stuff when the baby comes. Once we know whether we are having a boy or a girl," I said, taking a glass of orange juice and clinking it to everyone's glass. The women exchanged knowing glances.

"Think again. You are not going to have any time when the baby comes to do anything. I mean, you'll be lucky if you get a chance to brush your teeth. And take a shower each day. It's going to feel like a baby tsunami," Elle informed me.

"You're forgetting," I began. "Amazon Prime."

"You have no idea how many diapers you are going to go through a day," Annabel said. "You will need to become a 'diaper hoarder.' You think you have a lot of diapers—you have no idea how much comes out of their little bodies. And if it's a little boy you can use two diapers within the span of five minutes."

I must have appeared faint because Reggie came over and embraced me. This was beginning to feel more like an intervention than a baby shower. Everyone sat down. And it was Regina who spoke first. She was serious. I always listened to her. She fanned her arm around the condo, which was starting to look very small.

"Bailey, you need a house. You would be surprised at how much room an eight-pound baby takes up. All their stuff. Babies do not travel light," she said, giving me a hug that I didn't know I needed until now. "Griffin?" Reggie turned to Griffin and everything dawned on me. When my voice came out it was barely above a whisper.

"Did you buy a surprise house for us?" I asked, remembering how Griffin had secretly purchased this very condo and asked me if I liked it and did I want to decorate it for him. I realized five minutes into it that he was just bluffing and had already bought it.

"No, I haven't. Yet. Besides, this time you would have to sign the papers since your name is going to be on the deed." He paused and let me take in the legal ramifications. "This house, unlike the condo, would be ours. However, I have done some legwork," he said.

"Why can't we just open presents and play stupid baby games?" I asked.

"Why don't you let us go buy some of the essentials? I know you probably want to buy the baby clothes and other stuff. But there is still so much, like a changing table and strollers, that we can help you with," Elle suggested.

I started crying. I was beginning to feel like a failure as a mother before the baby even arrived. That must be a record. I remembered when I was going through my divorce with Elliott and what I learned about acceptance. It is very important to accept ourselves where we are. It is also important to accept others and their kindness. It is like receiving their love. I knew that I needed their help, and I also knew that they needed to feel like they were helping me. Sometimes shutting your mouth and just saying "Thank you" was the hardest thing and yet the best thing to do.

"Okay, do your best or worst." I suggested Griffin's card knowing that I had just purchased that dress from Mimi Thrift with my credit card. Divorce is hard on one's credit. "Well, let's get shopping then!" I cheered. Now it was Griffin who came over to me and hugged me and said, "Thank you, Bae." I realized Griffin needed validation too.

We all scattered like field mice. Some baby shower. The girls left to hit every baby store in Atlanta. Griffin and I drove to the destination in almost complete silence. He parked in front of a house on a beautiful cul-de-sac. I knew immediately what drew him here. The street reminded him of our house growing up. Before we got out of the car I took his hand.

"Before we look at houses, I really need to ask you something. It's been on my mind since the intervention with Henry. You said you could buy Henry out with no sweat. That takes a lot of money. Do you really have that kind of money?"

"I hope you're not saying you married me for my money. But yes—it would be hard but I could buy Henry out. I would need a wife who works her ass off, which coincidentally I have. Hopefully Henry has straightened out. Don't worry about these houses, they are all within our price range."

I had never even thought of Griffin's money. He lived so simply.

"I've started with my favorite house. It is a four-bedroom, four-and-a-half-bath house. The neighborhood is a big draw."

"Why do we need such a big house?" I asked. I noticed a woman coming out of the house waving at us to come in. She must have been the real estate agent working with Griffin.

"It's actually smaller than your dad's. We'd have a bedroom, the baby would have a bedroom. Another bedroom for maybe another baby, and another for a guest room or office. Not so big." He got out of the car.

It resembled Daddy's house, but a 2.0 version. Instead of a living room, it had a giant great room on one side and a dining room on the other. The staircase was at the back of the great room. I gravitated toward the kitchen, but Griffin led me upstairs to the bedrooms. Each was a good size and connected to its very own bathroom. The master bedroom had a massive walk-in closet—the kind you see on commercials, with recessed lighting and enough room for a piece of furniture. I loved the natural light and I loved the bones of the house. If Griffin had not gone into the cooking industry, he could've been a real estate tycoon. He certainly knew how to choose quality.

"Okay, you can go back downstairs and look at the dining room and kitchen," Griffin said. We made our way downstairs and he leaned into the doorframe of the kitchen and just waited.

The kitchen was huge. But at the end of the kitchen was a round breakfast room. I had never seen a round room before. I had seen bay windows. I had seen round tables in square rooms, but never a round room. Beautifully made windows. The sunshine streamed in and you could almost envision a family having a raucous mealtime, full of conversation.

"The sellers will leave the table if you want. It was custom-made to fit the space." He smiled. He knew he had me.

"Damn you. You always know what I like. Who's ever seen a round breakfast room before?" I went over and embraced him.

"And I hope you noticed the prerequisite banquette," Griffin pointed out, hugging me back. "Through the butler's pantry is a laundry room."

I hadn't even noticed the butler's pantry. "I like the idea of a cul-de-sac because it's not a cut-through street. I drove by earlier this week and saw kids riding their bicycles." He chuckled. "It's a safe place for kids to play outside."

I said just three words: "Make an offer."

"I will. I was waiting on you. I didn't want to make any unilateral decisions," Griffin said.

It occurred to me that families are not born. They don't just happen. They are stitched together over time. They are stitched together with each decision that is made. To get married. To have a baby. To buy a house. And they are fortified by memories. I remember how happy Griffin had been when he showed me his condo. If anything, he was happier today. I took one final look around the neighborhood and reflected on the normal-looking houses. I wondered who our neighbors would be and whether we would become friends. Would our children? Sometimes you don't know what a gift you have when you buy a house. Because you are also buying a neighborhood. And neighbors.

"We may be buying a house today, but we better get home to see what kind of damage the girls are doing with your credit card!" I said, maneuvering myself back into the car.

After some legal wrangling the house became ours and we moved in two days before Valentine's Day.

The crib with the green gingham check looked right at home in the room we had selected for the baby. Thanks to the girls, there was furniture, clothes, mobiles, and lots and lots of diapers. We did look like diaper hoarders.

For the last month of my pregnancy, I became what I'd heard about: a nester. I spent all my time on my computer looking at fabrics, bedding, and everything in between. While I loved all of our stuff, it looked tired in this new house full of light. Griffin complained occasionally when I would be up at night surfing through Etsy, Pinterest, and all my other go-to websites.

As we both woke up in the early dawn on March 21, I knew we were going to have a baby that day. Before we left the house, I looked at Griffin and stood as close to him as my belly would allow.

"You know, when we return to this house, we will be three. It won't be just us anymore. I have loved you, Griffin, before anyone else, and I know I will love you after everyone else. Let's go meet our baby because we have the chance to love it before anyone else."

I heard the scream. It sounded bloodcurdling. It also sounded healthy. Dr. Sutton and Griffin were at the end of the table where all the action was taking place. Griffin looked happy. But he also looked concerned.

"It's a good thing we didn't go on your instincts, Bae," he said, with the kind of joy reserved for the ringing in of a new year. "It's a girl!"

"I'm going to order a pint of blood," Dr. Sutton said in a soothing tone, like she was ordering a cappuccino. She moved swiftly and so did everyone at that end of the table.

"Oh my God, that's a lot of blood! Is that normal?" Griffin cried as they were pushing him out of the way.

"You need to move away, Griffin. Bailey is hemorrhaging."

"Blood pressure is dropping," the nurse said. She removed the cuff from my arm.

"We need to get her to surgery and perform an emergency D&C."

"I want to see the baby," I said, but I felt weak. I held it together long enough to see our daughter wrapped up and put in her father's arms. And that began my relationship with my daughter. Even during the birth process, we were estranged.

I learned later that I lost a lot of blood and passed out. When I finally got to hold this baby girl, I really couldn't believe how beautiful she was. She had a head full of dark hair like Henry and big eyes the color of indigo. Both Griffin and I had lighter hair and green eyes. I thought again about genetics and DNA. Maybe she looked like Hank Edgeworth. I couldn't wait to show him his granddaughter.

"Aren't you going to get tired of holding her?" I asked Griffin at the end of the day. It'd been a long day. I was having a hard time nursing her and every time Griffin put her in my arms she started crying again. Only when Griffin held her did she settle down. I was already fearing dramatic scenarios of mother-daughter clashes. I realized I was just a little crazy.

"So, Jack Hardwick and Robert Hardwick are out. Have you thought about what we should name our daughter?" Griffin asked, meeting my eyes and sitting close to me.

"What about Charlotte Edgeworth Hardwick?" I said. Hearing it for the first time myself.

"I like it. Why?"

"Well, Charlotte may have been where she was conceived. I'd also like to think that Charlotte was the place that I learned a proper work-life balance, and when I was growing up my favorite book was *Charlotte's Web*. I loved the friendship and I hoped one day to have a friend like Charlotte. I want that for our daughter."

"It's a strong name. You are full of surprises. Even on the day our daughter is born I've learned something wonderful about you." And he kissed me.

ॐ

Henry and Lea pretty much camped out at the hospital. I think Henry was as smitten with Charlotte as he was with his daughter Maggie. I watched both Henry and Griffin take turns holding her and talking to her. I was struck again by the caregiving gene that both of them had inherited. We had called Elle and Reggie and sent pictures. Annabel sent flowers and said that Charlotte and her daughter, Whitney, would be the best of friends. Reggie called me later and said she would come for a couple weeks after I had been home for a few days. I was so grateful for Elle and Reggie, and I drifted off to sleep thinking about Charlotte and Wilbur. Reggie and Elle.

Reggie was good for her word. A week after I came home from the hospital she came and was as welcome as Mary Poppins was into the Banks' household. She calmed everything down. Especially me. Sometimes only good friends can come into your chaos and restore a beautiful order to it. She kept the washer and dryer buzzing, held Charlotte so I could take a shower, and spent the better part of the day loading and unloading the dishwasher. She even had a calming effect on Griffin. She made hot tea and dispensed sympathy at just the right times, like when it was determined that I would not be able to breastfeed Charlotte. I fretted over her development because of my own shortcomings. Reggie's voice soothed me in ways that Griffin's could not. Although, bless him, he tried. She stayed three weeks, and I was so grateful to her for that. I hated to see her pack up and go.

"Charlotte is four weeks old. There is nothing you have done that is going to send her to therapy. I promise," Griffin said as he embraced my body that hadn't had a shower in two days. My inferiority brought us closer. He laughed when I told him that one night.

Reggie and Griffin encouraged me to nap when Charlotte went down for a nap, but I couldn't. I would tiptoe into her bedroom and watch her sleep. I studied how her nose would crinkle. I hoped she was having happy baby dreams. I may not have passed the BRCA gene onto her, but I wondered what sort of genetic cocktail Griffin and I had infused her with. Would she inherit the addictive gene from Griffin or me? How would all our traits knit together in Charlotte? Would our love and our devotion to one another somehow outweigh any bad fugitive genes?

"Bae, you need to come to bed. Parenting 101—sleep when the baby sleeps," Griffin urged on a nightly basis. I would reluctantly leave her and promptly fall asleep when I crawled into bed.

I engaged a builder to build me an office in part of our backyard. I could give up my expensive Buckhead office and be closer to home. He also built a playhouse for Charlie. Charlie—that's what I started calling her.

About three months later, I decided to take my first job out of town. Mac had decided to expand in Chicago. Mac had been one of my first clients when I went out on my own and he and I had become good friends. He had given me a lifeline and a job during the whole Elliott fiasco when my clients were jumping ship, and I had given him legitimacy as a restaurateur when he opened up his first on Madison Avenue. Mac was a true Southern boy and had the prerequisite twenty-five navy blazers to back it up. He had gotten married, had children, and moved into our neighborhood. I never used the term "settled down" to describe Mac because it never fit. He and his wife, Cassondra, could have chosen to live in Buckhead close to his sister, Annabel. I was so glad he lived close by. He used to laugh that it suited him because it was easy to drop off a retainer check and make me happy.

I was looking forward to working more than I even wanted to admit. Staying at home was hard. I wondered if it would always feel this hard. Motherhood did not come naturally to me. I was looking forward to getting my feet back into work, where I felt much more confident. Griffin and I had done the arduous process of hiring a nanny for Charlotte. Her name was Tabatha, and she was a godsend. She was young, full of enthusiasm, and, most important, Charlie seemed to love her. She cooed when she heard Tabatha's voice in the mornings. For me, it was like having a wife. She washed and folded clothes, loaded and emptied the dishwasher, and even ran errands.

That's when it happened. It had been one of the nicest evenings in June in Atlanta in a while. We took a blanket out into the yard for a little picnic supper. I poured my wine liberally, making up for lost time. I had read several parenting books while I was expecting, and damn, they were boring. It was like reading a textbook on some esoteric theory.

Some of the theories stuck, though. For instance, babies needed a schedule. Some of the books were conflicted on the matter of quality time versus quantity. I preferred to go with the school of quality time. There were some subjects where there was universal agreement. Like family rituals. Having dinner together. I wondered if regular people had these kinds of nights every night. Normal families. This was so different for both Griffin and me. It was nice. Griffin took to fatherhood so effortlessly. He was good with Charlie. Unlike me, he could read those books as if he were reading about sexy cocktails. I took to calling him Mother Goose and then shortened it to just "Goose." The nickname amused Griffin. I could tell, he secretly loved it.

As we were getting ready for bed, I put on my long-sleeved nightgown. As I approached the bed, Griffin just looked at me.

"Is there something going on with you that you're not telling me, Bae?" I shook my head no, but Griffin continued to pry.

"You've got on that wretched winter nightgown again. Aren't you hot?"

The truth was, I *was* burning up. But I didn't want to show Griffin my body. I didn't want him to get any ideas. I had seen my body naked. I wouldn't have wanted to make love to it. It was squishy and soft. I had lost the baby weight, but nothing was where it was supposed to be.

"I'm fine," I lied. We crawled into bed and he turned out the light.

"Would you tell me in the dark what's wrong?"

"This is just my first big project since having Charlie. I hope I still have my edge."

That wasn't completely a lie. I was worried that I had lost some of my vision.

"Bullshit. You and Mac have worked together before. You enjoy Mac." Griffin made his move. He began trying to kiss my neck and I pulled away.

"I'm just so tired," I protested.

"Somehow you can spend untold hours watching Charlie sleep in her crib. And then you can go to your office and spend untold hours there. Are you afraid to have sex?" he asked, in a slightly raised tone, withdrawing his advances.

"No." But it was a weak response.

"You talk to Reggie and Elle about this?"

"Do you think I am incapable of managing my own sex life now? I know I'm not doing a good job raising our child, but now do you think I should consult them about our sex life?"

"Are you having postpartum depression or something? I'm worried about you."

"I knew I would have a hard time with the whole motherhood business, but now I'm not even a very good wife," I said.

Griffin put his arm around me as comfort. "You have always been hard on yourself. I love you. I am not one of those guys."

When I looked at him, he continued, "I don't want a wife who looks like some Barbie doll with artificial everything. You're real. And you're my whole world."

Damn that man and his honesty. I felt my resolve falling away.

"I don't know if I would want to have sex with me. I don't look like myself anymore. I know my clothes fit but just not the same." For a few moments we just looked at each other, wondering what would happen next. Griffin moved a fugitive hair off my face.

"You're actually sweating, Bae." He was laughing. "Why don't you put on one of my T-shirts? At least you won't be hot."

And I did. I leaned over and kissed him good night.

Several nights later I was wearing one of Griffin's T-shirts. He kissed me good night. I didn't pull away.

"Want to try this?" Griffin asked. He waited. I took the T-shirt off. Griffin didn't change expressions. He wasn't repulsed by my body the way I was. We started kissing again. He was tender. Romantic. He uttered "I love you" again and again. He smiled as if to reassure me that I was everything he ever wanted. It reminded me of our first time. My first time. When I started out so cocky, wanting to have sex for the first time with Griffin. It had been important to him that he made it okay for me. This time was no different. Except for the memories that had been made and stored throughout our years. Together. Our bodies behaved like homing pigeons coming home to one another as they always had. Only now we had a baby. Afterward, we embraced and stayed connected.

"Do you want to put on your nightgown?" Griffin asked.

"Hell no. I'm burning up!" We went to sleep laughing, both of us happy in our connectedness.

Mac lost the first several buildings he looked at. It was going on three years now and he hadn't found the "perfect" location. We kept flying to Chicago and looking at buildings only to get beaten out by higher bids.

Mac was growing frustrated.

"Queenie, you may just have to lower your standards." Queenie was the nickname that I had come up with because he was just the figurehead in all his restaurants. He was amused by his moniker.

"And get rid of you? Never."

We talked every few weeks and he sent me addresses and I would comment on them. It was during this five-year time that I had returned to my roots, so to speak, flying up and down the East Coast designing my beloved cafeterias. I had even been written up as the "go-to" premiere restaurant designer to transform institutional eating halls. I had my fingers in so many of the Ivy League schools I could've almost received a diploma. And then there were the smaller liberal arts colleges that had sought me out. I developed a special affinity for them because they had thrown me a life jacket when my life and career were drowning. On many occasions, I donated part of my design fee to establish scholarships for deserving candidates. Motherhood had made me realize that there were so many children out there who were well deserving but incapable of funding expensive tuition.

I was still gone most of the week, but I would return on Fridays to be with Charlie and Griffin for the weekend. I would lay a blanket down in my closet and call it "Mommy Fort" and read to Charlie.

I would talk to her and say, "I love you, Charlie." I never wanted her to feel the absence of those words like I had as a child.

She would look at me and smile. And I wondered if she knew what those words meant. Other times I would say them, and she would just gesture back to her book, wanting me to read to her. I would carry her out to my backyard office and show her fabric swatches. "Aren't they beautiful? See how they go together?" She would just pick up the binder of fabric and bang it on top of my desk and smile. She loved the noise it made. Charlie would throw the binder on the floor, I would pick it up, and she would repeat this action. The game of "Mommy fetch" amused her the most.

She was a mysterious being. I wondered if she thought of me in the same way: mysterious. I commented on this phenomenon to Reggie and Elle.

"You're like the daddy who only comes home on the weekends," Elle said.

"Is that bad?" I asked. "Why is it so acceptable for men to travel during the week but not women? Griffin is here. And so is Tabatha. You still work, Elle." I was having those thoughts more and more. Why were working men acceptable and working women weren't?

"Yes. But at least I come home every night," Elle said, like a slap in my face.

"Elizabeth!" Reggie chastised. "Bailey is right. There is still some stupid double standard. But just keep a good eye on that Tabatha. When I was there the last time she wasn't exactly dressed like a nanny if you catch my drift."

I had to laugh. "Please. You know Griffin is not that kind of guy. I could be roly-poly and he would still love me. We are still trying to get pregnant despite the miscarriages," I said, because I knew how lucky I was. Annabel had already had a face-lift after years of altering the terrain of her face. She looked ghastly. And old.

"It will happen. Just relax," Reggie said in her maternal tone. I thought about the rituals cited in the books. It was a Thursday in the early evening when I got home from Chicago with Mac. Tabatha was about to give Charlie a bath before bed.

"I think I'll take Charlie to the Y to burn off a little energy and swim," I said, going upstairs to put on my bathing suit and shorts.

"Now?" Tabatha asked. "It's close to Charlie's bedtime."

"I know," I said. "But it's still light. I thought I would take her to the pool and just play in the water and get her tired. I will take her pajamas and night diaper." I welcomed the opportunity to bond with my daughter.

When it got time to leave, Charlie did not want to abandon Tabatha.

"Do you want me to go with you just in case?"

"No, we're good."

ℬ

When Charlie saw the pool, she became so excited. I loved the glee that the water elicited from her. The rest of the people were not as happy to see us. The occupants of the pool tilted to an older demographic. They were not too excited to see a rambunctious baby. I decided to stay in the shallow end.

Suddenly, Charlie came undone. She started crying and screaming. How could she be happy and splashing the water in one second and having a meltdown in another? I quickly made a calculation and got Charlie out of the pool and took her to the locker room. The geriatric crowd seemed to be happy with my decision. I took Charlie's swimsuit off and turned on the shower. It was ice water and that just made her howl even louder. I took her into a bathroom stall to change our clothes. She was squirming. I was growing impatient. As was Charlie. I got in a hurry. I jerked on her night diaper so we could leave. When I did, her chin hit the lavatory. Blood gushed everywhere. Charlie became hysterical. I couldn't get the bleeding to stop. I fumbled in my purse to call Reggie. She told me to take her to the emergency room because she might need stitches. Stitches? I decided to call Griffin since Charlie was screaming his name. "I want Da Da!" I could barely hear Griffin amid her screams.

"What the hell? I'll get there as soon as I can get the bar covered. We're shorthanded tonight." He sounded frustrated as he hung up the phone.

At the hospital, I did everything to distract her. I jostled her on my knee. I tried to get her to focus on something. She continued crying. And bleeding. The nurse came in and bandaged it until she could get a doctor. About that time, Griffin rushed in. He looked frazzled.

"What the hell happened, Bae?"

I reconstructed our evening for him.

"Why the hell were you taking Charlotte to the pool at eight o'clock at night? Her bedtime is at seven or seven thirty!" Charlie's chubby little arms reached out to him, and he embraced her. He soothed her. "It's okay, Sprite. Daddy is here," he said, using his nickname for her. A doctor and a nurse came in and confirmed stitches. Griffin interrupted.

"We have a nanny who usually puts Charlotte to bed," he assured them, as if I was incapable of looking after my own daughter. We both approached her and told her how brave she was as the nurse and doctor worked.

By the time we got home and put Charlie in bed, it was ten o'clock.

"Why would you go to the pool so late?"

"I was trying to bond with our daughter. I know she likes the pool."

"Not at her bedtime."

"The parenting books say you should have fun events with your children."

"Not at bedtime, Bae."

"I don't like your tone."

"Where was Tabatha?" Griffin snapped.

"I let her go home. I just thought it would be fun."

"To upset Charlotte's routine? Parenting 101—'establish a schedule,'" he said in a know-it-all fashion.

"You don't have to be so snarky!" I snapped back. We heard Charlie cry out and we went to her. It was going to be a long night. When she saw me she cried even harder. It broke my heart. I heard my phone. Reggie's ring.

"Go take it. I'm sure she is concerned. I'll stay in here with Charlotte." I glanced back at them. The bars on Charlie's crib looked like a jail, imprisoning her away from her concerned father. It made me sad for both of them. It made me sad for me. Would I ever learn this motherhood business?

"What happened, honey? I was worried after you called."

"Charlie had to have stitches in her chin. Why am I such a screw up, Reggie? You would've known not to take your children to the pool so late. You should've seen all the blood."

"We've all been there, Bailey. Just because you ended up in the emergency room doesn't make you a bad mother," she assured me. "I remember little David was at the playground and he was sliding down the slide and busted his lip wide open and lost his front tooth. It didn't grow back until he was about eight years old. I thought he was going to get a complex because he didn't have a front tooth for so long. He was without a front tooth in all his pictures until his permanent tooth grew in. Every time he smiled it made me feel bad. Don't beat yourself up."

"You're such a good mother, Reggie. I feel like I never get it right. Even Griffin told the doctor we had a nanny, as if that would ease her mind that our child was in good hands the rest of the time."

"Charlie probably won't even remember," Reggie said.

"Unless I've left her with a permanent scar."

"Bailey, I love you. Go to bed."

I hung up the phone and went into Charlie's room. Her night-light was on and Griffin was curled up beside her crib. I knew he was tired. I got the extra blanket and went in and covered him. I went to bed then and said a silent prayer that one day Charlie would understand the difference between good intentions and bad parenting.

Charlie's first word was "Da Da." Followed by "Tay," which was her nickname for Tabatha. She then uttered the word "Bae" followed by "Goose." The very idea enchanted Griffin and made him fall in love with his daughter even more. I was not immune to Charlie's voice either. Sometimes it just amazed me that her little voice could do such things to my heart. I think my heart had split just down the middle between Charlotte and her father. It was a rare occasion that she would look up at me with her blue eyes and say "Mommy." It was usually when I was going out the door to catch a plane on Monday morning. Somehow in her little baby brain she knew this was her best play that she could use to inflict the most guilt.

Sometimes, when I came home on a Thursday, I would find them together in the kitchen. Charlie and Tabatha playing and Griffin preparing dinner. Griffin and Tabatha having a glass of wine. To an observer, they looked like this was a routine. A habit. They looked like they were enjoying each other's company. They looked content. They looked like a family.

I wondered if the same thing could be said for us. If Charlie and Griffin were as happy in my company. Even though there were three of them, it seemed to be an even number. If you added me to the mix things were off. The Sprite was now four years old. On one particular Thursday night, I was assaulted by the familiar pangs of guilt. I had guilt because I liked working. I also had guilt because I never felt as confident in my own house as I did designing impersonal buildings. But it gave me an idea. The books had suggested family trips.

I put my rollaway suitcase in the living room away from the stairs and walked into the kitchen.

"Hi Bailey," Tabatha greeted me. Charlie didn't even look up. Until Tay nudged Charlie to look up.

"Hi babe," Griffin said. "I'm just finishing up supper. Veal scallopini. Wine?" He reached into the refrigerator. Then went out to the butler's pantry. "I don't have any Sausalito's finest. You want to try Tabatha's favorite?" I was a little taken aback. He always had my wine. Now he was stocking Tabatha's.

"I'll just take Charlotte upstairs and get her ready for bed," Tabatha said.

"Nonsense. Stay for supper," I said. "I will take Charlie upstairs and give her a bath." When I reached down to grab my daughter, she began reaching for Tay.

"Go with your mommy," Tabatha urged.

Once Charlie was secured in my arms, she relaxed. "Mommy doesn't get to do this as much as she wants to," I said to my daughter, and I meant it. After I had run the water and before I put Charlie in I decided to make it a magical adventure. She loved her revolving night-light with stars and the moon. I brought it into the bathroom.

"Would you like to bathe under the stars tonight, Sprite?" I asked. Charlie's eyes lit up. I turned the night-light on and carried her over to the light switch and turned the lights out. She was transfixed by the ceiling. I lowered her into the tub and started splashing. She started crying. She reached up for me. The darkness had scared her.

"It's okay, baby girl," I said, trying to soothe her. She was not happy. I hadn't bathed her yet, so the dilemma was how to leave her for a second to turn on the light. I jumped up, turned the lights on, and went back to Charlie. I was so relieved she hadn't drowned. I wasn't sure Griffin would ever allow me to be around Charlie and water again. I washed her enough and wrapped her in a towel. My shirt was covered in water. I hoped I had gotten the soap out of Charlie's armpits. I decided to take her downstairs so her daddy and Tabatha could kiss her good night. I heard them laughing and drinking wine. If the three of them looked like a family, then Griffin and Tabatha looked like a couple. I made my presence known. Griffin's attention quickly turned to his daughter. His eyes lit up. It made me the slightest bit jealous of my daughter.

"Sprite!" He reached out and took her from me. She cooed with delight as he smothered her with kisses. It brought me joy. I let Tabatha kiss her good night and then I took her upstairs to put her to bed and read her a bedtime story of *Wynken, Blynken, and Nod*.

Later, when Griffin and I were in bed, I closed my laptop.

"I have a proposal for you," I said.

"If it is a proposition, then my answer is definitely yes." Griffin leaned into me. I swatted him away.

"It isn't that kind of proposal. The parenting books suggest a way to make memories is to have family trips. Fourth of July is coming up and I thought it would be nice to go to New York. We could stay in the city at my corporate apartment. Go to Serendipity and Sara Beth's. Maybe spend a night or two with the girls."

"I'm guessing by the way you girls operate my answer is a foregone conclusion," Griffin laughed.

"Well, I had to make sure they were going to be in town."

"That actually sounds like a good idea. We could spend two nights in the city and then two nights in Connecticut. Now back to your proposition."

❧

It was great to get out of Atlanta and away from work for a few days. We adopted carefree versions of ourselves and tried to see this crazy city from a four-year-old's point of view.

Serendipity was a hit. Charlie ate the ice cream so fast that she ended up wearing as much as she was eating. She was enthralled by me. I guess that made us even because I was enthralled by her. She wanted me to eat her ice cream with her. I suppose I would be considered the "novelty parent." The parent who is not there all the time, day in and day out. She watched me. Did she approve of what she was seeing? We walked around Central Park and Griffin put Charlie atop his shoulders. How many couples had strolled through the park in a similar fashion? We looked perfectly normal. It was not lost on either Griffin or me that our childhoods did not look like our daughter's. And we were glad. We were making a conscious effort to go in the opposite direction.

The weekend with the girls was also a big hit with Charlie. She was the center of attention. Elle had a pool, of course, and Charlie loved it. Susan, Reggie's daughter, and Kendall, Elle's daughter, were there. They were both approaching adolescence, and Charlie was transfixed by them—especially Kendall, who had purple hair.

"Okay, Elizabeth, if my daughter dyes her hair purple when she is thirteen years old, I am sending the bill to you."

"Trust me, purple hair will be the least of your worries. Just wait until Charlotte hits the teenage years." Everyone laughed except for Reggie and me. Reggie knew how much I fretted about my abilities as a mother.

"How about I whip up a signature cocktail?" Griffin proposed. "A summer spritzer—a little white wine, watermelon and lime juice, simple syrup, mint, and tequila. A Firecraker."

"Make mine a double," Robbie said. Everyone laughed as Griffin served as the mixologist extraordinaire. He also offered to prepare dinner one night. He grilled hamburgers with a twist. He made a pineapple, mango, and heirloom tomato salsa for the burgers. He also whipped up a peach sorbet for dessert.

The morning of our departure Charlie seemed chipper—unlike us, both a little hungover and wearing sunglasses—but she didn't want to board the plane, refusing to cross over the gateway. People brushed past, their luggage bumping against us, causing me to lose my balance and temper. I tried to scoop Charlie up in my arms and she dodged my grip. Griffin let me handle this because I had become the favored parent this weekend and he thought I could get her to comply. The flight attendant dangled a lollipop toward Charlie and she cooed. Charlie reached for the sucker and missed. It fell to its death through the sliver of daylight between the gate and the plane. Charlie took a step back, planting her little stubborn legs, refusing to budge. I was growing impatient. I yanked her arm to get her across the threshold. She let out a bloodcurdling cry.

"Fuck, Charlie! Come on! We've got to go." I caught myself, but it was too late.

"Bae!" Griffin admonished. When Charlie was born, we had agreed not to swear in front of her. Not only had I been the first to drop the F-bomb in front of our child, but I had done it in front of a plane full of witnesses. Talk about bad parenting 101.

We had become *those* people. The ones who everyone stares at when they get on the plane last. The reason the plane hadn't taken off a few minutes before. Passengers were cowering in the fear that we would be sitting near them. It didn't make any difference. Charlie screamed so loudly that even the people in first class were not immune to her cries.

Griffin took Charlie on his chest and tried to soothe her. I tried to distract her with a tone-deaf lullaby. She did not want to hear the "Wheels on the Bus" or any other song. I reached in my bag to get a baggy of Goldfish crackers. She swatted it out of my hand and it landed in the lap of the man sitting closest to us. Charlie did not stop screaming. We were asked to deboard first.

"Bae, Charlotte's shoulder is swollen. I think we may need to take her to urgent care," Griffin said. Parenting 101: Don't yank your child's arm.

"Mommy hurt me!" Charlie screamed, pulling away from me. She wouldn't even look at me. We drove straight to urgent care. In silence. My head was throbbing. I tried to make the moment light.

"I don't know how other working women do this. Every. Single. Day," I said.

"I do. Because this is my life. Every. Single. Damn. Day." His voice dug into me in that tiny cubicle.

The attending doctor came in and surveyed our current situation and Charlie's arm. It just happened to be the same doctor we saw the night of the pool incident.

"Her shoulder is dislocated," she said after examining her. "We need to pop it back into place. Who wants to hold her?"

"Bae, you yanked her shoulder out of the socket?" Griffin asked.

"I don't think you said it loud enough for the other rooms to hear, Griffin," I snapped. I was already a wreck and feeling all kinds of guilt.

"I just need to know which one of you is going to hold your daughter for me?" the doctor repeated, pretending we were not having a domestic dispute. Griffin held Charlie, and when they popped her shoulder back into place it made a sound, like when you crack a knuckle, only worse, like some disjointed refrain. I don't think I will ever forget that sound. Charlie didn't stop crying.

"Does Charlotte have any allergies to medications?" The doctor looked at me expectantly. So did Griffin. Charlie stopped crying long enough to look at me too. I didn't know. Add that to the heap of guilt. I wondered if she was going to call social services.

"Not any that we are aware of. We are in the Providence health network," Griffin said.

"I think Charlotte has been through enough tonight. She is going to be in pain for a couple of days. Her shoulder is going to be tender. I am going to give her a splint and I would recommend some baby Tylenol for the pain. And be careful with her for the next few days." She tried not to look directly at me, but I felt guilt and shame boring into me like a drill bit, leaving shards of my dignity behind.

ூ

When we got home, Griffin carried Charlie inside. In his arms she seemed to calm down.

"How about some apple sorbet?" Griffin asked her softly. Charlie lifted her head from his chest.

"Shouldn't we just put her to bed?" I whispered to Griffin.

"Apple sorbet!" Charlie said.

"Apple sorbet is her favorite. She needs something in her stomach to take with the baby Tylenol," Griffin whispered.

"When did apple sorbet become her favorite?" This was news to me.

"About a month or so ago. I was playing around with recipes one day and she was my guinea pig. There's a whole bunch of containers in the freezer," he said. How did I not see this in the freezer? I completely forgot that she needed something in her stomach to take the Tylenol.

I remained on the threshold of the kitchen. Watching them. Any time I got too close to Charlie she started crying, cowering in fear. If there were a contest for worst mother of the day, I would win.

I had dropped the F-bomb in front of my daughter. I had yanked her shoulder out of its socket. I had lost my patience because I was slightly hungover. I didn't know what her favorite food was. I forgot that she needed something in her stomach to take Tylenol. The pièce de résistance: My daughter was afraid of me. Job well done.

I stood there watching them. Doing nothing. Doing everything I could not to move and draw attention to myself. Doing everything I could to make my daughter not hate me. She threw her spoon down to indicate she was finished. It was this motion that best described what Charlie did with my self-confidence. I had gone back and forth in my parenting, from trying too hard to just giving up.

Charlie was almost asleep when we walked up the stairs. I whispered to Griffin, "What about the baby Tylenol? I thought you were going to give her some."

"In the sorbet," he mouthed. Of course it was. As much as I felt like I was a complete failure, Griffin was a success. Griffin carefully removed her clothes as if she were a patient and he was changing a bandage. I was jealous of his ease. Would I ever have confidence as a parent? I felt more confident in my job than I ever did around Charlie.

Griffin was a caretaker. He would always be a caretaker. I was grateful in that moment that he was Charlie's caretaker. He put her nightgown on her, but didn't want to put her arm through the sleeve. So without forcing it, he just left it. With her other hand she took his hand in hers and laid it across her tummy like one of those weighted blankets that serves to calm and ensure a good night's rest. His hand acted as a paperweight protecting her fragile little body. As if he would move during the night. I could've told her that her daddy would not go anywhere. Even if his own arm were sore for days to come. Love and guilt engulfed me. I didn't realize I had pulled her arm so hard. I tiptoed into her room with a blanket and a pillow for Griffin. The way he was sitting made it impossible for him to lie down.

"I know you want to kiss her good night but I just got her to sleep . . ." He didn't finish the rest of that sentence. He didn't have to. The sight of me would traumatize her all over again. I realized he was Charlie's very own sentinel. Watching over her throughout the night. Throughout her life. I loved him. But the cocktail I was swallowing was hard and bitter.

I went into my closet and called Reggie.

"What happened? You sound terrible. We had such a fun weekend!"

I explained the plane ride. "Do you think they're going to report me to social services? This is the second time I've done something stupid and ended up with my daughter in the emergency room. She still has the scar from the swimming pool incident."

"I think a lot of parents have that very same thought, Bailey. How many times can we go to the emergency room without social services being alerted. I don't think it works like that. You weren't drunk or anything."

"Reggie, I was hungover and ill-tempered and I probably took it out on Charlie."

"You didn't want to miss the plane. I remember when Susan refused to get on an escalator in London. And the only other way to the subway was walking down six flights of stairs. Which we did. I have never been so hot and sweaty in my life. She has never gotten over her fear of escalators."

"My dear Regina." I paused, using her real name. "The difference between you and me is that you never lost your patience and yanked her on the escalator. I hope I never have to see that doctor again. Or else I am going to have to go to a different emergency room." Reggie laughed.

"Do you realize I didn't even know the Sprite's favorite food?"

"Take that off your list. My children changed their favorite foods weekly. Honey, you just need to relax. You have no confidence and Charlie probably senses that."

I put on my nightgown and got my pillow and blanket and carried it out into the hall. If the people I loved were in the next room, I was going to be as close as I could without distressing them. I heard Charlie snoring. She was probably the only little girl on the planet who snored like a freight train. I always loved it about her. She looked so delicate and fragile, and then she would go to sleep and make these otherworldly noises. For the longest time, Griffin and I thought there were animals crawling in our walls, until we discovered it was our precious baby girl. I fell asleep listening to Charlie snore, which served as my own lullaby.

"Bae? Did you sleep there all night? I almost tripped over you," Griffin said the next morning.

"I wanted to be close in case either one of you needed me. How are you feeling this morning? Can I make you some breakfast?" I embraced Griffin. I may not always know how to love Charlie, but I loved this man with bloodshot eyes, messy hair, and day-old stubble more than anything in the world.

I needed a do-over. Griffin and I had our do-over at Martha's Vineyard. I wanted that for our family.

"I think we should go to the beach over Labor Day." We were in bed with our respective laptops.

"Who have you been talking to this time? Reggie or Annabel? Or have you been consulting your parenting books again? Because I don't think I can take another trip to the emergency room because of your books," Griffin joked.

"That's not funny. I just want to give Charlie a better childhood than I had."

"When did you become a beach person?"

"Exactly my point. All the people in my class went to the beach. I didn't get to share in those experiences."

"I'm not sure I can take the trifecta of you, Charlotte, and the ocean." He laughed again. I didn't find it amusing.

"Will you just humor me?" I pleaded.

"Okay, fine." He closed his laptop.

"Annabel suggested this resort. Sea Island." Griffin's ears perked up when I mentioned the word *resort*. I pulled up the website and showed him the pictures. "It's not that far from Atlanta. We could drive. No planes." I looked directly at him as he took my laptop away from me. "They have lots of activities for children of all ages. If the Sprite doesn't like the ocean there's plenty of other things for her to do. Plus, her shoulder should be just about healed by then."

"This is some resort. Whoa, look at the price tag," he said. But in the end Griffin relented, and we even got an oceanfront room with a balcony.

The few nights leading up to us leaving for the beach were a flurry of buying things like sunscreen, beach toys, and an inner tube. I spent a part of each night showing Charlie pictures of the beach, seashells, and sea glass. She seemed transfixed. I was excited for her to see the ocean. After we checked in and before dinner, we went out on the balcony. Charlie just stared out onto the ocean, trying to take in its majesty. I knelt down to be at her eye level. Griffin followed.

"What do you think, Sprite?" Griffin asked. Charlie looked around and then at the walls of the balcony.

"Where's the switch?" she asked.

"What switch, Sprite?" I asked.

"The switch that turns the ocean on and off."

I laughed in utter amazement. Naturally, our daughter would want to know how the waves came in. And went out.

"That's just what the ocean does. That's Mother Nature," I explained.

"Doesn't she get tired?" Charlie asked.

"Mother Nature is old and wise. She knows exactly what we need all the time, and lucky for us she never gets tired. She makes sure the sun comes out. She makes the moon come out every night. She allows the seasons to change so we can have just enough warm weather to appreciate the cold. She gives us rain so we can have all the beautiful flowers and lush green grass. She works all the time. Mother Nature has a big responsibility, and we need to take care of her."

"Mother Nature has a big job like you, Mommy," my daughter said, and Griffin burst out laughing.

The next morning Charlie and I were on the beach. I was under an umbrella watching her play in the sand. Watching your child be carefree must lower your blood pressure because it did my heart good. Griffin was up in the room talking to Henry. The Sprite would dig a hole with her little shovel and see what little sea urchin would burrow deeper to get away from her. I loved watching her and allowing her the freedom and independence to discover the Earth's magnificent bounty.

"Mommy!" I heard her squeal with delight. She came running toward me. "Look what I found." She was clearly proud of her discovery.

"Sprite! You've discovered sea glass!" I held it up to the sun. "Look at all the pretty colors. It looks like the ocean. It is said to be very lucky for those who find it. It is one of the most priceless things the ocean can give us," I told her, spinning my tale. I loved the colors that were woven into the glass.

"I'll go look for some more." She hurried off to her little spot to see what she could retrieve.

About that time, I saw the unmistakable shadow of my husband.

"What are you two up to?" He sat down beside me. Charlie looked up and ran to him.

"Daddy, Daddy!" she yelled, displaying another piece she had discovered. "Bae said it's lucky."

"She did? Your mom is very smart," Griffin said. He turned to me and said, "I have to hand it to you, this was a great idea."

"I don't think I heard you above the sounds of our little Marco Polo," I laughed. Griffin leaned over and kissed me.

That night at dinner Griffin took the children's menu away from Charlie and proceeded to tell her some of the offerings on the regular menu. I don't know if it was because she was an only child or because she was the daughter of a chef, but she just ate the way we did.

"Why don't you order the grilled grouper, Sprite? You like that." The waiter turned to Griffin for Charlie's order. Charlie interrupted, using her manners, "Thank you. I'll have the grilled grouper please." She declined to color. She declined to order off the children's menu. The waitstaff seemed to be amused by our daughter. I couldn't believe how much she had grown this summer.

I woke up in the middle of the night only to discover her bed empty. I was suddenly wide awake. I threw off the covers and jumped up. I looked around. There Charlie was, her face pressed up to the glass of the balcony door.

"What are you looking at, Sprite?" I asked, walking over to her.

"The ocean is still working," she said. I loved her sense of wonder. "Where is my sea glass?"

"I put it in a plastic bag so it wouldn't get broken. Do you want to sleep here? We can just crack the door so we can hear the ocean."

She looked up at me and there was my answer in her smile. I got our pillows and a blanket and cracked the door. We went to sleep with the refrain of the ocean's love song.

❧

The next Valentine's we were in bed. "Santa left me a little something." I patted my belly. "I am about two months pregnant." I could see the delight register on Griffin's face.

"I suppose you want to name this child Prancer or Vixen or something," he said.

"No. I was thinking more like 'Ocean Breeze' because I loved our time at Sea Island. Breeze Hardwick. Now that is a strong name."

"It's a stupid name. But luckily, I have a few months to convince you otherwise," Griffin said. "I guess it will do no good to tell you to take it easy."

"I will take good care of myself. But I don't want to tell Charlie just yet."

❧

The day Mac and I found the perfect building and secured ownership was the day I told him I was four months pregnant.

I hoped the fifth time would be the charm for both of us. We had been flying to Chicago so much I had almost memorized the flight schedule.

"I can't believe it took me four years to find this place," Mac said. He had gotten married and had two children in the intervening years. I was still trying to have a sibling for Charlie. I loved the space right off Michigan Avenue. He paid a pretty penny for it but lucky for him he had a few of those. He wanted to do an establishment the way we had on Madison

Avenue but with a Chicago vibe. Again, I was struck by the architecture of the building he had chosen. Both Mac and Griffin had unerring eyes when it came to locations. I loved what fatherhood had done for Mac. He had a boy and a girl, but he could still be a little rascal, and I loved that about him.

"Go home and work some of that Bailey magic and let me see what you come up with," he said. We were drinking cappuccinos at the bar in our hotel. I had confided to him that I was pregnant.

"Can you believe we are celebrating our collaboration with cappuccinos and not our favorite cocktail?" I raised my cup to toast Mac, but my brain was bouncing all around with ideas for his new place. It was ricocheting between Mac's location and the recent binder that Charlie had been playing with. I was getting excited. I would convince Mac to change the name.

"Maybe Thompson will want to date your Charlotte."

I took a slow sip of my drink, savoring my small dose of caffeine for the day.

"Not if I have anything to say about it. That apple doesn't fall too far from the tree. No offense," I said.

"None taken. I see motherhood hasn't tamed you one little bit." We both laughed and returned to our separate hotel rooms. We were flying out early in the morning because the next day was Charlie's birthday. Her official party would be the following day. I was anxious to get to my room, pack, call Griffin and Charlie, and scour Etsy.

"I'm trying really hard to remember if there is something special happening tomorrow," I said on the phone to Charlie, feigning ignorance.

"It's my birthday, Mommy! Did you know that you gave me the biggest present of all? Even Daddy doesn't know what's in it!" Charlie said with a joy and curiosity that I would never grow tired of hearing.

"No peeking or shaking until I get home," I warned.

"I love all the colors of purple you wrapped it with," Charlie said.

Clearly, the presentation gene had gotten passed down. I had taken her present to a place in Atlanta that specializes in beautiful wrapping. For once, the wrapping cost more than its contents. Charlie was always borrowing a certain kind of pen in my office to write her name. I bought her a package of her very own pens and I had it wrapped in about three separate boxes, one inside of the other like Russian nesting dolls. I heard the phone being passed off as if it were a baton in a relay race.

"I don't know how Charlotte is going to sleep tonight. She's so excited about your present," Griffin said.

"I don't think she is going to be as thrilled when she sees that it is a box of pens," I laughed. Suddenly, I could feel the cappuccino coming back up.

"How did you even know about that?" Griffin asked.

"Every time she's in my office, she picks up a pen and starts writing her name over and over." I felt a stabbing pain in my side. It seized my entire body and I had to hold on to the edge of the sink so I wouldn't fall over.

"Bae? Bae?"

Everything went dark.

NOW

I strolled into the conference room to find Floyd Potts on his cell phone. "And that's conclusive? Can you send me a copy of the report?"

"Where's Jake?"

I sat directly across from Floyd.

"Jake is doing his job," he said into the phone. "I am doing mine. This is strictly a criminal defense case from now on." Floyd was grim. "That was the autopsy on Elliott. They have called the time of death two hours after you left the building. The cause of death was a knife wound followed by trauma to the head when he hit the kitchen island."

"That's good news, right? That will exonerate me since the tape shows that the time I left the building was two hours before Elliott's time of death?" I asked.

"That doesn't completely exonerate you. Yes, theoretically you are outside the window of his time of death. However, your DNA is all over his apartment. It has been my experience with juries that they pay more attention to the DNA evidence than the timeline of death, and your DNA is on the murder weapon."

"I just wish there were something positive," I said.

"You are going to have to watch and rewatch the video of people coming and going from the building," Floyd said.

"Why? I've already told you what I know. I studied the video."

"Bailey, you do not have the luxury of not looking at the video again. All the evidence is against you. Let me tell you how this could play out. You came to retrieve the pictures. Elliott was hiding them from you. You tore his apartment up looking for them. You two got into an altercation. You got mad, threw a vase of flowers. Elliott pushed you. You scratched him, stabbed him, he lost his balance and hit his head on the marble island as he fell. That is what the prosecution is going to say. I need you to study that video frame by frame. This is your job. Because your life depends upon it. Besides Griffin, I want you to look at every single hoodie. Take notes. Ask questions."

"I was there to protect my child," I said. "I didn't want her career or her life ruined by some pictures."

"For goodness' sake, you can't say that on the witness stand. You were so desperate to protect your daughter you would've done anything . . . even kill Elliott. By the way, your DNA was also found on shards of the broken glass from the vase. If those flowers were so defenseless, why is your DNA on the vase?"

"I moved the flowers to the island. I was trying to look in the cabinets for a Band-Aid for my paper cut from the manila envelope. Don't I look like a sympathetic figure, a mother trying to protect her daughter?"

"No. It makes you look guilty. A restaurant designer who has every measure of success can't get what she wants for her daughter. I know you think I'm not nice, but I am playing devil's advocate. Bailey, here is the deal," he said, a bit softer. "I think you are innocent. My instincts say you are not a killer. Very rarely have my instincts been wrong. So let me do my job for you. My job is not to be nice. My job is to get you acquitted." For the first time since I had met this enigmatic man, he smiled at me. He looked human. Very handsome. The next morning, I came in carrying a cappuccino and several pages of notes.

"By the way, I would be happy to bring you a coffee or cappuccino when I come," I said, handing him the pages of notes I had taken the previous day from watching and rewatching the video.

"I'll stick with my tea." He pulled a container with avocado toast and a black, neatly folded linen napkin from his briefcase.

"Do you always travel with your own napkin?" I asked.

"Yes. I am not a big fan of paper napkins. Besides, you can reuse these, and they don't add to the carbon footprint."

I managed to laugh. "You are full of surprises. Look at you, doing your part for ecology."

"I gave up alcohol and caffeine years ago," Floyd said, examining the pages.

I was about to say something glib like "You must be the life of any party," but I could tell Floyd was not to be toyed with. He glanced up from looking at my notes and smiled. His perfectly veneered smile.

"You surprised me, Bailey. You noticed things I hadn't." Just as I was getting comfortable, he looked me in the eye and leveled his question.

"I'm about to ask you a question and I need you to be honest. Your DNA was found on Elliott. I know you didn't have sex with him because I've heard the way you talk to your husband. What went on between you and Elliott?" I pondered how to answer the question.

"We fought. I scratched him."

"I know you probably noticed a few of those hoodies who look like your daughter. Have you seen your daughter on the footage? I need you to be truthful." Was that Floyd's subtle way of saying he didn't trust me?

THEN
EIGHTEEN YEARS AGO

I woke up to Mac sitting at my bedside in the hospital. He wore a pained expression.

"I lost the baby, didn't I?"

For a minute Mac didn't say anything. His eyes, which could be so full of mischief, were now pools of compassion. He nodded.

"I'm sorry, Bailey." He paused. "I called Griffin. He took the first flight out. He'll be here soon."

"I wish you hadn't. It's Charlie's birthday tomorrow. I can't have her waking up on her birthday without a parent. Call him back. Tell him not to come. I'll be fine."

"It's too late. He's on his way. He's worried about you," Mac said. What he didn't say was that he had to persuade the front desk to use their key to open my room. What he didn't say was that he found me in a pool of blood. What he didn't say until much later was that if Griffin hadn't called him, I could have died.

"I just don't want Charlie waking up without a parent on her birthday." About that time Griffin barged in. He looked disheveled. Whatever had transpired, he had gotten here in a hurry. His hair going in a million directions. I allowed myself this moment. I had always found Griffin endearing when he appeared in such a desultory fashion.

"Bae." No matter when and how he said my name, my heart always seized and stopped just a little bit. He went to the other side of the bed.

"Glad you are here. I'll let you be with Bailey," Mac said, shooting Griffin a look of sympathy mixed with worry. "I'll call you tomorrow, Bailey. Let me know if you need anything." Griffin and I thanked him in unison.

"You've got to turn around and go home."

"I'm not just leaving you here all alone in the hospital," Griffin said, kissing me on the forehead and looking at me with alarm. I realized that I must really look weak.

"Yes, you will. This is important. Charlie can't wake up on her birthday without one of her parents."

"Charlotte will understand. I'll just tell her you're in the hospital."

"You will do no such thing! And scare her on her birthday?" I remembered when I was about three months pregnant, Griffin wanted to tell Charlie she was getting a brother or sister. I had cautioned him about doing so. I'd had enough experience with miscarriages. It could get dicey explaining to a five-year-old that Mommy and Daddy's baby went to heaven. I wanted to wait until she asked me why Mommy was so fat.

"Listen to me Bae. Henry will be there. Tabatha, Annabel, and Whitney and Sally and Lucy."

"No. You listen to me Griffin. None of those people, no matter how much they love her, are either of us. Who is watching her right now?"

"Henry, of course." And this brought a smile to my husband's face. From the time Charlie had entered the world, it was like she was part Henry's. He adored his niece. Sometimes he just came over to bring her a piece of cake or something he whipped up just for her. He loved his daughter, Maggie. Yet there was some magical connection between my daughter and my brother. I was lucky that the men in my life were such fierce caregivers. "Henry will make her a special birthday breakfast."

"One more time, Griffin. I need you to get home. I can fly out the following day on the 1:55 flight in time to make it home for her four o'clock birthday party. I know that's cutting it close. But I will get out of here in time."

"I don't feel right about leaving you until I talk to the doctor. Things happened."

"I know. I lost a lot of blood." About that time a nurse came in to check my vitals. Griffin asked if she could summon the doctor, which she did.

When the doctor appeared, Griffin stood up and shook her hand.

"Griffin Hardwick. Can you tell me what happened?"

"Sit down, Mr. Hardwick. My name is Dr. Sha Patel. Your wife came in hemorrhaging badly. Her friend said that she was about four months pregnant. I'm sorry we were not able to stop the bleeding and save the baby. It was a boy. We performed a D&C. Your wife will be fine, though."

I tried to assimilate this information quickly. Tried to let it not absorb into my heart. I tried not to let Griffin know how this news affected me. I had a job to do. It was to be with my only remaining child.

"Dr. Patel, thank you for taking care of me. But tomorrow is my daughter's fifth birthday and I need to get out of here by Saturday for her party. Early."

Griffin was about to interrupt and ask a bunch of questions that to me seemed irrelevant. Dr. Patel broke out in a sly smile.

"I have heard many excuses for wanting to get out of the hospital early, but a daughter's birthday party ranks right up there with high priority." She had a pretty smile.

"I think that can be arranged. Mrs. Edgeworth, I have eaten in a few of the restaurants you have designed. What you do is beautiful." I didn't think I could feel anything but empty, but somehow Dr. Patel made me feel validated. Yes, the compliment on my restaurants made me feel good and would've been everything in the past, but the fact that she understood that I needed to get home for my daughter's birthday was, as she put it, the high-priority compliment.

Naturally, my flight back home was delayed. By the time I landed and took an Uber home, the party had already started. I was at least a half hour late. I saw everyone's faces.

And then I heard the little voice.

"Mommy!" She looked at me expectantly. And then she frowned.

"How's my big birthday girl today?"

"Daddy and Tay decorated, and Uncle Henry made me a cake!"

I hugged her. Griffin came up to me and whispered, "You look pale. You should go lie down."

"I'm okay. But my suitcase is on the sidewalk. I just couldn't roll it any farther." I tried to blend in, but the adults and their expressions were not making it easy.

Charlie opened my present last, with glee and a sense of merriment. Her eyes grew wide at all the boxes until she got to the very end and opened the box containing her pens.

"Mommy!" she exclaimed. Our smiles met each other and our eyes locked. There was a twinkle in hers. "I get to write my name anytime I want. And yours too, Bae."

The party continued but I held on to the moment.

As Charlie was getting ready for bed, I was making her brush her teeth and say her prayers. I had incorporated saying prayers at the suggestion of Reggie and Elle. And Sally, my next-door neighbor. Her daughter, Lucy, was Charlie's age. I wanted Charlie to be grateful. Wanted her to be kind. She was in her bathroom brushing her teeth when I noticed something. The pens I had given her for her birthday were in her trash can. She had thrown them away unopened. I realized she was mad. She was mad at me. I had not been there on her birthday and been late to her birthday party. And she didn't know why. She probably thought I had chosen my work over her—again.

It didn't matter that Reggie and Elle had agreed with me. That I was right not to tell Charlie I had been in the hospital. It would prompt too many questions. Seeing them in the trash broke my heart. I fished them out and put them on the side of the trash can. I pretended that she had just missed when she threw them and maybe she would have a second thought about them. I put in a prayer that she would understand.

When she said her prayers, she mentioned me last. Like an afterthought. An insignificant postscript. Griffin was still downstairs, and I was glad to have a moment by myself. I went into my closet and closed the door and cried.

I cried for the son that would not be part of our family. I cried for Griffin that I hadn't been able to carry our baby to term. I cried that my body was defective in some way. I cried for my daughter that somehow even in her young age she was building up a hostility against me. I prayed that one day she would understand and that we could have a better relationship. I cried for myself. I gave myself permission to have a pity party that my daughter had thrown away my present and thought about how much it hurt. And then I stopped. I didn't want Griffin to see me like this. I took out my phone.

"Hey, Mac. Two things. I just wanted to thank you for all your help in Chicago."

"Bailey, I'm just so sorry. I was glad I was there to help."

"I've been playing around with some ideas."

"Really?" Mac asked.

"How about a week from Wednesday at your office? I want to check on a few other things." Mac had given up his New York office for an office in Buckhead when he married.

"That sounds good," Mac said.

"Prepare to be amazed," I said with a bravado I didn't have.

"You always amaze me, Bailey."

I smiled. My vision was coming back. I really hoped Mac would like it. It allowed me to think of something happy. Something I was actually good at. Something I had control over. And I realized the thing about life all over again. Sometimes we have great sadness and disappointment and it can sit side by side with something that brings us joy. We have to be grateful for both and dwell on the joy.

ॐ

The next morning, before Griffin went to work and while Charlie was outside playing with Whitney and Lucy, he sat me down at the kitchen table.

"I know it's useless for me to tell you to slow down and recover from this," he said.

"I'm trying to survive the only way I can. Work heals me. I love you, Griffin."

"I know you do. As I always say, always have. Always did. Always will." He came over next to me and took my hand. He met my gaze and our lifetime of memories made me smile. Temporarily. He continued, "That's why I've made a decision. I want to have a vasectomy. I can't go through this again."

"You can't make this decision by yourself. Who's to say we won't get lucky?"

"Those are some big ifs—do you realize that? If you and I hadn't been on the phone. If Mac wasn't in the hotel with you. If he hadn't gotten you to the hospital in time. Do you know what would've happened? You would've bled to death in your hotel room. I don't want to take that chance again. I am not going to ask you to stay at home. But I can't be panicking all the time. I don't want Charlotte growing up without a mom. Do you? I don't want to lose you."

"You know I don't. And I don't like psychological warfare. You know that's my greatest fear."

"Call me crazy, but I don't like thinking about my wife bleeding to death. We need to be content. We are all healthy. We need to be grateful for what we have."

I had said that a thousand times to Charlie and he knew it.

"Well, this has been a couple of shitty days."

Griffin embraced me. He held me tight. He held me for a long time. He would've made an excellent attorney or comforter-in-chief.

"I feel so lucky to have you. Bae, you have given me a wonderful family. You are my life." We continued to embrace.

"Damn you, Griffin Hardwick!" But we were both smiling, and soon he was kissing me with a love that had multiplied over the years.

NOW

I had been summoned to the office by Floyd. He sounded agitated. "There is a time discrepancy between Griffin's and Lady Jane's versions. Griffin's time is over an hour before Lady Jane's statement," he said.

We watched the tape and stopped it when I saw Griffin and Jane appear. "There they are. Jane comes in, meets Griffin in the lobby, and they leave together."

"Are you entirely positive?"

"I am completely positive—that's Griffin." I got up and walked to the screen and pointed to his wrist. "You can blow up pictures but those are his bracelets. He wears them all the time. I gave him a couple."

"You just backed up Lady Jane's testimony and contradicted your husband's," Floyd said as he slid the two police statements over to me so I could read them. He had circled Griffin's time against Lady Jane's time. "Does Griffin have a good sense of time?"

"He is never late. In the restaurant business, you hate patrons who show up late for their reservations because it throws off the entire book."

"Bailey, I know this is a sensitive subject matter. Why would your husband lie?" I sat there for a few minutes trying to recalibrate that night.

"Let me put it another way. Does he have any prior history of making decisions without telling you?" Our past experiences came cascading over me. I didn't know much, but Griffin's love was unimpeachable. He would never let me take the blame.

THEN
EIGHTEEN YEARS AGO

I walked into Mac's office with a satchel full of ideas and a proposal for his new restaurant in Chicago.

The truth was, I had pouted. I had pleaded. I had even prayed that Griffin would change his mind about the vasectomy. I pulled out my own psychological warfare, asking him, "What if something happens to Charlie? Wouldn't we want to try to have another baby?" My husband did not budge. In between my attempts to cajole Griffin into changing his mind, I came up with a solid vision for Mac.

"Can I get you anything, Bailey? Are you sure you're up to this?" Mac seemed worried about me.

I nodded. Truthfully, I was on much firmer ground pitching ideas than I was with Charlie.

"I'm good. Let's get to it. Before we begin, take a deep breath," I instructed. I had completely changed my vision for Mac. This was not going to be anything like his place in New York. I pulled out the bluish-teal jewel-tone piece of velvet first. It was rich and vibrant.

I watched as Mac furrowed his brow. This was not a color we had ever talked about. Not the color. Not the velvet fabric. I waited until his expression relaxed before I continued.

"I found this incredible black-and-tan zebra-inspired fabric. The two fabrics together make the other pop." I carefully laid it on top of the velvet.

"And so we begin," I started. I had to pitch it right so he could see it.

"The two fabrics together are sleek. Sophisticated. Unexpected. The tan and black do look like a zebra," Mac said and smiled.

"Hold that thought. I know you wanted something similar to your establishment in New York, but I think you'd like to pump it up a notch. This is very sophisticated. And different."

"I love it. I can see these fabrics with the molding. How did you know I would like it?"

"It's my job. Besides, I sensed your yearning."

"Hey, I'm married now." He laughed his hearty laugh. The real one.

"Let me finish with the presentation, then you can ask questions. I know the velvet looks very expensive, but it's discounted. I was thinking of putting it on the booths in your restaurant. I would put the zebra fabric on chairs and stools. Fortunately, it comes highly recommended for wear and tear. Unfortunately, it is expensive, which is why I am suggesting we use it sparingly on the chairs and stools. And—wait for it—I would like to name your restaurant Zebra." I stopped for a minute. I wanted to catch my breath and gauge Mac's reaction. I had thrown a completely different concept at him, complete with a different restaurant name.

"We could have a zebra motif throughout the restaurant." Mac was on board.

"Not exactly. I am *not* re-creating Elvis's jungle room here. I could see some zebra motif sprinkled about."

"I love it, Bailey. I don't know how you did it, especially with . . ." He didn't finish.

"I'm sorry you had to be the one."

"I'm just glad I was there to help. Poor Griffin. I've never seen him that freaked out. How is he holding up?"

"He's okay." I didn't say he was at home sitting with a bag of frozen peas on his privates.

"I know it's noon. Is it too early to open a bottle of champagne and toast our newest collaboration? To Zebra." He smiled. I could tell he had warmed to the idea of my proposal and name change.

"It is a little too early for me. I'll take a rain check. I need to research some paint colors." I was thinking of a dark eggplant color to make his beautiful moldings pop with the same basic tones as the velvet. I figured he could only stand so much outside-the-box thinking for one day. My phone buzzed. Mac motioned for me to take it. I stepped outside his office.

"Really? Thanks for the recognition!" I hung up the phone and had a major happiness freak-out. "Mac!" I shouted.

"Are you alright?" Mac heard my screaming and poked his head out of his office.

"That was *Architectural Digest.* They want to put me on the cover! Do you know what this means? I will be the first restaurant designer ever to grace their cover!"

"That's so exciting. Congratulations! Bailey, you're the best," Mac said. We hugged and I thanked him, but I made no motion to leave.

"Do you have more ideas?" he asked.

I waited a customary amount of time, and then it dawned on Mac.

"Ah, yes. The thing that always makes our friendship bloom a little sweeter." He opened his desk to retrieve his checkbook. I smiled. And then I went home.

When I approached the threshold of my kitchen they were both there. Griffin sitting at the table and Henry at the stove. It steadied my heart. It always steadied my heart. I allowed myself a moment. I allowed myself to let the memories wash over me. It was as if I were instantly bathed in sunlight and happiness. My memories and my men.

"What took you so long? We've had champagne on ice since your call." Griffin poured me a glass. Henry stuck to his sparkling water. Both men clinked glasses and toasted, "To Bailey! Restaurant designer to the stars!"

I walked over to Griffin and embraced him and kissed him, forgetting Henry was there. "Griff, you sure picked a lousy time for your procedure if your wife wants to celebrate tonight."

"Henry . . ." I grumbled and went over and hugged my brother.

"The girls are out back. They want to ride their bikes. Maggie wants to keep an eye on Charlie," Henry said with pride, then quickly switched topics. "I want you both to try something," he said, turning back to the stove to finish what he was doing.

"How are you feeling?" I touched my husband's hand and held it. He smiled.

"I'm good. How did your presentation go?"

"Mac bought it. I think I pushed him a little outside of his comfort zone, but he really came around."

"That's not surprising—Bailey working her magic," my brother said as I pulled out the two swatches. I put them side by side. Henry put plates of food in front of us. About the same time the girls came in through the back.

"Nobody told us Uncle Henry was cooking," Charlie complained, stealing the knife and fork from me to take a bite of the waffles with banana, figs, and maple syrup.

"Quit stealing my food, young lady!" My brother gave me a wink, probably remembering all the times that he had stolen food off Griffin's and my plates growing up.

Henry set another plate down for himself and a fresh one down for me and sat down across from me. With a little help from Maggie, Charlie wolfed the whole plate down.

"Can we go ride our bikes now?" Maggie asked.

"Be careful. Keep an eye on Charlie," Henry said, like a responsible parent.

"I am responsible for myself, thank you," Charlie said. Then they disappeared.

"Henry, this is really good. What is that flavor in the waffles?" I asked, not realizing how hungry I was. He smiled. He loved dazzling us.

"It's pistachio. But I thought it went well with the bananas and figs."

"I'm just going to go check on the girls," Griffin said, leaving us alone.

"I love these two fabrics together," Henry said, holding the two swatches. "Why didn't you save this idea for us?"

"I wasn't aware that you were talking about opening another restaurant." I put my fork down and looked at him. "Are you?"

"No. But you never know. I really love how these fabrics play together."

"Well, I don't know how you do it. Come up with these wonderful recipes on top of being a wonderful parent. I don't have that second piece down."

"Have you talked to Lea? Mothers and daughters are just hard, Bailey. I'm sorry. But Charlie is just a little love."

"To you and Griffin. Me, not so much."

Henry laughed and finished eating his beautiful creation. He took his plate to the sink and put it in the dishwasher. Then he came back and took my hand.

"How are you doing, Bailey? I know this is not what you wanted."

"No. I just wanted to give Charlie a sibling." And then I looked at him. "Can you imagine what my life would've been like without you, Henry? Can you see Daddy and me navigating my teenage years without your . . ." I paused, "input?"

"I'm not sure my input was completely appropriate for an impressionable adolescent girl. I sure as hell wouldn't want Maggie to hear the things we told you." He laughed.

"I would've been so lonely without you, Henry. And just think about it, without you, there would be no Griffin. The two of you have always been the best part of my life." I got choked up thinking that Charlie wouldn't have these kinds of conversations.

"Bailey, without you, I would've never met Lea. And you know for a fact she is a saint for putting up with me. You and Griffin saved my life." He was referring to both interventions.

"How are *you* doing, Henry?"

"I go to meetings every day. Those people get me through. Day by day. Did you really like my concoction?" He grinned. False modesty did not become him.

"I loved it."

"I am thinking about the restaurant you wanted to design for us. A diner . . . called Edgeworth's. How you wanted us to jump off the color wheel. It would be an homage to Dad."

I started crying again. "There's something I haven't told even Griffin." I hadn't had any practice delivering this kind of news, and I was almost afraid to begin. Afraid the dam would break and I wouldn't be able to pull myself together for days. It had already shaken me to the core.

"Spill it," Henry said. It had a nostalgic ring to it. He used to say that to me when I was having issues with Daddy and he would call from school. I can remember cradling the phone to my ear, trying to come up with the right words that wouldn't send him running for the hills. In all the times with every dilemma, Henry never hung up on me. Unless he was drunk and had to go throw up.

"Remember that guy Cliff Rushton who I designed for in Charlotte?"

"Sure, he was a real pain in the ass."

"You know he has the golden touch with restaurants. I designed Bravo for him. It closed after nine months. Poor traffic. His string of hits came to a screeching halt."

"I see where this is going. You want to take the blame for the whole failure."

"It *is* my fault. How can you explain that the most successful restaurateur in Charlotte suddenly had a failure? He knows how to hire chefs. He just hired the wrong designer. I have never felt so low both personally or professionally."

"Okay, I know you're all in on this pity party, but I don't understand how Cliff's restaurant has anything to do with your personal life."

"The place that I had my first professional failure is Charlotte. And personally, I am not having good luck with my daughter either."

"Shit, Bailey. This sounds like a conversation that I need to be drunk for, and I don't drink anymore."

"Just think about it, Henry. Charlotte, the place, and Charlotte, the person, have given me my biggest failures."

"Why don't you talk to the girls about this?"

"They would probably tell me to forget that jackass."

"I need some coffee." Henry got up and made us each a cappuccino. I took a sip, and it was surprisingly good.

"Even this tastes good."

"Be careful, little sister—your jealousy and insecurity are showing. It's not a good look on you." He smiled before continuing. "Do you know how incredibly lucky you are?"

I was about to protest, and he put his hand up to stop me. "As I was saying, do you realize that in all these years of you being a restaurant designer, you have never had a flop. Hit after hit after hit. No wonder you don't understand what to do with failure. I'll remind you. You just got the call to be on the cover of *Architectural Digest*."

"You've never had a flop either, Henry. All of your restaurants are successful. I feel like such a fraud. I mean the restaurant closed. Closed. The one I designed. I think some of my confidence left me once I had Charlie. How can something that I love so much throw me so off-balance?"

"Griffin and I have three, count them, three, restaurants. That is why we are so hesitant to open another one. It takes the both of us to manage three restaurants. You don't want to hear it, but you need to sit with this failure. Failure can be a gift. Failure can be freeing. It gives you another chance to do things differently and maybe even make it better. You need to let it transform you into something better. Because failure can transform your life just like beauty can."

"That brings us to Charlotte. I am a failure as a mother. Walls don't talk back. Children do."

"Yes, they do. Hank and I have our issues. He's fifteen, and while he's a good kid, I smell weed occasionally. I have to tell him he can't do it because of his addictive personality. It's tough. Kids don't like to think that they have inherited these genes from us. And he can smart-mouth Lea because she is not his 'real' mother."

"But you're a good dad. You're there. I don't know which is worse, not being a good mother or not wanting to be here to try and be a good mother."

"I can't say I completely relate to your dilemma because we don't travel. This might surprise you, but Griffin isn't the only one who reads. I enjoy reading Willa Cather. She said you can learn as much from the storm as you can the calm."

I thought Henry was out of surprises, but the fact that he read something other than recipes shocked the hell out of me.

"I should tell you the last of it. Cliff is opening a new restaurant, and he hired Nick Gallagher, my nemesis back from my days of working with Julian."

"So? You're not going to land every account. And quite frankly, I don't think you would want to work with that jackass again. It sounds to me like Cliff is trying to be something he's not. He's found the sweet spot, but he wants to do something different. I call that a recipe for disaster."

Some of it was true. But my mind had gone off course a bit. I thought about the quote. I had learned a lot about life through my divorce. I had become a better designer from all those years of being lonely when the boys were gone, Daddy was working, and I was eating every meal by myself.

"Get a grip, little sister. You should be happy today. You just made history by being the first restaurant designer asked to be on the cover of *Architectural Digest*. You're letting this one failure rob you of your joy. Never let anything or anyone rob you of your joy."

What would I learn about my failure from Cliff? And what would I learn from my daughter about my shortcomings as her mother? Time would tell.

"I probably need to check on Dad. Want to join?" I texted Griffin. He had everything under control. Henry had talked me off the ledge. I had pulled him out of the gutter. We were quite the pair of siblings. We were always better together.

We walked into the facility and found Dad parked in front of the window. He loved the sunshine. We rolled him out to the courtyard. He rarely spoke anymore, and his face did not change expressions. His cheeks were hollow from all the weight he had lost. Henry had wrapped up a waffle with all its trimmings. He patiently fed Dad small bites. Dad still had a pretty good appetite and enjoyed what he was being fed. He opened his mouth for the next bite.

"All gone," Henry said, showing him the empty plate. I took his hand and observed all the age spots and that his nails needed trimming. The thing that remained with me was the love and devotion that Henry still showed Dad. Without words, his love for his father was as apparent as any soliloquy ever recited. I needed to do a better job with him. Then Henry proceeded to tell Dad about the diner. I realized that Henry used Dad as a repository for his own secrets, wishes, and dreams. Just as I did.

"Did Dad ever make waffles like this?" I asked Henry.

"No. But he did make a waffle with rosemary that was delicious, which will be another item on the menu."

"Just how far along are you with the planning of Edgeworth's?" I asked Henry. At the mention of his last name, Dad looked at Henry, as if for an instant, and it was just an instant, he knew we were talking about him. Was that a blessing from the patriarch of the Edgeworth dynasty? The doctor said it could either be reflex or recognition. Who's to know? Today had been a good day. I chose to see it as a blessing. The last few days I had focused on all the things Griffin and I would never have. More children. A bigger family. A fuller house. But I realized that a key component to happiness was gratitude. In that moment, with the very first two men in my life, it was all enough.

❧

When *Architectural Digest* put me on the cover, it was not how I envisioned. I thought I would be in Zebra. With Mac. As it turned out, there were many setbacks with Zebra. So instead, I appeared with Mac and the Color-Wheel Boys. The cover image was taken at NOIR. It made Henry so happy.

NOW

Reflexively, I drove to NOIR. I just sat in the car. I didn't get out right away. I thought about what Floyd had asked me. Suddenly, I heard a knock on my window. It was Henry. I started crying. About everything. I cried for Elliott. I cried about the discrepancy in Jane's and Griffin's statements. I cried for myself for all the miscarriages I'd suffered. How did one thing trigger everything? My nose was running so much that Henry dangled the towel he always wore at his waist at me. It almost looked like he was surrendering. I smiled, opened the door, and grabbed the towel and wiped my face. I walked inside with Henry. We sat side by side in a booth. It was his brand of comforting.

"Hey, Lindsay, can you make my sister a sidecar? Tell me what's wrong."

"It's weird. I haven't thought about Elliott in twenty years. He was my ex-husband, but I didn't want him dead."

"I keep forgetting he was your husband."

"Floyd doesn't think I killed Elliott." Henry just looked at me as if a live wire were sitting between us. "He isn't so sure about Griffin or Charlie."

"That's a bad place for you, little sister."

"I know Griffin wouldn't let me take the blame. But Charlie . . ." I said. Henry met my expression, and we didn't say anything for a long time. And yet. It prompted my next question. "What do you know about Charlie?"

Henry just kept looking at me. My phone buzzed.

"We aren't done here." I got up to leave.

"Didn't think we were," Henry said, getting up too. I realized the thing about siblings all over again. Their mutual experiences knit together to form endless conversations. And understanding. I left feeling very grateful for Henry.

THEN
ELEVEN YEARS AGO

I got home from New York late Thursday afternoon. I had stayed an extra day to visit Elle and Reggie. Our conversations had shifted into talking about our children, namely our daughters.

Something had gone off track between Charlie and me in the intervening years. It had started with that horrible birthday. Now she was almost twelve. Where had the time gone? We were still moving around each other like we were foreigners who didn't understand each other's language. The girls told me to just relax. That was always their advice. But this cancer of discontent had settled in my bones. Was it too late for me to learn the language of motherhood?

I walked inside the house and rolled my bag into the hallway. I heard them—Griffin's and Charlie's animated voices. That was what was missing. Animation. When she talked to me these days, it was indifference I heard. I thought it was too early to blame hormones. I smelled chili powder and heard something sizzling on the stove above their laughter.

Griffin was at the stove and Charlie was sitting beside him on the counter. The sun was streaming in from the window behind her, framing her body perfectly. She looked like she had angel wings. I just stood there, listening to their happy reverie. They were laughing at shared jokes. Then I heard a click. It sounded like a binder.

At that moment, I saw that Tay was coming down the stairs. "Bailey!" she said, which started a chain reaction. Both Griffin and Charlie looked in my direction. I rolled my suitcase as if I was just coming in the door to my own house.

"I'm just getting home."

"I was just getting ready to leave," she said.

"No. Stay for dinner, Tay," Charlie's voice rang out. "It's Taco Thursday." I walked into the kitchen.

"What happened to Taco Tuesday?"

"I ended up having to work Tuesday night, and Tay was a lifesaver and stayed over," Griffin said.

"I was just changing the sheets in the guest room before I left. It smells good."

"Stay for dinner, Tabatha," I said, kissing Griffin and trying to kiss Charlotte before she pulled away.

"Mom! I'm practically twelve." I kissed her anyway as she pulled outside my grip.

"Sprite, what do you have there? It looks like a binder," I said, pointing to the purple notebook with three rings.

"It's a cookbook. Dad made it for me. He wanted me to know how to cook. Not like you."

"Sprite, I didn't say that, exactly," Griffin interrupted. "I've restocked your wine," he said to me.

The next night I went to say good night to Charlie. I carried the binder with me. The night before, I had flipped through the laminated pages that Charlie and Griffin had created together. It was a marriage of both their talents. Griffin had supplied all the ingredients. And yet I loved Charlie's descriptions. They were in her handwriting. For Griffin's brownies: *Always add a good dose of cinnamon. Cinnamon coaxes the chocolate to come out and play and strut her stuff.* Griffin's fish: *Soak fish in pineapple juice before cooking. It is like the necessary bath before bedtime for fish. It washes away the fishy taste. Like today's worries.* Her descriptions were clever and amusing.

"I wanted to say good night, Sprite."

"What are you doing with my binder?" Charlie demanded.

"I was reading your descriptions of Dad's recipes. They're really good. They are clever and apropos, and I can hear your voice."

She looked at me. I couldn't decide if it looked like I had invaded her privacy—like reading a diary—or if I had pleased her. She carefully opened the drawer of her bedside table. I took a quick glance inside and saw the writing pens she liked and the bag of sea glass. There was also a piece of paper. She pulled it out. It was as if we were about to share a secret.

"Did you really think my descriptions were good?"

I nodded, trying not to ruin our conversation with words. She continued, "Middle school is having a writing contest. The idea is to write something fun you do with one of your parents."

"Are you thinking about writing an essay and using the binder as a show-and-tell?"

"That's a good idea. I hadn't really thought that far."

"It's good, Charlie. You could call it 'Recipes for Life.' Or 'Recipes for Living.' Your dad is a chef, and that is how you make memories. Unless you think it's too corny."

"I love that title. Thanks, Bae. The winner gets $100. Maybe I could take you and Dad to the beach."

I loved her enthusiasm. And naïveté. I needed to do a better job teaching her about money. I flipped the pages to one of my favorite recipes.

"*Choose friends like you choose a piece of meat. Go for quality. They will always come through in any circumstance . . . like Reggie and Elle. Lucy and Whitney.* Who came up with that?"

"I did. You know Dad doesn't talk like that."

We shared a rare laugh.

❧

The next morning, Charlie came into the kitchen and sat down next to me.

"Will you read what I have so far?" She looked at me expectantly.

I closed my computer and read the first few sentences. "*My dad is the chef in our family. It is a good thing because my mom travels for work. I love cooking with my dad. It has come to mean more than just explaining recipes. He has a way of weaving in life lessons. Many people would think we just cook. I have learned a lot from him, from picking friends to understanding my mom.*"

"This is really good," I said. "I'll tell you what: If you win the contest, we'll take you to the beach and we will go to the bank and put your money in a savings account for college where it will earn interest." I explained the concept of interest and her eyes grew big.

"Interest is like free money?"

"Yes. It pays to save your money and to be very careful with it."

ঞ

At Christmas break it was announced that Charlie had won the contest. Griffin seemed surprised that their collaboration had garnered a prize. That afternoon we went to the bank together and opened a savings account. The teller asked Charlie whose name she wanted on the account besides hers.

"Dad. He's always here, and I think he could use the money more." I laughed that Charlie thought her father was practically indigent, when in truth he made more money than I did.

Charlie would go on to win a number of contests and prizes, even having an article appear in the Atlanta paper. Her junior and senior years she worked summers at the paper. I loved watching her transformation. It didn't take her very long to start learning her craft and the value of money. I told Griffin we were on the hook for taking her to the beach.

ও

This beach trip was absent of any sense of wonder and astonishment. It made me sad. I could still be moved by the ocean at my age. I didn't think I would ever outgrow my respect for Mother Nature and God. But Charlie, on the threshold of adolescence, had a jaded approach. A "been there, done that" attitude.

We were on the beach together, and Griffin was up in the hotel room on the phone with Henry. The fact of the matter was that Griffin did not like the beach. My phone rang, and it was Gabriel Modare, my favorite billionaire client from Brazil. We were discussing his new space.

"Where is Charlotte?" Griffin came up behind me. He looked to his left and right. She had gone down the beach. "I can't believe you let her wander off so far." He saw her and went after her. I got off the phone quickly. I heard them laughing as they neared me.

"At least this time I didn't end up in the emergency room with Bae!" Charlie said.

"I was just telling the Sprite about some of her emergency room visits with you."

I looked at Griffin as if he had betrayed me. I didn't like thinking about those times, which highlighted how I had fallen short as a mother.

"It's a wonder I didn't end up dead or as a ward of the state," Charlie said, laughing.

"Not as long as I am around, Sprite," Griffin said.

"I'm right here!" I snapped.

"I found a lot of pretty sea glass down the beach," Charlie interrupted, showing me her treasure. She laid the pieces out on the towel. "Bae, I still just love sea glass." I smiled, looking up at her and examining her collection.

"Me too," I said, looking at all the unique shapes and sizes and colors.

ও

That night at dinner, the snarky side of Charlie emerged.

"Good grief. Have you taken a good look at the prices? Can we afford it?"

"We never take vacations. We saved up," I said. I was secretly glad that she was observing the price of things. The waiter approached us. He looked at Charlie to see if she was going to do her own ordering. She did.

"I will have the tuna tartare and the beet salad," she said, closing her menu.

"Are you aware the tuna is prepared raw?" he asked her.

"Well, duh. We eat sushi all the time."

"Very good then."

Griffin and I completed our orders.

"That wasn't very nice, Charlie. The waiter was only doing his job making sure you knew what you were ordering. He probably doesn't get too many sophisticated palates like yours."

"What is up with that, anyway? All Lucy and Whitney want to eat is chicken nuggets." Griffin and I could not suppress our laughter.

"The curse of a sophisticated palate. When your mom was your age, she took fennel soup to school with her," Griffin reminisced.

"I was the talk of the lunchroom and frequently ate lunch by myself," I said, turning my own tortured memory into something to delight my daughter.

"I still love the tater tots that Tay cooks for me. I guess that busts my gourmet cred."

"We all have our comfort foods. Your dad and I both like peanut butter and brioche." I looked over at Griffin and smiled at our inside joke.

"Nothing better," Griffin agreed.

"Y'all are really weird sometimes." Charlie pulled out her phone and began texting with her friends. The waiter came up to her once again.

"Miss, cell phones are not permitted in our dining room."

She put it away, ate her dinner quickly, and put her napkin on the table.

"May I be excused, please? This place is hell."

"Charlie," I warned. At the same time Griffin was handing over the key, giving in to her, and she disappeared. I ordered another drink.

"I don't appreciate you telling Charlie about my screwups in the emergency room. Parenting 101—present a united front to your child," I said to Griffin. It made me nostalgic for the people we were on our first beach trip.

NOW

I had been at the conference table for several hours. Looking and *really* looking at the tape. I saw where Griffin and Jane had left together. They had walked close together. Like a couple. Right down to the matching hoodie. I studied details, trying to see my daughter. There were a few prime candidates.

"When we were married, and I know that's over twenty years ago, Elliott was involved with a lot of unsavory people."

"What kind of defense attorney would I be if I didn't unearth every known association in Elliott's life?"

My phone rang. It was Gabriel. I answered it and told him I would have to call him back.

"Is that Gabriel Modare, the billionaire restaurateur?" Floyd perked up. "Is he one of your clients?"

I nodded. My grip on my confidence had been shaken by this legal drama. Much like it had been shaken by Elliott during and after our divorce. I was having a hard time keeping clients, just like when the mess of my divorce was plastered all over the papers.

"I sometimes forget how famous you are. Why don't you quit for today?" Floyd suggested. He was like the pope of the legal community dismissing me.

When I got out to my car, I called Gabriel back.

"It's time." He began. "I want you." I had to smile. Everything Gabriel said sounded sexual. It must be his Brazilian accent. Maybe that's what had attracted me to Elliott—his British accent.

"Are you really ready to design a restaurant in Brazil? Gabriel, I don't know if you're keeping up with things . . ."

"Yes. My little felonious friend."

"I had to surrender my passport. I can't fly to Brazil anytime soon. I didn't do it, just so you know."

"I know that. I was thinking I could send you pictures of my proposed space."

"I would like to see the vista—what you see from the windows of the restaurant. I can pull some swatches and put together some ideas for now."

"This reminds me of the restaurant you designed at Dana Point."

"If it has that kind of view, I can definitely work with that," I said, ending the call. I was grateful that Gabriel had given me a chance. This would be our fifth restaurant together. I knew from all our previous conversations that this one was the most important one to him. This was home. He still had a point to prove with the people from his hometown. Boy makes good and all of that.

As I was walking in the house, my phone was buzzing. It was Charlie. "Hi, sweetie. What's up?" Charlie rarely called me in the middle of the day. I suppose it was because I was always working.

"You are never going to believe this, Mom. It finally happened!" I smiled to myself. Rarely did she ever call me "Mom." And the way she said "finally" made it sound like she was sixty years old and had won the lottery.

"I just heard from a literary agent. She read the first three chapters of the memoir I sent and she loved it. She wants to represent me! And guess what she said—she loved the title *Trashed*. The title you gave me!" Charlie was elated.

I was so happy for her. This was happening so easily for her. I had to agree, however: she had a compelling story.

"Charlie, that's terrific! I suppose writing is your vision. I am so proud of you. What did your dad say? And Bishop?" I just hope she didn't do something stupid and drive him away like I had done with her father briefly.

"I haven't told them yet. I called you before anyone else. I guess I can get this out of the way, Bae. They want me to play up our relationship. You are kind of famous. I guess you were right about the *Devil Wears Prada* angle." She paused. I paused. In fact, I sat down at the kitchen table. Then I got back up again and went to the pantry to get a bottle of bourbon. The more successful I had become, the more expensive my bourbon had become. I was drinking Jefferson's and on rare occasions Jefferson's Ocean. I had locked it in my office while Charlie was at home, but I had moved it all back inside when she left for school. I got a glass out of the cabinet, poured liberally, and threw it back. It made my throat tingle.

"Your dad is going to be so happy and proud," I managed. But it was all I could do to keep my heart from leaping out of my chest.

"Guess what the agent said?" she asked.

"I don't know—what did she say?"

"Your mom must be a number-one bitch!" Charlie said with glee.

I shuddered. Did she think this was like a badge of honor for me? Why couldn't she wait until I was dead?

"But you and I both know how the story ends."

"How does it end, Charlie?"

"You'll just have to read about it like everyone else." She sounded confident. She sounded happy. She sounded sober. I guess I would give it all away for her continued happiness and sobriety. I closed my eyes and remembered the crack in our relationship after the pen incident. Although nowadays, in Charlie's mind, her birthday pens had shape-shifted into a happy memory.

A few weeks later, I was doing some preliminary searching for Gabriel's restaurant in Brazil. I knew how important this was to him, so my inner perfectionism was coming through. I knew Gabriel didn't care how much time or money I spent. He and I both agreed that the vibe needed to reflect the Brazilian culture and food. I was studying the history of Brazil when my phone rang.

"You're not going to believe this," Charlie said. "A big publisher already bought my memoir! My agent, Gail, was surprised that it got snapped up so quickly. They love my writing style. Stephanie, my editor, is a recovering alcoholic herself."

"Whoa, Charlie. This is happening so fast. Have they given you contracts to sign?" I was getting nervous that my daughter was getting carried away.

"They sent contracts over via courier this morning. I haven't signed them yet."

"Let's patch your Aunt Elizabeth in. Would you mind if someone in her office looked at them for you?"

"That would be great, Bae," she said, and I patched Elle into the conversation and briefed her on the developments.

"Congratulations, Charlotte! I have a better idea. Want to have an early dinner so I can take the soon-to-be best-selling author out before she is too famous to hang with her aunt?"

Charlie agreed. I was glad once again for Elle. I knew from the past that Charlie sometimes had a better ability to talk to Reggie and Elle and even Sally than she did with me. I was glad she had women in her life to give her advice. I was glad that she was not left to her own devices to live out some reckless behaviors.

About that time, Griffin strolled in carrying dinner. It was early. That had always been a sign that we would turn in early. I watched him. He came over and kissed me and then he unpacked dinner.

"I stopped by NOIR. Henry prepared a lovely Dover sole with tarragon and lemon cream–stuffed gnocchi." Dover sole was my favorite.

"You're laying it on a bit thick."

"And . . .?" Griffin was already smothering me in kisses.

"Food as foreplay is always a good place to start. Besides, when have I ever turned you down?" I paused. "Well, recently?" I decided to keep the contradiction in his and Lady Jane's statements and my growing doubts about Charlie to myself. For now.

THEN
TEN YEARS AGO

I walked into the house on a Wednesday night. Mac and I had a fruitless day of waiting for inspectors to show up who never did. Griffin, Charlie, and Tabatha all looked up and registered surprise. It was like I had caught them doing something they were not supposed to be doing.

"This is a surprise!" Griffin said, straining his neck to give me a kiss as he was cooking. Then another.

"Yeah, you're not supposed to be home until tomorrow night," Charlie uttered, barely looking up.

"Don't sound so excited, Sprite." I didn't want it to hurt my feelings, but it did. "What's Wednesday's dinner?" I was used to their father-daughter collaborations. Meatless Monday. Taco Tuesday or Thursday. I had forgotten what Wednesday was.

"Wednesday Wonder. Dad creates a concoction and he gives me the name, and I try to figure out what it is. It's also the last night of the week that Tabatha gets to eat with us."

Another hit. Charlie was twelve years old and had already developed a healthy animosity toward me and my job.

"What's tonight's dish called?" I looked at Griffin. Charlie interrupted.

"You can't play. Just Tay and me."

"That's not nice, Charlotte. Let your mom play. The dish is called 'green submarine.' Any guesses?"

Griffin looked around at all of us. I didn't dare guess. I went to the refrigerator and got a glass of wine. I kept the bottle handy.

"You're not supposed to peek, Bae," Charlie chided. Lettuce wraps, avocado, and green pea risotto were some of the guesses. I looked over at Tabatha. She was dressed in a black dress, nicer than what I was wearing.

"Sprite, Tay may have plans tonight. You look really pretty, Tabatha," I said.

"No plans. All my Lululemon's are in the laundry." She laughed and took a sip of her wine.

Griffin brought us back to the guessing game. "I think you're going to be underwhelmed tonight, Sprite. I didn't have a lot of time to think about this. It is a hollowed-out zucchini stuffed with chicken and sautéed mushrooms in a béchamel sauce. I put two sprigs of rosemary on top like torpedoes."

It sounded delicious to me. Charlie's eyes lit up. "Yum, Dad! It rhymes. 'Green submarine.' It's like a crepe in a zucchini. You are the smartest dad ever."

I felt a little green myself. Green with envy at the ease Griffin had with our daughter. Charlie asked Tabatha to stay, and she did. After dinner, when Griffin and I were alone, I helped him clean up. He playfully bumped into me occasionally as we cleaned.

"How do you do it? Why does she hate me so much?"

"I don't think she hates you exactly, but I noticed her attitude. I am really glad you're home."

My hands were wet as they cupped his face and I kissed him. He embraced me.

"She's only twelve. What's going to happen when she's a teenager? She really is a junior terrorist."

❧

Soon after that, I was working on the West Coast, where Gabriel Modare and I were doing our third restaurant together. I had been so happy.

When I strolled around his beautiful building overlooking the cliffs at Dana Point, it took my breath away. I knew almost immediately that the vibe was minimalistic. I wanted it to complement the view, not compete with it. For my pitch to Gabriel, I suggested painting the walls a marigold color by Farrow & Ball. I wanted it to resemble the color one associates with sunset, and not to interrupt the vista of the eye. I didn't want to obstruct the breathtaking views with drapes, but recommended a fabric done in the marigold color, a rich orange to mimic the setting sun and a blue-green to mimic the ocean color. It was a beautiful fabric, and it looked great at the top of the windows.

It was an elegant seafood restaurant. It all complemented the natural surroundings of this extraordinary place. Gabriel's wooden artifacts stood out. The place was beautiful and soothing.

At the opening, just like at all his other restaurants, there were wall-to-wall people and wall-to-wall cameras. I had purchased a lace shrimp-colored dress to wear to the event. Griffin did not want to leave Charlie or pull her out of school for two days to see California. I tried to entice him into creating "new" grand opening memories. I offered previews of "coming attractions." Even Henry tried to persuade Griffin, saying it would give him a chance to spend some one-on-one time with his favorite niece.

But Griffin didn't budge. He encouraged me to visit Thomas and Beth Wilson. Their restaurant looked as tired as ever, but the food was never lacking. I offered my services but they both agreed they preferred the "run-down" look. I missed Griffin, so I cut my visit short.

I had gone straight to my office to put some additional orders in for some extra things that Gabriel and I had selected once we saw how crowded and successful it would be. We had become the "odd couple" in the culinary world.

When I got home, I walked into the kitchen and heard Tabatha and Charlie in the great room. "Precious, that's just not the way your mother is wired. Some women, like your mom, want to work. They prefer to work rather than staying at home with their kids. If you were my daughter, I would stay home every day and be there for you and your sweet, understanding daddy."

"I just wish she loved me more," I heard Charlie say.

"I suppose she does, in her own odd, roundabout way. She is just a bit selfish."

I froze listening to this conversation. I closed the door discreetly and went back to my office. I called Reggie.

"You've got to fire her ass. Now. This is one for the committee. Let me patch Elizabeth in."

I had told them about Griffin stocking Tabatha's favorite wine.

"Do not pass 'Go'—you need to fire Tabatha," Elle said. "I told you years ago I would've never hired her. If Griffin were a different kind of guy, I promise you she would've made her move on him. And who's to say she hasn't. But Griffin only has eyes for you."

"Guys, if I go in there right now and make Tabatha leave, you know Charlie is going to blame me. That will backfire on me. What I really hate is her feeding Charlie some old-fashioned notion that women who stay home with their children must love their children more than women who work."

"Bailey makes good points," Reggie said in her maternal tone. "How about the next time you are out of town, Griffin does it, so Charlie can't blame you? But Bailey, this has got to happen. There is no telling how she has been undermining you with Charlie. This was always my worry. I wonder if this explains some of Charlie's behavior towards you."

"What she said isn't altogether wrong. You know I haven't been a great mother to Charlie. You know I'm gone with my work. I'm racked with guilt, but I still do it. And let's face it, children are not like rooms that I can go in and transform. Here I have complete control. When it comes to Charlotte Hardwick, I don't have any control. Walls don't talk back or make you cry."

We were silent for a while. My guilt poured out at my feet like a leak that wouldn't stop. I had farmed out my most important role to Griffin, Henry, and Tabatha. And sometimes Annabel and Sally. I just didn't have a vision for parenthood. Charlie and I seemed to be at odds from the moment she entered the world. I had loved her with reckless abandon and somehow it all went terribly haywire. The girls had been right. I had no idea what Tabatha had been saying all through the years. I knew they were right about letting her go. No matter how hard it would be on all of us. Charlie would be mad and sad. Griffin would shoulder the blame and I would have to stay at home until we could find someone else. I felt the centuries of women's struggles happening within me all at once. I wanted things to be different. I wanted to teach Charlie that working was important. It was never a measure of how much a mother loves her child.

As usual, the girls had been right. They always made me feel better, even when I felt like a complete failure. I got in my car and drove to VERT. I wanted to have this discussion with Griffin face-to-face without the danger we would be overheard.

"She can hit on me all she wants—it won't work," Griffin said, as we sat in his office behind the bar. I took a sip of my sidecar and realized how much I needed it.

"Wait a minute. Has she hit on you?" He didn't say anything, and that in and of itself was a tell. I continued, "It's Charlie I'm worried about. Tabatha is her security blanket. It might be a rough go in the beginning. I'll try to be at home more."

"Bae, you know as well as I do that's not going to happen. And that's okay. You're giving our daughter a great role model for working women. But Tabatha runs our house so smoothly. Maybe it'll pass." He was starting to sound a little like Mr. Banks in Mary Poppins. And I knew one thing for sure, I was no Mary Poppins. "When are you going to let Tabatha go?"

"I'm not. I've got to be out of town at the beginning of next week. I thought you could do it so Charlie won't blame me." I smiled at my husband and drained the glass. I realized he was a workaholic too. But at least he was based at home. "This is about saving my relationship with my daughter."

"Let me change your mind. This is going to be really hard on me and Charlie." He came around his desk and embraced me. "You want to test the sofa out? See if it's still got it? It's been a while. Before all hell breaks loose."

"Griffin, it's the middle of the afternoon." He was already kissing me.

"I figure you owe me." We locked the door. We fell into the sofa and into each other. It had always been that way. Our bodies colliding into each other's nooks and crannies. Even our clothing was in a heap of togetherness on the floor.

NOW

Some days it felt like just yesterday and other days, like today, it felt like quicksand. Floyd reviewed his notes before beginning. "Your ex-husband has a history of dealing with unsavory characters."

"Even now? With the success of his TV cooking show?" I asked.

"It looks like Elliott had never fully given up his affinity for drugs, alcohol, and women. What I don't understand is why Lady Jane ever took him back in the first place. Then they had a son, who, of course, you're familiar with—Desi. But he must not like his father too much because he goes by the name of Turner," Floyd said.

"Well, that threw me off."

"There's something here, Bailey. I just don't know what yet . . ." He almost sounded reassuring.

"Have you checked with Rex? I've forgotten his last name but he was a sous chef to Elliott."

"He hasn't worked for Elliott in ages. And I am guessing you know about the mobster Tony Esposito?"

"Not much. I just remember he was involved with the mobsters at the end."

"Did you ever meet his parents? Did he have any siblings?" Floyd looked at me. These were such basic questions. I worried that my impetuous marriage would never turn me loose.

"I never met his parents. I know Elliott had a volatile relationship with his father." I thought about it. "I never met any of his siblings. I only met Lady Jane the one time. She and Elliott had a tempestuous relationship. Maybe he liked it like that." I thought about how little I really knew about Elliott. How I could just rush into something as serious as marriage because of my racing hormones and my hurt feelings over Griffin.

"Let's see what the private investigators turn up. Bailey, you may have just been in the wrong place at the wrong time." I thought about it. I just may have been in the right place in order to protect my daughter.

*

Something nagged at me about Griffin. The contradiction in Jane's statement. He had denied killing Elliott. And yet . . . he could be so mercenary when it came to his family. I had viewed it as a noble thing. There were times when it wasn't. Would Griffin really lose his temper and stab Elliott?

About that time Floyd strolled in. He was carrying his briefcase in one hand and a cup of hot tea in the other. "I'm surprised to see you here already. I thought you may be doing your design work," Floyd said, as he began to set up shop.

"Apparently a murder charge really hurts business. I'm doing Zoom conference calls and mailing swatches of fabric. It isn't ideal but my current situation isn't ideal either." I took a sip of coffee.

"I'm looking into Desi. We are looking into whether Elliott or Elliott's father set up a trust fund. Getting your hands on inheritance is an age-old motive. Desi has an alibi but that doesn't mean he didn't do the deed. I need to ask you something. Have you talked to Charlie? Does she remember anything about the night of Elliott's murder?"

I didn't know how to have "the talk." One that begins with, "By the way, did you murder my ex-husband?" I didn't believe there was a book on the shelf that addressed this delicate topic of conversation.

"Are you completely sure that your daughter did not kill Elliott?"

I thought about everything his question contained. The years of ups and downs with my only child. Would it even matter to me if she had killed Elliott?

"I don't think so," I said, trying to steady my voice.

"She has a permanent job now at the *New York Times*. And she just got a book deal to publish her memoir about her road to sobriety. I wonder if all that would be in jeopardy if her publishers knew she had been drinking the night of Elliott's murder. I'm guessing that they would reconsider if it came out, she hadn't been entirely truthful. I don't know much about book deals, but I do remember there has been some brouhaha about the veracity of memoirs in the past," he said steadily. "It would be prudent if you could get her to postpone turning in her manuscript. I will leave that to you."

I looked at him. "How do you know about the job at the paper? And how did you know about her book deal?"

"Elliott isn't the only person I am investigating," he stated. "Are you entirely certain that the only people who knew Charlotte was drinking were you and Charlotte?" This frightened me. Did he have dossiers on all of us?

"Bishop knows. Her boyfriend. That's it. And Henry. I do know that Charlie is back on the wagon and attending meetings."

"Yes. I know that too." Did he have private investigators always following us?

"The only reason I bring this up, Bailey, is because your life has been an open book. You really don't have anything to lose except your freedom. Look at your daughter—what would this do to her new job and her new literary career? She has a lot more to lose if the truth came out than you do." With that, Floyd got up and left.

Instead of happy ideas ricocheting in my brain for restaurants, the life events with my daughter were ricocheting in my brain instead. There were times that Charlotte had hated me. Would she really let me go down for murder? Memory was a powerful thing.

THEN
TEN YEARS AGO

I walked around Zebra to inspect the final product before the grand opening. It had taken seven years. There were termites, electrical problems not being up to code, moving walls that needed to be fortified, and building permits that took forever.

I had changed my mind on several occasions. Vision requires adaptability. I loved the two fabrics together so much that I had put the velvet on the seat of the booths and the zebra print on the back. I thought it made a more effective visual if the fabrics were almost touching, holding hands. That's what the patrons would see when they walked into the restaurant. It was a stunning visual. Arguably, this had been the second most beautiful restaurant I had created in my opinion besides NOIR. When I had finished with NOIR, I had such a feeling of joy and unbridled happiness. Today, my heart was carrying around a suitcase of worry. My thoughts went back to Charlie and Tabatha. Was I really doing the right thing in letting her go despite admonitions from the girls? I knew who would tell me the truth. I went back to my hotel room so I could make the call.

"I was wondering if I would hear from you today," my brother said.

"I know this is a horrible time to call you."

"Let me duck into the office."

I had purposely told Griffin to wait until I gave the final order to fire Tabatha. I sounded like some four-star general making a life-and-death decision. But it felt that way to me.

"Tabatha," Henry said astutely. "I have heard a lot about her over the course of the last few days. Your girls think it's a good idea because she's undermining you with Charlie. Even Lea thinks that. Lea definitely thinks she's hit on Griffin a time or two. Of course, your husband only has eyes for you."

"What do you mean?"

"Let's just say sometimes she's come dressed not looking like a nanny."

"I'm not sure Griffin is completely on board with firing her. And Henry, what is this going to do to Charlie? Tabatha is her lifeline. Her security blanket. Can we just rip that away?"

"Bailey, I can't tell you what to do. I do have a feeling that she is undermining you. And in the long run, it is not a good thing for you and Charlie. None of us knows what she tells Charlie."

"She told her I was selfish. You think I'm selfish when it comes to my career?"

Talk about a pregnant pause. I could see diners at NOIR eating their meals and paying the check in the length of time it took my brother to come up with an answer. I realized in the vacuum it was an answer. He was just trying to figure out the best way to answer it. I smiled to myself. Henry would rather be cooking, and I would rather be designing, and yet here we were, brother and sister, trying to figure out the right strategy.

"You can't help it, Bailey. Just like I can't help being an alcoholic. When you were young, you could've come back to Atlanta. But no, you went to New York because that was exciting, and you could really stretch your wings there. You have built a very successful career." Henry was just getting started.

"How successful am I if I can't even raise my only daughter?"

"Here are some facts, Bailey. When you were growing up, there was just me, Griffin, and Dad. Charlie, on the other hand, has a mother, a father, wonderful aunts with Reggie, Elle, and Lea, some great friends with Whitney and Lucy, cousins with Hank and Maggie, and let's not forget—the best uncle in the world!" He made me laugh. He *was* the best uncle in the world. "Let's face it, that's damn more than what you had going for you and you turned out pretty great, little sister. Personally,

I think if you were home all the time, you would drive Charlie crazy. And she would drive you crazy. And I'm guessing you would drive me and Griffin crazy too."

After I stopped laughing, I began to cry.

"My God, what now?" Henry asked.

"I wish Charlie had this. A brother. I'm so lucky to have you."

"It's taken you a long time to think that. You and Griffin have bailed my ass out of trouble for as long as I've lived. I would probably be in a gutter somewhere without a family if it weren't for you two. I haven't exactly made things easy."

"I would do it as many times as I needed to."

"Not sure your husband feels the same way. I really pushed him to the breaking point sometimes. But that's what we do. We're better together."

"How do you do it?"

Again, Henry paused as if considering what to say next.

"I come home every night. I take the kids to school." Henry had turned into a father to be admired. Whereas I was a shit show in the motherhood department.

"I need a wife. I'm just not that person."

"Blame your DNA. You do sort of have a wife."

"Tabatha?"

"I was referring to Griffin. Griffin is at home every single night, so you have a wife. It's just role reversal. You are letting your daughter rule you. Bailey, I've seen pictures of Zebra. It's gorgeous. It may have had a lot of stops and starts and moments when you wondered if it would even happen but look how it turned out. It's probably your most beautiful creation. I love everything about that restaurant, right down to the zebra figurines you picked up at that estate sale. I just wish that it was our restaurant. You should be incredibly proud. I want you to be proud. I tried to talk Griffin into flying to Chicago to support you. I figured you could plan a strategy and then present a united front. Your husband is stubborn when it comes to your daughter. Charlie is almost thirteen. You are letting her rob you of your joy. Don't feel guilty because you are good at and like your job. Enjoy tomorrow night."

I was going to interject that Charlie was my most beautiful creation. Maybe we were all just beautiful disasters. Some days it tilts more toward beauty and some days it tilts more to disaster.

❧

The next night, I walked into Zebra and immediately heard flashbulbs going off like I was a celebrity. I guess in the cooking world, I *was* a minor celebrity. Mac was preening for the camera. I had worn my Valentino dress, which still fit—thankfully. It had been a long thirteen years, but the dress was still in style and it still looked like its price tag.

Mac motioned me over and we took several pictures together along with his wife, Cassandra, and Annabel. The truth was, I hadn't seen as much of Annabel lately. Whitney and Charlie were still good friends, but Lucy, the girl across the street, had become a better friend to Charlie, even though at times Charlie called Lucy "a geek." I think I preferred Charlie hanging out with nerds over the popular kids.

Mac went over to the bar and motioned to the bartender. "Ms. Edgeworth's champagne please?" He handed me the flute and we toasted. I heard more cameras going off. This place was wall-to-wall people. I put the champagne to my lips.

"I've known you a long time, Bailey. I've learned what your favorite champagne is. Only you and Cassie are drinking it so feel free."

I loved that he knew my champagne, but his wife and I had a great deal in common. Their son, Thompson, was one of Charlie's best friends. There was Thompson's best friend, Bishop Bellamy, who was always around. He had a Griffin-like quality that I recognized. I tried to relax. I tried to take Henry's advice not to let Charlie rob me of my joy tonight.

I tried not to look distracted when people talked to me. But all I could think about was Charlie. The confrontation. The anger. My phone had already buzzed five times tonight. All calls from Charlie. I wasn't quite ready to talk to her. I wasn't quite sure what I was going to say. I wasn't sure I had had enough champagne.

When my phone buzzed a sixth time, I finally excused myself and went to Mac's office and closed the door. I had even made his office beautiful. I had done the chair in a darker tan-and-black zebra print. I had chosen a cool animal-print wallpaper that I thought was just enough. It had the effect of a gentleman's study. I sat at the desk and answered the phone.

"*You* did this! You're the one who fired Tabatha! She said you probably would. It's *your* fault!" Charlie was livid. She was letting me have it. I tried not to let the guilt pour over me. I was the mother, after all. I needed to take charge.

"When did she tell you I would probably fire her, Charlie?" I took a sip of champagne. There was a pause in the conversation. Was it years ago? Was it several months ago? Maybe it was a few weeks ago. But clearly Tabatha had had the upper hand for a while. "I'm waiting," I said, with more confidence than I felt.

"She knows you don't like her." She ignored the question.

"How does she know that? I'm never there. She has been your nanny for over ten years. If I didn't like her, she would've been gone. I told her I would write her a glowing recommendation." I didn't tell Charlie that Griffin and I had decided to give her two months' severance. Sally and the girls thought that was beyond generous, but I needed it to be generous.

"You're writing her a glowing recommendation?"

"That's what I said." I was not going to cede my advantage to my thirteen-year-old junior terrorist.

"Tay was more of a mother to me than you will ever be," she said and hung up on me.

I didn't know it, but my year from hell was just getting started.

ঌ

"What are you doing?" Charlie asked with an accusing tone of voice.

"I just took out a batch of Heath Bar cookies."

"*You* made cookies?"

"Your Uncle Henry made the dough. I baked them." I smiled. I still couldn't cook my way out of a paper bag and Charlie knew it. "It's about time for a tea party. I thought you and your friends may want to have a snack."

"I'm too old for tea parties, Bae. Besides, this is not like when I was five years old, and we were having tea parties in your Mommy Fort."

About that time the back door opened. It was Lucy, followed closely by Thompson, with Bishop bringing up the rear.

"Cookies!" Lucy exclaimed as I was plating the cookies and putting them on the table.

I could see Charlie was giving in to the group.

"Would you like a glass of milk or water? Or if Lucy can keep a secret, I'll give you a little Coke . . ." I offered. Her father, being a dentist, did not like her having sugary drinks. Lucy, along with her mother, Sally, frequently came over and raided my refrigerator if they needed a Coca-Cola fix. I knew I had Sally's permission.

"Wow, Mrs. Hardwick—these are delicious!" It was Bishop. No one ever referred to me that way.

"You can call me Bailey. I'll wrap up some cookies for you to take home."

"Yeah Bishop, my mother never goes by her married name like most mothers." Charlie added her little dig.

The little tornado that was this pack of children disappeared as fast as they had appeared. What I held on to from that encounter was that Charlie, like me, had remembered all those afternoons in my closet with the door closed and the flashlight on, having our tea parties and having magical adventures together.

Well into the second week after firing Tabatha, when I started thinking I had gotten this motherhood business figured out, Charlie came into the kitchen as I was taking some brownies out of the oven.

"I googled you," Charlie announced.

"You must've been pretty bored," I said, putting the brownies on a cooling rack with my back to her.

"No, Bae, I googled you," she repeated. I still had my back to her, cutting the brownies.

"Bored?"

"I *googled* you," she said again. I thought about what she was saying. I finally realized what she was *really* saying.

For a parent, three of the scariest words in the English language if you had any sort of past are "I googled you." I stepped away from the stove and looked at my daughter. I realized she was talking about New York. All of it.

"Sit down, Charlie," I instructed. I realized she was talking about Elliott. I realized she was talking about a marriage that didn't involve her father. I realized she had seen all the sordid stories about me on Page Six. I saw the look of anger flash across her face.

"I guess you are referring to my brief marriage to Elliott," I said. It was clear to me Charlie was in charge of this conversation.

"How the hell could you do this to me? How the hell could you do this to Dad? What were you thinking?" The last question was the only question I had thought about a million times myself.

"Language, young lady." I sat down opposite my daughter and took a sip of my coffee. I hadn't planned to have this discussion this afternoon. I hadn't planned to have it alone. Without her father. Maybe that's the way it happens. Having serious conversations with your daughter in the Chick-fil-A drive-through, on the way to practice, or just driving home from the store. I hadn't rehearsed any of this.

"I can't believe you had sex with Dad for the first time and then married someone else." My daughter's revelations had given me vertigo.

"How did you know that my first time having sex was with Dad?" I had gotten distracted.

"Dad told me. He told me how you fell in love. You made the decision together. He told me he never loved anyone but you."

I tried not to look shocked. I wanted to strangle Griffin. Who gave him permission to discuss the most intimate piece of our lives with our daughter?

"I'll get to your dad."

"I can't believe you were married to the guy with the TV show," Charlie said. In the intervening years, Elliott had become one of those chefs with a TV show. He was charismatic that way.

"He didn't have a TV show when I met him. We were both starting out. I designed his very first restaurant."

"Oh my God, Bae, are you famous?"

"I'm not famous. Not now. Not then. Neither was Elliott. He was just starting out in New York trying to establish his first restaurant."

"What about Dad?"

I took a deep breath. I decided to slow the conversation down. I decided to talk about her father and me. I decided to talk about Griffin, my way. I lifted the lid wide open and let the memories wash over me. My shoulders relaxed. My whol body relaxed. I realized how tense I had been, reliving my life with Elliott. But discussing Griffin Hardwick broke my heart wide open. I wanted her to know that this love I had for her dad had made her.

"Oh Charlie, I loved your dad before anyone else. Your daddy was the first person to teach me how to drive. Your daddy was the first person to recognize I had design talent. Your daddy was my first crush. He was my first kiss." I stopped for a moment. "Your dad is the one who came up with my nickname, Bae . . ." I paused. I wanted to relive those memories. They brought me such happiness, and I was just getting started on all the "firsts."

"Wow, you loved Dad from the beginning," she said.

"Yes. I did love him, always."

"What happened?"

"I was living in New York. Your dad was here. Somehow things went haywire. Dad rejected me. It broke my heart. I shouldn't have, but I rushed into an impetuous marriage with Elliott."

"You eloped?"

"Yes. Without telling your Uncle Henry or Dad. Or even the girls," I added.

"I bet that didn't go over well," she said.

It was like we were discussing a book and she was engrossed in how it ended, although she already knew. It was strange to have my daughter so fascinated by such a tragic time in my life.

"No, it didn't go over well. I've never seen your uncle so mad at me."

"Yikes. What did Dad do?"

I wasn't going to do to Griffin what he had just done to me. This was too private. Too painful. "He didn't speak to me."

"I can just see Reggie, and Elle in her Louboutins kicking your—" I looked at her sharply and she said, "fanny."

"They were on board with the marriage in the beginning. Men like Elliott are charming. But it's all surface. You must be with a man long enough to see his heart, the stuff that's really important, like kindness. How they treat other people. How they manage crises. Whether they have friends."

"I like when you talk about Dad. You look younger. Even beautiful," Charlie said.

I laughed. Nothing like your teenage daughter to give you perspective. I decided we were not done with this conversation. I knew the moments of intimacy with my daughter were rare. And this is one subject where I could linger.

"It was raining the first night your dad and I were together."

"You remember that?"

"I remember everything about that night. That is one reason I love rainy nights. Do you remember the flannel shirt I wear sometimes—the blue-and-green one? Your dad was wearing it on that night. When he got dressed, he just put on a T-shirt, and I kept his shirt like a memento. Like some lovesick girl." I stopped.

Charlie started laughing.

"Sorry, Mom. I just don't see you as a lovesick girl."

"As you said, I've loved Dad from the very beginning. Ask your Uncle Henry." I realized that as the years had multiplied, so had my love for Griffin. I stopped talking and Charlie reached across and took my hand. This gesture, not an insignificant one between us, proved to be my undoing. I got teary. But I needed to finish my story.

"Did Dad know you kept his shirt?"

"Eventually. I always kept it in my bag. During the day I could reach down and touch it. I guess that really does make me a lovesick girl."

"Kinda. I just can't believe you were married to that guy on TV."

"He can't hold a candle to Dad. But Charlie—what we just talked about—your dad should not have been discussing our private life with you. That's not okay. Are we clear?"

"I think that's nice, Mom. I can't believe you kept Dad's shirt all this time." A rare smile spread across her face. "Anytime you want to talk about you and Dad, I'm here to listen. I like hearing about you as a lovesick girl. And how Dad rescued you."

"No, Charlie. I rescued myself. I wasn't running to your dad. I was running away from Elliott. It's important that you realize that. Men don't save us. We save ourselves."

We sat in silence for a time. I enjoyed dwelling on those early memories. I could tell Charlie was enthralled. It was as if we had just shared a deep, dark secret that had bonded us. Was she recalibrating her opinion of me? My voice contained the authenticity of a young girl reexperiencing her first love. Her true love. Her only love.

ஃ

That night in bed, I scolded Griffin.

"What were you thinking, telling Charlie about our sex life?"

"I just wanted her to know that your first time was with me. And that we were in love."

"That's not okay. I told Charlie our private life was ours. She was much more animated when it came to discussing my first husband." I watched Griffin's eyes open wide.

"That must've been a fun afternoon for you," he said, laughing.

"No more talk about our sex life to our daughter, okay? You better hope she doesn't google you."

"I'm not worried about Charlotte googling me. The only person I'm linked to is Henry!" We both laughed.

ஃ

Several nights later, Griffin and I were in bed. I was on my computer working on a proposal for Gabriel. Griffin was reading articles on the new trends in cocktails when we heard a rap at our door.

"Come in," I said.

"I wanted to ask you guys something. The last semester of my ninth grade, they are offering a study abroad. It's in Switzerland. Whitney's parents are letting her go. I have always wanted to go to Europe. What do you think? Can I go?"

Just as Griffin said, "Sure that sounds like a great idea," I said, "I don't think so." Both Charlie and Griffin looked at me.

"I think y'all better consult the parent guidebook. You're supposed to be on the same page. It sends the kid mixed messages," Charlie said.

"We will talk it over and get back to you," Griffin said, and she came over and gave him a kiss and blew me an air kiss.

"What was that about? Going to school for a semester in Switzerland sounds like a wonderful opportunity. She will be in high school," Griffin said.

"Exactly my point—she will barely be in the ninth grade. Her second semester. Who knows what goes on during those studies abroad? I know they're chaperoned, but how conscientious are they? Sally isn't letting Lucy go."

"You and Sally have become that tight? Best buddies?"

"Reggie and Elle suggested I get a 'voucher mother.' A mother who has children Charlie's age who has done a good job raising them. I've gotten to know Sally. I like that Charlie hangs out with Lucy. I think she's a good influence on our daughter. Even better than Whitney. Sally said there was no way in hell that she was letting Lucy go on that trip. She said that there have been instances in the past of drinking, smoking pot, and God knows what else."

"I'm still trying to understand this 'voucher parent' concept."

"She's the real deal. We walk and she can drop the F-bomb here and there. And she likes to throw back the wine. She's cool. I'm not sure I totally trust Annabel and Whitney anymore."

The next week, when we told her that she couldn't go to Switzerland, Charlie gave me, not Griffin, the silent treatment. But not before she yelled at me. "Why don't you just go back to work and leave me alone!"

But my instincts would be correct.

NOW

I was propped up, still trying to do some research on Brazil for Gabriel, when my phone rang. It was Elle. "I just had a delightful dinner with your charming daughter," she said, as I heard the familiar gyrations of her getting out of her shoes and pouring a glass of wine.

"Cheers. What did you think of the contract? Does it look legit?" I asked.

"Yes. It looks good. They want Charlie to explore your relationship." She laughed. I didn't. I shut my computer off so I could concentrate. I also took a gulp of wine for the rest of our conversation.

"That's just great. I really had hoped Charlie would be over all this by now. Clearly, no one can hold a grudge like my daughter. You are so lucky with Kendall. All you had to deal with was rainbow-colored hair."

"You must not remember that it took forever to get the maroon out."

Mothers all think their stories with their daughters are the worst.

"Don't even get me started. Did she tell you everything?"

"Yes. Not only did she send over the contract, but she sent the opening chapter. She is a good writer. She has your sense of humor. I don't know if she's going to reveal her stumble."

"Did she talk about her intervention and the 'uninvited guest'?"

"Bailey. Stop it. We don't have enough time or wine to hear that one for the sixty-fifth time. But can I ask you something?"

"You just took my daughter to dinner and didn't charge her anything, so yeah, you can ask me anything—as if you needed my permission?" This time I laughed, and Elle didn't.

"Do you think Charlotte could have killed Elliott the night she was drinking?"

Just then, Griffin walked in the door and broke my attention. But as I went to bed, Elle's question lingered like a smoke ring.

THEN
EIGHT YEARS AGO

I had just gotten in from Chicago. Mac had decided to sell Zebra. He was going to make a huge profit.

I was picking up Charlie from Annabel's house. Charlie and Whitney had not spent a great amount of time together lately because Whitney was so popular and moved by the whims of the popular crowd. Charlie often felt left out and would hang with Lucy. Lucy wasn't popular, although she was very pretty and nice. I would never understand girls at this age. I thought Lucy would be crawling with friends and boyfriends. The only one who was interested in Lucy was Thompson, which was a good thing because Lucy was interested in him. I often thought Bishop and Charlie just got thrown in the mix. I observed the way Bishop stared at Charlie when she wasn't looking. I would've given anything to have the kind of relationship where I could've just sat on the edge of Charlie's bed and asked her "So, what do you think about Bishop?" But Charlie herself had told me more than once that we just didn't have that kind of relationship. It would shut me up and make me sad.

One time I did get brave, and I asked her what could we do to have that kind of relationship. She rolled her eyes and told me it was too late. I walked away, not pressing things. How could it have been too late when she was barely a teenager? I reflected on my own teen years. What I would have given to have had a mother come in and sit on my bed and ask, "How was your day?" Yet isn't that the whole pursuit of life itself each day? To have another chance to get things right. To do better than we did the day before. Maybe the trick was to not give up until one day Charlie would relax on her bed and begin to tell me about her day.

On the way home from Annabel's house, Charlie told me about

Whitney's new boyfriend, Cooper, and how they had been to the movies together.

"You're fourteen!" I said.

In the back seat, I caught her eye roll. If I had a conversation for every eye roll that she had given me throughout the years we would have been the most communicative mother-daughter duo in history.

"Today is about the happiest day in my life!" Charlie declared when we got home. I kicked off my shoes and was hoping that this might just be that day when she would confide in me.

"That's wonderful, Charlie. What happened today?"

"I might not be an only child after all!" she said, before continuing. "You know how I blamed you for not giving me a brother or sister?" She paused. I had never told her that her father had a vasectomy. I had never told her that I had suffered many miscarriages. I had never told her I almost died. I never told her because I never wanted her to worry.

"Well, today Whitney told me that we could be sisters," Charlie began. I was envisioning the girls pricking their fingers and sharing blood to become blood sisters or something equally dramatic. I was still looking at her with keen interest.

"How's that?" I asked.

"She said that Dad could be her dad."

I sat on the edge of the bed. I was beginning to have a sense of foreboding.

"I'm not sure I follow," I said.

"We may not have the same mother, but we have the same dad," she said.

I realized it was not that day. Not by a long shot. This was the day that my daughter was lashing out at me. Being cruel. I tried not to show anything but calm.

"Why are you and Whitney launching such tales?"

"We're not. Annabel told Whitney that Dad might be her father. That they got together before you guys married."

I kept my face steady. I knew this was virtually untrue. But there were so many other layers to this that made me want to cry.

"Who in their right mind would have a discussion with their daughter about this kind of thing?" I asked.

"The same kind of parent that tells his daughter about the first time he and her mother had sex together." Charlie was gleeful.

"This is entirely different," I said, although I still wanted to strangle Griffin for telling our daughter that story. "Charlie, your dad and I were already together. Your dad would never cheat on me. And for the record, I would never cheat on him."

"Whitney is older than I am. It could definitely have been before you guys got married and that is not considered cheating."

"Charlie, if you know nothing else about your dad and me, you should know we have eyes only for each other."

"Yes, I know you love each other. Everybody knows you love each other. But this happened before y'all got married."

"You're forgetting one tiny little detail. Annabel was married at the time." I thought this should be checkmate. Annabel and Whitney's dad had gotten a divorce very soon after Whitney was born. I didn't believe any of this, but something was unsettling in my stomach, like I had eaten something that didn't agree with me.

"Oh, I don't know. It would have been nice to have a sister," she said. Giving up. Two mean girls under one roof. I didn't think I would be able to stand that. One was quite enough. I toyed with the idea of telling her she would've had a brother. But she was already walking out of the room. Disinterested in any more communications with me. I let her go. I needed to let my insides settle. To tell Griffin. I knew he would have something to say. I heard her close her bedroom door and I went into the bathroom and took a shower. I cried. The water had always mixed well with my tears. And no one could hear me. Confusion cascaded down on me like water pellets. I knew so much to be true, yet uncertainties swirled around me.

I heard Griffin coming into the bedroom as I wrapped myself in a towel. He knocked and came into the bathroom. He leaned in and embraced me.

"How was your day?"

"Not so good," I said. I told him about Charlie's big revelation. His eyes grew big. He looked at me in the mirror. He took a deep breath. Then he closed the bathroom door. Firmly.

NOW

My phone rang. I hadn't finished my first cup of coffee. It was Charlie. "Sprite. You're up early," I said, with artificial gaiety.

"Mom, do you think there is a possibility that I could have killed Elliott?" There it was. It wasn't an admission. It was a question. I was juggling how to answer. She continued talking. "I am a blackout drunk. Are you protecting me?" She sounded so frightened. I wanted to go to her. We stayed connected, adrift in our silence.

"Charlie, do you remember anything about the night that Elliott died?" I had seen the footage so many times and observed so many hoodies and still I wasn't sure if one of those was my daughter.

"I vaguely remember drinking and calling Bishop. I'm scared."

"Do you need to go to a meeting?" I asked.

"Yes." She severed our connection, but maybe our bond was growing stronger.

Several weeks later I was at my desk when my phone buzzed.

"Hi, Bae."

"Hi honey. What's up?" It was very rare for Charlie to call me in the middle of the day.

"Is now a good time?"

"Sure," I said. I could tell from the tone of her voice she had something troubling on her mind.

"Mom. I've been thinking. Do you think I should tell my editor about my relapse?"

"That has to be your decision, Charlie. Maybe you should talk to Elle."

"She didn't tell you. I told her about the relapse."

While Elle had told me, I wanted Charlie to know she had a safe place for her secrets.

"I gave her a dollar to engage her services."

"I can tell you right now, that's the best dollar you ever spent," I said. "Why don't you confide in your agent? She should be able to guide you. I don't know much about the publishing world, but nothing creates a scandal more than some memoir that isn't true."

"Does Dad know yet?" There was a pause in the conversation.

"Not yet. He knows something is wrong. Remember, this is not our first rodeo, as you like to say." Another break in our discussion.

"Thanks, Bae."

"Charlie?"

"Yeah, Bae?"

"Do you still wear those hoodies all the time?"

"Like the one you brought to me at rehab?" she asked. "Why don't you just ask me the question? You're being passive-aggressive again." She always accused me of this when we were arguing, which was often.

"I wasn't trying to be passive-aggressive. It's just not exactly in the mother-daughter handbook." She actually laughed. It did my heart good.

"What have you and I ever done that's textbook, Bae? I remember Bishop. He flew in to sober me up and support me the night of the murder. I wasn't exactly honest about one thing. It took me a few tries to get sober. I have a few white chips from AA. Shit, it's hard." There was a long pause and I thought we were done.

"We're back together," she continued. "He wants me to choose sobriety before I choose him. Bae, he's forgiven me."

"I'm glad, Charlie." I heard the deep well of emotion in her voice. "Let me know how you come out when you talk to your agent. I think you're making the best decision."

My daughter and I were starting to get closer when I was on the verge of getting convicted for murder. And she hadn't answered my question.

THEN
EIGHT YEARS AGO

"How did Whitney hear that?" Griffin asked. He had neither confirmed nor denied anything. I closed the toilet seat and sat down on it. He sat down on the floor beside me. I noticed the grout needed to be cleaned.

"Apparently, Annabel and Whitney have the same sort of relationship that you and Charlie do—discussing each other's sex lives."

"We're back to that again. You can certainly hold a grudge."

"Like my daughter." I was trying not to feel defensive.

"I need to tell you something," he said.

I hated those words. The only unimpeachable thing in my life had been Griffin. He was steady. His love was rock solid.

"It's not what you think," he continued. "Remember when you were married? And I was a mess?" I waited.

"One night, Annabel was in the bar when I closed. I was pretty wasted. I let her take me home. It only happened once. Your brother hit the roof. He said it was one thing to sleep with patrons, which we had never allowed. But to sleep with a married one? Your brother threatened to call you. Threatened to put me in rehab if I didn't pull my act together. Looking back on it, your brother was not persnickety when it came to his women. He probably slept with who knows how many, but none were patrons. He did draw the line. After that night I got sober. That's when I wrote you that letter."

I exhaled. I didn't realize how tense I had been. How terrified I had been. I was married to someone else, and Griffin was a disaster.

Tears welled up in Griffin's eyes. And mine. He wiped them on the edge of the towel. I leaned over and kissed him on the side of his face.

"How do I make this better, Bae?"

"How many other women do I know who . . ." He stopped me. It was painful for both of us.

"None. I thought about telling you. Henry and I decided it wasn't a good thing because Annabel was your friend. And she didn't want me telling you because of her husband. Technically you were married and . . ."

"I get it."

"Are we okay?"

"I'm relieved. I'm sorry that my impetuous marriage has had so many ramifications."

"I would never even look at another woman. You are my life. You know that, don't you?" I smiled for the first time since he had gotten home.

"I told Charlie that."

He reached over and hugged me tight. "About her—I need to go deal with the 'junior terrorist.'"

"She's going to know I told you." I wiped myself off and threw on one of Griffin's T-shirts.

"I don't care." And I could tell by his tone that he was angry. I followed him to our door and stayed put. I wanted to listen to Griffin's big parenting moment.

He knocked on Charlie's door, and when she told him to come in, he stood in the doorway.

"I just wanted to tell you good night, sweetie," he started. I could hear her moving and she went over to embrace Griffin. "And you're grounded for three weeks."

"Is this because of what I asked Mom earlier?" she asked.

"You know damn well. I can't ascertain your motives, but my guess is you were trying to hurt Mom—"

"But—" she interrupted.

"Don't interrupt me, Charlotte. If there is one thing you should be very sure of it is the fact that I love your mother. She is my life."

"Everybody knows that, Dad."

"And I am her life. She probably has loved me longer than I have loved her. And yet you decided to hurt her like this. I can't tell you how disappointed I am in you. The most important thing in my life is my family. Trust is a very fragile thing. It has to be earned. With your little maneuver, you could've done such destructive things between Bae and me. I wanted to raise you to be kind. Compassionate. You were just cruel to your mom. She and I were a family, and with our love we invited you in. I want you to be proud of this family. I want you to love it like I love it. You can't treat it casually. You don't know what I'm capable of when I am pushed. I won't even feel guilty."

"Okay . . . I'll go say I'm sorry."

"No, you won't. I want you to really think about your actions tonight. And when you are sufficiently sorry, then you can apologize to your mom. Understood?"

I backed away from the door and jumped into bed and got my laptop out as if I hadn't just been eavesdropping. I heard Charlie crying. Griffin came into our bedroom and closed the door. He turned on the noise machine to drown her out.

"I almost feel sorry for her," I said.

"Don't. She had that coming. No one better hurt you or Charlie. I won't be a nice person." It sent a chill down my back.

I tried to lighten the mood. I leaned over and started kissing him. Seriously kissing him. He pulled away.

"You're weird. Are you getting turned on because I slept with a married woman?" He leaned in but I pulled away.

"No. Let's be perfectly clear here. What is a turn-on is your little soliloquy about family."

"In that case, I will be prepared to give you a soliloquy on family every night. And just for the record, you are the only married woman that I want to kiss." He laughed and we finished what we had started a minute earlier. I couldn't believe that this night had ended with kisses instead of anger. I felt lucky. I felt grateful, and I said a prayer that we had come through yet another storm together.

❧

About ten days later, I was sitting at the kitchen table doing invoices. This was perhaps my least favorite aspect of my job. But because one of my favorite parts of the job was getting paid, it was a necessary evil.

I heard Charlie before I saw her. Over the course of the previous week, we had maintained a cordial relationship. It wasn't great but it wasn't the worst it had been either.

"Hi."

I glanced up from my laptop and saw she had taken her seat directly across from mine. I closed my computer to give her my full attention.

"Hi, yourself," I said back to her.

Charlie rubbed the side of her face just like her uncle. It always surprised me when a trait or personal mannerism from her father, Henry, or me revealed itself. Suddenly, the words just tumbled out, as if Charlie herself was putting the words together in a spontaneous fashion.

"Mom, I'm sorry. I don't know why I said that about Whitney. I knew it wasn't true. Everybody—I mean everybody—knows how you and Dad feel about each other. I kind of count on that. Maybe Dad was right, and I wanted to get back at you. I don't know. Maybe I wanted to be popular in Whitney's eyes," she said.

When someone asks for forgiveness, and it is sincere, then we need to have the grace to accept it.

"Thank you, Charlotte," I said, using her proper name. "You are a teenage girl. With hormones. Half the time you won't have a clue about some of the things that come out of your mouth." She looked relieved.

"I can't picture you ever not knowing what to say, you're so confident," she said. It made me sad that my daughter didn't know me well at all.

"In my case, I just didn't say anything. That has always been a problem between your dad and me. That is probably why I rushed into that marriage. Because your dad and I did not talk. In a weird way, our relationship is a lot like yours and mine. But just so you know and have no doubts, I love you. Very much."

"Yeah, I know that Bae." She relaxed a little bit. But she didn't make any motion to leave.

"You want to have a tea party? I have some snickerdoodle cookies."

"Only if Uncle Henry made them and we don't have to go upstairs to your Mommy Fort. I'm too old. Besides, the way things have been going, one of us may not come out alive." She laughed. I wished I could have returned the laughter, but it was just too close to the bone. I decided to offer her something else instead. I got up to get the plate of cookies. I had my back to her when I said it.

"I wanted to give you a sibling. The last time I had a miscarriage it was a boy. You would've had a brother. I got really sick and ended up in the hospital." I put a couple of cookies in the microwave. It made the cookies taste so much better and it allowed this information to settle between us. I put the plate closest to her. "Do you want some, Sprite?"

"Cookies so close to dinner and Sprite? You are going soft." But she didn't refuse, and I was already getting a glass out of the cupboard, trying to make the moment last. I poured us each some Sprite and put a maraschino cherry to make it festive.

"Cheers, Bae."

"Cheers to Uncle Henry and his famous snickerdoodle cookies." Our glasses touched. I could see that something was on Charlie's mind.

"Was it around my fifth birthday?" It surprised me. I assumed she would have had no recollection of that, but then she elaborated.

"I vaguely remember you coming in late for my birthday party and how everyone looked at you. I thought you were hogging the attention away from me on my birthday. It made me mad."

"That was exactly when it was. That's why I wasn't here on your birthday—I was in the hospital. The doctors didn't want me to leave the hospital. But I had to make it for your party. And then you threw my present away." That last part slipped out and I hoped our honesty would be enough.

"I was so mad. How you just sashayed in and stole all the attention. How did you know I threw your pens away?"

"Because I saw them in your trash can when you were brushing your teeth. Along with my bruised feelings. I fished them out and put them on the side so it would look like you just missed."

"I would've fished them out. I always wondered how they got on the floor." She took her dishes to the sink and turned around to go upstairs. She stopped in the doorway.

"I'm sorry about the baby. I'm sorry I hurt your feelings. Thanks for telling me, Mom." And then she disappeared.

I sat there for a long time thinking about this encounter. I had always admonished Griffin for being too honest with Charlie. But maybe sometimes they need to know we are real people with real feelings.

And then it came to me. Mothers aren't humans. We are trash cans. We are the receptacles for our children's emotions. We get their anger, their disappointments, their anxieties, their frustrations, their fears, their insecurities, their sadness, and their shame, all rolled into one ball of discarded aluminum that hits the bottom and makes a thud. On rare occasions, if we're lucky, we get an apology or a thank-you.

❧

It was August. The end of summer and the beginning of a new school year. For me, I was hoping it was going to be the end of the "year of hell." After

Charlie googled me and discovered that I had been married before. After we didn't let Charlie go to Switzerland with the "popular girls."

After the big revelation about Annabel and Griffin, I noticed that Charlie had put distance between herself and Whitney. She started hanging out more with Lucy. She even went to Sunday school with Lucy sometimes. Lucy would often remark, "Mom and Dad *make* me go. What's your excuse?" Sally told me they enjoyed sitting together in the pew, and we had even started to talk about going together as a family to the Christmas Eve service. But it was late August, and I knew a lot could happen before then.

ॐ

One night when Griffin and I were in bed, each of us on our respective laptops, we heard a knock at the door.

"I just wanted to say good night," Charlie said. She usually sat on Griffin's side of the bed. When she deliberately sat next to me, I felt suspicious.

"I know it's still early, but I know something I want for Christmas. But it's a big thing."

"You're too young to get a car. And too old to get a pony," Griffin said, and we all laughed.

"Actually, this is for Mom." I was right to feel dread. "You know I'm almost fifteen. I would like a grown-up bedroom."

"What do you want me to do? Is this some kind of trick?" I wished that last question stayed in my brain instead of coming out of my mouth.

"Why do you always assume the worst? I want you to decorate my bedroom!"

The dread was realized. I would rather design restaurants for Cliff Rushton for the rest of my life than design one bedroom for my daughter. The very idea petrified me.

"I don't do that kind of thing," I protested.

"You decorated this house. And I know you decorated Dad's condo."

Griffin chimed in. "It's true, Bae. You did a killer job with my condo. And I love our house."

"You're no help. Besides, I don't even know your style, Charlie, or your color scheme." I looked back and forth between my husband and my daughter. I thought a teenage girl would make a terrible client.

"Green . . ." she began, knowing that green was my favorite color. She looked at me and smiled. It was a fake smile and I realized she was plotting yet again. "And . . . purple."

"Charlotte, your mom is not a miracle worker," Griffin stepped in. She smiled. I was seemingly hesitant. I could fake it too.

"Can I get back to you in the next few days?"

"They say you're the best. You can prove it." She kissed me on the cheek, like Judas, went to the other side of the bed and kissed Griffin, and then left us.

After she left, I turned to Griffin. "What you don't know, and what Charlie doesn't know, is she has chosen a very elevated color palette. Very sophisticated. I know exactly what I am going to do." Instead of sugarplums dancing in my head, I dreamed of swatches.

❧

I had just returned from a job at a small college in Maine. I had been to the state a couple of times in the past and in my estimation, it was one of those undiscovered gems.

No one was home, so I went to my office out back. I was very anxious to get swatches and begin putting color schemes together for my daughter's approval when my phone rang. It was Mac. "I am ready to open Zebra in Atlanta," he said.

"Where?"

"Buckhead," was all Mac said. It was all he needed to say. I also knew it may not go over well with Henry and Griffin.

"Can I get back to you?" I hung up the phone and dialed my brother at NOIR and my husband at VERT.

"I need to see you both in person," I told them.

We decided to, because of Henry's perfectionist prep work, meet at his place.

"Hell, no!" Henry's answer was short but not so sweet.

Griffin, on the other hand, didn't say anything. Why should he? Henry did all the talking. "You knew I loved that color scheme when you showed it to me. You should have given it to us first."

"I don't know what it looks like," Griffin said.

"Don't you ever take a look at your wife's portfolio?" Henry asked with mild irritation.

"The last thing on my mind when my wife is home is her portfolio."

"It's beautiful."

"You two don't own me," I said. "And the last time I checked with either of you, another restaurant was out of the question. And if you did open another restaurant it would be a diner. The color scheme is not exactly conducive for a diner. You can't keep Mac from opening a restaurant. I wanted him to retain the name in case he wanted to open up Zebra in some other location. I didn't dream it would be Atlanta." I pulled out my phone.

"Let me make a quick call. I'll be right back." As I walked away, I heard Griffin and Henry talking. Henry was very animated. For the first time, so was Griffin. I called Mac.

"Listen, I have a situation. You and I are friends. Our kids are friends. Would you consider opening your restaurant in Dunwoody? You would have the prettiest restaurant there," I proposed to him. I was trying to keep the peace with all the people I loved, including my daughter. She'd already had a falling-out with Whitney. I didn't want her to lose Thompson too. I liked him a lot.

"Here's what I will do," Mac said. "Give me a couple of days to look around. That may even buy you some time with Henry and Griffin."

"Thanks, Mac." When I arrived back at the table they were still talking. Neither one looked too happy.

"This was just one reason I didn't want to work in Atlanta," I said. "Technically, Mac can open a restaurant where he pleases. And yes, I suggested to Mac to retain the color scheme and name of Zebra for this exact reason. Mac didn't even need to ask me about it. That was a courtesy to you guys. I suggested Mac open his restaurant in Dunwoody. He's going to look around, and we're going to talk in a few days. You guys don't own me."

"I don't think we need to say anymore. We are all going to say things we regret," my sensible husband said.

"Could you just let another designer execute your plan?"

"Henry, that's like saying you come up with all these phenomenal recipes but give them to another restaurant in town."

That night as we were having family dinner, Griffin finally conceded. "I do realize you're in a tough position. I looked at your website this afternoon. Wow, Bae, the color combo is beautiful, but I don't see it in any of our restaurants. You really do amazing work. I'm so proud of you."

"You looked at my website?"

"My beautiful and talented wife." Griffin always knew what to say. I squeezed his hand, letting my hand linger on a freshly acquired callous. Charlie looked over at us and rolled her eyes, and then she smiled.

"Guys. I'm right here," she said. "You didn't have to text me about a meeting, Bae."

I had worked the afternoon looking at swatches for our daughter's room. I was in my own happy bubble. Even though Charlie and I were under the same roof, I texted her and suggested we set up a time for her to meet in my office to discuss design elements. Like with any client, I wanted her to be blown away by my vision. Like with any other client, I had my fair share of nerves and excitement.

Three days later Mac texted me the address where he wanted me to meet him. Later that afternoon I was to have my meeting with Charlie in my office.

When I got to the address and just looked at the outside I smiled. I had no idea what the inside looked like, but I loved the location. It was nestled off the beaten path, away from Perimeter Mall. I recognized the green Jaguar parked next to me. I tapped on the window. Late August in Atlanta could be brutal. I was in a sleeveless shirtdress that I had purchased at a consignment store on Buford Highway. Mac held up a set of keys and we walked inside.

"How do you do it?" I exclaimed. I continued walking around, looking at the incredible architecture of the place.

"This was once a home. Custom-built by a doctor for his wife. They fancied themselves as architects. I love the architecture. What do you think?"

I was so busy walking around and gazing at the molding and natural light it was hard to say anything at first. We walked all the way back into the kitchen, which still had green appliances. My mind was doing flip-flops and somersaults all at the same time.

"Please tell me this place is already yours." I turned around to look at him.

"Now that I know you're sleeping with the competition, I had to snap it up." He chuckled. It must be nice to have that kind of money to just write out a check on a whim. "Alon's is close by. Why don't we grab a cup of coffee and discuss our business? I'll drop you back off at your car."

"Sure. Let me take a few pictures first." As I snapped pictures, I made a mental note to get in touch with my contractor, Phil Richards. This place was going to be beautiful. Memorable.

I enjoyed negotiating with Mac. We clicked our cappuccinos to our joint business agreement.

"Considering I have already technically paid for your design fee, I think that should be waived on this project. And I should get an accommodation because I am solving your domestic turbulence and sibling rivalry," he said good-naturedly.

"That's fair. But if you had bought in Buckhead, you would never have found this place so . . ." Mac smiled.

"True. I'll give you twenty-five percent of your design fee for Zebra." He stopped. "Did I lose you?"

"I'm just thinking."

"That always costs me money."

"Hear me out. What was the couple's name who owned this house? I just don't see this being Zebra."

"It belonged to the McDuffies."

"No." It came to me like a lightning bolt that split my brain in two. "Whitney's." I watched the smile spread across Mac's face.

"Well, look at you. What about our zebra motif?"

"How about this—let me work up something for Whitney's. That will buy me some time to convince Griffin and Henry to let you enter their domain and open Zebra. And collect my full design fee on that project."

This elicited the hearty laughter from Mac that I had come to enjoy. He merely took out his checkbook, stroked the check, and handed it to me.

"I just need half. Besides, I need you to be able to go outside your comfort zone on this. I think I am seeing more of the colors in a well-appointed house. Like your mama's."

He laughed again. I had only seen pictures of his mom's house, but I had been in his house. Cassie had decorated their house in mainly neutrals. I saw rich textures and colors.

"I see beauty. But not stuffy. Stuffy is out."

As we were driving back to my car, my mind mentally walked through each room in this house. Ideas came in and escaped like my brain had an open window or secret door.

"You're awfully quiet."

I fished around in my purse to get my keys but mainly to gather my thoughts.

"You do know this is the first time in my career that I have turned an existing house into a restaurant. That poses both unique opportunities and potential drawbacks. For instance, do you want to keep all the rooms as they are now?"

"Damn."

"And you really need to think about a budget. I think it might be kind of cool to have three beautiful but different rooms." I paused, thinking about all the possibilities and how this neglected house was awash in potential. "How do you feel about me engaging Dexter Common to look around?"

"The famous architect? You think you can get him? I heard he books six months out."

"Not for me. We went to school together. He actually invited me to prom."

"Really? I heard Dexter was gay."

"He is. That just indicates the level of my popularity in high school." I laughed. So did Mac. "You wouldn't have taken a second look at me. That's okay. I already had my eyes set on Griffin."

My brain was swirling with ideas like a sandstorm on the beach. Whirling with joy and passion for my job.

"I have an idea. You have these peaceful woods in the back. So much lush greenery. I know it's Atlanta, but what about if we built a stone fireplace so it's cozy and it provides accommodation for all four seasons of the year?" I saw a big smile cross Mac's face. It was the smile that I had recognized when we were in sync.

"May I borrow your keys? I'll get another set made for me so I can bring Dexter. I will drop these off later at your house. It's nice to be neighbors," I said as I got out of his car. I started to get into my car when I turned around. "In each room we'll introduce some subtle zebra, leopard, or cheetah print. That will be your brand. You did it in Chicago and now you're doing it in Atlanta. I know you probably don't see yourself as an animal print kind of guy, but maybe you should go with it. Visions and brands require adaptability." I was grateful to Mac for giving me back my joie de vivre.

I headed home for my second meeting with a client—my daughter. I realized I was nervous. The last couple of years I had allowed my stress over Charlie to interfere with my love of my job. I realized that, as I was pulling up into our driveway, it was Charlie, not Mac, who had given me my joy of design back. I loved the sketchbook I had prepared for her. I was grateful that she had trusted me to do it.

Charlie knocked on my office door and came in carrying a Slurpee. Ordinarily, I would've frowned. I had become one of those mothers who hated that artificial sugar and fructose combination, especially in sixty-four ounces. But today, Charlie was not my daughter—she was my client, and I wanted to treat her like I would treat any prospective client.

I'd had a second cappuccino in preparation of our meeting. I wondered, having drained the last drops of my cappuccino, if I would get any sleep that night. What if the meeting didn't go well? I had prepared three storyboard ideas. The first one could be done at the local fabric store. The second one was a hybrid of one and three. The third was high-end. Top dollar. Our master bedroom had not cost as much as this proposed bedroom would.

When Charlie came closer to my desk, I motioned for her to sit down and extended my hand.

"Really, Bae?" She put that wretched Slurpee on my desk and it was all I could do not to find a napkin to put under that red dye number forty.

"Yes. In this office you are my client. You're hiring me for a job. I want to project a professional demeanor. So let's get to it. First of all, Charlotte," I used her real name, the one I rarely called her. "I want to thank you for giving me this opportunity to work for you."

I paused and opened a bottle of Fiji water. The cappuccinos had left me dehydrated. I flipped over the first storyboard, the one with the fabric that could be purchased in the local fabric store. I could see her reconsidering her own color choice.

The second storyboard was a hybrid. Now I was beginning to see a little interest spring to life on my daughter's face. She still hadn't asked a single question. I found that a little disconcerting, but I gave her the benefit of the doubt. She had never been in one of these meetings. I took another sip of water. This was my moment. I really wanted her to be blown away by my third and best storyboard.

"This is a purple and green floral print. I think it would make a beautiful headboard. The second one has scallops. You see from this picture in the magazine the top is finished by all these layers of pleats." I looked at my client. Was it wishful thinking or did I see her eyes light up a bit? I was about to introduce the bed skirt when she interrupted.

"The detailed one. Most definitely the detailed one."

"This is definitely your focal point. I have purposely chosen this green-and-white polished cotton gingham for the dust ruffle, so it will not compete with but will enhance the headboard." It was the color of green apple and white. I pulled out examples and put them before Charlie. I had no idea really what her taste would be.

"And on the other side by your windows, I would put two club chairs. And in the middle, instead of a table, I would suggest an ottoman, done in this rich purple damask." I produced the color swatch of the purple damask. I thought of the musician Prince. He would've loved all this purple. She picked it up and rubbed it against her face. I knew she liked this fabric.

"Could we use this purple on the dust ruffle?" Charlie asked. It didn't surprise me. Often a client would be drawn to an accent color. It wouldn't have the same effect without the combination of the other fabrics.

"That's always an option, Charlie. I agree with you. This purple is so special I don't really see it on the floor. It needs to pull your eye to it. What we could do is put it on some pillows on your bed if you like it that much. I think the green-and-white gingham being on the dust ruffle anchors the room and allows your eyes to focus on the other two truly extraordinary fabrics. What are your thoughts?"

"The last one is definitely my favorite."

"Me too."

"I think it's very sophisticated. No one else will have a bedroom like mine." Now this was my daughter. She liked being unique.

"Would you like to engage me to redesign your bedroom?"

"Do I have to pay you or something?"

I laughed. Charlie was astute enough to start understanding business.

"Ordinarily, a client would write a check for half of my design fee. Because this is your Christmas present, it's on me. I want you to be happy with the design." I looked at her for final approval.

"I love it," she gushed.

"Really? That makes me so happy, Charlie." I meant every single word. "One last thing. When we begin the installation, you'll have to move to the guest room, and then when we are finished, we can have the big reveal."

"Like on one of those TV shows?"

I had to laugh again. She got up to go but lingered in the doorway. She turned around. "You're good at your job, Mom." She flashed a smile. A smile that had been dormant since she was five years old. I had missed it. I had looked for it. I had even prayed for it, and here it was. Like sunshine.

It was the first time since she landed in my arms as a baby that my job had brought us together rather than being a source of tension and strife.

&

I called the various showrooms to proceed with my orders. I was so glad I had my own credit card. If Griffin had seen this bill he would have flipped.

Before I went into the house, I called Dexter and told him about Mac's project and the address.

"The old McDuffie house in Dunwoody? I'm familiar with it. I just hated when that beautiful house was zoned commercially. I was so afraid someone would tear it down or open up a nail salon in it."

I laughed out loud. We agreed on a time to meet the following week and I hung up the phone. I looked at the date, August 22. I sat at my desk for a few minutes longer just basking in the events of the day.

Is that how it happens? I hadn't been aware that I wasn't happy. Maybe joy and happiness just erode little by little over time until you live a certain way and forget that you used to live this other way, with joy, passion, and laughter. Today I laughed a lot. I laughed with Mac. I laughed with Charlotte. I think she and I set a record for laughter. We had not laughed much together in the last decade. I drew a circle deliberately around this day on my calendar. Like some people would an anniversary, first dates, birthdays, or maybe the day they first fell in love. I was old enough now to realize this was a special day. In both my professional life and my personal life, I had rediscovered my raisons d'être. It was a happy elixir that collided together on a beautiful afternoon.

NOW

I had just gotten finished a tense conversation with Gabriel. I pulled all the samples to show him. He was going to fly here, even though he didn't want to. I was going to meet him in his suite to go over the proposal. Ideally, I would've flown to Brazil to get a firsthand look at the space. Nothing took the place of being able to walk around and take pictures. I enjoyed letting my eyes linger on spots the camera might have missed. I wanted my passport returned to be able to travel freely. I didn't want to spend large chunks of time with Floyd. I wanted my life back. I was closing Gabriel's folder when my phone rang.

"Hi, Bae," Charlie said.

"Is anything wrong?" I asked.

"I talked to my agent. She didn't seem bothered by the idea of me relapsing for a few days. She mentioned some father-son memoirs that dealt with the son's addiction. She said I could write an epilogue. It just means coming clean. I guess it could give people hope."

"*Hope*. That's a powerful four-letter word, Charlie. The memoirs you are referring to are by Nic and David Sheff, called *Tweak* and *Beautiful Boy*."

"How do you know so much about this stuff?" Charlie asked me.

I read all these things while she was gone. I wanted to know what my daughter was going through. How she felt. And then to stumble upon a father's perspective was very refreshing. I wanted to feel close to my daughter. I wanted to understand her. I wanted to be able to help her when she returned home. I felt guilty about my role in her addiction. I think Charlie was just so relieved that her book contract didn't fall through because of this revelation. Maybe she was even surprised I had read so many books. I kept a few. They were still under the bed in the guest room.

"I guess you and Dad weren't having any candlelight dinners while I was away," she joked half-heartedly. We said our goodbyes and hung up the phone. I realized Charlie was more like me than her father. How we deflected situations with humor. How we both preferred to keep our private feelings bottled up.

THEN
SEVEN YEARS AGO

I was nervous. I had put together a detailed proposal for Mac. I included drawings from Dexter and a proposal from Phil Richards of the Richards Group. Mac and I sat at a card table with two chairs that I had brought in so I could study the place and the lighting as it grew dark. Griffin had complained because he felt like I was in the woods all by myself. He talked about raccoons and critters to the point it made me laugh and once again call him a "Buckhead snob," which he was.

"Before we begin, I want to thank you, Mac, for giving me this opportunity to design the restaurant for you and for being patient so we could find a space."

"You're welcome." He tried to get comfortable in the padded chairs. We looked ridiculous. Mac was in his uniform—one of the thousands of blue blazers he owned. He had on a collared golf shirt and a pair of pressed slacks with colors you might find at Martha's Vineyard. It was September in Atlanta, so it was still very warm. I had on a Bohemian dress that I enjoyed in the summer because it didn't fit tightly.

"First, let me show you Dexter's architectural rendering so you can follow the color and concept."

He reached over and carefully perused the pages that Dexter had designed.

"What I wouldn't give for a gin and tonic about now," he said. I hoped he kept his sense of humor when I showed him the bill on the renovation.

"There are a lot of moving parts to this design, as you can see. You have this wonderful outdoor space, complete with a stone fireplace. The three color palettes I have selected for each room flow into the other very nicely. In the main dining room, I would suggest painting the walls a gunmetal gray." I gave him the storyboard for the room.

"I think this color is cozy and inviting, and the stone for the fireplace will have undercurrents of gray," I continued. "I would like to do the booths in a warm vermilion. On the chairs at tables I found this interesting pattern that combined the vermilion color, a warm beige, and the hint of the gray of the walls."

Mac just nodded.

"I would suggest a deep teal for barware and light fixtures. Because the fabric is a print, you really see colors of gray and beige and teal."

Mac interrupted.

"This nondescript fabric, is it as expensive as the zebra fabric?"

"No. I first found a specific pattern and it was exorbitantly expensive. I carried that swatch around until I found this one. I don't think you sacrifice beauty," I explained, and continued with my storyboard.

"I will address the private dining room next. This room can hold a maximum of about sixty people, which would be a nice size for a party. I would suggest a whisper shade of lavender for the walls." I pulled the paint swatch out. "The pink flows nicely off the gray, since they have the same undertones." I paused. I wanted to gauge Mac's reaction. He liked the lavender color of the walls. I pulled out the drawing and the swatches for the private dining room.

"Remember I suggested we choose a teal for the barware in the main dining room? I would incorporate that same color idea here, except with a seafoam color velvet against the back wall. I think the seafoam against the lavender wall is a marriage made in heaven."

Mac smiled and I continued. "We can put a long banquet-size table against the seafoam cushion back. And then for the chairs, we will have a green-and-black cheetah fabric. I have a wonderful watercolor painting in mind on hold to go over the fireplace if you go with the color scheme for this room. If you like the painting, I could contact the artist in Highlands about doing some similar abstracts for the other two rooms." I paused and took out my phone to show him the picture of the painting I had in mind.

"Bailey, I love it. I think people will want to have parties here. I also love the gunmetal gray and the vermilion."

"I saved the last dining room for my boldest color suggestions. I would do a golden-yellow vinyl for the booths, finished in a bright-green cording, and then the chairs would have this great green, with pink-and-yellow accent fabric. A sunroom." I pulled out three fabrics and kept explaining.

"I know this can be overwhelming, so I tore out three pictures from my magazines to give you an idea of what your eye will be looking at. These are not the exact fabrics, but I hope you can get an idea. I want all three rooms to be pleasing to the eye no matter where you sit. I want them to all flow into each other quite naturally like they belong together. What do you think?" I stopped.

Mac chuckled.

"You talk about fabrics and colors like they're partners or lovers."

I smiled. "I guess in a way they are. I want them to be compatible. I want people to want to return. You may have questions or want to change something around. I also took the liberty of asking Phil Richards to work up a quote. If he could get started now you might just be able to have a Yuletide opening or New Year's Eve at the latest!"

"I see your game, Bailey Edgeworth. You want me to fall in love with the design and then you lower the boom on the price of the renovation from Phil."

I didn't mean to laugh but I did. That's exactly what I was doing. It was an expensive renovation. The biggest thing I had ever done. I reluctantly pulled out the last sheet of paper and gave a silent prayer.

"Are you kidding? That's like building a house!" Mac's eyes roamed up and down the two sheets of paper with Phil's letterhead. The little card table had gotten crowded with pictures and designs. And thoughts.

"I know you have to think about it. It's a lot. This is probably the biggest job I've undertaken. Three designs under one roof, plus a patio." I pulled out the last document.

"I engaged Mary Margaret Dalton from Harry Norman to do a market comp valuation. Factoring in the renovation, the cost of your project falls smack dab in the middle." I set the document down and took a sip of water. I needed that gin and tonic. The papers were all scattered in a desultory fashion except for the three magazine pictures. I watched Mac review drawings, review renovation prices, and then return to Dexter's design. After reviewing every document, Mac's eyes would return to the three magazine pictures I had torn out for him. I realized a picture does paint a thousand words. Each time I looked at them my heart smiled. A strange combination of satisfaction and calm settled into my bones.

If I were being honest, it was a little disconcerting for me seeing all those scattered pages on our tiny card table. I knew that Julian had done this once in his career. The project where he lost money. It was before my time. I didn't see how he executed his plan, but maybe I had just come on too strong.

"I appreciate the time you put into this, Bailey. Thank you for doing the real estate comps. Mary Margaret is a pro."

I wanted to go with someone who Mac recognized as an authority. This was not the time to toot my own horn or even make a joke.

"Think about it. If we do move forward, I want you to be all in, as they say."

"Thank you for that, Bailey. Julian told me you were too nice. That's okay. I don't think Julian could have done this. Each room is beautiful, but together it is a feast for the eye," he added.

I didn't know if Mac would approve the budget or project. I had to be content knowing I had created something he loved.

"You could really be an interior designer for more than restaurants."

"Don't tell anybody, but I am doing some interior design for a certain teenage girl's bedroom. She may make the worst client ever." I laughed, thinking about Charlie as my boss.

"Oh, God. Amelia is going to want me to hire you to turn her bedroom into a palace. These girls." Mac had no idea. Amelia was just eleven. She was not a demanding teenager yet.

By the time I got home, both Charlie and Griffin had gathered in the kitchen for dinner. The rule was no cell phones. It was our chance to come together as a family and give each other our undivided attention. When I came through the door, I heard Griffin start mixing a cocktail for me. Talk about role reversal. He would greet me with a kiss and then we would all launch into our various stories of the day.

Griffin and I had come to love these moments. Griffin never had parents who were present, so it was very important to him to be present for our child. For me, Daddy would bring me to the restaurant and either put me in a back booth to eat by myself or, if Henry and Griffin were home, we would eat in the dining room. That became one of my favorite moments of childhood. Being at the table with them.

Charlie was telling us that Lucy's crush on Thompson, Mac's son, was about to be reciprocated. I was just waiting for her to tell us how she felt about Bishop when my cell phone buzzed. I pretended it wasn't making noise and Charlie shot me a big eye roll. I thought eye rolls and Charlie were synonymous with each other. At least so it seemed to me since we couldn't get through a single conversation without one. I let the phone ring. Ten minutes later it buzzed again.

"It's okay, Bae, we are practically done," Charlie said. I looked at Griffin and he nodded.

"I'll be quick," I said, jumping up from the table to silence my impatient caller.

After I hung up, I walked back to the kitchen table.

"Well, it looks like I am going to be working for the rest of the year right here in Atlanta. I have two jobs lined up."

Griffin looked at me in a quizzical fashion.

"Mac just hired me to do his job and then I am doing the bedroom for a certain daughter of ours."

Charlie met my gaze. Her expression changed. I couldn't tell if she was happy or horrified.

ॐ

I entered a period of domesticity. I hadn't spent this much time at home since Charlie was a baby.

After VERT, and the sordid mess with Elliott was resolved, it was a time of unimaginable success. I flew all over the place and spent a great deal of time in my corporate apartment in New York. It was a good central location for visiting colleges in the Northeast, and LaGuardia had easy flights to Chicago and the West Coast.

Griffin didn't complain much. Especially after we hired Tabatha and had come to an agreement over Cliff. I was always on a plane back home on Thursday or Friday afternoon. I tried to fly back on Tuesday to give me long weekends with Griffin and Charlie. I hated missing some of her milestones, like when she said "Da Da." I would've loved to have seen Griffin's face light up. I realized not only was I missing the milestones, but I had missed them through his eyes. That was my biggest regret. Griffin enjoyed being a dad. It was seeing him cradle our daughter that had such a memorable effect on me. It was during this time that I came up with the nickname "Goose." I was lucky. He didn't even complain when my achievements eclipsed his and Henry's. I knew in my bones that I was only a mediocre mom. The girls reassured me that as long as Charlie had Griffin, she would be fine.

"Besides, men do this all the time. They are gone during the week but return on the weekends. At least when I'm home, I am present for Charlie. She and Griffin are like a mutual admiration society," I would say to the girls when we would go out to dinner on nights I spent in New York.

And now here I was, fifteen years later, driving a carpool! Bailey Edgeworth, daughter's carpool service, cookie maker (as long as Henry provided the dough), fort builder, tea party enthusiast, and all the other various jobs the word *mother* entails.

Charlie, Lucy, Thompson, and Bishop were in my SUV. They were laughing, and I caught a look at Charlie in the back seat. She was the only one not laughing.

"Care to share, Charlie?" I asked. When they looked at her, she looked at Bishop.

"It's just kind of strange to see you driving a carpool, Mrs. . . . I mean, Bailey," Bishop said.

"It seems a little strange for me too, Bishop. But wait for it—I also made cookies for you guys to have for schoolwork."

"Yeah, that Uncle Henry made," my Judas daughter said. Bishop nudged Charlie's shoulder as if to chastise her. She shrugged and mouthed, "True." You have to love a boy who has great manners and sticks up for you with your daughter!

"Well, I just took them out of the oven so they still should be warm. They're snickerdoodles." It was Charlie's favorite, but the boys were salivating.

My day would always start out the same way. We would all eat breakfast in a hurried fashion, Griffin would either head to the market or do carpool with Cassie, Mac's wife, and I would generally go on a long walk with Sally. Neighbors I had never met before I met through Sally.

"We really have a good neighborhood, don't we?" I remarked one morning.

"Chad and I will never move. We'll just keep adding on. Cassie and Mac could've lived in Buckhead. I really like Cassie a lot. I think she could be a lot like her sister-in-law, but she is really down to earth and wants to raise both Thompson and Amelia to be grounded and unaffected."

"I hadn't thought of it but you're right—Mac could've lived in Buckhead near Annabel . . . but I am glad they are here. I'm partial to the Four Musketeers." We both laughed at what our children had affectionately nicknamed themselves.

"I always thought the friendship between you and Annabel was interesting," Sally said, without going into detail.

"She was the first friend I made in Atlanta. She was able to take me all over the place. But things change."

"She didn't try to hit on Griffin, did she? She has that sort of reputation."

I let the statement pass. She had inflicted very little harm to our relationship.

"I will confide this to you now. My friends thought I needed a 'voucher' mother," I told her.

"What the hell is a 'voucher' mother?"

"A person I admired and thought did a good job with her kids. Like you. You did a great job with Ward and Lucy and sometimes even Charlotte!" I told her.

"It's a good thing I didn't know you picked me. Half the time I am just winging it. Bailey, most mothers are just trying to keep their kids alive and in school. The rest is just gravy."

"Don't say that, Sally. Being a mother is a hard job."

We ended up at my house and said our goodbyes. Then I dashed inside to take a shower and jumped in the car to see what issues awaited me at Whitney's.

Phil Richards's crew had already commenced their day. I grabbed the hard hat and goggles that Phil forced me to wear. We were knocking down so many walls and erecting others that it felt like we were building a brand-new house. After I put on my hard hat, I recognized Dexter's Audi in the parking lot. I tapped on his window.

"Girl, what took you so long? I've been waiting on you to show up for about half an hour," he said.

"I wasn't aware we were meeting." I hated keeping Dexter waiting.

"No. I just assumed you would be here when the workers showed up.

I didn't expect you to be the kind who lingered in bed unless it was an opportunity you couldn't pass up." He laughed.

"Please. Griffin left the house ages ago. What do you have for me?"

"The private dining room has a real fireplace. What if we transitioned to gas logs?"

"Let's run it by Phil."

When we walked inside, Mac was already there with a woman I recognized immediately, although we had never met. I had spoken with her several times on the phone and bought at least one painting from her for this establishment. It was Bennett Ramsey, the abstract artist. I could tell Mac would be easily convinced to use her paintings throughout.

Phil thought gas logs was a great idea. Dexter and I waited for Mac to disengage from Bennett.

⁂

After Dexter and Bennett left and it was just the workmen and Mac and me, I took him aside. "This is none of my business, but what is going on between you and Bennett?"

Mac's face turned red. "She's charming. She's beautiful. She's . . ."

"And you're married."

"Wow, Bailey. How do you read people so well?"

"I can see rooms. But when it comes to you, I can see where your thoughts were going. You better stop that immediately."

"You're right. I'll behave. Good catch on the fireplace."

Phil ran us off after lunch. It gave me time to devote to my next job. I went to a store off Buckhead Highway, and I found the most beautiful tiered-prism chandelier that I wanted to put in Charlie's bathroom.

On the way home, I stopped by VERT. I was going to hide the chandelier in Griffin's office. He told me to order dinner and that he would be home later because he had to cover for one of his bartenders.

When Charlie came down for dinner later, she noticed that I had set only two places at the table. "Where's Dad?" she asked, opening the pizza box and sliding a piece out onto her plate. Charlie's favorite pizza, like her dad's, was arugula, prosciutto, and fig. I watched her eat a bite of fig. I had decided to have the halibut and white bean on a bed of quinoa. I had grown accustomed to long silences with my daughter. We could have been strangers thrown awkwardly together at a table or two people at a meditation retreat practicing the vow of silence. We had made it through the entire meal almost with exchanging only a few questions.

"I found something for your Christmas present today," I threw out to see if I could elicit her curiosity. It worked.

"What is it?" Charlie asked.

"You'll have to be surprised."

She met my gaze. "Bae, how did you know you were in love with Dad?"

That caught me by surprise. A meteor dashed through my head. Was this Charlie's way of telling me she was in love? Or did she see it as a chance for conversation? I decided to go with both and took it as an invitation to tell a story I was so comfortable with. Loving Griffin had been one of the easiest things in my life. Well, not easiest. One of those things for which I was most grateful.

"Oh, sweetie. I thought I loved your dad when I was eighteen. That was just a fraction of what I feel for him today. At eighteen I thought I knew stuff. I knew my heart beat faster when he was around. I knew he made me laugh harder. I knew he knew all my faults. He liked me anyway. But now? I love him more now than I ever thought possible. He gave me you. Our life is possible because of your dad. How many dads do you know whose wives traipse all over the United States? He always greets me with a smile."

"No shit, Sherlock."

"Charlie, we don't say those words at the table," I said, although I knew that it was one of my, Griffin's, and Henry's go-to phrases. She must have overheard us. "Your dad always puts me in a good mood. Even when I had that fiasco in Charlotte. I know we are very lucky."

"What happened in Charlotte?"

"Some man who was very successful hired me to design a restaurant for him. He was very accomplished. I tried to please him. To the point that I never came home. Your poor dad had to come visit me to keep me from going off the deep end. The restaurant I designed for him closed after nine months."

"Ouch. I thought you were always successful, Bae."

"In Charlotte I learned work-life balance. I needed to learn it. I know you think I work all the time now. In the beginning it frustrated your dad. Actually, that is how we named you."

"You named me after your failure? Gee, thanks."

I laughed. "No, I named you after the place I learned my most valuable lessons. It's okay to fail." I paused, remembering what Henry had told me. "Failure can be freeing. You are never going to please everyone. Always go with your instincts. Never be afraid to say no to a client. Always put your dad first. I probably shouldn't tell you this part." I watched her lean in.

"You were conceived in Charlotte because I never came home. I loved the name. It was so strong. Growing up I loved the relationship between Charlotte and Wilbur in *Charlotte's Web*. I wanted you to have a friend like Wilbur."

She was quiet for a while. I suppose giving her the origin of her name made her introspective. "Well, your love is epic, Mom."

"Charlie, do you think you are in love?" I was very tentative in asking my daughter this question.

"I don't know. That is the one thing I like about you, Mom. It's obvious how you feel about Dad. I like it when we talk like this. I loved

Charlotte's Web when I was little. I always thought it would be cool to have my name come from that book. I guess in a way it did. Thanks for telling me, Mom." She smiled. I smiled back.

"I don't take it for granted, Charlie. Sometimes your dad and I joke that we may be the only living couple in love with each other that suffered poor communication skills." I laughed. I wish I hadn't.

Autumn slipped away. The browns and oranges gave way to barren trees and gray skies. Inside, I was bursting with excitement. I had two jobs that were bringing me fulfillment and they were both at home. I enjoyed being home at night with Griffin and Charlie. They made me laugh. One night, the happy reverie came to an abrupt halt.

"Mom!" Charlie shouted. I went upstairs to find her standing outside her bedroom. Because of all the work that was being done inside, and mainly because I wanted it to be a surprise, I had put a lock on her bedroom door when I moved her into the guest bedroom. I leaned against the wall.

"You rang, Charlie?"

"You locked my bedroom door!"

"I told you to get everything you needed out of your bedroom. Phil Richards's men are working there. You wouldn't want to peek inside before Christmas morning, would you?" I pulled her to me and gave her a big bear hug and kiss. After a few seconds she pulled away and gave me one of her eye rolls and then stomped back to the guest room. I understood my daughter's curiosity. Her dad had been that way when I was designing his condo. I crossed my fingers and held my breath that her room would please her the way Griffin's condo had pleased him.

It might have been more than a week before Christmas, but it felt like Christmas to me. It was the Saturday night grand opening of Whitney's. I felt nervous and excited. I had changed outfits three times until Griffin grumbled.

"Just who are you trying to impress? It better not be Mac."

I laughed, giving the only man I had truly ever had feelings for a kiss.

"I am trying to color coordinate my outfit with the rooms. They're all different colors."

"I think you're the only woman who would dress to impress paint colors." He embraced me, giving me a proper kiss.

I settled on a black dress with some funky beads. I decided if my picture was taken, I would choose the lavender room with the abstract painting with the watercolors and black lines. My dress would make the painting pop.

When we arrived at the restaurant, it was in full swing. Mac looked like a proud papa. He walked over to the bartender and fetched a champagne for me and a Saratoga for Griffin.

"Your favorite champagne, Bailey. Cheers, to the best restaurant designer in the business!" Mac spotted a new guest and excused himself.

I was about to show Griffin around when we practically bumped into Annabel. I hadn't seen her in a long time, especially since the information came to light a few months earlier about her and Griffin. I wanted to be nice but brief.

"Oh sweetie, you have really outdone yourself with my brother's place! You logged so many hours together I joked that you two were having an affair." She smiled as she said it and gave me air kisses.

"Thanks, Annabel. I'm sure Dexter's husband thought the exact same thing." And then we parted company.

"You can hold your own with Annabel," Griffin laughed. "She's right about one thing—this place is amazing. I can't believe you designed a whole house."

A photographer wanted to take my picture with Mac, and I led him into the private dining room in front of the fireplace and abstract painting.

"This is my favorite restaurant you designed." I wondered if he would call this picture "Moneybags and his Muse." I laughed, and that's when he snapped the picture. After, I took Griffin's hand and we went home to celebrate another grand opening.

Christmas morning began with a banging on our door. It took me back to when Charlie was a little thing and still believed in Santa Claus.

"Seriously?" Griffin whispered. "Let's tell her she's got to go back to bed."

I leaned over and smoothed out the hair in Griffin's eyes. "I'm excited myself." I smiled, sharing my daughter's sense of Christmas wonder.

"Hold on, Sprite," Griffin said, getting up and dressing. I met him in the closet and embraced him and gave him a Christmas kiss.

"Merry Christmas, Goose," I said.

"Merry Christmas, baby. You sure have relaxed your standards about mistletoe," he laughed.

"I have a legally binding document that says married people don't need mistletoe. Come on, I'm excited to see what Charlie thinks."

Griffin stopped me. "Don't be too disappointed if Charlie isn't completely overwhelmed by your creation."

I didn't tell Griffin, but I had been awake all night worried about the same thing. We met her at her bedroom door.

"You took your sweet time. I want to see my bedroom."

I loved the fact that my daughter was impatient. Like me.

"Oh no," I said, searching in the pockets of my lounging pants. "I don't think Phil ever gave me back the key." I watched as Charlie's expression went from excitement to anger. I waited. Even Griffin looked at me. After a minute more I said, "I'm kidding. Merry Christmas, Charlie!"

"Not funny, Bae!" She stepped aside so I could unlock the door. She just stood on the threshold looking at her bedroom. I wondered if Griffin was right. She took one step into her bedroom as if the bedroom cast a magical spell and if she entered it would disappear. I felt Griffin's hand on my back.

"I love the headboard!" she said as she dashed over to touch it. "I love how you did the dust ruffle. You were right!"

She walked over to the other side of her bedroom to survey the chairs, which I had done in green and finished with a coordinating purple fabric. In the middle was the ottoman. I had also used the fabric for a big pillow for her bed with her initials. Her hand grazed the ottoman and she sat down in a chair.

"This purple fabric is the best." She turned around smiling and walked back to embrace me. It was the best Christmas present I thought I would ever get. I wanted to hold on to her. I wanted to hold on to this moment. This must be how mothers and daughters feel every day. It bordered on something religious. Spiritual.

"But wait, there's more!" I walked over and showed her the eiderdown at the end of her bed. It was done in the same floral as her headboard and I had backed it in purple. I knew that that was her favorite fabric.

"Mom," Charlie said. I heard joy. I heard happiness. I heard all the things you want to hear from your child.

"Check out your desk." I had her desk painted in a cream color with green accents. I found a notebook that said "Make it happen," which was done in gold letters.

"This is for you to put in your backpack so when you come up with an idea or a phrase you can jot it down."

"I'm going to write down the word . . . *awesome*," she said, knowing that I thought that was an overused word.

"It's Christmas so you can write anything you want. Tomorrow you can write *amazing*." I laughed with her. "One last thing." I motioned for her to look at her bathroom.

"You did my bathroom too?"

I was very interested in her opinion of the tiered prism chandelier. She peered into her bathroom and then walked in. Griffin and I joined her. I heard the twinkle as she touched the colored prisms. "Nobody has anything like this."

"I found it at an estate sale. Is it too much?"

"I love it. I really didn't know you could do all this with purple and green." She walked over to me and embraced me. "This is so me."

"Did you notice the monogrammed towels? One set done in green and one in purple."

"I can't wait to show Bishop and Lucy!" She returned to her bedroom, touching everything, sitting on her bed and rolling around like a five-year-old. It made this past year from hell bearable. We had gone to church the night before with Lucy and Sally and cooked dinner for them. Today Henry and his family were coming over, and we had invited Bishop and his mom to join us. I noticed the subtle shift in order in Charlie's statement. She had gone from "Lucy and Bishop" to now "Bishop and Lucy."

About that time the doorbell rang. We heard Henry let himself in downstairs. Griffin and I left Charlie to explore.

"I bet this set me back a little bit."

"This one is on me. I'll find some mutually agreeable form of payment." I embraced him and extracted treasured kisses before reluctantly letting him get dressed. "You know I always get paid."

"You can even charge me interest."

I was in the process of "extracting payment" when Henry yelled up at Griffin. As he pulled away, he said, "You made our daughter happy."

"What would make me happy is one of your cappuccinos."

"It will be waiting for you."

Henry and Griffin, with little or no fanfare, went to work. I sat at the island sipping my cappuccino, watching these men. We were at our usual posts. Henry at the stove, Griffin at the sink peeling and washing things for Henry, and me in the position that Dad and I used to occupy. This was my second Christmas present of the day, just being in the kitchen with Griffin and Henry. The three of us together. We were always better together.

"I guess Maggie is going to want you to design her bedroom now," Henry said.

"I'm not sure I want to get into the business of designing teenage girls' bedrooms. Besides, I don't know if you can afford me, Henry!" I laughed.

"I'm guessing as long as I'm cooking for you and giving you cookie dough, I can afford you," he joked back. I loved the playful banter that had always been between us.

"You can put it on Griffin's tab."

"Henry, it's Christmas Day. Can we try to look halfway normal?"

"I love messing with you."

"Do it for Charlie." The way Henry and Griffin worked together they could win a gold medal.

I heard Lea, Hank, and Maggie at the back door. It was still hard to believe that Hank was in college, following in his father's footsteps. I heard the girls scamper upstairs. On my way to change my clothes, I went over to Griffin, took his head in my hands, and gave him a long kiss.

"Stop distracting Griff."

"I love messing with you too," I grinned, nudging Henry, and disappeared upstairs.

❧

Bishop and his mom arrived a little after one thirty. We served lunch at two o'clock, our customary time. Amy was very nice and quiet. Charlie wanted to show them her room. I had given Bishop the idea to give Charlie a Moleskine journal for her Christmas present and I had a package of her favorite pens to go along with it for him. Charlie had given him a bunch of gift certificates to some of his favorite places.

When we said good night to Charlie, she was still gazing at her bedroom. It made me happy.

ঌ

The kids were all going to spend New Year's Eve at Mac's house. They would walk home a little after midnight. Griffin and I decided to spend it at home. It had become our custom. It was quiet. Unlike all those extravagant New Year's Eves I had spent in New York. I much preferred our way. We toasted with my favorite champagne. I went first.

"Here's to the year of hell being over."

Griffin laughed. "To my wife and her brilliant vision."

"You are such a good toastmaster. You ought to do it more," I said, as I squeezed Griffin's hand and kissed it.

I thought about the year. It had started with Charlie being mad with us because we wouldn't let her go to Switzerland with Whitney to study. It was followed by the revelation from Whitney that Griffin and Annabel had slept together prior to my moving back to Atlanta. Then, that was all followed by Charlie googling me and finding out that I had been married before Griffin. I had hoped that by designing her bedroom it would put us back on track.

ঌ

Later, when we were in bed waiting for Charlie, my cell phone buzzed. It was Mac.

"Listen, we have a situation. The kids got into bottles of tequila and the girls are tipsy. I am driving them home. I already called Sally, and I'm relieved. I was worried about telling Sally the most, but she thought it was pretty funny. I don't think she is going to punish Lucy but I just wanted to tell you, "he said before continuing, "I don't know how they got into the liquor cabinet. I am speaking to Thompson about that. Thank goodness they are good kids."

I relayed the conversation to Griffin. He was not amused.

"Listen, Bae. We have deeper concerns than the other parents. We have strong alcoholic tendencies in our DNA. Charlotte needs to know that Henry is an alcoholic."

About that time Charlie barged into our bedroom. "What do you mean, Uncle Henry is an alcoholic?"

I took charge. "Come in, Charlie. Sit down for a minute." I motioned to the end of the bed. It was clear she was drunk. "We need to talk about what happened tonight. First, you never barge into our bedroom without knocking, is that understood?"

"I could tell nothing was going on." She was loud.

"Lose the attitude," Griffin snapped.

I wrestled with what to tell my daughter. It was Henry's story, after all. I knew that Griffin was ready to tell her everything if I didn't. It was a dangerous cocktail of anger, fear, being drunk, and the lateness of the hour that weighed on my heart. I wanted to get this right. For Henry. For Charlie. For our family.

"Henry is an alcoholic. He hasn't had a drink in about sixteen years. It's a daily decision for him."

"I can't believe you guys kept this from me. If he hasn't had a drink in sixteen years, he's not an alcoholic anymore."

I closed my eyes. I could see it happening. The long arm of history was reaching out to grab Griffin and strangle him. We think we can outrun our history. It is always lurking around the corner to set us straight.

"That just tells you how much you know, Charlotte. For Henry, one drink tastes good but the fiftieth tastes even better until he passes out. He's a mean drunk. He makes bad decisions. Did you pass out?"

"What is wrong with you guys? What bad decisions?"

"Henry wasn't picky about who he slept with," Griffin said. "When Hank was three, his mother died. She had listed Henry on the birth certificate. My parents—your grandparents—were raging alcoholics. They died in a fire because they were passed out."

We were all quiet for a moment. I glanced at the clock. It was one thirty.

"I basically know nothing about my family. My uncle is a drunk. And your parents were drunks. Some shitty family tree. Why did you even have children in the first place?"

"Charlie, we had you because we love each other and you. I think your dad just wants you to be careful," I said.

"No. I want her to stop drinking!" Griffin barked. Sigmund Freud could really have a heyday with us. Past is prologue and all of that.

She ran in our bathroom to throw up. I reached under my bed to get a bottle of water.

"I guess I am starting the new year grounded," Charlie mumbled.

Griffin took over. "For starters, I want your phone. I'm putting a tracking device on it. Underage drinking is nothing to play around with. You cannot drink. Do you understand me? I don't care what everyone else is doing. In this house you're grounded. I don't even want you hanging around those friends."

"Griffin . . ." I warned.

"You're *not* serious? You guys are the worst parents on the planet! I'm used to having a disappointment as a mother, but not some dictator as a dad!" She slammed our door, and I just stared at Griffin. He was wide awake with rage.

"Despite what you said, they are good kids. Other kids their age are experimenting with weed, alcohol, and sex. I was drinking at fifteen. I was drinking with *you* at fifteen."

"I don't care what you were doing. We don't know what kind of addictive genes Charlotte may be carrying."

"You are driving her into the arms of Jose Cuervo."

"You just don't get it. It just means I'm going to have to be home in the afternoons. What I wouldn't give to have Tabatha back."

"Are you still holding that over my head?"

"You just overreacted to Tabatha."

I interrupted him. "Like you are overreacting about Charlie drinking."

"I told you it didn't matter how many times she hit on me."

"If you recall, it was mainly about her undermining me with Charlie. That was the main reason, but what if she got you drunk like Annabel?" I was instantly sorry I said that.

"What's the point in forgiving if you're not going to forget?" He cut off the light without kissing me good night.

❧

We entered the season of warfare. The whole house suffered. We were a hothouse and every plant was turning brown. Occasionally, I would just stop at the market for some cheerful flowers.

Charlie moped around. She floundered. She was missing her best friend. She missed the person she had always had the easy relationship with, her dad. Griffin had grown suspicious. If Charlie laughed a little too loudly, he would eye her as if she had been drinking. He even had grown distrustful of me, as if I were in some way enabling her.

I missed Griffin too. It was like an invasion of the body snatchers. None of us were acting like ourselves. I became intentionally happy to try to bridge the gap between Charlie and Griffin. Sometimes I would say something snarky just to provoke the dreaded eye roll from Charlie. I was looking for something familiar. Even the easy intimacy that Griffin and I enjoyed had abandoned us. I felt like I was just a chore on his to-do list. A job requirement: "Satisfy Bailey." Sometimes I thought he was just satisfying his own anger and frustration.

Charlie became increasingly moody, spending most of her time in her bedroom with her headphones on.

One night Griffin was trying. He knocked on her door and opened it. "Sprite, do you want to pick a recipe out of your binder and we can make it for dinner?"

"No thanks. Hormones. Get your wife to help." Griffin closed the door. I met him on the stairs.

"I'll help you cook." I was trying too.

"No thanks. I was just trying to get Charlotte interested in something other than sleeping and music."

One afternoon I was going over to Sally's to make margaritas, and I noticed it. A bottle of tequila was missing. I went to the butler's pantry and took an inventory of all the liquor that was left and where it was. I showed Charlie the diagram. She looked surprised, startled. Then she begged. She pleaded. She promised. I relented. I acquiesced. I didn't do it as much for Charlie as I did for the household. I just hated the anger. I didn't want to live like this. I was firm. I was jeopardizing one relationship for another.

"Don't make me sorry, Charlie. And don't try to kid me. I have been married to an addict."

"I promise. You'll see." Valentine's Day, the Four Musketeers were getting together at Mac's. Griffin made him promise he would keep a better eye on the kids.

She missed her curfew by fifteen minutes. Griffin was waiting at the door. Ready to pounce. My insides were churning. We had had the worst Valentine's since I left Elliott. I hated to admit it, but I was having a severe case of PTSD flashback to New Year's Eve.

"You're late, Charlotte. Let me smell your breath," Griffin demanded.

"I texted, dictator-in-chief," Charlotte snapped back.

"I didn't get a text."

"That's because I texted Mom." Charlie looked at me. "Really, Bae? For once you're not glued to your phone."

I checked my phone and confirmed Charlie's story. I could tell Griffin doubted me, so I showed him my phone.

"What's going on between you two? I still want to smell your breath."

Charlie complied. She made a sound like a cat's angry hiss. It was clear she was sober.

We all went to bed. It didn't feel like a victory or anything bordering on satisfaction. In fact, it felt just the opposite. I still had the churning inside my stomach and around my heart. This wasn't my parenting style at all. Maybe parenting is an evolution. When one parent goes too far in one extreme you are reluctantly pulled in the other. I had become the parent of choice. Not because she liked me any better, but because she was missing her dad.

NOW

"We have another problem," Floyd said as I walked into the conference room the following day. I dropped my satchel on the chair next to me and took a sip of my coffee. Floyd handed me a piece of paper.

"This is Tucker Landon's statement. He has been out of the country. He was walking his dog when he passed Jane and who I'm guessing was Griffin as they were leaving. He and Jane exchanged greetings. He also noticed some inebriated kids. This is good news for you. The more doubt we can cast the better the odds of getting you acquitted."

It never ceased to amaze me how cavalier Floyd was about my life.

"I don't want to doubt my husband or daughter the rest of my life. I just hate that we can't see their faces. It's like everyone thinks they are being watched."

"It is not my job to save your relationships. My job is to get you acquitted."

I drove to see Henry. He had a cappuccino waiting for me.

"From your voice on the phone it sounded like you could use this. You look pale. Hey Rusty, can you bring my sister some of the swordfish with the mushroom brûlée?" he called back to his chef. "Don't forget the balsamic reduction over the swordfish." He turned to me. "Now tell me—what's the matter? Do they have more evidence against you?"

I sipped my cappuccino. It tasted like Griffin's. Rusty arrived with a beautiful plate of food. I was interested in sampling the mushroom brûlée. It looked like crème brûlée but was meaty and full-bodied. It went perfectly with the simple swordfish. But Henry took his towel and wiped the edges of my plate.

"Rusty, you can do a better job on the drizzle next time." My brother, the perfectionist.

"This is delicious, Henry," I praised, taking a bite.

"What's troubling you?"

I took a breath in. "It looks like Lady Jane's account has just been backed up by an eyewitness. Floyd is frustrated with me. I know Griffin. I know he would never let me take the blame for something he did." I stopped mid-bite to look at Henry. "We need to talk about Charlie."

"Your daughter is a blackout drunk. If she was drinking that night, and we both know she was, she won't remember."

Henry drained his cappuccino.

"If that wasn't bad enough, Floyd asked me if Griffin ever made a decision for the family unilaterally."

"You better be glad I don't drink anymore. Because little sister, you're screwed."

NOW

When I walked into the conference room, I realized Floyd and I were not alone. Jake was sitting at the head of the table, his customary spot. The men exchanged looks. This was the first time Jake had sat in on deliberations since this nightmare began.

"Jake? To what do we owe the pleasure?" I said, sitting down.

"I just thought I would sit in on the meeting," he responded. Floyd slid some papers over to me.

"What is this?"

"A plea bargain," Floyd said, and filled in the gaps. "The prosecution will reduce your sentence to five to ten years if you plead guilty to voluntary manslaughter." He said this as if he were ordering a sparkling water.

"Charlie will be beginning her life. She may be married and have children. I don't want to miss any of that. Besides, you keep forgetting I didn't do it!" Thinking about all my daughter's milestones, I began to cry. Jake came over and comforted me, and I realized that was what he was doing here in the first place. Griffin came through the door about that time. I hated for all three men to see me cry.

"Tell them I didn't do it." My eyes pleaded with Griffin's as he knelt beside me and rubbed my back. A memory flashed of him doing this with Charlie. I was right bestowing on him the nickname Goose.

"We are legally obligated to tell you about any plea bargains. The prosecution is overplaying their hand." Floyd began pulling the document away from me and back toward him. I held it back. "I guess the main question is, did anyone know you were meeting with Elliott?"

"Just Griffin and Charlie. I don't know who Elliott told," I said.

"Griffin, did you tell anyone?"

"Lady Jane contacted me to discuss the situation and that's why I went to New York."

"How often do you talk to Lady Jane?" I looked at him quizzically.

"Never," Griffin said.

"I need to be on a conference call, so I'll walk you out, Griffin," Jake offered. The two of them left together. It was just Floyd and me.

"This is how the prosecution is going to paint you. As a privileged white woman. A career woman who is driven by ambition. They will introduce witnesses who heard you and Elliott argue and that your argument became heated. You stabbed and pushed him. His head hit the island and he died. You neglected your daughter in your drive for professional accolades. She ended up in rehab at sixteen—"

I interrupted Floyd. "Would they use Charlie's alcoholism against me?"

"Probably. Even though Charlie was a minor at the time. She's not a minor anymore."

"Would they call her to testify against me?"

"They might treat her like a hostile witness. It might come out that she fell off the wagon the night of Elliott's murder." Floyd said. It petrified me.

"What about the time difference between Griffin's and Jane's version of events?"

"The police think they have the real killer—you. But I am not giving up. I don't want to lose.

"Do you see how moving flowers and cutting your finger is going to be a really hard thing to prove? It just sounds flimsy. I need to go follow up on some leads. One more thing. You should probably get your affairs in order." And just like that, Floyd Potts was gone.

I sat and looked at the four walls. I wondered how I had gotten here. I should be gazing at the beautiful shoreline in Brazil rather than studying plea bargains. I should be spending my days convincing Gabriel about my vision rather than trying to convince my own attorney of my innocence. I should be scavenging estate sales for unique pieces instead of spending another second wondering what happened to Elliott. What if Charlie had killed Elliott? What if the plea bargain was the best chance to save my family?

I was sitting at the kitchen table drinking bourbon when Griffin walked in.

"My God, Bae. How are you holding up? What is that?" He sat down next to me and removed the glass from my hand.

"The top document is the plea bargain. The second document is my last will and testament and power of attorney that Meg Murphy, our estate attorney, drew up this afternoon. I'm lawyered up." I tried to laugh.

"I didn't think you were going to consider the plea bargain."

"Don't worry. I'm leaving all my worldly possessions to you."

We both knew that the things not being said were screaming to be heard. But how should I begin this conversation? We sat there for so long that Griffin poured himself a bourbon and threw it back like medicine.

"Damn, I hate the taste of bourbon. Just tell me what is going on."

The sun was setting on the day. It seemed an apt metaphor for what was happening at the kitchen table.

This time I took the bottle away from him and put it on the counter. Again, we settled into a prison of silence. Of secrets. Of strange truths.

"There are some facts I haven't told you."

He looked at me and went to the butler's pantry and got a bottle of cognac. "If I need to be altered for this conversation, I might as well drink my beverage of choice."

"My DNA was found on the knife. My DNA was also found on Elliott. Elliott's DNA was found on me."

There was a long pause. Griffin stared at me. I could see his jaw tense. We were both choosing our words carefully. We knew they were the most destructive weapons. We had used them on each other before. It had taken a long time to heal. But there is a thing called death from a thousand cuts.

The gloaming of the day had begun.

"You were arranging flowers? Elliott got your DNA because you were dancing. Who the hell is going to believe that?"

"A jury, I hope."

"I'm not sure I believe it."

"Floyd believes me. If I can't even get my husband to believe me, what are my chances with a jury? Elliott and I got into a bad argument. I scratched him. Elliott's DNA was found under my fingernails."

"Did he hurt you?"

"No."

"I told you we should have gone together." Before I could tell him about Charlie, Griffin got up and left.

ꕥ

I slept on the couch, if you could call it sleeping. I heard Griffin coming in. He looked rough.

"I think it's time to replace the sofa in my office." Was he speaking metaphorically? He went to the cabinet and got some aspirin. I'm not sure I'd ever seen him hungover. I was scared to say anything. I watched him swallow the aspirin. I watched him make coffee. I watched him watching me. He noticed the plea bargain still on the kitchen table. Unsigned.

"I'm not sure how I'm going to explain my hangover to Henry." Before I could say anything, he was gone again.

ꕥ

Jeri, the head nurse—and my favorite one—greeted me.

"He isn't having a good day today. He is still in bed."

"Thanks. I won't stay long."

When I entered his room, it was dark. I opened the blinds to let some sun in. I sat by his bed and took his hand. It was cold. He moved his head to face me, but his eyes were closed.

"Dad, it's me, Bailey. I am in a bad spot. I really need your advice. I have this plea bargain. I don't know what to do. My daughter could have killed Elliott. She admitted to being so drunk she doesn't remember. Then there's Griffin. I have seen him in a blind rage before. When Charlie was drinking. I also remember what he said to Charlie about how he would take out anybody who threatened his family. Both Charlie and Griffin were in New York. He was in the apartment building right before the murder. In my heart of hearts, I think Charlie could have done it." It felt good to say it all out loud.

I paused as if giving Dad a chance to think about it. I smiled. I know what he would tell me to do. He would tell me to take one for the team. He would tell me to bargain like I used to do in those consignment stores. He would tell me it was time for me to show my family how much I love them. He would tell me to protect my family even if it meant surrendering my freedom.

THEN
SEVEN YEARS AGO

As we approached March 21, Charlie's sweet sixteenth, things were almost back to normal. For her birthday, Charlie just wanted the musketeers over to have a cookout. Hamburgers, tater tots—which were an unfortunate carryover from Tabatha's tenure but a food group Charlie adored—fruit, and a birthday cake made by Henry.

It was fun to see Charlie so happy again. We had invited Lucy's parents, Sally and Chad, over to eat with us inside. We gazed at the kids outside. Both girls were sitting in their respective boyfriend's lap. I could tell it rankled Griffin.

"Why do they have to sit so close?"

"Young love. I would've sat in your lap if you had only offered," I said. Griffin chuckled. It was marvelous to hear him laugh again. I felt like it had been years since I heard such an unguarded laugh.

"And give your brother the satisfaction? No way."

I smiled and nodded toward Charlie. "The birthday girl is ready for her cake."

Charlie was in a good mood. I loved to see her like this.

We all went outside, and while Griffin was lighting the candles, I took a bite of the watermelon, which was almost gone. I tried not to register any emotion but clearly I didn't try hard enough. Griffin put down the lighter with only half the candles lit and took a bite of fruit. It was spiked. Apparently, the only thing lit at our daughter's party was our daughter. Needless to say, the party ended abruptly. Griffin's mood changed immediately.

"What the hell, Sprite?"

Charlie was equally combative. "Do I even get my birthday presents? It was just tequila."

"How long has this been going on? It doesn't matter. Do you know what you're getting for your birthday? Drug testing! I am going to drug test you from now on randomly. You're grounded!"

"Why the hell should my birthday be any different from any other damn day? How long are you going to make me live in a police state? I should just move in with Lucy. Her parents are understanding."

All the kids were drunk in our backyard. I just thought they were happy. I cursed my naïveté one more time.

"Another thing. You can't hang around Bishop, Lucy, and Thompson anymore, do you understand that?"

"Griffin. That's a little harsh," I interjected.

"No worries, Bae, I'll just hang out with the druggies and the boys who want to have sex with me."

I was on the verge of tears. I watched Griffin's jaw tighten. I could tell he was holding his tongue. I hated what this was doing to my family. Charlie stalked off to her bedroom after relinquishing her phone. I went upstairs and I heard Griffin downstairs making a jarring symphony out of washing pots and pans. I heard him when he came to bed.

"Despite what you think, those are good kids," I told him.

"I'll be damned if she ends up like my parents."

"She's not. I know you're doing your best but be careful. I love you."

"Me too," he said, turning his bedside lamp off. As I tried to go to sleep, my mind landed on Emily Dickinson and her poem about hope and how it was the thing with feathers that perches in the soul. No offense to Miss Dickinson, but that seemed a little too flimsy for what we all needed. We needed something sturdy, some kind of armor to protect us and our tender hearts. I needed an all-weather coat made of a more stubborn fabric like faith.

Charlie failed the first few drug tests. Over the course of the following nineteen weeks, a season and then some, Charlie passed Griffin's tests. After Charlie's birthday, it was clear that Griffin did not approve of her hanging out with the Four Musketeers. She began hanging out with Whitney again. I found this to be a troubling development. Whitney was extremely popular, had lots of boyfriends, and periodically Charlie would spend the night with her. I didn't like the way Charlie looked. She looked dissipated. The way Henry had back in the day, when he was mixing alcohol and drugs. Her clothes just hung on her. I found myself snooping in her closet and drawers to see if I could find any evidence of pills or weed. Occasionally I would ask Charlie about it.

"Why don't you hang out with Bishop and Lucy anymore?" Or other times, "Charlie, talk to me. Are you drinking?"

"You're as bad as Dad. I'm sure you search my room every day. And the dictator drug tests me every other day. I don't know what you want. I passed your damn tests," she said.

"You look so thin. Are you sure you're not taking drugs?" It pained me to ask her questions. About that time Griffin strolled in with dinner.

"What? Are you taking drugs now? I want you to go take a test right now!" Griffin barked.

"I took your damn test this morning."

"That's why they call it random." Charlie marched upstairs and took another test. It came back clean. Occasionally I would go in her room at night just to say good night and she would snarl and me.

"You want to check under the mattress, Bae?"

"I just wanted to tell you good night, Charlie. I am always here for you."

"Big deal. Just leave me alone. I think Dad needs to see a shrink. He is out of control. I can't talk to him anymore."

I noticed my hair started falling out. It had fallen out when I was so stressed about Elliott before we divorced. Maybe Griffin and I *were* the problem. When we were getting ready for bed I tried to talk to Griffin. Maybe we were making her thin.

"Griffin, maybe we should see a family therapist to help deal with Charlie better," I suggested.

"Oh, dear God, you've been talking to Charlie." He would turn off his light and turn away from me. I wondered where our little girl was and what had happened to all of us.

❧

Nothing seemed good enough for Griffin. I was scheduled to fly to Rhode Island to meet with the dean of a beautiful campus right outside of Providence. I went by VERT.

"Griffin, would you like me to postpone my trip?" I put my arms around his waist, but he backed away, citing payroll. Had addiction robbed the playful nature that we once enjoyed with each other?

"I've got things handled, Bae. We're fine as long as Charlotte keeps passing her drug test. I still don't trust her."

Things had even become a little cool with Sally, and I hated that estrangement.

"Just how long are you going to keep testing her and searching her room when she's at school?"

"Until I am convinced. I told you before—addicts are sneaky."

I knew better than to disagree with him. I wanted him to grab my hand and say "I miss us," or "let's try out the sofa before you leave." But he didn't.

❧

I came home from my trip to an empty house. I wondered if maybe Charlie was with Lucy. I texted Charlie. I texted Griffin. No one answered. I went into the kitchen and there was glass all over the floor. Then I noticed a cell phone swimming in a vase of flowers.

I heard the front door. It was Griffin.

"Hi—I've been trying to text you all night. Any idea where Charlie is? And what happened in the kitchen?" I met Griffin and noticed he had a black eye. "Oh my God—what happened to you?"

"Sit down. I need to talk to you, Bae."

"What's wrong? Where's Charlie? How did you get the black eye?"

He sat next to me and took my hands in his. It was one of the most intimate gestures we had exchanged in months. "Charlie is safe. That's Henry's cell phone in the water." I felt a sense of foreboding.

"Henry? What does Henry have to do with anything? Did you get in a fight with him?" I remembered their fisticuffs when we were younger. "Is he back in rehab? Where is Charlie?" I asked again.

"Promise to just listen to me." I nodded.

Griffin continued. "Charlotte is in rehab. We took her there just a little while ago. She needs help."

"What do you mean rehab? She was passing her tests."

"No, she wasn't. You remember it doesn't take a lot of urine to do a drug test. She had urine to give us as samples. She was keeping them in the guest room. I found those, along with empty bottles of tequila. Charlotte confessed. She admitted she has been drinking at school. Charlotte skipped school today. Her tracker said she was here, and when I found her she was passed out. It's bad. Henry and I had an intervention with her. I took her to the rehab facility where Henry was. They have a juvenile section. I told you addicts were sneaky. She's been using her allowance to pay some guy for tequila."

"And the glass in the kitchen?"

"Henry and I got into a fight while Charlotte was passed out. I shoved him and he lost his balance and knocked over some glasses. He wanted to call you. I took his phone away and threw it in the vase of water. Henry has a black eye and a few bruised ribs. You can talk to your brother."

"How can I talk to him when his phone is in our kitchen?" I felt my voice rising, my nerves fraying.

"I did the right thing."

"I want to go to her."

"You can't. We can't see her for at least seventy-two hours until she detoxes."

I was silent. Stunned. The truth hit me like daggers of the broken glass. I pulled my hand away.

"Are you saying you had an intervention for *our* underage daughter and put her in rehab without even letting me know or asking me if I wanted to be a part of it?" The shock of it all was wearing off and anger was setting in.

"There wasn't any time. I was afraid she would run away. Henry and I had her, and we did it this morning." He was talking about our daughter like some wild animal that he caught and took to animal control. It made me sick to my stomach.

"You kidnapped our daughter."

"No, I didn't. You know exactly where she is." Griffin didn't even seem apologetic.

"You did something with our underage child that I was not aware of. Something drastic. Kidnapping. Did she wonder where I was? Was she scared? How could you do this? I am her mother!" I stopped. I knew our words were only going to be weapons. I got up, took my suitcase, and left the house. I went to a hotel and checked in under the name of Bailey Mayberry, after the *Andy Griffith Show*, our favorite growing up.

ॐ

The next day, I went to see Henry. He looked worse than Griffin. I imagined what those rehab people must've thought seeing two grown men with black eyes checking a sixteen-year-old into rehab. They must've wondered if they should call the police.

"Griff owes me a phone," Henry said when he saw me. He sat down gingerly. He looked like he had taken the brunt of the abuse this time around. "I know you're mad," he continued. "You have every right to be mad. I tried to get Griff to call you. At least to let you know what was going on. I have never seen him like that before. He went into some blind rage that I didn't recognize."

We looked at each other for a few moments. Addiction had claimed a seat at the table once again.

ᘛ

I came home three days later. Griffin wasn't at home. I went upstairs and moved some of my things into the guest room. My anger was still hot. I didn't recognize my husband. How could he do this to our daughter without even telling me? Did he disrespect me so much as a wife and a mother that he didn't bother to let me know something this important? I was angry. I was hurt. I felt shame. The emotions ricocheted inside me until I thought I was going to throw up. My phone rang.

"Is this Bailey Edgeworth?" the voice on the other end asked. I answered in the affirmative. "Would you accept a call from Charlotte Hardwick?" I answered again in the affirmative.

"Mom," was all she said. Her voice sounded weak, stripped bare of any confidence she possessed. She started crying. I slid to the floor, just trying to keep us connected until she stopped. "I guess you heard. I think you and Dad are coming tomorrow. Would you mind bringing my favorite gray hoodie and some underwear? Dad didn't do a good job of packing my things," she said. I wanted to ask her so much.

"Sure. What if I bring a couple of your Moleskines so you can write, and maybe some of Uncle Henry's snickerdoodle cookies?"

"Thanks, Mom." She sounded so young. So scared. "There are other people needing to use the phone. I've got to go."

I panicked. I wanted to say so many things to her. I wanted to tell her I would always be there for her. I wanted to say something important, something she would remember, something wise.

"I hope you eat fruit every day." I looked at myself in the mirror. My only child was in a rehab facility and I was worried about her getting scurvy or rickets? I wanted to tell her I loved her when I heard the phone click. I felt like an idiot. Why hadn't I done better? I started to cry.

I had an armful of clothes that I was taking into the guest room when I almost ran into Griffin.

"Are you still angry with me?" he asked.

"You still don't get it. In case you forgot, she's as much my daughter as she is yours. I had every right to know."

"That's what Reggie and Elle said when I talked to them looking for you. They are certainly upset with me."

"I haven't even talked to them. I didn't want to put them in the middle of our . . ." I paused. I remembered the phrase that Mac had used during my divorce from Elliott and his own. "Domestic turbulence."

"You haven't talked to them? They were saying some of the same things you did. By the way, we have a family therapy session tomorrow with Charlie."

"Thanks for telling me, but Charlie already told me."

Griffin disappeared.

That night, sleeping in the guest room, I had company. A ménage à trois of me, my shame, and my sadness. I felt shame that I had been such a neglectful mother that I didn't even see my daughter's drinking. Had all my years of working and being absent from Charlie turned her into an alcoholic? There was a part of me that felt shame that I cared what other people thought. *She is this famous designer but her daughter was an alcoholic before she got her driver's license? What kind of screwup is that for a mother? The kind that says eat fruit every day!*

And then I felt consumed by sadness. What kind of life and journey would this be for Charlie now? Our culture was so driven by alcohol. She was an alcoholic at sixteen. I was sad that her innocence had been taken; it had been detoxed over seventy-two hours. What kind of person would she come out as? Could she be around others who were drinking and not be tempted?

Later that night, I was joined in a ménage à trois with guilt and anger. I could not get over the guilt in my shortcomings as a mom. All the years that I was designing beautiful spaces in every city in the world and my own daughter's spirit was decaying right under my nose.

I was angry. I didn't know I was capable of such anger toward Griffin. He made me feel as though I didn't matter as a mother. He didn't even see that he was in the wrong. How could I forgive him when he wasn't even asking for it? He was so close. I could hear the floor creak as he walked around closing doors. I could hear the shower running in our bathroom. And yet. How could I feel such loss over someone who was just thirty feet away?

What had I become? My life was in crumbles at my feet. I thought of the poem "The Guest House" by Rumi.

> Welcome and entertain them all!
> Even if they are a crowd of sorrows,
> Who violently sweep your house
> Empty of its furniture,
> Still, treat each guest honorably.
> He may be clearing you out
> for some new delight.
>
> The dark thought, the shame, the malice,
> meet them at the door laughing,
> and invite them in.

Be grateful for whatever comes.
Because each has been sent
as a guide from beyond.

I turned it over and over in my mind. I was exhausted. I was ready for them to leave.

ℬ

The next day, I felt like I was arriving at a prison. I had to stop at the desk and give them Charlie's backpack. They searched it.

"I'm Bailey Edgeworth. I'm here to see my daughter, Charlotte Hardwick."

The lady looked up from behind the desk and smiled.

"You must be Henry's sister. We love Henry!" She made it sound like a hotel and Henry was their favorite guest. "He comes back every week and brings cakes or cookies. I'm Daisy."

"Daisy, it is nice to meet you. There are some cookies in there for my daughter but there is a package of cookies for you too. Is that okay to say?"

"That's cool. That must make you Griffin's wife. We know him too. I'm sorry about your daughter," she said as she handed me back the book bag. "Go down the hall and it is the last door on your left."

A woman greeted me at the door. Griffin was already inside. She had arranged our chairs in a semicircle.

"My name is Linda Noris. You can call me Linda. Next week we will include Charlie, but I thought it would be good just to get an overview from you both. I see that you have different last names. Is that professional?"

I nodded. She continued. "I understand you were not a part of the intervention. Was that your choice?"

"I didn't know about it. If I had been consulted, I would've absolutely been at the intervention. I have attended both of my brother's interventions."

Her face remained unreadable. "Griffin, is there a reason you didn't include Bailey for her daughter's intervention?"

"You know the drill, Linda. Addicts are sneaky, and when I found out Charlotte had been stockpiling urine for her drug testing, I hit the roof. Her school called and said that she had missed school. I knew she would run away if I let any more time pass. Henry came over and we had the intervention in our kitchen. Bailey was out of town so there was no way for her to get back in time."

"Is this the way you generally operate?"

"I'll go first," Griffin said. "I think Bae underestimated the situation. She has been too soft with Charlie. Too much of a friend."

"That's rich. Says the man who told our thirteen-year-old daughter that the first time I had sex was with him."

"Addiction strains any marriage. If your wife had been in town, would you have included her?" Linda asked Griffin.

"Probably. She underestimates the disease."

"You're punishing me because I wasn't in town?"

"There wasn't any time. I had to act fast—it's our daughter we're talking about."

Linda looked at us. "You may want to consider couples therapy. I see we have a lot to unpack here. We will meet again next week with your daughter. She is very bright and articulate." And with that, we were dismissed.

ঙ

The session with Charlie wasn't pretty. Her frustration, anger, and consternation were directed at me. The slice of anger she reserved for Griffin was dismissed as "the alcohol talking."

Linda took copious notes. I noticed during Charlie's interactions that some of her memories had shape shifted. The memory of me giving her the pens for her birthday had gone from a bad memory to now a good memory, which had inspired her love of writing. Maybe that's what memories do over time. They change and transform into different things entirely.

Linda dismissed Charlie, which left just Griffin and me. We hadn't spoken much over the past few days. We had exchanged housekeeping matters.

"Do you want me to bring home supper?" he asked. Only once did Griffin veer into the personal. "How long are you going to sleep in the guest room?"

I didn't have an answer.

ꕥ

The following week it was just the two of us, without Charlie. We both shifted uncomfortably in the chairs. Linda must have picked up on our acrimonious vibe.

"I take it there is still a strain between you two?"

"You can say that again. Bae is still sleeping in our guest room." Griffin made it sound like this was my fault.

"Bailey, Charlotte leveled some pretty serious shortcomings at your role as a mother. What do you have to say?"

"I really don't dispute too much. I am a working mother. I am gone a lot. Griffin and I have made it work. We have switched roles. I like to say I am the dad who travels during the week and Griffin is here. He is excellent with Charlie. I didn't have a mom, so I thought because Charlie had such a hands-on dad, plus my brother Henry and a host of aunts, she was well cared for and loved." I may have been mad at Griffin, but I could easily dip into my own well of memories to describe his favorite job and the one he did so well. "Linda, I can say without a doubt that Griffin is the much better parent."

"I put Sprite—that's my nickname for Charlotte—first. Always. That is why I would do what I did over again. I have no regrets," he said.

I sat there in silence. I could almost feel pieces of my heart breaking away. I prayed that Linda would not call on me. But she did.

"Bailey, suddenly you're very quiet. Do you put Charlotte first?"

I shook my head in the negative. "I always put Griffin first. I always loved him." Even as I said it, I realized I had put it in past tense. I couldn't look at Griffin. I was in danger of breaking down. After that, the session ended with no fanfare.

❧

One afternoon, after one of these disastrous sessions, I was trying to get some work done in my office. It was impossible. My thoughts kept unraveling, landing on Griffin. Questions swirled inside my head. Was I a bad wife? How did we get here? Could we ever get back to the way things were? Then they ricocheted to Charlie. Could I be a better mother?

I took a cup of tea up to Charlie's room. I studied my creation. I had been so happy with Charlie's reaction. I wished I could transform my daughter the way I had her room.

❧

"Griffin, we haven't explored the roots of your frustration with what you thought was best reconciled with Bailey's ideas," Linda started our next session.

"With all due respect, I am the one with all the experience in addiction and arranging interventions. I recognize it when I see it. It has given me confidence to know what is best for my daughter," he said.

I lost it. "This is not some 1950s edition of *Father Knows Best*. We are supposed to be partners in this."

"You gave up that right when you let Charlie have a bottle of tequila."

So that was it. Griffin knew. I guess Charlie threw me under the bus.

"Bailey, would you like to respond?" Linda offered.

I took a deep breath in. "I can't remember when, probably after Valentine's Day, I noticed a bottle of tequila was missing. I asked Charlie about it and she told me the Four Musketeers took it one weekend. She begged and pleaded with me not to tell her dad."

"I assume you didn't tell Griffin. Is this how you both operate? Putting Charlie in the middle, trying to use her to gain advantage over the other parent?"

"It does look like that doesn't it, Linda?"

"Who are you? That's not what I was doing at all. I know Charlie prefers you. I never had a problem with that, Griffin. You were grounding her, taking her phone away, and I didn't think that was working too well. Besides, clearly Charlie was drinking right under your nose, and you didn't notice." I had landed a blow. Was that what we were doing to each other now?

"Giving an alcoholic a bottle of tequila certainly would make you the popular parent!" Griffin snapped.

"Stop it. Trust me, I have beaten myself up for giving in to her. I don't feel like a very good parent right now. I should've told you. I'm sorry. I didn't know she was an alcoholic. But we are supposed to be in this together."

"This isn't Henry we're talking about. This is our daughter."

"Griffin, do you think you're still dealing with emotions from your past?" Linda asked.

I had come to the same conclusion myself. But I wouldn't dare mention it to him. I knew his past had come back to bite him. I could only imagine what it was doing to him watching his own daughter go down the same path. It was the only reason I was still in the same house. I understood about the heavy toll it was taking on Griffin. My heart ached for him. But the situation had turned him into someone I barely recognized.

"Both of my parents died in a fire passed out because they were raging alcoholics. I'll be damned if I let my own daughter drink herself to death like my parents."

I thought the sessions with Charlie seemed to be a time of healing and reconnecting. Unfortunately, when it was just Griffin and me, I felt like we were as distant as ever. Serving up leftover animosity that never tasted any better than it had the first time.

ꕥ

Griffin's fiftieth birthday loomed. Despite the chilliness between us I wanted to at least recognize his birthday. Henry offered to cook and let us be his guinea pigs for his new tasting menu. We were going to have a family dinner with Henry's family, minus Charlie. We were meeting with Linda. I had called her earlier to see if she would allow Charlie to call her dad at dinner.

Halfway into the session, she closed her notebook. "Are you still sleeping in separate rooms?"

"Oh, yes. But you should see the guest room. Bailey has worked her magic. She redecorated the whole room. She even commissioned an artist to do artwork for it." Griffin's voice dripped sarcasm.

"Really?" She seemed surprised. "We haven't made much progress on your issues." She stopped and looked at both of us. "Have either one of you discussed divorce or engaged attorneys?"

"Bae can have whatever she wants."

I sat there dumbfounded. I knew Griffin was hurting, but I was too. I wanted to tell him all I really wanted was him. Why is it that hurt masquerades as anger until it ceases being the costume and becomes the uniform?

ꕥ

As I opened the door, wonderful smells assaulted me. I stood there, taking it in like cleansing breaths. Henry was already hard at work. I walked closer and found him happily cooking away. Counters were covered with fresh ingredients, every burner on the stove bubbling over with some wonderful aroma. The kitchen island was blanketed with cutting boards, and the scents of various herbs danced merrily in the air in a lovely marriage of flavors and smells. I went over and hugged him. He gave me a peck on the cheek.

"Hold that thought," I said, and I ducked into the butler's pantry to get a shot of Blanton's. Henry was watching me.

"That never solves the problem."

"But God, it helps," I said, sitting at the island. "What's on the menu?"

"An appetizer crostini with blue cheese and fig. The first course is something I'm calling 'Lobster Confetti.' It has chunks of boiled lobster, mango, and red and green bell pepper tossed in a citrus beurre blanc sauce. The red, yellow, and greens look like confetti."

I smiled as he continued. "The main course is a hanger steak finished with a bing cherry reduction and maque choux—creamed summer succotash. This is followed by a mint and cucumber sorbet to cleanse the palate. The pièce de résistance is an espresso chocolate birthday cake and coffee ice cream. I grabbed a couple bottles of champagne to toast the birthday boy. We *are* toasting the birthday boy?"

"Of course." For once I did not confide my inner turmoil to Henry. He put so much hope into our marriage. He was having too much fun for me to spoil his evening.

❧

Griffin walked in with Lea and the children. I still referred to Hank that way, even though he was already a man, following in his father's footsteps.

Griffin came over to me and gave me a peck on the cheek. Had we become those people? We had become actors even with our own family. Even that made me sad.

We were sitting down for dinner when Griffin's phone rang. He excused himself.

"Thanks for remembering your old man's birthday, Sprite," we heard him say. After a bit he walked back in. "Bae, she wants to talk to you."

"Everything's fine. Thanks for calling. It meant a lot to Dad. We both love you very much, Sprite."

Later, after a happy evening and many courses, Henry presented his cake to the birthday boy. With great aplomb Griffin blew the candles out. I wondered what he wished for. Had he wished for Charlie's sobriety? Maybe he wished for peace to return to our house.

"What does a girl have to do to get a cappuccino around here?" I lightly lobbed the question in Griffin's direction.

"I'm the birthday boy. I have the night off," he responded. It was tinged with determination. Conversation came to an abrupt halt.

"Bailey, I've gotten rusty," Lea said. Henry surveyed the situation.

"I guess preparing five courses isn't enough for this beleaguered chef. I'll be happy to make it, Bailey."

I looked at Henry with so much love. He understood. It wasn't about the cappuccino. It was about trying to establish some historical connection to my husband. Was it historical? The truth was Griffin hadn't prepared a cappuccino for me since this ordeal started.

Later that night, I heard Griffin rap on my door. He leaned on the doorframe. Was he waiting for an invitation? He slid down and sat right on the threshold.

"I just want to thank you for tonight. I know you put it all together. Thanks for the presents."

I had found him a flannel shirt that was blue and green and looked very similar to the one that I had appropriated from him years ago. At a different time, this would've been viewed as a sentimental gift. I had also given him a blue-checked shirt from Charlie. He liked the kind with a pocket for his pen.

"I'm sorry that I made that crack about the guest room. You've done a nice job. I love the paintings. The watercolors really go together." He looked around the room.

"Thanks. I guess this is the best of birthdays and the worst of birthdays."

"How's that?"

"Your daughter is safe and sober, but your wife is sleeping in the guest room."

"I would do it all the same way again," he said. He was still so damn limber, standing up in one fluid motion. He closed the door. I heard the floor creak and the sound of our bedroom door closing. Separating us even more.

ॐ

Several nights later we were eating takeout from VERT. We had become one of those couples who rarely talked over a meal. We were stumbling through a polite fog of silence. Occasionally, it would be interrupted by cordial exchanges covered up by good manners.

"Did James cook this? He has come a long way."

"I'll tell him. Can you pass the salt, please?"

"Sure." I put down my fork. "Would you mind if I took a few days off and went to see Reggie and Elle?" Even my questions were timid.

"I think that would be a great idea."

ॐ

We all decided to congregate at Elle's Connecticut home. Dual incomes had given her a lifestyle to which she had been just waiting to become accustomed. After dinner and cocktails, we settled into the business of my fractured life.

"I have a question for you both. Who do you put first? Your children or your husband and marriage?"

They answered at the same time. But with different answers. Each was confident.

"I put my children first," Reggie said. "Dave understands that. They are part of me."

"I put Robbie and my marriage first," Elle said. "I want my children to see a loving marriage. I think that's the best gift we can give them. What do you say?"

"I have always put Griffin first. I told Linda that as an only child I wanted Charlie to know the world did not revolve around her. I wanted her to see a healthy working marriage. Griffin puts Charlie first. I guess in some ways that is okay because I am gone a lot."

"I have always seen Griffin as the caregiver. But it sounds like he hasn't taken very good care of you lately." Concern filled Reggie's voice.

"He is my life. What am I without him? Why is it that couples talk about whether to have children or not, but no one ever discusses parenting techniques before they have children? I spent years reading about how to be a good parent. I didn't think I needed the ones on how to be a good partner." I paused. "If Griffin is not going to ask for forgiveness for putting Charlie in rehab without my knowledge, what does that say about his respect for me as a parent?"

"He's gone a little crazy. I've tried talking to him, Bailey," Reggie said in her compassionate voice.

"Are you still sleeping in the guest room?" Elle asked.

I nodded.

"Are you kidding me? You haven't slept together since this thing started? Griffin is fifty. He's not dead."

"Elle! Bailey feels bad enough."

"Reggie, that's why I pay her the big bucks," I laughed. "I mean, what's next? Griffin is going to have Charlie's wedding without me because I don't approve of the destination?"

We didn't solve my problems. We never solved problems. But we enjoyed being together. We laughed a lot, drank too much, and forgot we were adults for just a little bit.

I went to bed that evening thinking about Griffin. Would our collective memories carry us through these choppy waters?

I went by to check on my dad. Jeri, his nurse, told me I had just missed Griffin. For once I was relieved. I unburdened my soul. I had found the joy of being in his company. I could honestly say his dementia was not my fault, unlike just about everything else in my life now.

I texted Henry and decided to stop in at NOIR. I took my customary place at the back booth of the restaurant.

"You're just in time to sample the Dover sole. It's beautiful. I am featuring it with a blueberry orzo."

I figured I could eat with Henry, do some work in my office, and duck into my bedroom and avoid any unpleasant exchanges with Griffin.

"I can't visit long because I am preparing for a full house tonight," Henry told me. "What's on your mind? I hope you and Griffin have figured things out. I can feel the strain. I need you to be okay."

"Let me ask you a quick question. Who do you put first? Your children? Or Lea and your marriage?" I asked.

His answer was quick. "Lea. She puts up with all my shit. I didn't want to just marry a mother for my kids. I wanted a partner. Like you and Griffin. Do you want a piece of pistachio cheesecake to go?"

"When have you ever known me to turn down food?" I kept our conversation about food. I hated that so many people were counting on us to make it.

ঞ

"Charlotte will be leaving us soon. Have you thought any more about your living situation? I don't want all this to come as a surprise to her, threatening her sobriety," Linda said.

"We are going to do everything we can to support her. We are under the same roof. I think that's all Charlie needs to know. I don't want it to be her job to fix us. That's our job."

"Bae and her precious privacy," Griffin scoffed.

"I want her to have her own life. Not be so invested in ours."

And so it went. I sometimes wondered what we could agree on. It didn't seem like anything.

ঞ

A week later, things started differently. Linda allowed us to sit in silence for what seemed to be most of the session.

"Charlotte is due to leave in a week. I would like to know how you're feeling about each other. Griffin?"

"I don't have a lot to say. Bae thinks she has a clue about what's going on with Charlotte. I bet if you added up all the time she has actually spent with our daughter, it would add up to about a year."

"Fuck." I closed my mouth before I uttered, "you." It might've all been over. Instead, I said, "If you are going to list all my transgressions as a mother, don't bother. They run through my mind on a nightly basis. I'm a little sick and tired of you always saying you are putting Charlie first. I think you're just guilty because you know that the Sprite was drinking on your watch." I was instantly sorry.

"You can bet I will always put her first. You're jealous. You can have whatever you want. Except for Charlotte." He got up and left, leaving Linda and me exchanging stunned looks.

That afternoon I was boxing up bottles of wine and booze. I was amazed by how much wine and alcohol we had acquired. I took one box out to my office. I was going to keep it out there from now on. Griffin came home.

"What are you doing?"

"Removing temptation. Taking all the alcohol out to my office. Do you want to grab a box and help?"

"Sure."

The closet door was ajar with the other boxes. Griffin looked around. "Wow. Is this shelving new?"

"Yes. Phil Richards came over and put new shelving in and a bigger refrigerator, which required upgraded electrical and locks on the door."

"I would've helped. Are those all your awards? Have you redecorated out here too?"

I didn't tell him that the awards were just a few of the ones I had received.

"They are just paper and other people's opinion. When I repainted everything else looked a little tired. I would really like to add a second floor for customer orders, things I find at estate sales, and samples, but that's like building a new house. I'm a little tapped out."

"No need for any false modesty. I told you I would contribute to the Sprite's bedroom."

"That's okay. I didn't mean anything by it."

"All that's missing is a stove."

"You forget. I don't cook."

Griffin laughed. It felt like a meteor sailing across the sky and landing on my heart. His laughter had been dormant for so long I had forgotten what it sounded like. It made me miss him even more. He took a seat on the other side of my desk.

"I'll give you a key to my office and the closet," I said.

I couldn't tell whether he was paying any attention to me. He had shifted in the chair and adopted a serious expression. It scared me. I realized whatever he was about to say was something so bad he couldn't bring it in the house.

"Bae, I don't think we're going to make it." He stopped. He looked me dead in the eyes. He must've noticed the color drain from my face. He added, "I'm not going back to Linda." He got up and left, closing the door behind him gently.

My insides exploded the violent way you would crack open a pomegranate to get to all the flavorful seeds. I looked around. Everything looked the same except everything was different.

No. He couldn't just waltz in here and say, "I don't think we're going to make it, Bae." We couldn't *not* make it. Griffin was my "before anyone else." He was supposed to be my "after everyone else" too. Wasn't this just domestic turbulence? I wouldn't abdicate my life without a fight. Parenting 101: our child needed both parents. If I had to fight with Griffin from now until one of us surrendered, then that's what I would do. Fuck Griffin and his soliloquies on family. Soliloquies don't show our daughter what a real marriage looks like. Soliloquies don't get you through this shit.

ঙ

Over the next few days we were cordial to one another, as if not wanting to offend. The day arrived when we were to get Charlie. I was nervous. What would her life look like now? She was so young to be "living one day at a time," marking days by chips rather than simply days. I had seen a drawer with all of Henry's chips. The most important was the white one. Henry had two white chips.

We had agreed to take the same car. A united front and all that. Over dinner, Charlie regaled us with stories. They were sprinkled with humor. It was good to have laughter back in the house. At dinner, she described the weak and tepid coffee: "I mean, why even bother?" The plastic mattresses: "It's bad enough that they were stained and smelly, but every time you move, the plastic crunches. Why were they plastic? Because so many people have thrown their guts up. I don't want to know how many." And the harshest criticism she leveled at the food: "Even the rats are malnourished." I caught glimpses of Griffin, who was enjoying her stories immensely. He took his bites slowly so he didn't have to look down at his plate to take his eyes away from her. I got up from the table briefly. I handed her a pen.

"Write that down," I said.

"You think it's funny?"

"Sprite, no need for false modesty with us," Griffin chimed in.

⁂

At bedtime we retreated to our separate quarters. Charlie came into the guest room to tell me good night.

"Oh my God, Bae, did you redecorate in here? Is this your room now?" She walked all the way in and looked around before settling on the twin bed closest to the door. I occupied the one that most resembled my side of the bed in our room.

"They say you should sleep in your guest room every few years to see what your guests experience. Your room inspired me." I stopped. I was wrestling with how to answer her other question. The difficult one. The one I didn't have an answer to. I decided I could talk to her and give her something else tonight: my humanness.

"You're always talking about our epic love. Well, Charlie, this is what it looks like." I noticed she kicked off her shoes and stuck her feet under the duvet cover as if I were about to tell her a bedtime story. She even pulled the pillow out to rest her head.

"There were times your dad and I weren't even in the same house, much less the same zip code or state. I was even married to somebody else. This isn't bad, Charlie. Epic love is not about never having rough patches—it's about getting through those rough patches together. It's about sticking it out when you are in the middle of something hard, but you do it because you're together. Being a parent, it's almost 'transactional love.' You take that kid here, I'll take this one there, and it's hard. It's like Mount Kilimanjaro. It is a struggle to get to the top. When you get there, the air is so thin you can barely breathe and you wonder how you're going to make it. Then you look out and you witness this incredible view. This life. Our life. It's about holding on when there's nothing to hold onto except a mutual determination to get through it together. It isn't about love. It's about endurance. This is what you call 'happily ever after.'" I wondered if I said that for her benefit or mine. I looked over and she was sleeping. I turned off the lights. The next morning, I noticed that the duvet cover had been pulled up around her shoulders. Did she get cold during the night or did Griffin come in to check on his girls?

For the next few weeks, we all settled into our respective routines. Separately. Things did not revert to the way they were. We were establishing a new normal. Griffin was still on edge. I could tell he was keeping a watchful eye on Charlie. For her part, Charlie was a bit more guarded and tentative around Griffin. Their relationship had been fractured. It wasn't beyond repair, but time, I prayed, would work its magic for them as it had for Griffin and me over so many years. I would see flashes of their old ease with one another and then they would remember. It made me sad. Griffin and I made an effort when Charlie was around to be "normal," whatever that was. I hoped time would repair our relationship too. I would touch my worn tattoo, *repair*, that I had gotten after Elliott, when Griffin and

I were mending our relationship. The only relationship that had a semblance of recognition to me was between Charlie and me. When she gave me her first eye roll, I actually smiled. How could something so mundane bring a smile to my face when in the past it had annoyed me so much? I was grateful to see it and the accompanying "Oh, Bae."

I was in my office working on a proposal for a small university in Maine, which I was going to present to them in a few days. I heard a gentle knock on my door and my heart seized. I was petrified it was Griffin, ready to resume the last conversation we had here. His words, "Bae, I don't think we're going to make it," kept reverberating in my heart. But it was Charlie. She sat down in the chair and threw her leg over the arm. I hated this posture. It was in a lackadaisical fashion that reminded me of a slacker. The words *pick your battles* were tattooed into my tongue. I kept my mouth shut.

"Hi, Mom." She waited. "Mom."

I stopped what I was doing. This must be her amends to me. I closed my laptop. I noticed she had a notebook with her. Was she about to launch into a speech she had prepared? I realized in that moment she was as much a mystery to me as the day she was born.

"I saved you for last," she started. She grabbed a few strands of her hair between her index finger and thumb. This had always been a nervous habit of hers. I recognized it. Instead of scolding her that her hair was going to fall out, I found her habit endearing. I smiled at her. I wanted to make her feel at ease. Make her feel as if whatever she said was safe.

"I'm sorry, Bae. I'm sorry I tricked you and Dad with the drug tests. I'm sorry I have been so mean and sneaky. I'm sorry I threw you under the bus about the tequila."

"I should've never put you in that position, Charlie."

"Dad was just acting so crazy."

"Yes. But I knew why he was acting crazy. His past with his parents and Henry were coming back to bite him. You are the thing he loves best in this world. I should've told him."

"That's pretty much what he said. He's still a little wacko. Here's the rest of your amends. The beginning of my memoir." She thrust her Moleskine at me. "Read it."

I put on the tortoiseshell-and-bamboo reading glasses I had begun needing. I read the first two sentences and glanced up and met her gaze.

"From the first two sentences, you really get the picture your mother is a bitch. This is some amends, Charlie."

She laughed.

"The bitch has a sense of humor. Besides, you've just started reading."

"Is that supposed to make me feel better? Because I'm not feeling it." I wanted to say that she should read my joke memoir, *How to Live With a Junior Terrorist*, but we were still in the early amends stage of our own relationship. Amends. Repair. I was torn with not wanting to read it and reading it until I had consumed every word.

"You will have to change the title. *Smashed* is taken by another teenager who's written her memoir on alcohol addiction." She cocked her head and raised her eyebrows.

"I have a whole library under my bed of memoirs written on addiction," I told her.

"Which bed?"

"The guest room. You're free to borrow them."

"Thanks, Bae."

"Hey, do you want to go to Maine with me in a couple of days and be my assistant? It's beautiful up there."

She laughed. "Uncle Henry and Dad told me they loved me and you're offering me a job. Typical. I asked Uncle Henry about a job as hostess."

"You and your uncle are best buds. I'm offering you the glamour of traveling."

"And schlepping around your stuff. Don't you think that's a lot of togetherness for us?"

"Just think of it as research material. It didn't turn out so badly for the author of *The Devil Wears Prada.*"

❧

In the end she capitulated and worked for me for the rest of the summer. We had fun in Maine, except for one unexpected incident. I was coming out of the bathroom in my underwear so she could take a shower. She stopped dead in her tracks, pointing at my hip bone.

"Is that a tattoo?" She was walking toward me and I backed away. I was grateful for my "granny underwear," as Elle described some of my cotton underwear.

"Don't invade my personal space, Charlotte."

"How long have you had it? What does it say?"

"The stupidity of youth. Long before you were born. It is the word *repair*. After all that mess with Elliott I was suffering from a broken heart. Your dad told me that it wasn't broken, it just needed to be repaired." I touched it. It reminded me of the lesson I needed to be reminded of in this very moment. "The bathroom is yours," I said, ending the conversation. Charlie was having none of it.

"Does Dad have one?"

"You'll have to ask him yourself."

"Is it your name?"

"You'll have to ask him."

"That means he does." She was clearly delighted with herself and her investigative abilities. I heard her humming in the shower, and I guessed I could suffer a little humiliation if it made my daughter happy.

❧

Over the next couple of months, the new contours of our home life emerged. Charlie and I would travel with my job. She made a good assistant. I enjoyed her company. She learned to appreciate not only what her dad and Henry did but also my profession.

"You're a rock star, Bae. I like how you put designs together. I see your fabrics and sketches in your office, but they really come alive when we get into the space. You are really good at your job," she said, as if her pronouncement was the crowning achievement of my career. In a way it was.

"Thanks, Sprite," I said as we were sipping our cappuccinos, waiting for the plane to board.

"I still prefer the way Dad likes to travel," she said. Clearly, she had inherited his propensity to stay at five-star establishments.

"It's good for you to see that not all hotels have bellmen and concierges. I've been meaning to tell you—you've really done a good job. You're a natural with my Instagram."

"Duh, that's not saying much, Bae."

After a trip, we would arrive home and Griffin would have dinner waiting for us. We looked like one of those normal families. But each night we retired to our separate quarters. Griffin and I had not revisited what he had said in my office before Charlie came home. He and I adopted an affable demeanor similar to the aunt you see only at Christmas time.

The relationships that did seem to spring back with ease were with our friends. The Four Musketeers resumed hanging out together. I noticed that the three of them were all invested in Charlie's sobriety, offering to take her to and pick her up from meetings. It made me happy that she had found her little village, as I had with Reggie and Elle. And Sally. Sally and I had stitched our frayed relationship back together. We even started walking again. I was grateful that she was able to forgive some of the ugly moments.

"My daughter still prefers you to me," Sally said one morning.

"I don't think you have anything to worry about. I'm not going to be winning any Mother's Day awards for having a daughter in rehab before she acquired a driver's license."

"Lucy loves the way you dress," Sally told me.

I had started wearing lounge pants and a tank top at night. I had discovered these cool kimonos I could throw over my rather drab ensemble to create something with a little panache. Some of my favorite vintage stores carried some funky ones that pushed the limits with my family, like the pink one with purple, orange, and black dragons.

"Do you have a side hustle that we don't know about?" Griffin had asked good-naturedly over dinner one night. He did everything that way these days. Good-naturedly. I couldn't tell if he was trying or had just given up.

I was wearing my favorite blue, yellow, and green one that reminded me of confetti one night when Charlie came home from Lucy's. She sat down next to me. She took my hand and it frightened me.

Reflexively, I pulled my hand back. It was as if by breaking our connection I was also severing whatever she was about to tell me. She took my hand back. I didn't think we had ever been this close. She cleared her throat like it pained her as much as it would me.

"Mom, I need you to do something for me," she said. "I need you to forgive Dad. I've been trying. I really have. But it's really hard seeing you and Dad not together."

"Have you been talking to your uncle? This is something he would tell me."

"Yes. We both depend on you to be rock solid. He asked me how things were going. I told him."

"Henry has no business putting you in the middle of this."

"He said you would say that."

"I'm glad you have each other."

That was the easy part. I took a deep breath and ventured into a conversation I didn't want to have with my daughter.

I leaned back into the sofa. Getting comfortable. Charlie got up and sat on the ottoman, where I had propped my legs and closed my computer.

"Charlie, you can't ask me to forgive Dad. That's like asking Henry to do your amends. Forgiveness works a lot like an amends. It works between the two people."

She nodded. Conversation faltered. I noticed she had been biting her nails. A nervous habit. Like me. Charlie reached over and squeezed my hand. She was giving me her flimsy strength. I loved her so much in that moment.

"Are you guys getting a divorce?"

Tears welled up in my eyes unexpectedly. Tears welled up in her eyes.

"I don't know. I hope not," I answered honestly. I thought about what I would say next.

"This is tough. Here's the thing about forgiveness though, Charlie. It's like a green banana. It isn't good to forgive someone before you're ready. That doesn't do you or the other person any good. By forgiving prematurely, it can turn into a grudge. But forgiveness also has an expiration date. If you wait too long, it's like a brown banana. The person you need to forgive . . . well, they might not care anymore." Was that where Griffin and I were? He didn't care anymore. He had already given up on us? "But after you offer forgiveness, you must also be willing to forget. And sometimes that may be the hardest thing of all." I had made that error of not forgetting. She got up and threw herself into my arms. I was comforting her. In her own way she was offering me the same thing.

"I love you, Mom," she whispered in my ear. I don't know when, if ever, she had said it first.

"I love you too, Charlie." We wiped our eyes.

About that time, Griffin walked through the door. He surveyed the scene.

"Everything all right here?" he asked.

"Just hormones, Dad." Charlie was no idiot. She knew how to make her father scamper from the room.

ॐ

A few nights later, I found myself alone downstairs—a rare occasion. Griffin had turned in early because he had relieved one of the bartenders, and Charlie frequently turned in early because that was what she had become accustomed to at rehab.

I took the opportunity to go out to my office and fix myself an adult beverage. Griffin had taught me how to make it. He called it a "fig smash." It called for Larceny bourbon with muddled mint, freshly squeezed lemon juice, and a fig simple syrup topped with sparkling wine. I loved the twist of fig. Griffin was still the best mixologist I knew. In fact, I was on my second. It felt good. My mind hadn't really strayed from the conversation that Charlie and I had. I took my drink upstairs, leaving my computer open. I noticed the light was still on in Griffin's room. Was that the way I was referring to it now? I made a pit stop to spray a little perfume for good measure. I hated brown bananas.

I knocked on the door and cracked it open.

"Griffin, may I come in?" I waited.

"Sure."

I opened the door. I was prepared to walk over to my closet to retrieve an article of clothing and put my drink down. Something unexpected caught my attention.

"Are you sleeping on my side of the bed now?" Thoughts swirled around in my head.

"In the beginning, it smelled like you. Then I just got used to it," he said. His admission was endearing. I walked over to my side and sat down on the edge of the bed.

"Griffin," I started. The expanse of his name contained years. It contained memories. It contained milestones. It contained love. Lots of love. It contained everything that was most precious in my life.

"Griffin, I don't want to be angry anymore. I'm so tired of being angry." I smiled, even though I was very nervous. In turn, he gave me his nervous smile. Even this recognition brought me comfort. I breathed in and out. And then I leaned in to kiss him. Not forcibly, but gently as an act of kindness. He returned my affection. Then just as quickly, he stopped. He pushed me away and adjusted the sleeve on my kimono that had fallen off my shoulder. He traced a finger to his lips. Committing it to memory. The way he had at Martha's Vineyard. Before he had rejected me. Before my domestic turbulence with Elliott. Before Griffin broke my heart. I adjusted myself. I felt his ankles cross under the covers.

"We need to talk, Bae."

NOW

"Did you discuss Tucker Landon's statement with your husband?" Floyd asked.

"No. There are just things I know to be true. I have faith in Griffin."

"I get that. But how do we explain the contradiction? That brings us back to Charlie. You're still not sure about her." I couldn't be sure about the hoodies. I could tell Floyd was frustrated. He knew I would take the blame for my daughter. I could render his only loss in the courtroom.

Before I could think about it, it was time to meet Gabriel. He had come to Atlanta to go over possible designs for his restaurant in Rio de Janeiro. I was to meet him at his hotel suite. He had promised a surprise.

When I rang the doorbell of Gabriel's suite, he answered the door himself. I was immediately aroused by the smells coming from inside. "Because you can't come to Brazil, I brought Brazil to you. I always travel with my personal chef. She has prepared lunch for us. Complete with Caipirinha, which is an alcoholic beverage of Pinga and lime."

"I never drink during a presentation," I said, putting my bag down and walking over to the dining room that was set for two.

"This, my dear Bailey, is nonnegotiable." Gabriel flashed his winning smile. "Carolina, we are ready." A beautiful woman in a white chef jacket came and disappeared. She reappeared, bringing drinks and a carafe of water. I pulled out my notes.

Gabriel held a chair for me.

"For starters, I love your location. I don't want to clutter it up with a lot of unnecessary color or stuff. Your home country is the best decorator. My idea is to use the richness of your country's colors." Before I continued, Carolina brought in the first dish.

"Coalho. Cheese squares." Gabriel took one and then a sip of his cocktail. Carolina also brought tapioca, which I learned was very plentiful in the rainforest.

It was obvious that Gabriel was proud of his heritage. The cheese was delicious, and the tapioca did not resemble what we have in the States at all. There was a break between courses. I used it as an opportunity to show Gabriel the pictures of these funky white light fixtures that looked like the balloon of a hot-air balloon. Gabriel smiled.

"I also have these flat light fixtures for the walls that look like starbursts with mirrors in the middle that can reflect the vista of the breathtaking landscape. Speaking of which, you have magnificent views of Atlanta from your perch here."

He motioned for me to get up and walk to the windows with him. Even though we were in Buckhead, you could see all of downtown. He walked up behind me as if to see what caught my attention.

"What is troubling you? Where is my jovial Bailey?"

"A murder rap will kill any joviality. No pun intended."

He laughed as we walked back to the table. He pointed to the pictures of the light fixtures. "These are perfect. Another Caipirinha?"

"No, Gabriel!" I laughed. After a time, Carolina appeared with a second course. It was served in a clay pot.

"Moqueca. A fish stew. It is served with a plate of tucuma, which is a fruit typically found in the north."

I watched Gabriel to see which utensil he picked up. There was a large spoon but also a fork.

"Since we're among friends, why not?" And he took the spoon and dived into the stew with gusto. The flavors were so full-bodied. "What do you think so far? The coffee is brewing. Did you not like the drink?"

"The drink is delightful. It is the middle of the day that I have a problem with—and driving home," I explained.

Carolina brought in a silver pot of coffee. You could smell the richness.

She poured me a cup. The aroma permeated every olfactory gland I possessed. I noticed how beautiful she was. Beauty right under Gabriel's perfect nose.

"That's why I have a private plane. I travel with my own coffee beans and grinder. I want to have a fresh cup of coffee whenever possible. Whenever I want."

"You're used to getting whatever you want," I said, looking at one of the wealthiest men in the world. He smiled.

"Not everything. Look at you. You're immune to my charm."

"Not at all. I'm just much more attracted to your money."

This solicited spontaneous laughter from Gabriel.

"These look like chocolate truffles," I suggested.

"Brigadeiro," Gabriel announced. "Which are exactly chocolate truffles."

The pairing of the coffee and the chocolate was delectable. It was the perfect way to end a perfect meal. We took our coffees to the sofa. We talked casually.

Carolina brought in a stainless steel attaché case and put it on the coffee table between Gabriel and me. I was immediately curious. What would he carry around in a stainless steel attaché? Diamonds? Some other priceless gems? Gabriel punched in the memorized code on the lock. He carefully and proudly opened the case. Sea glass. Lots of it.

"Gabriel, you are full of surprises. May I touch it?"

Gabriel fanned out his hand for me to study it. I was impressed. I could tell it delighted him.

"It's so beautiful. My daughter used to collect this when she was a child. Hers isn't as beautiful as yours."

"My dear Bailey, some things, like true beauty, require age and weathering."

"I didn't know you were a philosopher too. I just thought you were a pretty face," I joked. I took the pieces out and rearranged them in the words *sea glass*. He studied it for a few minutes.

"What do you think?" I asked him.

"You surprised me. I thought, for sure, this would be 'Ipanema.' But I love it. You're taking the color of the water and incorporating it with my collection of sea glass. Thank goodness you've left me a few pieces." He laughed again and turned serious. "Have they still not found the killer of your ex-husband?"

I debated about whether to tell him any more.

"Some new evidence has come to light but I'm not sure it will be completely helpful."

Gabriel studied my face, and I wiped my mouth to make sure I did not have any stray chocolate crumbs.

"It's your husband, isn't it? He did it."

"Why would you even go there?"

"I am not bragging, but you're the only woman my charms have not worked on. Not even when you are trying to land my account. Don't get me wrong, Bailey. I respect you. You are a driven career woman who just happens to be devoted to the man she married. You would protect him."

We were about to say our goodbyes when he continued. "My parents have been married for over fifty years. I find that kind of devotion extremely sexy. Beautiful. But be careful the prosecution doesn't use it against you."

I left thinking about what Gabriel had said about how real beauty requires age and weathering.

THEN
SIX YEARS AGO

We need to talk," Griffin said again.

I didn't want to hear it or "I don't think we're going to make it." We were adults. We might even be considered middle age. I noticed, for the first time, strands of gray hair had invaded his longish brown hair. Had this season of separation been so long that he had acquired gray hair? Would he just propose that we rock on until Charlie leaves home? Couples did that every day. It was a half-assed life. I would choose the half-assed life with Griffin over fireworks and terms of endearment any day.

We looked at each other. As if we were surveying strangers. I needed to be ready for whatever he said to me. But I was afraid. Terrified even.

"Okay." I nodded.

"I need to say some things. Some of the things I said to you were all about my projection. Things I wish I had told my parents but never got the chance. I'm sorry." This didn't sound like Griffin at all.

"Wait a minute. Have you been seeing a therapist?"

"Yes. I talked to Linda's partner. That was one reason I didn't want us to go back. She wouldn't see me unless we were no longer her patients. She helped me see things from your point of view. I realized I acted unilaterally. That was wrong. I stopped putting you first and started putting Charlotte first. I don't know when that happened. When you told me you put me first, it broke my heart."

I stopped him. "This isn't all on you. I abdicated my role to you and Henry and Lea. Even to Tabatha. I gave up. I was a crummy mom. Part of me knew you were putting Charlotte first—that's what allowed me to be gone all the time. I knew she was in good hands with you, Goose." I stopped.

"I'm sorry I hurt you. You aren't a crummy mom. You are a role model. I think I have enough space for both you and Charlie. If that's okay? I love you, Bae," he said, and then he smiled. A real smile.

I could have said so many things: "It's about damn time," "I've been waiting." Instead, I repurposed the words he said to me so long ago.

"Always did. Always have. Always will."

"Thank you." And then he leaned in and pulled me to him. He kissed me gently. With tenderness. Even this surprised me. Considering our time apart, I thought we would be fast and furious, eager to make up for lost time. Griffin kept his gaze fixed on me. I kept mine on him. I was so grateful just to be with him. We had been together countless times. And yet perhaps this time was one of the most important. This time marked one of the greatest breaches in our relationship. Our fusing back together had been about faith and forgiveness. About desire and devotion. About supplication and grace. I wanted to consecrate this moment. At the altar of all things sacred.

I woke up on the sofa with a blanket covering me and Charlie standing over me. I adjusted my eyes from sleep to wide awake.

"You fell asleep on the sofa again, Bae," Charlotte said. But my mind was on the blanket covering me. Had Griffin grown tired of waiting for me and found me asleep and covered me? I remember sometime during the night I had said, "I need to go downstairs and charge my computer."

"Why should tonight be any different?" Griffin kidded. "You can take that dragon kimono with you."

"I'm surprised after tonight it's not your favorite." We had laughed.

I propelled myself to the present. I pulled myself up to meet my daughter's gaze. She came around and gave me a hand up.

"Thanks, Charlie. Let's go put on the coffee. How do you feel about pancakes? I will even put some butterscotch morsels in them for you. Why don't we put blueberries in the rest for your dad? Maybe he will even make us cappuccinos."

ঌ

After breakfast Charlie got up and put her plate in the dishwasher.

"I just need to make some notes and then I am going to a meeting."

"Is everything all right?" I asked.

"I like this meeting. Mom, I wrote some more of my memoir. If you want to read it, it's on my bed."

"What about me, Sprite? I think I am going to hang around here for just a little while," Griffin said, looking at me and smiling.

ঌ

I wanted to see what new revelation Charlie had written about me. But instead, I found her diary open. These were her private thoughts. I toyed with reading them, but curiosity got the best of me. Today's entry read "This is all I know."

The door of the guest room was open, and it looked like Mom hadn't slept there. Dad's door was closed. Sleeping on the sofa was nothing new for Mom, but something was different. Mom seemed lighter. Easier. In fact, our whole house had a different vibe to it. Had Mom forgiven Dad? Had everything somehow gotten put back into place? Realigned? Were the bones of the house actually my parents?

"Griffin?" Mom called. "You better get in here before your daughter puts butterscotch chips in all the pancakes."

Dad looked like he'd gotten caught doing something. He gave his goofy smile. The one he flashed when he was about to say, "I love you." He never cared that he looked goofy.

"How about I make a round of cappuccinos?" Dad proposed.

Dad got busy. The sound of the familiar steamer whistled. I always loved the way he made cappuccinos. Mom said he made the best in the country. I tended to believe her on this topic.

I sat down at the island waiting for breakfast. Mom put an end to that.

"Charlie, why don't you set the table." I gave her an eye roll. Not because I was perturbed. I knew she was expecting it. She even smiled back when she saw me do it. Dad finished the first cappuccino. I reached out.

"I think Mom gets this one." I watched their handoff. The fake out. I had seen it a million times. Their playful nature. The way their fingers touched . . . Just for a moment . . . As if no one was looking. To an observer nothing looked amiss. Dad finished with my cappuccino. I saluted him and took a sip. Mom plated the food and put it on the table.

"Do we not have any mint to decorate the plate?" Dad asked.

"When did you turn into Henry?" she quipped.

All this was perfectly normal. Maybe that's the point. I hadn't even noticed until now. This morning things had been normal. We had just been living in this other way for so long I had forgotten what our normal looked like. I had taken it for granted. I don't know if Mom had forgiven Dad. Maybe it didn't matter. What Mom said was right. It was between two people. We had somehow gotten back to the place that I recognized. Uncle Henry's pancakes and Dad's cappuccinos were my favorite breakfast. I had decided in that moment to go to a meeting. The real truth was part of my recovery was gratitude. Gratitude for each day that I remained sober. Today I was grateful for my parents. They had given me a normal day.

A few weeks later Charlie knocked on our bedroom door.

"Lucy and her family have asked me to go to the beach with them for fall break. I really want to go. There are meetings at the beach. I have already checked."

Griffin and I looked at one another. We had learned the hard way not to answer instantly.

"You need to have Sally call me."

The next morning, Sally told me about the conditions. No boys. No liquor. I thought Charlie had earned it after the summer of us working together. We gave Charlie the green light. Griffin had other ideas.

"You realize we haven't gone away just the two of us since Charlie was born? I think it is high time we rectify that. I tentatively booked a place in the mountains waiting for your okay."

I laughed. We were acting so grown-up and doing things bilaterally.

"I don't know if I see us as mountain people," I said. Griffin quickly pulled up the website and assuaged all my worries. This was a five-star resort with opulent accommodations in the mountains of Virginia. I laughed. "I forgot how you travel."

"One of the up-and-coming chefs works there. The Sprite has clued me in on how you two travel."

"I think she inherited your 'five-star accommodation' gene." We laughed.

Griffin was right. This place was just delightfully decadent, complete with afternoon tea.

We were having dinner one night. Greg, the chef, came out and chatted with us and recommended the magret duck with a blueberry lemon thyme jam, in a veal demi-glace reduction, Swiss chard, and sweet corn. The jam's sweetness really brought out the succulent flavor of the duck. If there were food gods, they had certainly answered our prayers that night. I could tell that Griffin was relaxed because he ordered a cognac.

"Question. What was the high point of your year last year?" Griffin asked.

"It's so unlike you to be so reflective," I told him.

"Just answer the question. And I mean the previous year, not the one we have just been living."

"That's easy. Designing Charlie's bedroom for her and her liking it," I said. The smile came from the inside where all good memories reside.

"That's the right answer." He reached in his sports jacket and pulled out a little box and put it before me.

"Is this a ring box? Have you been cheating on me?" I still hadn't reached for it.

"No. What is it with you and ring boxes?"

I laughed. Inside was nestled an exquisite ring. It was a rectangular-shaped amethyst with peridots on either side encased in a beautiful gold setting. I loved it instantly.

"May I? How did you do this?" I slipped it on and marveled at how unique it was.

"Behind any jewelry purchase lurks Elizabeth and Reggie," he said. "They said you deserved it for being so low-maintenance and putting up with me. They said to tell you that you have the right to use it as an instrument against me if I get out of hand again." He laughed. "Apparently Elle went to school with this jewelry designer who has quite the following. Her name is Brent. When we spoke on the phone my idea was to have the peridot in the middle, but she convinced me to reverse it because she had this beautiful amethyst. She texted me pictures. I've been working on this for a while. You may have to consider this part of your Christmas present," Griffin laughed.

"I love it. So, no matching earrings for Christmas?" I laughed.

"When I told her your favorite peridot and diamond earrings, that's when she convinced me to do the amethyst so it wouldn't look too matching. I know what you say about that and letting the experts do their job. I called the girls soon after we got back together. I wanted to have something made that reminded you of the joy between you and Charlie but also you and me. That we had made it through this ordeal together. It serves as a reminder to never to take us for granted again." He was serious when he said it. I took his hand in mine with the newly minted ring on it.

"My sentimental husband."

"I've decided forgiveness is the greatest gift you can give someone. I was so stubborn. Holding fast to my conviction that I knew what was best. I came so close to losing the thing I value the most. Our family. I'm so ashamed. Thank you for forgiving me."

We walked to one of the sofas and sat by the fire. It was cool in the mountains. We each ordered another drink and were enjoying each other's company when an older couple sat across from us.

"Are you on your honeymoon? We came here on our honeymoon and have been coming ever since," the woman told us.

I couldn't suppress my laughter. Was it because I'd had too much to drink or because we had been on the brink of divorce a few months beforehand?

"We have been married almost seventeen years. But I feel luckier today than the day we married. I wish our daughter were here. She would roll her eyes."

The couple bid us a good night as my cell phone was ringing. It was Charlie.

"You're where?" she asked.

"We're in the mountains. We've been hiking."

This elicited laughter from Charlie as I knew it would.

"I'm sorry—I must have the wrong number."

"I'll take some pictures. We're at a five-star resort, thanks to your dad. Our bedroom is the size of our bedroom and the guest room combined."

"When do I get to go?"

Griffin couldn't stand it anymore. "You would really love this place, Sprite," as we shared the phone.

"This would definitely be a great graduation present for you, Charlie, complete with afternoon tea."

"You gotta love Dad's idea of traveling." She waited before saying, "It sounds like you're good."

"We really are," I said. I was grateful that I could give Charlie this validation. I was grateful that our family had been repaired. Then Griffin and I added the drinks to our tab and went to our room to pretend we were honeymooners.

We stayed connected and intertwined after we were done. I noticed Griffin had a new soap. I wanted to discover all the new things I had missed about him.

"Do you think we could have avoided the separation if we had taken trips together or had date nights? Henry used to tell me that I should go with you to openings. I just thought because we loved each other and were faithful, it was enough." He was running his chin along my shoulder blade.

"We were so busy reading about how to be good parents we neglected how to be good partners. I told Charlie this is what happy ever after looks like."

"I'm glad our love is sturdy. If it were flimsy, we would've never made it," Griffin said.

I drew his arms tighter around me. I thought about faith. I had to have faith that we would make it. Yet it was the hope in us that allowed my faith. Albeit shaky at times. Like Henry's and Charlie's sobriety. Hope. It is truly the gateway drug.

NOW

I was sitting at the kitchen table, thinking.

"Bae?" I jumped out of my skin. I had my hand on my cell phone and I pushed it off the table.

"Jumpy much? What's the matter?" Griffin began unpacking our dinner and plating it. He put before me a beautiful halibut with a summer tomato and olive tapenade. I waited for him to sit down. He poured a glass of Sausalito's finest.

"This should calm your nerves. And if it doesn't, this should." He bent down and kissed me.

"I think it may take more than that." But I took a sip and took a bite of the succulent fish.

"Out with it."

I noticed Griffin hadn't touched his food yet.

"Here goes," I sighed. "There's a discrepancy in the facts. The time you said you left Elliott's apartment is different from the time Lady Jane says she left. And she has a corroborating witness."

"That's impossible. The Starbucks receipt will give the time and back me up." He sounded sure. Confident.

"All I know is Lady Jane has a witness. It was a man coming in with his dog as you were leaving."

"Let me have your ring."

I reluctantly pulled it off my finger and handed it to him. I didn't know what he was about to do, and a little chill went up and down my spine. Griffin simply put it back down in front of my plate.

"What?" I asked.

"Your ring is a reminder to me not to make unilateral decisions. I didn't murder Elliott."

"I'm not sure that falls under the heading of unilateral decisions. 'I'm going to take a secretive trip to New York, go by Starbucks, and while I'm in the neighborhood, kill your ex-husband." I slipped the ring back on my finger before he changed his mind.

"I may not know much, but I told Floyd you would never let me take the blame. That much I know for sure." I said with conviction.

"I didn't see any damn dog."

Later in bed, Griffin had his arm around me. He kissed me. I never took these moments for granted. I could hear his heart beating.

"Thanks for having faith in me, Bae." I felt his chin, fresh with stubble, against my shoulder blade.

"Don't you know by now? I always have faith in you."

"I'd like to strangle the person who killed Elliott," he said. My mind drifted to our daughter as I pulled Griffin even closer.

THEN
FOUR YEARS AGO

Both couples of the Four Musketeers were quarreling. They seemed to have a similar problem, only in reverse. Thompson wanted to spend more time with his buddies and less time with Lucy. Bishop was upset that Charlie kept texting a couple of guys from rehab. Charlie did seem to text quite a bit with a guy named Desi. Before I talked to Charlie, I talked to the expert on rehab relationships, my brother Henry.

"That's really not unusual. It is very similar to AA itself. People in the same boat with you. Dealing with the same issues and the same desires."

The way he said desires made it sound sinister. It was a Thursday afternoon and I had just flown in from Chicago. I had been summoned by Russell Sanders, the guy who bought the restaurant from Mac. He wanted me to "refresh" my design.

"Charlie talks about Desi often. Do you have any details on this guy? Where he lives, that kind of thing? I can see why Bishop is a little jealous," I said.

"Nothing her mother wants to hear." Henry chuckled.

"Is he that bad?" I asked.

"I think he was. He's cleaned up his act just like the rest of us." He stopped. "All I know is that he lives in New York and went to rehab to pacify his mom."

"That's interesting. Charlie was accepted to New York University, and she is dying to go there for their writing program. You think the two are connected?"

"I have no idea. But I wouldn't be getting a monogram 'Bishop and Charlie forever.' I'm still trying to pry Maggie away from this fraternity boy she likes."

"What's wrong with the frat boy?"

"He's a frat boy. He will probably go to law school and practice with his dear old dad."

"Excuse me. What's wrong with that?" I sometimes did not understand my brother's logic. "I would welcome Charlie being married to an attorney to support her writing habit!" We both laughed.

"And give up on the lowly craft beer maker Bishop wants to become after college?"

"I'm just not sure my alcoholic daughter should be around a husband who makes craft beer all day long." So much could happen to Charlotte and Maggie, but it made for amusing conversation. "We're terrible," I joked.

"Hey, listen—not to change the topic here, but Griffin and I have been tossing around the idea of refurbishing NOIR. I don't want you giving away any ideas we may want to use."

"That's news to me. Griffin hasn't even mentioned it."

"FYI, I loved the richness of the purple damask in Charlie's bedroom . . ." he hinted.

"I'll keep that in mind." Ideas were already ricocheting around in my head.

THEN

FOUR YEARS AGO

One night, Charlie knocked on our door. I was reading a book written by a talented new chef. In truth, I was as much informed by these culinary geniuses as I was by mentors like Julian. Griffin was looking at a spreadsheet with numbers. Looking at spreadsheets before bed would guarantee me nightmares.

Charlie came bounding into our bedroom wearing a goofy smile. I recognized it. She had inherited it from her dad. She was happy.

"Bishop invited me to go with him to the prom!" she exclaimed, sitting on the edge of our bed.

"He didn't ask us first," Griffin said.

"Dad!" Charlie yelled, just as I said "Griffin!"

"That's not the kind of thing you have to get permission for. Tell him, Mom," she said, looking at me.

I noticed that she had been calling me Mom a great deal lately. I liked it.

"That's great. Sprite, what about Lucy? Is she going to prom?"

Lucy and Thompson had recently broken up and it had caused all sorts of drama within the ranks of the Four Musketeers. It had put a strain on Bishop and Charlie and forced them to choose sides. I tried to tell Charlie this kind of thing happens all the time. Then Charlie told me that Thompson was taking some "slutty" girl. I had baked some of Henry's cookies and offered tea and sympathy to Lucy and Sally.

"Lucy has her own problem. She is going to the prom with Steve Collins, who is a bad boy. I told her we needed to double date. Bishop and I want to keep an eye on her, but especially on Steve."

"I think that is very thoughtful," I said, and I meant it.

"Duh, Bae, someone needs to keep an eye on him. He's the kind of guy that would slip something into Lucy's drink," Charlie said. Griffin perked up. When Charlie became a teenager, Griffin had begun lecturing her on making sure she watched her drink being poured. He had seen enough of the bar scene to know that guys and girls can slip things into each other's drinks very quickly.

"Charlotte, I don't know if you need to be hanging out with him. He could slip something into *your* drink."

"Dad, I am on high alert thanks to you. I am not going to let someone like Steve do that."

"You better keep an eye on Bishop too."

Charlie got up from the bed and looked at me. "Bae, you better get control of your husband and his wild ideas."

I cracked up laughing.

ぁ

The night of the prom should have been renamed the day of the prom. Charlie and Lucy spent all day together getting their hair and nails done, and then spent the rest of the afternoon upstairs in Charlie's bedroom getting ready. I remembered the night of my prom and was glad that I had not gone through all those machinations!

Sally and Chad came over to take pictures when the boys arrived. The girls came downstairs. I immediately noticed their shoes. Charlie was wearing black Converse high-tops with white laces, and Lucy was wearing white Converse high-tops with black laces. Their footwear was the equivalent of a black-and-white cookie.

Bishop and Steve arrived separately. I took one look at Steve and could tell he had already been drinking. Sally and I exchanged worried looks. After pictures were taken, Griffin pulled Charlie aside.

"You need to be really careful. And keep an eye on Lucy," Griffin told her.

Charlie walked over to Sally with assurance. "Bishop and I have this covered."

I looked at my daughter and thought she looked so grown. They had all wanted to go to an after-party. We used Charlie's addiction to nix that idea. In a few months we would have no control over curfew, but until then, we were the "square" parents. I was surprised when Charlie didn't put up a protest.

Charlie knocked on our door at precisely a minute before curfew. She came into our room and went over to her father's side of the bed. "Do you want to smell my breath?" She breathed on him anyway. The scars of that period in our life still resurrected themselves on occasion.

"Sprite, that's okay. Did you have a good time?" Griffin asked, but I could tell he appreciated knowing she was sober. I realized parents live one day at a time, just like the addicts do.

"Bishop and I had a good time. I would say Lucy didn't have a good time except for at the end of the evening, when she and Thompson started making lovey-dovey eyes at one another. Steve was completely trashed." She got up and kissed her dad and blew me an air kiss.

"Night guys." And she went to her room.

After a few minutes I got up and noticed her door was cracked, so I went in. I sat down. She was taking a shower.

"Shit, Bae. You came into my room without knocking?"

"The door was open. I just wanted to check in."

"Can't this wait until tomorrow?"

"Nope, I don't think it can. You said Steve was trashed."

"Some guy brought some bourbon and weed. What a wretched combination."

I almost laughed. I wondered if it had been tequila if she would have had a different viewpoint.

"Good bourbon should not be mixed with anything."

"Bae, you know as well as I do it wasn't your kind of bourbon."

"You said Steve was trashed. Did he drive? How did Lucy get home?"

"Don't worry. Bishop and I drove her home. Are you going to sit there? I need to put on my nightshirt," she said, with a towel still wrapped around her. I already knew the answers to the questions I was asking her. I wanted the answers to the ones I didn't know yet. Griffin had filled her head with all sorts of romantic notions of our first time.

"Do you want me to close my eyes? These chairs I designed are so comfortable. I could sit here all night," I said. Charlie grabbed her nightshirt, went back into the bathroom, and put it on and came back out.

"So, when did you and Bishop drop Lucy off?" I looked directly at her and that's when she realized where the conversation was now heading.

"Okay. We dropped her off about an hour or so ago. We just drove around after that."

"Where did you drive around?"

"Is there something you want to know?"

"Yes, Charlie. And I am prepared to sit here until I'm satisfied."

"When did you get this mom ESP thing?" She waited before answering my question. I didn't really know the answer. In many ways I hoped I was wrong.

"How did you know? Do I look different?"

"How do I know what?" I could tell she was trying to decide if she wanted to tell me. I realized I wanted her to tell me. I also realized it was her business now.

"You tell me these things are private."

"What things?" I realized my voice had changed. Charlie's demeanor had changed. We were about to have a conversation that was serious.

"Bishop and I had sex. You can't say anything because it would make you a hypocrite."

"Are you okay? Did you use protection?" I could tell Charlie relaxed a little bit. I'm not sure I would've told my mother, but I would've told a good friend. I just wanted to be there for her because there were so many times I wasn't.

"Of course we did. We went back to Bishop's house—"

I interrupted. "I don't need details!"

"I love Bishop. He loves me. We made this decision together. I don't regret it. I'm glad Bishop was my first. He is the best."

I let out a deep breath. As casually as I entered this conversation, it was anything but. "I'm glad Charlie. You're right. I can't say anything. I am glad your dad was my first. He made it all right for me." This was the most intimate detail I had ever shared with Charlie regarding my personal life.

"I'm glad you told me. Bishop made it right for me."

This was the only detail I truly cared about. "I appreciate you telling me, Sprite." I got up to go to bed.

"Hey Mom, can you not tell Dad about this?" she asked with big eyes, and I went over to her and hugged her. It was an uncommon occurrence between us. I broke away.

"I think that can be arranged. I am not sure your dad would've wanted me telling my dad that I had sex with Goose when we did."

We both let out knowing grins. I was glad my daughter told me before anyone else.

Sleep eluded me that night. I threw on clothes and went out to my office to work. My creative muse didn't show up either. I was lost in thought. I didn't even hear the door open.

"Shit, Charlie! You scared me half to death." I watched her sit down and, as usual, throw her leg over the arm of the chair. I wondered if she was okay. "You okay? Do you want to talk about tonight?"

"I'm okay. I just couldn't sleep, and I saw the light on in your office. I was surprised."

"In the future, it's not a good idea to come out here if you think there's a burglar."

"What would a burglar want? A scrap of fabric? Really?" she joked. She was as wide awake as I was. We lapsed into silence. It was Charlie who spoke next.

"Could you not sleep because of what I told you earlier?" she asked, looking directly at me.

There were so many directions my answer could've gone. My child had just admitted that she had had sex. How does one sleep after that? I looked at the clock on my computer. It was a quarter to two in the morning. I couldn't remember the last time I was up this late.

"It just occurred to me that you are going off to college in less than three months. You are going to be on your own. Making all kinds of big and little decisions. I don't know if I have equipped you with enough decision-making tools."

"Don't make me sorry I came out here. I didn't think you would be all self-reflective at this time of night."

"This may sound crazy, but do you want a cup of Nespresso?" I offered.

She nodded. I got up to fix us both coffees. I unlocked the closet to get another sleeve of pods.

"So that's where you keep the booze," Charlie observed, as I locked the door again and started the coffee. We were silent. I gave her a cup first. She took it black, like her father. I put cream and sugar in mine to imitate a cappuccino. I raised my glass.

"This probably should be our little secret too." What kind of mother was I letting her daughter have a strong coffee at two o'clock in the morning?

"I just think about how good I had it. And then I threw it all away and became an alcoholic. I'm such a mess."

I looked at my daughter. She would always struggle with her demons. I wished I could take them away and bear them myself. I thought about Henry. I thought about Griffin and me.

"I read the beginning of your memoir. It's good, Charlie. Really. You wouldn't be *you* without your demons. They make you unique. Your demons are like an uninvited houseguest. You may be sorry that the gene showed up, but you have learned from that. And it has given you creativity. Maybe you wouldn't have this creativity or viewpoint without it. So be grateful for it. It has made you *you,*" I said. I didn't know how articulate I could be at two o'clock in the morning. I would text her the Rumi tomorrow.

"Thanks, Bae. Sometimes I don't like going to meetings. I wish I could just lead a simple life."

"No, you don't. Simple is boring. I don't think you could write like this without having experienced it."

"I know Lucy and Bishop don't drink around me anymore. I hate that I've done that to them."

"They do it because they love you." I paused. I would be no good tomorrow with all this caffeine flowing in my veins. "You know Charlie, I sometimes wish I had been a different mom. A better mom. The kind of mom you wanted."

"I can say for a fact, no you don't. Can you imagine staying home all day? Every day? With me? We would've driven each other crazy. Besides, I've watched you. I've worked with you. You are really good at what you do. I've seen swatches scattered on your desk. They don't look like anything special. But you put them on your sketch board and you create something beautiful. Here," she said, thrusting a paper at me. "My college essay—'Lessons From my Mother.'" Charlie's essay talked about how I had taught her lessons about forgiveness and how to conduct herself in business meetings. I hadn't known I needed her to say that to me, but it made me feel better.

"Thank you, Charlie. I appreciate you saying all this."

"It's true. But I wouldn't want to work for you for a living," she said, only half kidding. She got up to leave. She would be able to sleep until noon, unlike me. "Thanks for making me feel better about being an alcoholic."

"You're welcome. Every one of us face some kind of demon. Our own shit. There's no such thing as a perfect life."

The currents of change swept through our house. Things I wouldn't have predicted happened. Thompson and Lucy got back together. Bishop and Charlie broke up. I was surprised by both developments.

Thompson and Lucy were both headed to Sewanee University. Apparently, the reconciliation began around prom.

Bishop broke up with Charlie. According to Charlie, he was jealous of her relationship with Desi.

"I don't know why Bishop is so bent out of shape. Desi and I text because we are each other's support system. He is going to be going to college in New York so we will probably hang out some and go to meetings together. Bishop is going out to Arizona to learn the craft beer industry. It's like he doesn't trust me. I don't know why he can't see this is my way."

"My guess is he doesn't trust Desi. Think about it from Bishop's point of view. You and Desi have a connection. One that Bishop isn't a part of. You go to meetings together, text each other, support each other. I'm not saying that you and Bishop should stay together during college. I think you should experience the whole of college life. And not just spend all your time with Desi."

"Don't worry, Bae. I want to study, make good grades, and be able to write. I want to establish myself as a writer. No guy is going to get in the way of that."

I almost laughed. Those were exactly my thoughts heading into college. I had wanted my own name. My own reputation. My own career. I just hoped she didn't make some of the same mistakes I did.

ঞ

The first week went by fine. The second week went by okay. It was the third week that got me. My heart felt wobbly. We FaceTimed with Charlie in her dorm.

"Desi and I have found a cool meeting to attend. It has a lot of creative types. Green hair. Covered in tattoos and piercings. My people."

"Sprite, not sure that gives Bae and me confidence," Griffin said.

"I agree with your dad. It sounds like you and Desi are spending a lot of time together."

"Mom!" The dreaded eye roll. "We don't talk about our personal life."

I tried to cut my gaze over to Griffin without being obvious.

"I can see you, Bae." She caught me. "By the way, I don't think I am coming home during fall break. The *New York Times* 'Modern Love' section is doing a contest for college freshmen. If you're selected, your piece will be published in 'Modern Love.' Do you know what that would do for my career? It may even get me an internship this summer with the paper."

"Are you publishing something from your memoir?"

"Yes. But it's the section where you drug tested me and Dad staged the intervention and basically saved my life."

Griffin smiled. "I would save your life any day, Sprite."

We severed our connection with Charlie. I couldn't help it. I thought, *Great, she paints me as a number-one bitch and Griffin as her savior.* But then it hit me: Charlie would not be home for fall break.

I wouldn't see her eye roll in person. How easy would other holidays be for her to miss? I went out to my office and I took out the Moleskine notebook I had given her to spell her name and write her letters as a child. Even in the beginning, her handwriting was confident. It didn't look like a child's. It was self-assured. And yet her *t*'s were crooked. Just enough to betray her all-out bravado. I began crying.

I had watched her sleep as a baby. And now that she was in college, it felt like she was really walking away. How often would we see her now? I reflected on when the boys went off to college. How sad I was. How I went into Henry's room. I had been afraid of Charlie's room. Afraid I would be engulfed in regret, sadness, and shame. Those houseguests who won't leave. My phone buzzed. It was Charlie. No FaceTime.

"Bae, I was just checking on you. I didn't want you to think I just credit Dad with my sobriety."

"I'm sure you credit Uncle Henry too," I said, half joking. "I'm looking at, I think, your very first Moleskine when you started learning how to write your name. I remember you said you hated having such a long name. Charlotte Hardwick." I traced my fingers over her printing as one would do a fine piece of velvet fabric. My heart smiled and hurt at the same time.

"I can't believe you have that. Are you in your office?"

"Just some loose ends before I call it a night."

"I miss you too."

A few weeks later I heard a knock at the back door. Except for Sally and Lucy, hardly anyone used the back door. It was a late Friday afternoon. I had just gotten home from Chicago. It was Bishop.

"Well, Bishop, Charlie didn't come home for fall break." I motioned for him to sit down.

"I know. We text. I am meeting up with Thompson and Lucy a little later and I thought I would come by."

I looked at him. He looked good. He had always worn his hair shaggy, but he had gotten it cut.

"You got a haircut. It looks good. Did Charlie ask you to check up on us?" Suddenly, I felt old.

"No," he said.

I could tell he was lying. "Is Griffin around? I wanted to ask him something."

"He's on his way with supper. Have you had supper?"

"No, I was planning on grabbing a protein shake before I meet up with them."

"You want to eat with us? You can talk to Griffin then." I texted Griffin to pick up some extra. I had never known Bishop to turn down food. Shortly after, Griffin bounded in with dinner. Bishop stood up to shake Griffin's hand. It was a firm handshake. He seemed to have grown an inch and he was as tall as Griffin.

We exchanged pleasantries about college before we got down to discussing Bishop's passion. Craft beer. It didn't interest me at all, so I excused myself and hoped I would have a client who was based in New York so that I could see my daughter. Charlie had dismissed me when I suggested we come to her over Thanksgiving.

Later, we were getting ready for bed.

"You and Bishop were talking a long time," I said to Griffin.

"Yeah, Thompson texted him a couple of times. Interestingly, so did Charlotte. I don't know who has a more improbable job idea, Charlotte or Bishop. Maybe it's a good thing they aren't together."

"Do you think he is really out of the picture?"

I heard my husband laugh. It was the laugh I loved. The laugh that brought me great joy. The laugh that contained everything that was my life.

"So, we have a daughter who wants to be a writer and Bishop wants to make craft beer for a living. How did we hit the jackpot?" he joked.

"Charlie's mother married a bartender and it worked out pretty well for her." I smiled.

"A mixologist. And don't you forget it."

❧

Over the next three years a pattern emerged. Charlie would see Desi, but when she was at home on breaks, the Four Musketeers always hung out together. Sally and I took bets on how soon after graduation Thompson and Lucy would get engaged. When the Four Musketeers were in the kitchen one afternoon, I caught Charlie studying Bishop. Seeking his opinion out. Apparently, she had given him pages to read. Sometimes, he would come over for dinner and they would spend hours discussing pages. Maybe this was their way of healing. Repairing. Maturing. When she was feeling stressed out or overwhelmed, it was Bishop she called. And yet, Desi lurked. It was as if he had a vise-like grip on her. I didn't hear her laugh when she was talking to Desi. Not like she did with Bishop.

I kept my opinions to myself, but even Griffin noticed it.

"Are Charlie and Bishop back together?"

"They're just 'friends,'" I said, with air quotes.

"Been there, married that," Griffin laughed.

When Amy, Bishop's mom, had to have shoulder surgery, Charlie flew home to be with Bishop. Charlie arranged meals for Amy. Signs of the junior terrorist were still there, like when she would spend all day in her room writing and then snap at me, "*Bae*, you don't understand inspiration!" I would be the one to give Charlie the dreaded eye roll.

"Just my job, Charlie."

❧

I convened the meeting. It was a Friday morning. As usual, I had flown in the night before. I had Fridays at home to pay bills, send invoices, and work on proposals.

Griffin walked into NOIR first. He was suspicious. Before he could ask me a question, Henry strolled in.

"Bailey, I am just a little curious. I know this isn't an intervention since I am sober, so what gives?"

"I'd like to know the answer myself," Griffin joined in.

"Henry wanted to know how I was going to decorate Mac's old space in Chicago."

"I still don't get the point of this. Does anyone want coffee besides me?" Griffin asked us.

I continued. "As I said, Henry wanted to know what beautiful design I came up with for Russell. I heard Henry's unspoken desire and I concur that NOIR needs a face-lift."

My husband handed a mug of coffee to Henry. "What the hell have you been telling my wife?" Griffin took a sip of his coffee and sat back down, but his lips were pursed like whatever I said next he was going to shoot it down.

"This has always been one of the most beautiful restaurants I have ever created. But thanks to Henry, I see that sometimes beauty needs to evolve. Beauty needs to be noticed so it won't be taken for granted—like a good marriage, for instance." I briefly glanced at Griffin.

"What is the most beautiful thing?" I asked them.

For once, Griffin played along. "My wife." He smiled and lifted the coffee cup to his lips to suppress a smile.

"No sarcastic answers," I said. Henry flashed a smile as if he enjoyed our playful banter.

"The most beautiful thing in the world is nature," I finally told them. "It's all around us, begging for us to look at it and be grateful for it, and we just take it for granted. Poets through the ages have written about daffodils, the glory of flowers, and how the seasons enchant us through their ever-changing landscape—" I was interrupted.

"Oh brother, this is going to cost us, isn't it?"

"When you're ready, I would suggest bringing nature inside. I would take down the paisley ceiling and, in its place, I would hire an artist to paint a beautiful trompe l'oeil on the ceiling to 'deceive the eye.' I can see beautiful bluebirds taking flight. I can see black trellises with redolent flowers laced with colorful greenery. Bees buzzing around and ladybugs resting precariously on flower petals. I see the birds with their feathers expanded in flight with colors of blue and coral. Picture a black gazebo and something whimsical . . ."

"Somebody better tell Bae that Michelangelo is dead."

I disregarded my husband's remark and continued. "I found two pieces of fabric. This beautiful green velvet that would make all the foliage pop or this periwinkle blue–toned fabric, the color of hydrangeas. These are not very expensive. You can choose one to put on the booths. You can keep all the black light fixtures."

"Thank God for small favors," Griffin said. I noticed that Henry had not said a word.

"And now for a menu suggestion. With each change of the tasting menu, I would add a line of poetry or a verse to anchor that particular menu. For instance, for your special New Year's Eve menu, I would incorporate Shelley's verse 'Ah, the dawn of the new year.'" I proceeded to finish it, omitting that the first time I had seen it was on a note written to me by Elliott. "You could select anyone—Mary Oliver has some wonderful verses." I concluded my little presentation and made direct eye contact with my husband, knowing I had just invoked one of his favorite poets.

"Shit," Griffin said. I knew that was because as much as he hated to admit it, he liked my idea. "You don't play fair."

"Is this some weird foreplay that I don't know about? I don't know poetry," Henry said.

"Henry!" I admonished him. "You'll just have to google it. I'll even do it for you. But you are the brains behind the nectar of the gods. I'm just creating a ceiling that has no limits but the sky. I probably won't even be able to get to this for another year."

"You should've run this by me first. I can't believe you turned Bae loose." My husband directed this to his partner. The funny thing was, I was doing this as much for Griffin as Henry.

Charlie would be graduating college next year. If Charlie were anything like me, and she was, she would be full steam ahead with her career. I knew Griffin would struggle with it. It made me a little sad. I wanted to give him a new endeavor. This was less challenging than opening a brand-new restaurant like Edgeworth's. It would allow Griffin to concoct beautiful and interesting cocktails and probably redesign the menu.

"We hadn't expected to overhaul NOIR," Henry said.

"No. We did not." Griffin was a little miffed at the both of us. I caught him glancing at the ceiling and I knew he was pondering the painting.

Later that night when we were in bed, Griffin finally turned to me and asked the question he had been wanting to ask. "Any idea what a commissioned painting like this would cost?"

"I don't. But I have a good idea who would." I kissed him, and he couldn't help but kiss me back.

~

I met Bennett Ramsey at BLANC. We each ordered cappuccinos and a slice of brioche with unsalted butter, the French variety that both BLANC and NOIR served, and some apricot marmalade.

"I was surprised to hear from you. I knew you didn't approve of my friendship with Mac."

"Mac and I go way back. We've done three restaurants together. We went through our own domestic turbulence together back in the day. Our children are friends. I like Cassie very much. I really like the paintings you did for his restaurant and for my guest room. Would you be willing to do this for a ceiling?"

"Any chance I can see the ceiling?" she asked. I signed the check and we drove the short distance to NOIR. I took out my keys, thinking no one would be there that early. When I opened the door, I saw Henry in the distance. He looked up briefly, looked back down, and then looked up again. What was it with Bennett and men? She had long gray hair in the shape of ringlets. It looked wild in a polished kind of way. She wore her clothes in what I would define as "Buckhead Bohemian." They were very expensive, like Neiman Marcus meets Anthropologie.

Henry came over to us. There was some weird connection.

"Well, Henry, we meet again."

"I didn't know Bailey had you in mind. When you are calculating, don't forget to give us a friends and family discount." Henry was jovial. We lingered and then we began looking around. I could tell she was ruminating over it.

"Let me work up a proposal and some sketches for you." She called out to Henry. "Any chance I could come by at different times of the day just to see the lighting?" This time my brother did not look up.

"Sure," he said.

❧

"I shared parts of my memoir with my boss at the *New York Times* and they want to offer me a job after graduation. It's entry-level with lousy pay, but it's the *New York Times.* I am good at fetching coffee aren't I, Bae?" Charlie said, bounding into the kitchen for supper. It was the week between Christmas and New Year. After dinner, she was going to hang out with Lucy, Thompson, and Bishop.

"When do we get to read this masterpiece?" Griffin bestowed a kiss on both of our cheeks.

"Sprite, that's wonderful. Well done!" I said, taking a bottle of sparkling cider out of the refrigerator.

After a round of toasts, Charlie ducked out. "I want to call Bishop."

Henry and Griffin had surprised me with a Christmas present. They were going to redo NOIR. It gave us all something to look forward to.

ॐ

Around spring break, Charlie announced that she and Desi were talking about moving in together for the summer. The only thing we knew about him was still just his name and that he had gone to rehab to pacify his mom. I wanted to meet him in person. They had seen each other very rarely in college. I had thought that maybe he was out of the picture. I went to talk to Henry, her confidant.

"Do you know anything about Desi? Did she tell you they want to get matching sobriety tattoos?"

"Just be careful not to alienate your daughter," Henry warned.

I had been working on a special gift I wanted to give Charlie. She had agreed to a lunch so we could meet Desi. I would give her my gift after our lunch, when we were alone.

ॐ

We met them at a little restaurant in Gramercy Park. Charlie had threatened us not to ask too many questions. She could still be a junior terrorist when it served her purposes. It would be hard because we knew virtually nothing about Desi Turner except that he was named for his grandfather.

He had dark hair and eyes. He looked rough.

"Where did you grow up?" I asked.

"Mom." Charlie glared at me.

"It's okay. California."

"You must miss it," Griffin said.

"I do. My mom is here now."

"What does your mom do?"

"Mom." Charlie gave me a look, and then looked surprised. "I didn't know your mom is here."

"She doesn't need a job," Desi responded.

I was finding it difficult to talk to him.

"Mom is here because of my dad." He didn't seem to be that interested in Griffin and me. Griffin squeezed my knee under the table.

"Your dad works here."

"Dad—I'm sorry, Desi," Charlie apologized.

"It's okay, baby. My parents have been estranged. They recently got back together. Dad is in the TV industry."

We ordered food. I needed a drink. In addition to those sobriety tattoos they were getting, he had just called my daughter "baby." Eek.

"I didn't know your dad was an actor?" Charlie was surprised.

"God no. He has a cooking show."

"Maybe Dad has heard of him," Charlie prodded.

"Sprite, cooking is the last thing I'm interested in when I turn on the TV," Griffin said in that easy manner of his.

"He has restaurants too." There was another lull in conversation. Why couldn't Griffin help me out here?

"You know, my mom designs restaurants," Charlie told him.

"Not my dad's. He talks about the 'bitch' that designed his restaurant."

"Do you have any idea where you will live?" I asked, changing the topic.

"Near the subway for Charlie and close to Dad's restaurant because I'm managing it this summer and doing the graphics. The outskirts of SoHo, probably."

"That's where I lived a million years ago," I told him.

"It was seedy when your mom lived there," Griffin said.

"I definitely think Graemmar's improves the place," Desi said.

Jarring pieces of a puzzle falling into an unimpeachable truth. The realization blooming on my family's faces simultaneously. I felt faint. My legs wobbly. I stood up, clutching the table for support.

"Who is your father?" I asked point-blank, forgoing good manners. There were no objections from my daughter.

"Elliott Graemmar."

I heard Charlie say "Shit."

"What?"

"Mom is the bitch who designed your dad's restaurant."

❧

I walked outside, pulling my phone out and trying desperately to hit the Uber app. Griffin shouted and caught up with me as the Uber approached us. Thoughts were swirling around so fast. The Uber pulled up and took us back to my apartment. Wordlessly, we entered the apartment.

"Is it possible Desi knew who we were all along?"

"That's a stretch, Bae," Griffin said. "They were in rehab together. Desi looked surprised."

"Not as surprised as I was." My phone buzzed. "It's Henry. Talk to him. I guess Charlie called him."

❧

Right about then, Charlie came in. She looked as dazed as I felt. I scooped up the contents of my bag with the abandoned gift for Charlie so she could sit down beside me.

"I'm sorry. I didn't know. I called Uncle Henry. It's a 'clusterfuck,' to quote him."

"Henry has a way with words."

She hugged me.

"Sprite, how involved are you two? I've never asked you to not see somebody on my account, but I'm asking now."

"We were talking about living together, Bae."

"I don't want you anywhere near him. You can always live here in the apartment."

Her phone was buzzing. "I kind of told the Four Musketeers. Bishop wants to know if you're all right."

"Maybe you can hold off giving them a play-by-play," I said.

"These are all texts and phone calls from Desi." She looked anxious.

Seventy-two hours later I would be arrested for Elliott's murder. Seventy-two hours later my nightmare would be beginning. Seventy-two hours later Griffin would look at me like I had betrayed him. Seventy-two hours later my daughter finally looked like herself.

NOW

I went to see my de facto therapist. He had a cappuccino waiting for me. Over the years he had perfected the designs that perched on top. Today I noticed he had created angel wings so pretty and delicate. And ironic. Given my current quandary.

"You sure got yourself involved with scum when you hooked up with Elliott. Charlotte is a blackout drinker. She doesn't even remember the night Elliott died," Henry said.

"I don't think she killed Elliott, if that is what you're thinking. I think she was passed out," he continued. "She promised me she was going to call Bishop. He called me himself when he was with her. Talk about history repeating itself."

"Charlie would be very lucky if Bishop turned out to be like Griffin."

"You're right about that, little sister. What would either of us be without him? I would probably be dead or in a gutter, and you would still be famous but royally screwed up."

We had all saved and transformed each other's lives throughout the years.

"I think you have done your fair share of saving us, Henry."

"No shit, Sherlock. Stating the obvious, little sister."

"I'm worried about Griffin and how he will take Charlie's relapse."

"I know Charlotte does not want him to know, but I think he deserves to hear it from you." He drained his coffee. I realized I hadn't touched my cappuccino. I had been too nervous. My phone buzzed. It was a text from Griffin.

"He said he might come home early for supper."

Henry just shook his head and smiled. "I feel for Griffin. This night isn't going to turn out the way he planned."

"When does it? I wasn't exactly thinking I would be facing murder charges at this point in my life either." I reflected on the man in front of me. He had fought and won so many battles with addiction. Now we were in another battle for my daughter. I was grateful that Charlie had Henry. I was even more grateful in that moment that I had Henry. Even though we rarely displayed signs of affection, I reached up and hugged him. "Thanks, Henry." I meant it.

I decided to take Henry's advice. It wasn't the first time that Griffin and I would argue about Charlie's drinking. But God knows, I hoped it would be the last.

I heard the sound first. The sizzle of melted butter. The smells were tiptoeing closer to me.

"I thought you could use a home-cooked meal," Griffin said, straining his neck to lean over and kiss me while he unwrapped the most beautiful scallops and tossed them into the pan. Many nights, when it was just the two of us again, he came home early to prepare a home-cooked meal, to accommodate my early bedtime. On these occasions when he would come home early, we still took pleasure in each other's company. We would turn in early, be together, sharing kisses, laughter, and a togetherness that our years of history had given us. Tonight, I wondered if we would even share a bedroom.

"That smells delicious."

"Sautéed sea scallops with saffron sauce and some red quinoa for some color." He kissed me again. Properly this time. I felt guilty.

"I would really like a drink. Could you make me a sidecar?"

"Was your day that bad?" he asked.

"Yep. Yours isn't looking so good right now either." I sat down at the table and just waited for Griffin to finish. He plated our meal. I loved how the golden yellow of the saffron sauce made the red quinoa look even more appealing. I started eating my feelings.

"Slow down." The years between us had taught him a thing or two as well. "This is going to be bad, isn't it?" Griffin said.

"If you know me so well, what's the topic?" He just looked at me and then put his fork down.

"Oh my God. Charlotte?" I put my fork down too. I realized he never got around to making my sidecar. Just a glass of wine. Which I downed. He refused to give me the bottle until I told him what was on my mind. I hadn't rehearsed any of this and it was going to sound really bad. His eyes caught mine and they refused to let me go.

"Remember how I stayed in New York to support Charlie? I thought she had gone to a meeting and then gone to her dorm to collect her things. When she showed up, she was wasted."

"Shit, Bae. Are you telling me that Charlotte is drinking again?"

"Charlie went over to Desi's apartment. He was drinking tequila and she just thought she could test her resolve. Desi told her he had taken pictures of her and if she didn't make up with him, he would put them on the Internet. She begged me to get the pictures. She was so fragile. She didn't want you to know that she had been drinking . . ."

"What the hell? If I had known this, I would've killed Desi or Elliott myself!"

"Exactly. I didn't know what you were capable of at that moment. I knew you'd be angry. You have a right to be angry. But I have gone with her to meetings and I know she is still going to meetings because of Floyd."

"How does Floyd know?" His voice was rising.

"Apparently Floyd has private investigators on Desi but also the rest of us. Floyd thinks Charlie is still a suspect because how would that look in her memoir if she had fallen off the wagon?"

"All hell was breaking in New York, and I was sitting at home in a fucking accounting meeting!"

I hadn't heard him say that word in a while. But if there was a time to use it, it was now.

"You said that she has been attending meetings regularly?"

I knew Griffin would be all over this from my first rodeo with Charlotte's drinking. He was always insistent on her working the program.

"Bishop and I went with her to some meetings and I made her promise she would go several times a week for as long as she needed."

Charlie's sobriety was as important to Griffin as it was to Charlie. I also knew that you couldn't make a drunk go to meetings. I was so relieved that Floyd's investigators had told me she was going.

"You sure know how to kill the mood, Bae. First you tell me that Floyd thinks Charlie did it, then that Floyd has investigators following all of us like we are common criminals, and now you tell me that Desi and Charlotte drank tequila. You're right. I would've probably killed both Desi and Elliott."

Griffin looked at me. He looked hurt. He looked confused. He was trying not to overreact like we had done with each other in the past when secrets came out.

"Who else knows?" Griffin asked me.

"Henry, Floyd, and me. And Bishop. Actually, Floyd thinks you could've done it."

"Fuck," Griffin said again. I hadn't heard it in years and he was dropping it left and right. He was shell-shocked. "Why am I the last person to know?"

"Charlie didn't want me to tell you. I told her it was only a matter of time. She just doesn't want you to be disappointed in her. PTSD. You need to make this okay for her," I told him.

"Of course, I want to make it right for her. She needs counseling."

"I took her to a therapist. I canceled all my appointments and went with her. I am worried that this will take a toll on her. I'm worried that she will turn back to her old friend tequila. I was insistent she keep going. So far she is humoring me."

"Is that it?"

"Damn, isn't that enough?" I paused. Griffin got up and threw his plate into the sink. I got up and touched his shoulder. He flinched. He grabbed his keys off the counter.

"I need some time. I'd like to call Charlotte. If you think that's okay."

"I think that would be nice. Are you coming home tonight?" There was a long pause and I realized I had stopped breathing.

"I'm not sure," Griffin said, and then he was gone.

Well past midnight, I heard the back door open and close and the stairs creak. I said a silent prayer that Griffin had come home. He was surprised to see me up. He leaned in the doorway. His eyes were red like he had been crying.

"You really need to replace the sofa in my office. I talked to Charlie. She said that you were a big help to her. She told me not to be mad at you. But this isn't about Charlie. This is about us." Griffin paused.

I wanted to say something. I wanted to fill the stubborn silence with apologies. But my throat closed. The weight of everything that had happened landing on my heart. I didn't give a flip about the murder or who did it. I wanted my family to heal. I hung my head in shame. My shame and inadequacy as a mother had been with me from the beginning. Griffin just stood there.

"Forget how the murder turns out. You know how this turns out." He made his searing indictment. I looked up and noticed he stood on the threshold outside our bedroom. Tears welled up in my eyes. I heard him leaning on the door frame like an exhale. I was so afraid.

"I understand now that this was your moment for reconciliation with your daughter. You wanted to prove to her and yourself that you could be a good mom. That you could be there for her when it counted. I know you worried about being a good mom before Charlie was ever conceived. Even before we got married. This was your greatest fear and why you turned me down three times." He stopped. Emotion stealing what he was about to say. I thought about what he just said. He was right. In doing so I had thrown away the thing that was most important to me: my marriage.

"How did you get so perceptive?" I said. Even now I was trying to dodge the uncomfortable emotions between us.

"Linda Noris is perceptive. Because you don't always talk to me, I need someone who can explain you to me."

This was one of those moments that I couldn't predict how we would end up.

"You're quiet," he noticed.

"I'm scared." Ironically there was so much I wanted to say to him. But I couldn't. I was terrified.

"It's about forgiveness."

When I looked at him, he added, "Charlotte isn't the only one who needs therapy. I know you are worried about her. You need to worry less about her and more about what's going on in this room."

I nodded. I thought about those green and brown bananas. Those houseguests.

I almost missed it. He crossed the threshold. He disappeared into the bathroom. When he returned, he slid into the bed next to me, cutting off the lights.

For a long time neither one of us said anything. I was grateful that our love had hobbled and bridged the communication gap once more.

"Charlotte mentioned Bishop. How is he dealing with all of this?" Griffin asked.

"He has been with her this whole time."

Sleep eluded me. Night inched closer to dawn. As much as I didn't want to entertain the thought of Charlie letting me take the murder rap, that was the least of my worries.

I thought about my little girl. How her first sight of the ocean had astonished her. I thought about how she took delight in writing her name and ripping open the pack of pens. I thought about how she enjoyed "Taco Tuesday" and cooking with her dad. I thought about her fragile sobriety, how each day would be measured by not drinking. This wasn't what I wanted for her life. I thought about Griffin. I loved him before anyone else. I would love him after everyone else. I had done a lousy job. I began sobbing. My tears wouldn't stop. There was no need; they found some company.

I felt Griffin take my hand under the covers. He squeezed it. I squeezed his in return. This was how we entered a brand-new day.

When I walked into the conference room, Floyd was actually smiling.

"Do you know Winston Webster?" he asked.

"He's a weird architect who lives in my apartment building and always wears argyle sweaters and smokes," I said.

"He is all of those things but he's just given you an airtight alibi. He was out smoking and saw you come in. Which I am guessing was after your acupuncture appointment."

"Would I not have the same problem of leaving again? What about my DNA?"

"We have been watching the wrong apartment building footage."

"What do you mean?"

"Your apartment footage. I have watched it many times. It shows you coming but never leaving. I want you to watch all three hours. It isn't the most exciting, but it is exculpatory for you."

For the next three hours I settled into watching my apartment building's footage. I saw myself coming in with Charlie's things. There was Winston lurking in the shadows. Floyd was sending texts. Then he got a phone call. He was very animated.

"The DA in New York is reviewing your apartment building's video too. Now you have an eyewitness and video footage backing up your story and your timeline. If it all checks out, they are prepared to drop the charges."

"That's terrific. What about Charlie or Griffin?"

"The police aren't looking at Charlie. I've asked Griffin to come in this afternoon to review the discrepancy in his and Jane's statements. I would like you to stay."

"Certainly. Notwithstanding my own family, I would've put good money on Jane. Are you positive Jane couldn't have done it?"

"Not anymore," Floyd said with a brief hint of optimism.

Charlie was excited to hear about the possibility of the charges being dropped. She wanted to come home to celebrate. With Bishop. I put her off. I wanted to make sure I was released and that her dad was innocent.

As I waited on Griffin, I reflected on the last year. While I was facing a murder conviction, my life had flashed before my eyes. Griffin and I getting married, our love being able to get us over the threshold of our marriage optional; our love creating Charlie; our finding this wonderful neighborhood with Sally, Chad, and Lucy along with Bishop and Thompson; our love finding its way back home again to one another. I didn't want to lose Griffin, so I halted my trip down memory lane until he could review the tape.

About two o'clock Griffin strolled in. He was carrying a cappuccino and two portobello mushroom sandwiches. One for Floyd and me. He leaned down and kissed me gently before taking a seat. Floyd had been on the phone.

"I have good news and bad news," Floyd said, waiting for us to tell him which news we wanted to hear first. At the same time Griffin said "good news" and I said "bad news." Our usual approaches.

"The good news is the DA has dropped the charges against Bailey. The bad news is that they're now looking at you, Griffin. I suggest we get down to business and look at the tape. Thank you for the sandwich." He pulled out his napkin and once again took delicate bites. We paused at the frame in question.

"See, there you are with Lady Jane," I pointed out. Griffin studied the freeze-frame. He got up and walked closer to the picture.

"That's not me," he said.

I got up and went to the frame. "Yes it is. There's your watch. Your wedding ring."

"I wasn't wearing a watch. And I wasn't wearing my ring. That's not me."

At this, Floyd jumped up.

"We've been working under the assumption that this was you and Lady Jane."

"Not my watch, not my ring. I didn't see a dog."

Floyd went back and rewound the tape to where Griffin said he left.

"Look at this portion of the tape and tell me what you see," Floyd said.

"There I am. Blow it up, you will see my serenity bracelet that Bae gave me." He pointed and sat back down. It was hard to see, but there it was. I thought that was a father and son leaving the building. We all watched the tape again. I thought I saw Jane and Griffin. She had changed hoodies.

"Do you think Jane could've hired someone to imitate Griffin?" I asked. "How did I get this wrong?"

"You were stressed. It's a common phenomenon known as optical or visual illusion." Floyd was already making calls to the DA about Griffin. He said he would blow up the frame with Griffin and his serenity bracelet and send it to the DA. Griffin was just sitting there, looking at the both of us. I was remembering the combustible arguments between Elliott and Jane. It all made sense. I took Griffin's hand in mine. I did so many things wrong, but I was right to have faith in my husband. Resilient faith. Stubborn faith. Rewarded faith.

"I need to fly to New York." Before I could get excited, I needed to finish this. I sent a text: *We need to meet asap.*

"Bae, why now? I thought we could celebrate. Sprite will be happy," Griffin grumbled. I barely heard him. I was waiting for a reply and punching in the last flight to New York today.

Meet me at the Starbucks at Broadway at 10 p.m. I want something you have and you want something I have. What Jane wanted was one of my dearest possessions: my peridot and diamond earrings. But earrings were not as important as my family's extrication from this nightmare.

"We can celebrate tomorrow night with Charlie. Why don't you book her a ticket?"

"What's so important?" Floyd glanced up for the briefest of moments.

❧

I went straight to the airport. After a pit stop at home. I needed to get my hands on the pictures of Charlie. I had texted Floyd the sudden reason for my departure. He was already on to me.

Be careful, Nancy Drew, he texted back.

I was going over what I would say to Jane. We had never been alone together. We only texted during my divorce from Elliott about the retrieval of my things from his apartment. We were an unlikely pair. Some may even say we were unlikely mothers. I would plead to her maternal nature. The man behind me was digging his knees into my seat.

"Excuse me, ma'am, could you put the seat in the upright position?" I would've been perturbed if I hadn't recognized the voice.

"You're not as clever as you think," Griffin said, getting up and joining me in the middle seat, which he hated. "You and I both know why you're going to New York and who you're planning to see."

"You can't see Lady Jane with me."

"Why not?"

"I need to get the pictures back alone. Mother to mother. You can wait outside."

"I don't want you walking into a trap. Mother to mother? Now that's funny."

Neither of us exactly fit the domestic profile.

"Fine. Let's go do this. Together."

Starbucks was the perfect meeting place. Half the world was in there. Tourists, Broadway theatergoers, and kids looking for free Wi-Fi. I didn't see her. Then I recognized the sunglasses. Who wears sunglasses at night—and a ghastly blonde wig? The kind of person who knows cameras are always watching. I walked over to her.

"I know you did it." I looked her in the eye.

"It was an accident. I pushed him."

"Here are your damn earrings. I want the pictures."

She smiled, scooping up my beloved earrings. She could have them just to put this nightmare behind us. "There were never pictures. Desi confessed to me afterward. You were already arrested. I took perverse pleasure in your predicament." Jane flashed a sly smile.

Then something caught her attention. Was it the police? I turned around and saw a young couple indecently making out. I wondered if they were drunk. I wondered if Desi and Charlie had ever done such a thing in public.

"Why should I believe you? I want the pictures. You owe me the truth."

"As I said, there were never pictures. Desi blackmailed Elliott for money. Elliott was furious to be played by Desi. I thought Elliott was going to hurt my son. I got angry. We fought. I shoved him. Then, I knocked him out of the way. He lost his balance, knocked over the flowers, and then hit his head. Besides, I would be the first one destroying pictures of my son and your tacky daughter. I wouldn't want my son exposed like that. I worry about his future too. They may settle for my deportation to England, which would be fine with me."

We retreated to our mutual corners of silence. I noticed a coffee stain on our small round table. Orders continued to be shouted out in the distance like some caffeinated cheer. They offered me a reduced prison sentence and they might offer Jane deportation. She sounded maternal talking about her son. I wanted to take issue with how she described Charlie, but there were other matters to discuss.

"Not so fast. I need you to assure me that Desi will not come near Charlotte ever again." This was as important to me as the pictures.

"I don't want my son near your flaky daughter. We aren't so different, Bailey. We have loved the same man. We love our children. We would both do whatever it took to protect them."

Freedom and sobriety. These issues intersected on this sad table just as the world intersected in this all-night Starbucks. The issues intersected and reluctantly connected Jane and me.

"Theodosia!" the barista shouted. Jane pushed her chair back, grabbed the coffee, and disappeared into the throngs of humanity.

What the hell just happened? I sat there, recalibrating the events that had transpired this past year. I remembered what Elliott had said and what Jane had said. We weren't different after all. The truth dawned on me. She hadn't mentioned stabbing Elliott. It's because she hadn't. Jane hadn't killed Elliott. Jane was protecting her child. The real killer. I jumped up and ran after her.

"Did you see which direction Jane went?" I asked Griffin.

"I didn't see her come out."

As we were walking back to my corporate apartment Griffin grabbed my arm.

"Don't you think it is a bit ironic it was my bracelet called 'serenity' that would be the thing that got us both off the hook for Elliott's killing?" Griffin said.

In the middle of the sidewalk, I threw my head back and laughed and then I kissed him as if we were the only two people in the world. Because in that moment we were. It was the very definition of serenity.

EPILOGUE

SIX MONTHS LATER

The Four Musketeers gathered in our circular breakfast room at the roundtable. Both couples were happily holding hands under the table. We had gathered for a belated celebration dinner with Henry's family. My mind briefly landed on how this room sold me on the house with the idea of having rambunctious family meals here. Of course, I had been thinking of our children, but these people were enough. No. They were everything. They were wearing "Justice for Bailey!" T-shirts. After dinner I excused myself and booked a flight to Brazil with my reinstated passport. I needed to put the finishing touches on Sea Glass. I had to travel to Brazil to see the stunning vistas. Sometimes visions require time to percolate. Time had sharpened my focus for NOIR. It had also allowed me to focus my attention on Griffin. I was old enough now not to take these moments for granted and to savor each one. Time has been kind to Bishop and Charlie. Maybe this interlude was their way of healing. Maturing. Repairing. When I looked up from my phone Charlie was hovering over me.

"Mom, Henry made a special dessert. Warm carrot cake with cinnamon ice cream." She spied something in my satchel as I came back to the kitchen. "What is this?" Charlie picked up the present I was going to give her the day we met Desi–before this whole ordeal started. It had been in the bottom of my satchel. It was pretty beaten up.

"It's a present for you to congratulate you on your book deal. I guess I can add graduation now. It looked magnificent when it was newly wrapped. Before my life was hijacked."

She picked up the smashed present and surveyed it dubiously. "Gee, Mom, you shouldn't have."

I pulled Charlie into the butler's pantry. I had envisioned giving her my beautifully wrapped present with a little soliloquy about how proud I was of her. Maybe there really are no perfect moments in life. Sometimes, the wrapping is coming undone. The box is crushed. And you're squeezed into a cluttered butler's pantry. She held it in her hands. It looked like a fancy pen box.

"It practically unwraps itself. The tape is unraveling at the edges," Charlie laughed. She opened it. Her eyes grew large. A big smile spread across her face. I knew she liked it. "Mom, I love this sea glass necklace." She was lifting her hair so I could put it on her. I had it made in sterling silver with one little sterling silver ball above it.

"That's not just any sea glass. This is the first piece of sea glass you ever collected on the beach when you were four years old. I've saved it this whole time."

"Like Dad's flannel shirt," Charlie said. She took a selfie and then looked at her own reflection. "This can't be that piece of sea glass. It's so pretty."

"It is. It is astonishing how time and weathering can bring out the true beauty of things. Over the years I would take out that little plastic bag and just look at it and remember. I was wistful for that little girl who wanted to turn the ocean off and on. Seeing you now, I know it's time to let the little girl go. You're amazing and beautiful, Sprite. You deserved a better mother than me."

"This says it better than I could." I thrust a piece of paper at her. It was stanzas of the poem by Cecil Day-Lewis entitled "Walking Away." She started to read:

> Behind a scatter of boys. I can see
> You walking away from me towards the school
> With the pathos of a half-fledged thing set free

Into a wilderness, the gait of one
Who finds no path where the path should be.

That hesitant figure, eddying away
Like a winged seed loosened from its parent stem,
Has something I never quite grasp to convey
About nature's give-and-take—the small, the scorching
Ordeals which fire one's irresolute clay.

I have had worse partings, but none that so
Gnaws at my mind still. Perhaps it is roughly
Saying what God alone could perfectly show—
How selfhood begins with the walking away,
and love is proved in the letting go.

I got choked up, all the words I wanted to say caught in my throat. Charlie stepped in to fill the void.

"Are you going to tell me to eat some fruit too? Because I really want some carrot cake," she said, her mouth crinkling into a smile. She reached over and hugged me, and whispered in my ear, "I got the mom I needed."

I pulled away and said, "If you thought the box looked rough, you should see that bag."

We laughed together and rejoined the others.

"Dad, I just caught Bae booking her flight to Brazil."

"Hold on. I thought you were going to redesign NOIR," Henry complained. I got up and went around the table to where Henry and Griffin were sitting.

"Gabriel was ahead of you guys. The good news is I really just need to be there for the install and then I will be all yours." I bestowed a kiss on Henry and put my arms around the two men who had been with me from the beginning. We were always better together.

The carrot cake and cinnamon ice cream were so delicious that there was a momentary lull in the laughter as silver spoons replaced forks to scrape the last sweet puddles from the plates.

"Are you trying to decide if it's polite to lick the plates clean?" Henry asked, pleased with his own creation.

Everyone laughed. Except Bishop. His plate was untouched.

"What's wrong, Bishop?" Not inhaling his food was uncommon for Bishop.

"Nothing. I just have some questions to ask Griffin about the craft beer industry. Maybe we can talk later."

❧

Henry's Family called it a night and headed out just as the Four Musketeers were about to leave for Thompson's.

Griffin and Bishop walked ahead into the den as I blew out the candles on the table. Charlie, Lucy and Thompson were out the door when Charlie suddenly ran back into the kitchen.

She pulled me into a tight hug, kissed my cheek, and said quietly, "You don't have to let me go. Not all the way. I'll always hunt sea glass with you."

She looked at me, blinking back tears, and then pulled me close, "Go easy on him Bae."

In a flash, she was out the door, yelling to Lucy and Thompson to wait up.

Bishop called from the den, "I would really like your opinion too, Bailey."

I took my place on the couch, and Griffin reached for my hand.

Bishop looked at us, resolute.

"This isn't about beer. It's about Charlie."

Griffin and I looked at each other with dread.

“Is she alright?” I asked.

“Is she drinking?” Griffin interjected.

“Sorry. This is so not like I had planned it.”

“Bishop,” Griffin implored. “What is the matter?”

“Nothing. Nothing is the matter. We love each other, and we want to take the next step together,” Bishop began.

“What are you asking?” I said, alarm rising to the surface.

I went on. “Whatever it is, you’re too young.” I said, looking at Griffin for help.

He was none. I couldn’t tell if he was in shock. I managed to choke out the next question, “Is she pregnant?”

“No, oh my god no . . . We just want to move in together. We want to get married when it’s the right time. We want to be young when we have children.”

I stared at Bishop, trying to envision my child a mother.

Bishop met my gaze and said slowly, “The most important thing is Charlie. I’ll take care of her. I promise to respect her sobriety.”

Griffin looked at me. This time, I was no help. Charlie’s kiss still felt warm on my cheek.

Bishop continued. “And I was serious when I said I wanted to talk to you about craft beer. I’ve figured out that a degree in finance might be a better way to build a life, so my plan is for us to live together in New York while I go to grad school and Charlie works at the paper and finishes her memoir.”

Griffin squeezed my hand. “Bae, I think what Bishop is telling us is that he and Charlie have the kind of relationship you and I did.” Griffin and I exchanged knowing expressions. Then, Griffin did what he did best. He defused the tension. “Bishop, it may be a good thing that you’re starting early. It took me three marriage proposals to convince Bailey to marry me. And then she was the one to finally ask. Charlie is like her mother that way.” We all laughed.

Bishop looked relieved. After he left, I could see him through the window, scooping Charlie up in a bear hug. I thought about the sea glass I had given Charlie. Weren't we all like sea glass? Very few of us start out complete and beautiful. We have sharp edges. Occasionally, we look flat and dull and go through phases that look ugly. We may wonder why we chose to keep some pieces to begin with. Family is like a mosaic of sea glass. Our memories, our marriages, our relationships shape-shift over time until they form a collage that represents our lives. If we're lucky, we can appreciate the texture, nuance, and complexity of what we see. The spaces represent unwanted houseguests. Learn from them and let them sit comfortably with the other pieces. Maybe, with time and weathering, we become beautiful like sea glass.

Or maybe the gaps represent the times when we didn't get it right. When we fell short. When we thought we knew it all. And didn't. Those separations remind us to try harder. To forgive when it is hard. And acceptance, which may be the hardest.

Later, I sat tucked in bed with my laptop when Griffin brought in a bottle of champagne.

"You still keep wine glasses in the closet?" he asked. I nodded. "I thought we could have a proper celebration." He was already taking the laptop away giving me proper kisses.

"Really? You want me? I'm on the verge of being someone's mother-in-law."

"I will want you when you're somebody's granny." He kissed me again.

"What would've happened if I had married you at twenty-two?" he asked, setting the glasses on the bedside table as he slipped in beside me.

"You would've dumped my ass on the side of the road at twenty-three. But I love you, Griffin."

He laughed.

"I'll say it again. Always have. Always did. Always will."

acknowledgments

How fitting that the first pages and last pages of this book would include the name of my beloved brother Robert. This book is dedicated to him, and here in the acknowledgements, I again want to honor him. Robert pulled me back from the ledge so often. I can still hear him saying, “Now, Les, it is going to be OK.” And it is OK, at least as much as it can be without him here to read it. For me, writing is working through things. I miss his chill personality that balanced my intense one. I missed the chance to tell him “thank you” for all the times he pulled me back from the ledge in his quiet and unassuming way. I hope I’ve made him proud.

When I began to write *Before Anyone Else*, I simply wanted to bring beauty into my own world, a world that was not so pretty at the time. In writing this book, I wanted to shine a light on the lifetime arc of love present in our sibling relationships. Our siblings are always there, with their knowledge of our past, to set us straight. I don’t think it was a coincidence that I was reading *The Dutch House* by one of my heroes, Ann Patchett, in the weeks following his death.

If Robert pulled me back from the emotional ledge, there were two people who pulled me back from the literary ledge. Time and time again, when self-doubt covered me like an unflattering uniform, Melissa Walker and Susan Lancaster read, reread, and proposed ideas. I think in their former lives they were high-powered senior editors at some venerable publishing house! Melissa, your idea about the epilogue was a great one, and Susan, thank you for sharing the lovely poem by Charles Day-Lewis. Your suggestions were so profound but maybe not as profound as your friendship’s effect on me. You are two beautiful souls, both of you!

In many ways, an acknowledgment is a retrospective; people I have met along the way and want to thank. As I was writing this book, I was simultaneously traveling for a book tour for *The Secret of Rainy Days*. I met so many wonderful people who became sources of joy, encouragement, and friendship. Zibby Owens (I call her #CaffieneDripNotIncluded), profound thanks to you for your friendship. Your recognition of *Before Anyone Else* was thrilling, and you ushered me into 2022 by including me on your podcast for *The Secret of Rainy Days*! Your smile is like a glass of champagne: fizzy, sparkling, celebratory, and ultimately thought-provoking. I raise a glass to you!

I'm so thankful for the wonderful women who have given their time to get out the good word about my books. They are evangelists and publicists rolled into one.

Many thanks go out to my dearest Lisa Harrison, Brenda Gardner, and Annissa Joy Armstrong for talking me up and having me on the gargantuan Friends and Fiction. Let's not forget Kristy Woodson Harvey and Patti Callahan for offering their beautiful words of encouragement and blurbs. Many thanks go to my dear friends who hosted parties for me and spread the news to their friends. Jenna Olsen, Sally Leath, and Cammie Monroe, thank you for your love, friendship, and dedication. And then there's Francene Katzen who not only hosted a beautiful party for me but posted tirelessly about my novels. I have come to depend upon our weekly cocktail hours. Thank you to Kimberly Mize who hosted such a beautiful party it needs to be in a magazine. I often tell her that she could run a small country, but I'm pretty sure she could run a pretty big country just like Zibby. Jaz Dillard, thank you for all your friendship and for another lovely party and celebration.

And then there are the bookstores and the book people. Oh my goodness. My first ever public event was at Parnassus in Nashville. It is quite an august stage to begin my very first book tour. Ann Patchett was there. I got choked up. I almost lost it. And yet in her grace (she is otherworldly, you know) she offered me a hug and some encouragement for a project. My hometown bookstore, Park Road Books, is always touting my books to customers who wander in. Bless you and thank you. I just loved being at Fox Tales in Atlanta. It was like being in a Hallmark movie that featured celebrity author friends who dropped in like Colleen Oakley and Kimberly Brock.

Thank you to Tanya Farrell and Emily Afifi at Wunderkind. You are two of the best in the business, and you made this book sparkle. I appreciate your great ideas and your good cheer.

Thank you to Kamie Rudisill for the beautiful note cards and bookmarks that go along with each and every book. I so appreciate your patience and creativity.

Stephanie, at Page and Palette in Fairhope Alabama, was just beyond delightful and encouraging. Angela, I loved being at my alma mater down in Auburn and being in your cozy bookstore, Auburn Oil Booksellers. What a fun night. Auburn is still the "loveliest village on the plains." Thank You Books in Birmingham felt more like a family reunion because so many people I know came. Elizabeth, thank you for putting me on the schedule and not running us off when we stayed beyond closing time. At least we were selling books! Finally there was my hometown crowd that welcomed me home like a hero with beautiful food and crowds. Venessa Lowry, Susie Almon, Elaine White, and Nancy Potts, you all have my appreciation for all the hard work. The tents and chandeliers felt as if I were getting married rather than just signing a few books which turned into *a lot* of books! Thank you for making the drum beat so people *came*.

Then there is Lew Burdette. In addition to being one of my first readers, he drove me all over Alabama during the book tour. We covered a lot of territory while you were "driving Ms. Hootie," but we never stop talking! And laughing. Thank you for letting some of our adventures grace the pages of *The Secret of Rainy Days*.

And thank you to all these generous authors who said *yes*! *Yes* to blurbs and special appearances. I so appreciate your support. Big thanks to Kevin Wilson, who always says yes. Jane Rosen and Lisa Barr said yes even though they both had big books of their own coming out. Rochelle Weinstein, you are an absolute genius for proposing the THEN headers. And Julie Chavez, for always dispensing good cheer and advice.. Besides being uber-talented, you guys have been so gracious and kind to me. Over and over again.

A special shout out to Carolina Lemos for the valuable information you provided me regarding Brazilian cuisine. Thank you for the late-night texts explaining this tasty and exotic food. Who knew that my trip to Nashville would yield a meeting with Ann Patchett and meeting you and your sweet family on the plane after you attended a Harry Styles concert!

And then there were the literary missionaries who were bloggers—who not only embraced my book but embraced me and in turn became good friends. I really hate to name names for fear of leaving anyone out. I will do a quick shout out to Katie Fulton, Cortney Wood, Christina Powers, and Christy Taylor. There are many others and forgive me if you don't see your name. It may not be in print at the moment but it is in my heart. About that . . . my memory is not what it once was, so if you think I inadvertently left you out, please let me know and I will mention you in the acknowledgments twice next time. I also want to thank Suzanne Leopold for your constant support, friendship and promotion of *The Secret of Rainy Days*. I don't know when you sleep!

There are not enough additives to thank the tremendously talented Emily Mahon. Each of your covers has been better than the one before. Seeing the "cover reveal" is still one of my favorite days in the process. I don't know how you manage to top yourself each and every time. I am grateful. So grateful.

I couldn't do any of this without my team at Leslie Inc. Kathy Wells who drives me around when she is not shopping at Talbots. I feel like Dr. Seuss *Oh, the Places You'll Go!* that don't always include Leslie Inc.

activities. Linda Howey is in charge of business and calendar activities. In other words, if it isn't on the calendar, I just might forget it! The youngest member of our team is Alexandria Buttgereit. As you might expect, she handles some of my social media and my desperate texts asking how do you post this? She always answers with good cheer never reminding me how dumb I appear.

And then there is a team at Turner. Todd Bottorff, Ryan Smernoff, and Lauren Ash, you are always patient and there to answer my numerous questions. You have made my dreams come true. And that is no small thing!

A final thanks go out to *you*. While I was traveling around, you were showing up, devoting your time, and reading my books. I don't take any of it for granted. I am too old to know that these things aren't a given in this business. I so appreciate your comments, your love, and—yes—your reviews. But especially your friendship. One of my desires in writing in the first place was so I wouldn't feel lonely. And if I have brought a little joy to someone else, that is everything to me. So don't hesitate to reach out. I am always here. Unless, of course, I'm writing the next book!

book club discussion questions

1. Why was Bailey reluctant to marry Griffin initially? What helped her make that decision ultimately? Who helps you work through big choices?
2. Bailey and Griffin have a decidedly "non-traditional" household. What are the advantages and disadvantages of their arrangement? Can either gender really have "it all"?
3. Was Bailey right to fire Tabitha? Why or why not?
4. Did Charlotte exploit Bailey's feelings of guilt and inadequacy? What were the consequences for Charlotte of Bailey's "mom guilt"?
5. Charlotte's addiction nearly shipwrecks her own life and her parents' marriage. How does addiction play a role in American life now, and do you think it is a chronic problem or one that has become worse in this generation?
6. Bailey and Charlie each crave a space that is uniquely theirs. What space in your home or life is uniquely yours, and what makes it special?
7. Griffin puts Charlotte in rehab without consulting Bailey. Was this the right thing to do? Why or why not? To what lengths will parents go to protect their children?
8. The family relationship in the book explores the hierarchy of loyalty for family members. Bailey puts Griffin first in her affections while Griffin puts Charlotte first. Should parents privilege marriage first or children first? What are the implications of each arrangement?
9. The novel also explores the sibling bond between Henry and

Bailey. Bailey says Henry has pulled her back from the ledge. How is sibling love vital in the novel, and who serves that role for Charlotte?

10. Bailey is comforted by Rumi's poem, "Guest House" and its image that anger, sadness and shame are emotions that have come to stay. What is a work of literature you turn to for affirmation?
11. By the novel's end, Charlotte is independent and stepping into her own adult life. What kind of life do you envision for her?
12. The murder of Elliot serves as a backdrop to explore young love vs. weathered love. What are the characteristics of weathered love, and what examples have you seen in your life?
13. The novel's title reminds us that there are only a few people who will stand with us under any circumstances. Who are those people for you?
14. Bailey gives Charlotte a sea glass necklace. What does this gift symbolize, and how is it appropriate for Charlotte, and for Bailey as well? What gifts have you given or received that mark a turning point in life?
15. Charlotte remarks "I got the mother I needed." How do you think our parents' influence our choices and decisions?

about the author

Leslie Hooton is many things: a fabulous friend, a powerful speaker, a flower enthusiast, and a lover of language. You don't want to miss her beloved novels, *Before Anyone Else* and *The Secret of Rainy Days.*

Leslie attended the Sewanee Writer's Conference and studied with Alice McDermott, Jill McCorkle, and Richard Bausch. Growing up in a small Alabama town, Leslie went on to earn her B.A. and M.A. from Auburn University and J.D. from Samford University. She became intrigued by people and discovered everyone has their own unique stories. Leslie resides and writes in Charlotte, North Carolina. Follow Leslie on Instagram and Facebook. Go to Lesliehooton.com for book clubs or speaking engagement contact information.